Also by Robert L. Wiggins

Fiction

The Council of Five: A Reckoning

Whiteout

Beguiled Child

Nation Torn Asunder

Nonfiction

Big Red...Our Time

This is a work of fiction. Names, characters, places, and incidents are either the product of the author's imagination or are used fictitiously, and any resemblance to actual persons, living or dead, business establishments, events, or locales is entirely coincidental.

Cover design by Jason Moser of
MaverickDesignWorks.com

THE COUNCIL OF FIVE:
RETRIBUTION

Robert Lloyd Wiggins

To my grandson, Carson Robert Shinebarger

It is not possible for us to determine the time, place, or the circumstances into which we are born. This is God's work.

Throughout our lives we are continually shaped and molded by our relationships and our experiences. Every aspect of our existence is determined by external forces...except our dreams.

Our dreams are our exclusive property, our personal choices. We imagine them, nurture them, and with perseverance we can come to realize them.

My wish for you is to dream big and dream always.
It is the least you can do. After all... you are your mother's dream.

Though the mills of God grind slowly,

yet they grind exceedingly small;

Though with patience He stands waiting,

with exactness grinds He all.

Henry Wadsworth Longfellow

Nemesis is the Goddess of Divine Retribution

ACKNOWLEDGEMENTS

I am indebted to the following family and friends who have helped me as editors or provided support in other ways during the creation of this, my second novel: Craig Devenport, my friend and college classmate; Francine Dimmick, my friend and extremely gifted editor; Christopher Austin, my computer expert and friend; Steve Shinebarger, my son-in-law and formatter extraordinaire; and lastly, my editors and greatest cheerleaders, my Aunt Florence, "the wind beneath my wings," and the originator of our secret "Oh Mys," and Uncle Barry Fabrey.

As always, I am also eternally grateful to my wife Coleen, my son, Robert "Rob" James, and my daughter Erin for their patience and encouraging words. Finally, I would like to thank my most beautiful grandson Carson Robert for not getting cheese puffs or Popsicle drippings on all my papers.

CONTENTS

CHAPTER ONE

1. Cold Case Investigator   13
2. Granny Carries a Gun   18
3. Rapture Ministries   23
4. Nights of the Round Table   35
5. Bad Choices   43
6. Financials   51

CHAPTER TWO

1. Profiling   55
2. Going Global   63
3. Bloody Baseball Bat   65
4. The Slow Moving Line and the Cliff   70
5. Tragedy in Oregon   78
6. Folsom Prison   85
7. A "Hectorism"   92
8. Retirement   99
9. The Catacombs   103

CHAPTER THREE

1. Ethan Cole Laningham   113
2. DNA   119
3. Sheldon and Jessica Lortz   125
4. Twenty Thousand   131

  5. Zenith Productions   141

  6. Shy Raymond   149

CHAPTER FOUR

  1. Sunday Morning   158

  2. Lolita's New Clothes   167

  3. Ferndale   175

  4. Preparations for G Day   184

  5. Help from HOT Software   194

  6. Unabomber   201

  7. Jewels   211

  8. T. Gator "The Touchdown Maker"   217

CHAPTER FIVE

  1. New Robes   228

  2. Goth Girl   235

  3. Jack Daniels, Neat   248

  4. The Promised Land   254

  5. Venus   261

  6. Admission   268

  7. Obstacles to Freedom   277

  8. Advance on the Inheritance   285

  9. 1896 Silver Dollar   295

CHAPTER SIX

1. Counting Cash   303
2. What's that Smell?   311
3. Full Circle   321
4. Tyler Hayes   326
5. Secret Desires   338
6. Antisocial Matthew   349
7. Flushing Matt   356

CHAPTER SEVEN

1. A Match of Old and New   364
2. Hotel Carretto   368
3. Emilio Scavo   376
4. Room 113   383
5. Shot Dead   389
6. Goodbye   394

CHAPTER ONE

1

COLD CASE INVESTIGATOR

Law enforcement may have a greater preponderance of obsessive-compulsive employees than any other industry. Police chiefs and detectives everywhere get a little nuts when high profile cases drag on, waste department resources, and yet remain unsolved. On March 1, 1932, Charles Augustus Lindbergh Jr., son of the famous aviator Charles Lindbergh, was kidnapped from his New Jersey home. Four years later, a man was executed for this crime. The baby's body was found badly decomposed two months after the abduction, and science had not yet evolved to the point where the evidence was of much help in solving the crime. The scene abounded with evidence, but it was next to useless. In the meantime, the entire nation was screaming for justice. This violation to one of our greatest heroes demanded vengeance. The pressure on law enforcement agencies must have been beyond belief. Ultimately a suspect was arrested, a trial ensued, and a man was executed in a New Jersey electric chair. By today's standards, this case would have cost the taxpayers millions of dollars. All this, and many believe we executed an innocent man.

To be sure, technological and forensic advances, along with the proliferation of surveillance cameras have given today's law enforcement officers an edge. However, advancements and improvements in technology are not the exclusive property of the

13

good guys. Perhaps computers are the best example. Computer technology has given law enforcement agencies the ability to share information and create databases which can instantly be searched and retrieve information germane to their case. From his car, any policeman can now tell if there are any outstanding warrants against you, or look at your history of traffic violations. Then, is it not ironic that the computer, which has been so helpful in catching criminals, is also responsible for more graft, thievery, and mayhem than anything ever invented? In the wrong hands, a few keyboard strokes, or the click of a mouse can steal more money than the greatest bank robberies in history. And now robbers don't need to wear masks because they are invisible.

Santa Molina FBI director Yolanda Tubbs was mulling over these philosophical questions when her train of thought was interrupted by a loud knock on her office door.

"Boss, we've given Martha Green an office on the third floor," said Agent Adam Franklin. "The computer people are setting her up now, so she should be up and running very soon."

"Thanks Adam," replied Yolanda. "Tell her to let me know if she needs anything."

"You bet." Said Adam as he backed out of Yolanda's office and closed the door.

Yolanda was unsure if it was a blessing or a curse to be old enough to remember the old days. Policemen used to walk beats. They knew everyone. Their visibility on the street served as a deterrent to crime, and they were respected. People liked having them around. They were associated with good.

Now, law enforcement officers are feared. That is much different than respect. Today, if you see a policeman, you wonder what's wrong or what did I do? The police are now associated with bad things. They are like dentists...you don't want anything to do with them, that is, until you need one.

And lawyers! Why do parents thump their chests and brag when their kid becomes a lawyer? Litigating attorneys intimidate witnesses, distort the truth, misrepresent the facts, and pervert the judicial system to their own advantage. Yet it is the police who are feared while the lawyers are revered. The practice of law is the only profession which is allowed to proliferate unchecked at the expense of society. Normally, the law of supply and demand has a bearing on a person's decision to enter a trade or profession, as well as dictating the financial remuneration for that job. If plumbers are scarce, they can charge more for their services. This, in turn, makes more people want to become plumbers. However, isn't it ironic that a law shouldn't have to apply to lawyers? While the law of supply and demand applies to all other jobs, whenever there is an overabundance of lawyers, they simply invent more work requiring the skills of an attorney. You used to be able to buy a home or a car, or take out a loan with one signature. Now you have to take half a day off from work to sign the required paperwork. Why does everything now require so much paperwork? Lawyers need stuff to do, and, thought Yolanda, don't even get me started on frivolous lawsuits! Everything is backwards. She decided that, in fact, it was a curse to be old enough to remember when things made sense.

Martha Green is a good example of the transitioning of the old days to the present. Martha represents a new kind of investigating FBI agent. She is a cold case detective. The

15

technological advances have come so quickly, that unsolved cases of the past are now able to be revisited. Old evidence can be re-examined using state-of-the-art forensic science. The cold case detectives have frequently brought justice, albeit delayed, to cases long forgotten. Of course, a caveat to the revisiting of old crimes is that we sometimes now find ourselves apologizing for the incarceration of an innocent man. While DNA evidence may prove a person's involvement in a crime, it can also be virtually conclusive in exonerating the innocent.

Yolanda had been working for the FBI for nearly thirty years. She has been the director of the Santa Molina division for the past six years. A recent nationwide directive has mandated that the FBI create and train these specialized cold case agents like Martha Green, and disseminate them across the nation. Yolanda was unsure exactly how Martha would be able to help them, but during these lean times, any new warm body was appreciated.

Martha Green and her cold case peers did some hands-on scientific analyses themselves, but their real value was in evaluating the available evidence and getting it to the FBI technicians who were the forensic specialists. Yolanda decided it was probably best to give Martha some time to acclimate to life at the Santa Molina FBI before assigning her a case of her own. She always found it helpful to rotate new employees around the office, and let them work with the others. Learning the personalities, as well as the strengths and the weaknesses of the other agents makes for a more productive and harmonious workforce.

Yolanda's secretary, Ruth, called her. "Hi, Yolanda, it is Judge Laningham on line two."

Yolanda answered, "OK Ruth, I'll take it, thanks."

"Hi, judge, what's up?" asked Yolanda.

"Can you meet with the Council for about an hour on Friday at 7:00 PM?" the judge asked.

"Sure," said Yolanda. "At your house?"

"Yes, "replied Judge Laningham. "Also, would you be kind enough to run a profile on a Reverend Thomas Hartsell from San Francisco and bring it along?"

Yolanda was puzzled. "Did you say reverend?"

"Yes I did," said the judge. "Can you believe it?"

Yolanda chuckled, "Are there no limits to the depths to which we may sink?"

"Apparently not," the judge answered. "See you Friday at 7:00 PM." He hung up the phone.

Yolanda entered the information required to look into the last thirty years of the life of Reverend Thomas Hartsell, pastor and CEO of Rapture Ministries, San Francisco, California. This is going to be good, she thought to herself.

2

GRANNY CARRIES A GUN

It had now been over two years since the Council was created. All five Council members, at one time or another, shared with the others their misgivings about Council activities. Each Council member was also a respected citizen in Santa Molina society. No one wanted to be thought of as a vigilante. Law enforcement and the judicial system worked just fine most of the time. But sometimes, high-priced lawyers found technicalities which set guilty men free. And there were, also, those who possessed such wealth and power that they were able to bribe or buy their way out of trouble. And then, there were the rarest of the miscreants who were able to inflict injury on others without breaking any laws.

No one in the Council doubted the good they had accomplished over the past few years. Lives had been saved, others had been spared financial ruin, and several very bad people had been shown justice in most unconventional ways. It wasn't that the Council felt the need to continue their activities. They were more concerned about the ramifications should their activities cease.

Yolanda thought it quite strange how the five Council members had managed to find each other. Outside the Council, they shared almost nothing in common.

Joel Harris was a very rich thirty-six year old computer software designer. His company, HOT Software, led the industry in the production of computer animated games. Joel moved to the

Silicon Valley from Detroit following the brutal murder of his parents and sister. The perpetrators of this horrific crime had never been found.

Hector Martinez was the owner/operator of a landscape business. His father started the business after moving to the United States from Mexico about forty years ago. Hector's father died of a heart attack last year, and Hector, who had worked with him, just kept on mowing. He served his country for fifteen years as a Navy SEAL and retired after he was wounded. At forty-three, Hector is the least cerebral of the group. He is profoundly patriotic and has a tendency to view problems as black or white. Most of all, Hector Martinez hates bullies in all forms. He has no compunction at all performing Council activities. In his eyes, he is simply making things right.

Dr. Jerry Woodson, together with Judge Lamar Laningham, were the masterminds behind the creation of the Council. They have been the closest of friends for forty-six years, starting when they played high school football together. Judge Laningham has very strict feelings for justice, and he takes it quite personally when the legal system gets perverted. The judge was pushed too far a few years back when an illegal immigrant raped an eight year old girl and was set free because he was read his Miranda rights in English, and the rapist spoke only broken English. The crime was especially heinous since he bound her tiny hands behind her back and raped her repeatedly over two days. He then left her in a dumpster behind his apartment. She was so deeply in shock that she could not speak for nearly a week. Her nightmares now require that her parents leave the lights on all through the night. After the case was declared a mistrial, the girl's father assaulted his daughter's attacker outside the courtroom and nearly beat him to death. Of course, while the rapist is a free man, the father of the young girl is still in prison.

With alarming frequency Judge Laningham had watched helplessly as inept prosecuting attorneys made rookie mistakes resulting in crucial evidence becoming inadmissible. And of course, there was the legendary Don Houdini, Vincenza Fortuna, who evaded justice no less than three times because of bribery and extortion.

It would be a difficult thing to try to find a kinder, gentler man than Judge Laningham. He had just been pushed too far, too many times. The formation of the Council was the by-product. A year ago, Judge Laningham retired from the bench. He decided that it was time for the younger guys to slam the gavel.

Dr. Woodson also has witnessed the tearing at the fabric of society. Greed has become all-pervasive. Corporations place profit above ethics and safety. Politicians line their pockets with lobby money and pass legislation based on remuneration. United States' drug companies send medications to Canada at deeply discounted rates while poor seniors in this country go without the same medications because they are too expensive. Doctors routinely order unnecessary tests because they own the equipment. And they rationalize this by saying that the patients won't be responsible since the insurance companies cover the cost. Teachers inflate student grades and have even been known to alter student's test scores to increase their state reimbursement rates. Like Yolanda, both Dr. Woodson and Judge Laningham felt it a curse to remember what it was like to have lived in a time without this greed. Of

20

course, in the long run, Council actions did nothing to alter the degradation around them. However, the five Council members slept better in the knowledge that they were at least not part of the problem.

Like the others, Yolanda sometimes had issues with her participation in Council affairs. Interestingly her personal demons did not arise from the fact that she was a law enforcement official. She wanted criminals to receive justice no matter how it was served. Yolanda was also a daughter, a wife, a mother, and recently a grandmother. Vincenza Fortuna was delivered Council justice. In addition to killing Yolanda's father, Vincenza had been implicated, either directly or indirectly, in the deaths of at least thirteen other people. Yes, he deserved to die. He had a wife and two daughters, and because of the actions of Yolanda and the Council, they were made to suffer. However, each of Vincenza's victims had families as well. What about them? Most of the time, Yolanda easily dismissed such thoughts from her mind, but not today.

As requested by Judge Laningham, before she left work, Yolanda prepared the dossier on Reverend Thomas Hartsell. She put the document in a folder and kept it in her car until Friday. As she approached her home and began turning into her driveway, Yolanda smiled. She saw her daughter Angela's car there, and this meant that little Warren was paying a visit as well. Being a grandmother changed Yolanda. The change was slow and subtle, but she could feel it nonetheless. Whenever she was with Warren, Yolanda could feel a calmness envelop her. Things which seemed important to her were suddenly forgotten. Her entire focus was on the two year old who had stolen her heart. Of course, she still loved her husband and Angela, but when they were all together in a room, it was like love for anyone else was put into suspended animation. Perhaps it was because children were so dependent. Perhaps it was because they were so innocent. Yolanda's protective instincts for her grandson were at least equal to what they were for her daughter when she was a child. Pity the person who delivers any harm to this child. Also, don't forget, granny carries a gun.

3

RAPTURE MINISTRIES

Hector was very much looking forward to the next Council meeting. After all, the Council was convening because of his call to Judge Lamar Laningham.

A week ago, Hector's mother, Rosa Martinez, received a frantic phone call from her brother, Julio Lopez, who lives in San Francisco. Julio was distraught because his wife Francisca had been donating excessive amounts of money to a church where she had recently become a member. Francisca and two of her friends had joined Rapture Ministries, a new church in the bay area which had been growing very rapidly.

Hector was just three years old when his parents, Juan and Rosa Martinez, immigrated to the United States in 1956 from Mexico. Like so many others from poor countries, Juan Martinez just wanted a chance at life. He was not seeking riches or fame. Juan sought opportunity. Somehow he summoned the courage to uproot his family and move them to a place where he couldn't even speak the language. To his amazement Juan found that, for the most part, his new country welcomed the Martinez family. Of course there were some who were unfriendly and treated them as interlopers with suspicion and even disdain. But there were always such people, even back in Mexico. Juan's optimism and affable personality usually won them over.

Juan's outgoing nature also helped his business. He started a very humble landscaping business with just a truck, a second-hand riding lawnmower, and a handful of garden tools. His hard work and dependability brought him more and more customers. Juan was not well educated, but his business savvy taught him that customer recommendations beat newspaper advertising every time. After being in the United States just a few years, Juan was able to provide a comfortable life for his family. They had a modest home, his two boys did well in school, and he was proud to be an American. In fact, he was so proud that he called his brother-in-law and convinced him to come to the United States and become a citizen.

Rosa Martinez recognized her husband as the family patriarch. She was old school and had no inclination toward contemporary feminist issues which had become so popular in California. Rosa loved her new life in America as much as Juan did, but it was more difficult for her to let go of her past. She missed her church and her family. Rosa was able to find a Catholic church with no problem, but she did not share her husband's outgoing personality. Rosa was shy, and her broken English didn't help matters. In Mexico she loved participating in church activities and cooking for various social events. But here in America, she felt more comfortable going home immediately after mass on Sunday.

There was nothing Juan could do about the church issue, but having Rosa's brother and his wife Francisca nearby would certainly make Rosa happier. Julio and his wife have now been in the United States for twenty-two years, and since Juan died last year, Rosa needs family more than ever.

Julio's frantic phone call to his sister was clearly the culmination of pent-up feelings which had been building for a while. He described to Rosa how several months ago, Francisca's friends had her join them in attending a new church which had been reaching out to the community. Rapture Ministries had been in town a little over one year, and the charismatic leader, Reverend Thomas Hartsell had descended on San Francisco like a whirlwind. He was on talk shows and his picture adorned billboards and buses, all inviting the public to worship with him at Rapture Ministries. Reverend Hartsell attended civic groups and he found his way into all of the social events. A handsome man to begin with, Reverend Hartsell wore custom made suits and kept his appearance perfect. It was rumored that his hairspray was guaranteed to hold in gale force winds. Everyone loved the good reverend, and he, in turn, loved his flock...or so it seemed.

The world is filled with clergymen of all religions and denominations who truly love God, and have His word as the primary focus of their lives. Their mission in life is to grow closer to God and to help others in doing the same. This is the noblest work a man can do as well as the most challenging. What work could be more rewarding than helping others find eternal salvation? God acknowledges these teachers as the most righteous of men. Yet at the same time, He clearly admonishes those who would be false teachers of His word. Over and over, the Bible warns against false prophets and teachers who pretend to do God's work and exploit the masses for their own personal gain. These are the lowest form of humankind and are promised a stricter form of justice than other men. We are all human beings, and as such, we all sin and make mistakes. God acknowledges this and forgives us.

There is something supremely evil in a clergyman who knowingly and willingly hides behind the veil of his most trusted position to satisfy his own lust or greed. This is why God promises such men special punishment. God takes men's souls and their salvation very seriously. He recognizes anyone who speaks with a false tongue in order to satisfy their personal greed as the most vile of men.

Sunday morning services at Rapture in the Round were a thing to behold. A monstrous pipe organ, specially placed high above the circular stage, led the choir of at least fifty men and women in songs carefully chosen to engage the congregation and gradually build it to a frenzied level. All of the parishioners wanted to believe that the spirit of God was right here, right now. No one knew that the entire production was specifically created and choreographed to intentionally bring the brethren to this fever pitch. And at just the right moment, the Reverend Thomas Hartsell, in all his splendor, was raised from underneath the stage onto a special platform to deliver his sermon. This, too, was planned to incite the crowd. He encouraged their participation and raised his arms to the "Amens" shouted from the congregation. Reverend Hartsell told the parishioners that they were special, they were the chosen, and they alone would ascend to heaven. And brother Hartsell would lead the way. Hallelujah!

Once the congregation was made pliable with song, and consecrated with the reverend's words, the organ would again lead the choir in the Rapture's signature song, *Rapture O' My Soul*. All of this was just in time for the collection of tithes and offerings. Once the collection was over, things took a dramatic turn downward. Upcoming activities and special announcements were followed by the doxology, and the flock, now hopefully a little lighter in the pockets, was dismissed.

While still intoxicated with the aura of the service, Francisca and her two friends, while slowly being herded toward the front door, were suddenly surrounded by a group of smiling men and women and directed to a small recessed area off the main aisle. It took a sharp eye to notice that the good reverend had the aisle specially designed so that it gradually narrowed as it got closer to the front door. Of course, this forced the crowd to move more slowly as they exited, and gave his specially trained minions ample opportunity to search for meek-looking men and women. Once identified, Hartsell's groups would steer these people in twos and threes into the aisle recesses. Here, smiling church members would warmly greet newcomers, introduce themselves, and goad them until they were ultimately cajoled into a promise to attend a Wednesday night prayer meeting. The mass of people slowly moving out of the church made it impossible to observe the fact that there were, in fact, several aisle recesses where the same coercion was being played out over and over again until Rapture in the Round was emptied of all parishioners.

Francisca and her two friends, Anita and Stella, talked about their decision to return to Rapture Ministries on Wednesday evening for prayer meetings. They agreed that it seemed like a good idea. After all, the nice people from the church thought enough of Francisca and her friends to go out of their way to deliver them a special invitation. Of course, they couldn't know that fifteen others had received special invitations as well. Besides, they were promised that they would be able to personally meet Reverend Hartsell. What an honor!

27

Several months later, all three ladies were regular attendees at Rapture in the Round as well as Wednesday evening prayer meetings. Only now, Francisca, Anita, and Stella were separately part of the small groups which descended upon the submissive-looking victims at the end of the Sunday worship service, inviting them to Wednesday prayer meetings. Unnoticed to the flock, the nature of the Wednesday evening prayer meetings had also gone through some subtle, almost imperceptible changes.

Reverend Hartsell had appointed a group of six men and women who were designated as Rapture's elders. These church leaders, supposedly further along the road to salvation than the others, had created a program which they call *"climbing the ladder."* This program singles out certain parishioners whom they believe are advanced in the spirit, and they are removed from their prayer group and sent to a group which represents a higher level of spiritual attainment. Those who are fortunate enough to move up are celebrated, and their achievement is duly noted on the *Wall of Attainment* located in the church vestibule. The church members who ascend to the level of attainment have their names listed in various untitled brackets or tiers. Of course, the impressive-looking *Wall of Attainment* is located where the entire congregation must pass it on their way out of the church. The message was clear enough. Those who successfully climb the ladder are indeed special, while those left behind are encouraged to work harder and seek guidance.

Following Sunday services and Wednesday evening prayer meetings, Reverend Hartsell routinely meets with Rapture's elders who, in turn, meet with the prayer group leaders. However, the topic of conversation is not God or salvation or prayer. The topic is worship, or more specifically, the worship of money.

The Reverend Thomas Hartsell was a master at mind control. He knew from practical experience that nearly anyone could be brought around to his way of thinking. The trick was learning how to get inside their mind. Everyone wants or needs something in their life which they feel is lacking. Some crave respect. Others want adulation. Some desire sex. Some just want to be wanted or needed. A desire for power is a common craving. However, most people simply want to be loved. Reverend Hartsell knew these things. He also had taught his elders how to ask key questions of parishioners so that they could quickly ascertain a person's secret needs. Having this information is like possessing their vulnerability, their Achilles' heel. And if you could convince someone that you were sincere and cared about them, they practically handed you the key to unlock their secret desire.

Mind control is not new. It has been around forever. Some companies, like life insurance companies, have used forms of mind control to sell policies to people who didn't need or could not afford life insurance. Insurance agents were trained to ask a series of questions unrelated to insurance which helped the agents warm up to the clients while honing in on personality traits which would ultimately help them sell policies. Reverend Hartsell's elders, while not as adroit as their boss in mind control, had skills which easily allowed them to manipulate and control parishioners. They used their skills to milk the congregation of money which many could not afford to give. The truth was, the real purpose of the Wednesday evening prayer meetings was a shakedown. Yes, prayers were said, and then, carefully prepared movies were shown depicting disease-ridden villages, both at home and abroad, which desperately needed the prayers, but more importantly, the financial support of Rapture Ministries. Sometimes, a before-and-after film showed the good which resulted from the donations. The parishioners were told that now their church needs to send these people Bibles. Perhaps a week later they might need a new roof on a building or a well dug. Other times, Reverend Hartsell was shown, without his expensive suit, helping to repair a building or feeding an emaciated child. If a parishioner was so moved by the good work which Rapture was doing, that they made a sizable donation, they *"climbed the ladder."*

Sometimes Reverend Hartsell appeared stern when he made it clear that his congregation was not doing enough. People throughout the world were clamoring for the word. If the parishioners could not dig deeper and give more, how could they expect that God would reward them?

Francisca, Stella, and Anita were separated into three different prayer groups. They were told by the elders that experience had shown that splitting up friends or family members hastens the climbing of the ladder. However, the truth was really found in the old divide and conquer axiom. While normally referring to the deployment of troops in a battle, the axiom also works well in any situation where a hierarchy exists. When a king's subjects are angry about an issue, if they are unanimous in their dissent and act as a unified body, the king can easily be overthrown. A smart king, however, will not allow unity. He plays favorites and keeps his subjects fighting amongst each other. By orchestrating various levels of compensation, and making the subjects compete against each other, jealousies are created. Hence, if the subjects keep competing and arguing with each other, they will never be able to unite and overthrow the king. For eons this practice has been used in politics, in the workplace, and sadly, in families. Reverend Hartsell well knew the value in keeping his subjects divided. Also, a little competition among his flock in the area of donations couldn't hurt. Yes, the good reverend studied the divide and conquer axiom, and he embraced it.

During one Wednesday night prayer meeting, Stella was overcome with the spirit of benevolence. She decided to donate the two thousand dollars which she had been saving for Christmas to the Rapture Ministries Relief Fund. Certainly Rapture Ministries could put the money to better use saving lives than she could buying clothes and toys for her grandchildren. Sure enough, the following Sunday morning, Reverend Hartsell announced to the entire congregation that sister Stella had climbed a rung on the ladder. And when Reverend Hartsell asked her to stand, the congregation gave her a thunderous applause. Both Francisca and Anita felt the pangs of jealousy. Divide and conquer. The feelings of jealousy were only compounded when they saw Stella's name on the Wall of Attainment in the church vestibule.

Throughout the next couple of weeks, the elders and others who had also climbed the ladder, fawned over Stella and gave her celebrity status. Stella was even invited to a closed preview of the Rapture Ministries' new global initiative which was delivered by Reverend Hartsell. Of course, the groveling behavior toward Stella was purposely done to beguile her into making greater donations, as well as to fill her friends and the other parishioners with envy. The elders had been taught well. They were masters of deceit. Divide and conquer.

Three weeks after Stella's coronation, Anita could stand it no longer. In her Wednesday prayer meeting, she donated five thousand dollars to the Rapture Ministries Relief Fund to help send Bibles to save the heathen souls abroad. However, it wasn't the spirit of benevolence which descended on Anita. It was the spirit of covetousness. And her source of funds wasn't Christmas savings. It was maxing out her credit card.

In a repeat performance, on Sunday morning, Reverend Hartsell announced that sister Anita Rodriquez had climbed the ladder. Amidst the hallelujahs and the amens, she was embarrassed by the congregation's applause. Anita had never been so happy...until she saw that her name was even higher on the Wall of Attainment than Stella's.

Francisca was utterly crestfallen. She had a serious dilemma. Both Stella and Anita were higher on the socioeconomic ladder than Julio and Francisca Lopez. After tending to their family's needs, there was very seldom any money left. Francisca and Julio were now having serious arguments over Rapture's effect on the family's finances. At first, Julio tried his best to be supportive, but Francisca was relentless. Julio said nothing in the beginning, but he watched Francisca's donations to Rapture grow larger and larger each week, and then she began writing checks on Wednesdays as well. The budgeting of the family's income and paying the bills was Julio's responsibility. At the rate his wife was sending money to Rapture Ministries, balancing the budget was no longer sustainable. Julio was heartsick. He didn't want to fight with Francisca, but they were drowning in debt. He had no choice but to confront her.

The elders were prepared for such situations. They told the dubious that you cannot out give God. The more you sacrificed and the more abundantly you gave, the more richly you will be rewarded. Tithing was considered an absolute minimum. The elders knew there would be family discord over donations. In a staged display, an elder's wife told parishioners how her husband had rebelled against her generous donations to help the poor and the downtrodden. However, after just two months of her generous donations, her husband received a big raise at work which included a bonus. He was so impressed that he felt compelled to donate the bonus check to Rapture Ministries. Their lives have been enriched ever since. One of the women explained that she and her husband fought constantly over her donations and were close to divorce. The elder told her that sometimes an enriched life started with a divorce.

Julio knew the husbands of both Anita and Stella. Having had no success in talking with Francisca, Julio wondered if the other husbands were having similar problems. It turned out that all of the men had been fighting with their wives over excessive donations to Rapture Ministries. After examining his credit card statement, Anita's husband went ballistic and threatened to cut up the card. Like Francisca, Anita said that perhaps a divorce was needed. At about this time, Julio called his sister. Rosa and Hector made the short drive to San Francisco to see if they could help. After listening to his mother describe what Julio had told her, Hector felt a hankering need to go to church.

Hector and his mother joined Francisca, Anita, and Stella and paid a visit to Rapture in the Round. It was quite a show, but the high point came in the middle of the sermon. Reverend Hartsell just stopped talking. After a moment, with tears streaming down his cheeks and his voice quivering, he announced that he had received a message directly from God which instructed him to have Rapture Ministries go global. Praise God! Reverend Hartsell was told to use the radio, the internet, and television to send the message of Rapture Ministries all across the globe. The donations promised to be in the millions. Cha-Ching and hallelujah!

4

NIGHTS OF THE ROUND TABLE

For the first time, Hector was not the last one to arrive at Judge Lamar Laningham's house for the Council meeting. Only Hector and the judge knew why the meeting was called, but after preparing the dossier on Reverend Thomas Hartsell and Rapture Ministries at the judge's request, Yolanda Tubbs had a pretty good idea as well. This only left Dr. Woodson and Joel Harris in the dark.

"Good evening, everyone," began Judge Laningham. "Hector has asked us to get together this evening, so I think I will let him fill you in." He motioned to Hector.

"Hi, everyone," Hector sat up straight. "A few weeks ago my mother got a phone call from her brother Julio. Julio is normally a happy guy and is fun to be around. My mother said that he sounded more upset than she had ever heard him. She feared that he was nearing a breaking point. He and his wife, my Aunt Francisca, have been arguing for months over her donating extravagant amounts of money to a new church which she started attending with two friends. This church, Rapture Ministries, is headed by Reverend Thomas Hartsell. Julio also told my mother that he called the husbands of my aunt's two friends, and they, too, were fighting over excessive donations. Folks, these are hardworking people who barely make ends meet." Hector paused, clearly upset.

Dr. Woodson spoke up. "How much money are we talking about?"

"Thousands," Hector answered. "In fact, my Aunt Francisca's friend Anita gave five grand in a single pop at a Wednesday prayer meeting."

"Ouch," said Judge Laningham. "Why did she give so much?"

"Folks, these aren't prayer meetings, they're shakedowns." Hector continued. "Family members and friends that come to church together for these prayer meetings, like my aunt and her friends, are separated into different prayer groups. In these groups, the churchgoers are shown movies of remote parts of the world in need of food, shelter, water, and medicine. Basically they need everything...and Bibles, too. Anyway, the guys that run these prayer groups manipulate these folks, slathering them with guilt, and browbeating them into submission until they give."

Joel asked, "I don't understand why they have to separate family members and friends that come together?"

"Manipulation." Hector added. "Aunt Francisca said that she and her two friends try to out give each other. If friends are allowed to remain together during the meetings, they would have courage in numbers and likely realize the insanity of what they are doing. Also, get this. The big donors are singled out by the reverend during the service on Sunday, and then they get to see their name in lights on some Wall of Attainment. Of course, this billboard is conspicuously located so the donors can gloat and the others can conspire ways to out give them."

"Wow, we're in the wrong business." Dr. Woodson laughed. "These people make bait-and-switch swindlers look like pikers."

Hector continued. "Since my father's death, aside from my brother and I, Uncle Julio and Aunt Francisca are all the family my mom has. Mom and I drove to San Francisco to try to calm things down. Francisca was excited that we wanted to go to church with her and her friends."

"You, in church?" Joel laughed. "Is that your first time since you were baptized?"

"No, I went to a wedding once." Hector answered. His self-deprecating humor was appreciated by the others. He continued, "I used to enjoy playing a game on Sunday mornings before we went to church. There never seemed to be anything good on television Sunday mornings. So while I had coffee, I would use the remote to surf from one preacher to another. The game was to quickly determine if the preacher was a charlatan or the real deal. You folks know that I take pride in being a pretty good judge of character. However, this game was child's play. All of the swindlers seem to share the same characteristics, the common denominator so to speak. First you look them in the eye. Would you buy a car from this guy or let him take your daughter on a date? Remember Eddie Haskell on *Leave it to Beaver*? I loved that guy. He would sweet-talk June Cleaver while he was stealing the silverware. Well, the phony preachers are cut from the same cloth as Eddie. They claim to be full of the spirit, but I would submit that they are full of something else. These guys usually look too perfect, from their porcelain crowns and one hundred dollar hairstyles down to their alligator shoes. It just seems to me that anyone who insists on looking that good cares more about the **me** than the **He**. Of course, then comes the delivery. There are a lot of wonderful Sunday morning preachers who stand there and look you in the eye and speak from their heart. These guys are sincere and in the business of doing God's work. Then there are the guys like Reverend Hartsell. They have an agenda, but it has nothing to do with God's work. They exhibit histrionic behavior and strut and dance around. They scream and rant trying to appear filled with the spirit and convince everyone that they are the chosen one. They alone possess the secret to salvation. Sometimes they may shed a tear or speak of a direct communication they received from God. Well, of all of the personal messages I have heard them speak, I never remember any which didn't end with cha-ching."

"This Reverend Hartsell may be the best one ever," continued Hector. "He is destroying marriages and depleting the life savings of humble people. Anyway, I think I have been pretty clear about what I would like to see done."

The judge, obviously deep in thought, raised his head. "I have asked Yolanda to look into Reverend Hartsell's past." He looked at Yolanda. "Did you come up with anything?"

The round table, around which the Council members sat, separated them from each other by only a few feet. Dr. Woodson always said that, like the *Knights of the Round Table*, it was round designating them as equals. There was no head of the table.

One by one Yolanda looked at the other Council members. She stopped at Hector. She reached down beside her foot for the file on Reverend Thomas Hartsell. She began, "Did I find anything? Well to start with, calling him reverend appears to be optional. It appears that he got his degree from Leavenworth University, Kansas. Yes, Thomas Hartsell was a guest of the U.S. taxpayers in a federal penitentiary for ten years ending in 1992. He grew up in Chicago and spent his first twenty years there. He came from a broken home, and like countless other black children, he grew up fatherless. He never attended high school. He has a lengthy rap sheet, mostly full of misdemeanors including stealing purses, assault, and a whole host of motor vehicle violations, which is impressive in itself, since he never owned a car. Then he went big time. He and two other guys ran a pretty lucrative credit card scheme. Back when a lot of businesses still used the manual credit card machines, a carbon copy of the credit slip was made when the store clerk rolled the bar over the credit card. This second copy was routinely discarded because it got ink all over everything, and most people used the cash register slip as proof of the transaction. Thomas Hartsell and his two henchmen would distract the store clerks and swipe the trash bag containing the discarded credit card slips. No one noticed or cared since they were essentially stealing the trash. Once home, they would use the cardholder's name and credit card information to make phone and mail order purchases. Before they finally got caught, it was estimated that Thomas Hartsell and his accomplices stole over a quarter of a million dollars' worth of merchandise. This was the offense which landed him in Leavenworth."

Hector was flabbergasted. "Wow, Yolanda, I could tell that Hartsell was a phony...but a convicted felon?"

A strange look came over Yolanda's face. "Just hold on Hector, you haven't heard the best part." She turned a page in the file. "Mr. Hartsell wasn't one to waste time pumping iron or watching old movies behind bars. I called the warden at Leavenworth, and he was kind enough to track down one of the guards on C block, where Hartsell's cell was located. The guard remembered Hartsell very well. He said that he was one of those inmates you never forget. Even though Hartsell never went to high school, he was an avid reader. His guard told me that the first several years of his incarceration were spent reading everything he could get his hands on about historical figures that had been known to use mind control and intimidation to control large numbers of people. You know, sweethearts like Hitler, Stalin, and Karl Marx. He devoured the stuff. He also requested books on our homegrown psychopaths, Charles Manson, David Koresh, and our own San Francisco boy, Jim Jones. To make a long story short, Thomas Hartsell was a model prisoner with kooky reading habits. For several years, all he did was read, study, and make notes. However, since he never bothered anyone, they let him continue and left him alone. Then, about seven years into his ten year sentence, odd things began to happen. His guard found it difficult to explain, but all of a sudden Hartsell came out of his shell. He became Mr. Sociable. He spent hours talking with the other inmates. Yet, unlike the other convicts, he could easily pass from clique to clique." Yolanda looked up at the other Council members. They appeared spellbound. "Now, I don't know how much you boys know about prison life, but intermingling between groups is virtually unheard of and can easily get you killed. Hard time prison life is about survival. The inmates band together into groups for protection. There are gangs of blacks, whites, and Hispanics and nothing in between. The fact that Hartsell, a black man, was able to move freely among all the gangs was uncanny. The guard, also, said that once Hartsell began coming out of his cell, strange things began to happen. One minute all of the prison groups were able to organize to protest no television after 9:00 PM. Then, two days later, the groups wanted to kill each other again. Two days after that, everything was wonderful again. The guard could offer no explanation for these dramatic shifts in the prison cellblock atmosphere, but somehow Hartsell always seemed in the middle of it. One last thing, I mentioned that calling Mr. Hartsell reverend was optional. Supposedly, his degree in theology was issued by the Koehler Seminary. I called them, and they have no records of any Thomas Hartsell ever attending there." Yolanda closed her file indicating that she was finished.

Judge Lamar Laningham asked, "What about the financial details on Hartsell and Rapture Ministeries?"

Yolanda answered, "They have only been operational a short time, so I didn't spend much time there. However, from the amount of donations which Hector has been describing, something isn't right. I can look deeper into the finances if you wish."

Dr. Woodson spoke up. "You know, I think that technically, at least from what I have heard so far, this Hartsell, reverend or not, has not broken any laws, with the possible exception of falsely representing himself as a clergyman. Are we sure that we want to get involved in this?"

Joel was thoughtful. "I agree with you Dr. Woodson, and this guy could easily continue to operate like this for years, and then what? Hartsell and his cronies ride off into the sunset with millions while families like Hector's aunt and uncle are destroyed financially and otherwise. I think we should look into this."

Hector, obviously upset said, "Cajoling people to give up their life savings sounds like bullying to me, whether he is called reverend or not."

Judge Laningham brought the discussion to a close. "OK folks, since my wife and I are now retired, I think we will pay a visit to Rapture in the Round this Sunday morning. Yolanda, keep looking into the Rapture Ministries' finances as well as Hartsell's. Hector, try to convince your aunt and her friends to stay home or attend another church for a few weeks until we can sort this out. Hector, maybe Colleen and I can pick you and your mom up to join us Sunday morning?"

5

BAD CHOICES

Yolanda sat at her desk Monday morning and began discreetly poking around the financial records of both Rapture Ministries and Reverend Thomas Hartsell. She also wanted to contact her peers in Chicago to see if they could add anything to her file on Thomas Hartsell. Hopefully she would be forwarded a mug shot of him. Yolanda found she could work better if she had a visual, a face to look at, while she did her detective work. But for now, Chicago would have to wait. Like many other businesses, law enforcement, including the FBI, utilized a diminished staff on weekends. Law enforcement officers were people too, which meant they had soccer games, family outings, church, and other family events to attend. Church. Yolanda smiled and managed a slight laugh as she tried to envision Judge Lamar Laningham in the congregation of Reverend Hartsell. Judge Laningham, the reserved, stoic, dignified man in a predominantly black church where they would be shouting to the heavens, dancing, and gyrating to music. She would have to remember to ask Colleen Laningham how that went down.

Anyway, back to work. Now that it was Monday and her full complement of staff was back at their desks, she could see what new work the weekend had brought her.

Martha Green had now been with the Santa Molina FBI for nearly a week. She started her rotation with the other agents, and so far the feedback from Yolanda's people was promising. The agents she had shadowed said she was professional, pleasant, and a team player. This was good. Yolanda detested working with anyone, although they were invariably men, who thought that they were crime solving superstars.

Today Martha was assigned to shadow FBI Agent Daniel Lockwood. Daniel was affectionately known throughout the office as Danno. This started shortly after he downloaded the *Hawaii Five O* theme music to his cellphone. Now, every time he makes an arrest, everyone says "book 'em Danno."

Martha thought that Danno didn't look like an FBI agent. He didn't have the piercing eyes or the square cut jaw like the G-men you see on television. Robert Stack portrayed FBI Agent Eliot Ness many years ago on television. Now there was a guy you didn't want to mess with! He never cracked a smile, and those eyes could look straight into your soul. Martha remembered that when she was a little girl watching *The Untouchables*, every time there was a close-up of Robert Stack, little Martha was ready to confess to not making her bed or brushing her teeth. She loved those old television programs. Back then, it was much easier discerning the bad guys. They looked evil.

Danno was forty-five years old, Martha's senior by fifteen years, yet she felt comfortable with him right from the start. He did not possess the pretentious testosterone-driven attitude frequently encountered in the macho male FBI world. And it was also obvious to Martha that Danno had no problem working for a woman.

Martha was curious. "Danno, pardon me for asking, but what made you want to be a cop? You are much different than the other agents. I mean that in a good way. Normally, whenever I have worked with other male agents, they are threatened by me. Some do not want to work with a woman, some think women can't do the job, and some are afraid I will do a better job than they will do."

Danno turned to look at her. "Sounds to me like those others you describe have job security issues. I am not worried about my job. The way I see it, there is plenty enough crime to go around and keep us all busy. Why did I become an FBI agent? I am not sure. When I was a kid, my sister was raped and beaten up pretty badly, so I received an early dose of reality. The police never seemed very interested in catching whoever did it, and my parents were so happy to have my sister come home after three days in the hospital, they never pushed it. Maybe they didn't want her to have to relive it in court. Everyone just wanted to move on. I do remember being angry with my father. He always told me that there were consequences to doing bad things, yet no one pushed the police for answers. Yeah, like every kid, I thought that it would be cool to carry a badge and a gun. Once I got to law school, I thought that the courtroom drama and the litigating would be fun, but it was not. I am more of a hands-on kind of person. Lawyers deal with things after they happen. So I went where I thought the action was, 'thought' being the operative word. So what do I do now? Ninety percent of the time I am on the phone or in front of a computer. It's the other ten percent which makes my blood pump. And that, Martha Green, beats life in a courtroom every time."

Danno was presently working on a child abduction case. A young man named Delano Reese picked up his eight year old daughter Amy from school and drove away with her. That was four days ago. He has not been seen or heard from since. The FBI became involved because it is believed that Del may have left the state. Friends, neighbors, and family were interviewed and asked where they think Del may have taken Amy. Del's wife and several friends believed he would head to Oregon. He is an avid hunter and goes to Oregon a couple of times every year. He has never failed to return without a deer.

Danno summarized for Martha the results which the investigation had produced thus far. Delano and Alicia Reese had been married eleven years. They lived in Forestport, California, a sleepy little hamlet where Del made a decent living working for a logging company, and Alicia cooked in a local diner. Three years into the marriage, Amy was born. By all accounts, Del had been a good husband and a doting father. That little girl was Del's life. Friends and neighbors alike said that Amy was like an appendage of Del's. He took her everywhere with him and loved showing her off to strangers and friends. Amy had a favorite swing in the park near their home. It was the green swing, and the people who frequently took their children to the park told us that Del could often be seen pushing Amy in that green swing until it was dark.

Life was wonderful for the Reese family until one Monday morning three months ago. Like always, Del drove his truck to the logging camp where he worked. He was surprised to see the other loggers congregated outside instead of heading inside to suck down coffee. Toby, one of his co-workers, handed Del a yellow paper which was encased inside a transparent plastic sleeve. Toby had been the first person to arrive at the camp and he found this note stapled to the front door. The logging camp's office door was locked, and the note, addressed to all employees simply said that their services were no longer required. All logging operations had been suspended and final paychecks would be mailed the following Friday. The reality of this life changing moment hit Del immediately. There was simply no way that the Reese family could survive on what Alicia made at the diner. Del had worked as a logger for this company since he graduated high school. He had no other skills, and there were no other places to work in Forestport or any place within one hundred miles. The Reese family did not even own a computer. The only option left for them was moving. They, of course, would have to sell their modest home and use the equity to live on until Del and Alicia could find new jobs. The prospect of being able to sell their home was extremely unlikely. Forestport was so small that the only realtor in town made his real living as the town barber. So the Reese family put their home up for sale and waited. Del and his logging buddies who, like him, had nowhere to go and nothing to do, began drinking. Alicia thought that the money Del was spending on beer could have been put to better use, but her heart ached for her husband, and she did not wish to nag him or make him feel even worse.

Danno thought about Del a lot. When a working man loses his job, it is like his entire world falls apart. A man is defined by his work. It gives him a feeling of worth and self-respect in the knowledge that he is providing for his family. These feelings are shared by men who earn salaries in six digits as well as those who can barely make ends meet. Married women who lose their jobs do not normally think of the experience as an assault on their dignity as men do. Women remain secure knowing that the loss of their job in no way reflects on their performance as a good wife or mother. Their job has no bearing on how well they keep the home together.

However, a man feels that he cannot be a good husband or a good father if he cannot provide for his family. A man's judging his worth as the head of the family based on his working, whether it is fair or not, goes all the way back to the caveman. If the caveman failed to bring home food, his family starved. It didn't matter if he was a good father or not.

Del was helpless as the days went by. His drinking with his friends continued unabated, and as his debts grew, he became more and more angry. He was not angry with his wife or his daughter even though they were the recipients of his hostile outbursts. He was angry at his life, his circumstances, and his helplessness. He hated himself. Ultimately Alicia had to ask Del to leave. He did so willingly. Even he could see just how desperate and pathetic he had become. Del took his clothes and his guns and drove away in his truck. One week later, he picked up Amy after school, and they have not been seen since.

"I hate cases like this," Danno told Martha.

"What do you mean?" Martha asked.

"My heart absolutely bleeds for this guy," said Danno. "I probably would have done exactly the same things he did. Del is not a bad man. Hell, he never hurt anyone. He never even got a speeding ticket. He is a good man who made a stupid choice. How does that song go? *When you ain't got nothin', you got nothin' to lose.* And, Agent Green, a man who has nothing to lose is the most dangerous animal on the planet. Now give that animal a gun and the likelihood of a happy ending approaches zero. I don't want to go after this guy. He loves his daughter more than life. My guess is that he took her because right now she represents the only good

48

thing he has left in his life. My gut tells me that if we left Del alone, the little lady with him would make him come to his senses, and in a week he would bring her home. Unfortunately, as far as the FBI is concerned, that option is not on the table. So, once we find him and start making demands of him, the situation will not defuse, it will escalate. Corner a rat and see what it does. Everyone knows that he is not going to harm that girl. Amy is not his hostage, she is his daughter. Once we have him surrounded, everything changes. His options become few. Now his best case scenario becomes jail. No, Agent Green, I hate these cases because Del is just like me, only I am lucky enough to have a job. I am a working man. Yes, Del did a stupid thing, but I do not wish to send him to jail or maybe kill him for one bad choice. All he ever wanted to do was go to work and provide for his family."

Martha asked, "Do you have any ideas where he may have gone?"

Danno was clearly frustrated. "That's another thing. Del isn't exactly trying to hide. He took his own truck, about a week before it was going to be repossessed. We have been following his trail using his gasoline charges on his credit card. And he has been staying in motels under his own name. No, I do not believe Del is up to no good. I think he just wants to see his little girl for a while. We have an all-points bulletin out on him now, and since where he appears to be headed gets increasingly desolate, he will have fewer places to choose from when he stops. I have a list of gas stations, motels and restaurants along the route he has been following. You and I, Agent Green, will be spending the rest of the day calling these people. Once we give them the descriptions of Del, Amy, and their truck, we sit back and wait. We will have him soon enough. Then comes the hard part."

6

FINANCIALS

Judge Laningham had called each of the Council members earlier in the week and requested that they meet at his home on Friday evening. Everyone was seated around the table, anxious to learn of the judge's experience at Rapture in the Round. Judge Lamar admitted that he was somewhat embarrassed to have participated in such a spectacle. He agreed with Hector that the service was carefully prepared to excite the congregation. Reverend Hartsell seemed skilled at being able to measure the response of the people and modify the delivery of his sermon to evoke the reaction he wanted. At times, he spoke very softly to the people, and they would have to strain to hear him. This was done when he was expressing sorrow, such as when he was nearly in tears speaking of the needs of the poor whom the church had been supporting through Rapture's out-reach programs. At other times during his sermon, the reverend was in a heightened state of agitation. He got so excited describing the looks on the faces of those that received Bibles that the unbridled joy spread to the parishioners who yelled out amens and hallelujahs. The man clearly knew how to play to the crowd. The judge, of old Southern Baptist tradition, found it quite odd that there was never any mention of scripture or Bible verses. Judge Laningham had attended church all of his life, yet he was unable to identify any of the spiritual references to which Reverend Hartsell eluded. The message was clear enough. The fast-track to salvation was through generous giving. Although the judge, his wife Colleen, Hector and his mother, all shared observations

51

with each other in the car following the Sunday service, the judge asked Hector to reiterate his thoughts to the Council.

Hector really could not add anything to what he had shared with the Council a week ago. He and Judge Laningham agreed that Reverend Hartsell was not what he pretended to be. He was just too theatrical. He tried too hard.

Yolanda appeared amused. "Did you boys get invited to the Wednesday night prayer meeting?"

Judge Lamar continued. "Thank you, Yolanda, I nearly forgot. As a matter of fact we did. I doubt that I will be climbing the ladder, but I am anxious to see how it works."

Hector told them that Francisca, Stella, and Anita agreed to stay away from Rapture for a few weeks at Hector's request. He told them that he wanted to check the reverend's background. He thought that the three women appeared relieved that they were abstaining together. Hector's mother wanted to go again after learning that the reverend had been a convicted felon. She thought that the whole business was rather exciting.

Hector interjected, "You know, I do have one more thing that bothers me. Reverend Hartsell goes to an awful lot of trouble telling us how important it is for us to give money to provide Bibles to third world countries in need of hearing God's word. Well, then why are there no Bibles in Rapture in the Round? Yolanda, I picked up a bulletin on the way out. It lists the names of the church's hierarchy, including the elders. I don't know if it will be of any value to you. You'll also note the church's projected budget versus the total of weekly donations to date. If you believe the numbers, the

52

donations fall very short of what the church is hoping to bring in." Hector handed Yolanda Rapture's bulletin.

Yolanda took a minute to look at the names listed in the bulletin. She looked up slowly, first to Hector, and then to Judge Laningham. She had that "I know something you don't know" look on her face. "Oh yeah," she said. "Two of the elders listed in the bulletin are the same two that worked with Hartsell in the credit card scheme back in Chicago. It appears as though all three have gone through a religious conversion...or not. Boy, the more you stir this stuff up, the more it stinks. I had a very busy week at the bureau, so I couldn't look as deeply into Rapture's finances as I would have liked. The church bulletin should give me some new leads. I was able to find out that Rapture Ministries has non-profit status. No surprise there. Reverend Hartsell pays himself a modest salary. And two of his elders are paid salaries as well. Does anyone care to hazard a guess which two? One holds a position as youth minister, and the other is the outreach director in charge of missionaries. It also appears that Reverend Hartsell has two homes. One is a modest two story colonial near the church, and the other, although I don't yet have a description, appears to be valued on the upside of one million dollars. This home is about an hour outside of San Francisco. That is all I have right now."

"Thank you Yolanda." said Judge Laningham. "Doc, do you now have any reservations about going after Reverend Hartsell and Rapture Ministries?"

"No, Lamar." Dr. Woodson responded, "Not since the last meeting. You had me at Leavenworth."

Yolanda laughed. The judge measured the Council members' looks. "Anyone?" he said. No one objected. "OK, Hector and I will go to the Wednesday night prayer meeting with Colleen and Rosa. Yolanda, keep after the finances, and give Hector the addresses of Hartsell's two homes. Hector, please try to find time to look at Hartsell's homes and get some pictures for us. Doc, work with Joel and see if you can come up with a game plan to expose this guy for what he really is. Let's meet again two weeks from tonight, here at 7:00 PM as usual. Thank you everyone."

CHAPTER TWO

1

PROFILING

Martha Green ended her rotation where she would likely be spending most of her time. On the third floor of the FBI building, down the corridor from her new office, was the forensic division. Here there were experts on firearms and ballistics, fingerprinting, DNA collection, blood and blood spatter experts, hair and tissue experts, rape studies, and environmental evidence (cars, furniture, carpeting, clothing, etc.). This was where Martha loved to work. Evidence could talk to you, but it never lied to you. Evidence could tell you what happened and how it happened. The agents on the other floors had the more difficult job. Their job was the *why*. The best evidence in the world never told you the *why*, the reason for the crime.

Thankfully, there were agents who loved determining why crimes happened. These were the "people" FBI agents. Stephan Dakeslee was such an FBI agent. The drama of the interrogation, the analyzing of body language, and the ferretting out of minor details to corroborate or destroy a suspect's story, was their job. Martha hated anyone to lie to her. She found it incredulous that there were detectives who actually enjoyed it when their suspects and witnesses lied to them. Stephan loved the challenge. The lie was like the starting gun in a race. As Sherlock Holmes would say at the start of a case, "Come Watson, the game's afoot." A lie signaled the beginning of the game, the test of one against another, the search for the truth versus the perpetuation of the lie. However, uncovering the lie did not always help you solve a case.

About ten years ago, there was a high profile case in which Agent Dakeslee was involved. Saul Robertson, a very expensive defense lawyer was found shot dead in his office. The lawyer's death, in addition to making many people want to celebrate, initiated an FBI investigation. What a case! The list of people with motives to kill Saul was like a veritable who's who of people that hate lawyers. Saul had been responsible for sending more guilty thugs back onto the street than anyone in recent memory. Prosecuting attorneys hated Saul because they could not beat him in court. Judges hated Saul for time and time again making a mockery of their courtrooms. The families of hundreds of victims who never got justice hated Saul. The tropical fish in his office aquarium probably hated Saul. The police joked that Saul had to be cremated because the family was unable to find six friends to be pallbearers. Stephan Dakeslee was given the assignment of interviewing Saul's family. Sadly, there were not a lot of family members who liked Saul either. Yet even though a lot of people criticized the man, the fact that he was a good provider was undeniable. His opulent home was a testament to the fact that good defense lawyers, not the court-appointed kind, made considerably more money than their prosecutorial counterparts. Saul had everything that you would expect to see in a movie star's home. What Saul did not have was a loving family. Surely they appreciated the lavish lifestyle he gave them, yet they spoke of him almost as an inanimate object. In addition to all of this luxury, Saul left a five million dollar life insurance policy to his wife Judy.

One by one, Stephan interviewed all of the members of Saul's family, and he decided to save Judy till last. Once again, like the other family members, Stephan found Saul's wife cold and remote. There were no tears or talk of fond memories. Most of Judy's answers to Stephan's questions were "yes," or "no". It became clear to Agent Dakeslee that Saul and Judy may have been married, but they did not seem to know each other very well. Stephan's instincts told him that Judy was lying about something. Agent Dakeslee thought that she may have five million reasons to keep her secret to herself. Two weeks later, Agent Dakeslee discovered Judy's secret. Judy Robertson had been having an affair with one of Saul's previous clients, a millionaire car dealer. The dealer was being sued because one of his car salesmen sold a Corvette to a ninety year old man with Alzheimer's disease. Ten minutes later, the old man drove the car into a bridge in excess of one hundred miles per hour and died. Saul got the dealer acquitted because the old man was having one of his "good" days and the salesman was unable to discern the illness. Stephan Dakeslee didn't miss the humor in the fact that while Saul was getting his client off, the car dealer was returning the favor with his wife.

After all of the notoriety and the hundreds of hours spent investigating this case, the solution to the crime was quite anticlimactic. Late one night, while Saul was sitting at his desk preparing a case, he was murdered for money. A very desperate and drug crazed addict went by Saul's fancy office building. One of the building's doors had been left open, so the killer simply walked in, shot Saul, and ransacked the office. Of course the irony was that Saul was the one person who conceivably could have kept the murderer a free man.

Martha's skills were analytical, not social. She appreciated agents such as Stephan Dakeslee. Martha knew that the process of interviewing suspects, witnesses, and others, was at least as important as her work. They were interdependent. The best police work always resulted when the interviewers and the evidence specialists worked in concert with each other.

The best forensic pathologists have said that a homicide victim or a crime scene "talks" to the investigator. Each victim has a story to tell, and the best detectives slowly and patiently look at every detail to understand both the crime and the killer. Was the murderer angry? Was he after control of the victim? Was the killer in a hurry? Did he hate women? Was this his first kill, or was he experienced? Was this a random act, or was the victim specifically chosen? Did the killer know his victim? Martha knew of one serial killer who always cut out the eyes of his victims so they could not witness the shame he felt during his brutalizations. Yes, the best forensic detectives were artists in their work. Slowly, painstakingly, they looked at each shred of evidence before coming to any conclusions.

The interviewers, the "people" detectives, have evolved over the years in their skills as much as the technology has in the collection of evidence. In the old days, at least on television, suspects were seated in a dark room and questioned under a spotlight until they confessed. Those days are gone. Today there are interrogation specialists. Every suspect or witness is different and unique. Recognizing subtle differences helps detectives ask questions in ways which will not alienate the suspect. A good interviewer does not take control, he pretends to give it. Interrogation specialists actually can make a suspect want to confess their crime. Being relieved of their secret is better than suffering alone in possession of it. And sometimes, once the confession is made, the floodgates open. Unlike years past, today's interrogator is more of a friend to the suspect than an adversary.

One of the most recent developments in the evolution of the interviewing detectives is the creation of the profiler. In the truest sense, the profiler represents a bridge between the evidence and the interviewing detective worlds. Although there are still many very good law enforcement officials who look upon profilers as hokum and black magic, the increasing success of the profiler in solving crimes has been nothing short of astounding.

One of the first serious attempts at profiling a serial killer was used in investigating Jack the Ripper. The evidence told the police that Jack was angry at prostitutes and most likely had sexual issues of his own. In addition, he exhibited a high degree of skill in surgically cutting open his victims. There was, also, evidence to suggest that he was not a commoner, but a gentleman. As he kept killing, the police unwittingly became profilers. Police files have illustrated that the Ripper detectives used methodology and techniques which are consistent with those now used by modern profiling investigators. Many television shows and movies have showcased police profilers and attested to their value in solving cases. Most notably, *Silence of the Lambs* brought profiling to the vanguard in the investigation of serial killers.

Martha had been told to report to Yolanda at the end of her new employee rotation. Yolanda's door was open, so Martha tapped lightly on the window of the door. Yolanda looked up and smiled, "Hi, Martha, please come in."

Martha sat in one of the chairs immediately in front of and facing her new boss. "Is this a good time, Mrs. Tubbs?"

Yolanda closed the file in front of her and laced her fingers together on top of the folder. "Please, call me Yolanda. I know that I am old enough to be your mother, but I prefer not to be reminded of it. I hope you enjoyed your rotation. As I told you previously, I think that it is a good way to have a new employee and my agents get to know each other. It is, also, helpful for you to become comfortable getting around and learning where everything is located. All the feedback I have received from my people about you has been good. Welcome to the family." Yolanda paused and Martha blushed. Yolanda continued. "I have spoken with the people in Washington that sent you here. As you know, the creation of your position was mandated from the highest levels in the agency. The technology has advanced so quickly that we need someone like you to help us keep current. We are kept so busy chasing vermin that we fall behind. We now have you, our very own cold case investigator. I see your mission here as two-fold. First, you are to use your skills to make sure that we make the best use of forensic science as it applies to the cases we are currently working on. I would like you to oversee the collection of evidence from our crime scenes whenever it is practicable for you to do so. Obviously, you cannot always be there, so use your talent to help us get better. Nothing makes me angrier than one of my people contaminating a crime scene. Secondly, and I think this is more in line with the mandate from Washington, we want you to take a look at questionable cases from our past. Whenever we are given a reason to re-visit an old case, do what you can to use today's science to take a new look at how we did back then. Nobody likes to think that we may have locked up an innocent man. Of course, the flip side to this means that a guilty man is still on the street. Our rudimentary skills in collecting evidence in the old days left a lot to be desired. Like everyone else, we did the best we could. But we are supposed to be about justice. I have taken the liberty of choosing a case for you to begin with. This is a case from sixteen years ago. It has always haunted me. Two young boys were convicted of attempted robbery and murder and both are now serving lengthy sentences at Folsom Prison in Sacramento. Talk about a rush to judgment, the community backlash was such that we likely could have convicted Mother Teresa if she had been in the store."

Martha asked, "What makes you think that the boys may have been innocent?"

Yolanda looked up. "I am a mother and a cop. I was there when they brought the boys in and were booked. If my kid stole a cookie, I could look them in the eye and know that they did it. These boys were so scared and pathetic looking that we could have had them confess to killing President Kennedy. Hell, Martha, the smaller one even pissed himself he was so scared. Every instinct in my body was screaming. 'No way.' Everything happened so fast, and it was just too easy. Anyway, here is the file. I thought this might be a good way for you to get your feet wet. Let me know if you need anything."

"Thanks," said Martha. She took the file and headed toward the door. Martha stopped abruptly and spun around. She walked back toward Yolanda and closed the door behind her. "Boss, I need to ask you something."

Yolanda could tell that this was not going to be an ordinary request. "Let's have it, Agent Green."

Martha was pensive trying to formulate her thoughts. "Boss, I understand that I will be given assignments like the one in this file, and that's OK. This is my job, and the reason why I am here. I am OK with that. What I want to know is whether or not I can work on other things that pique my interest. The assignments like this," she held up the folder, "are my priority. But if I have the opportunity, and the time, can I look into old cases on my own, or are you the kind of boss who wants to approve everything that I do?"

Yolanda was unsure where Martha was headed with these questions, so she was not sure how to answer. "I am not exactly certain where this is going. You are new here, and I have no desire to discourage you from taking initiative. I like that. We are all adults here. Yet I do not want renegade agents either. Let me just say this. An independent spirit in an FBI agent is a good thing. If you do not have the freedom to think and act for yourself, you cannot follow your instincts, and a good FBI agent lives by his instincts. I give my agents a lot of rope, but at the same time, I cannot have my people all running in different directions. This job demands organization. To summarize, I expect you to get your assignments completed in a timely fashion. If you want to look into something unrelated to your casework, go ahead. But don't go too far without my knowledge. Clear enough?"

"Yes, Yolanda." Martha was pleased. "Thank you."

2

GOING GLOBAL

A few days after the last Council meeting, Joel called Dr. Woodson and invited him to his home. They had been given the task of formulating a plan to expose Reverend Thomas Hartsell and Rapture Ministries for their fraudulent activities. Dr. Woodson had been to Joel's home several times in the past, but only with all of the Council members. Dr. Woodson accepted a glass of merlot and began the conversation.

"Joel, I think that I may have a solution to our problem, and it has been delivered to us by the reverend himself. Two Council meetings ago, Hector first told us of Hartsell and Rapture Ministries. At that meeting, before any of us got involved, Hector told us that Hartsell got all emotional when he announced to the congregation that he received a message from God instructing him to make Rapture Ministries go global."

Joel answered, "Yes, Doc, I remember that."

"Well up till now, everything at Rapture has been status quo. Week after week, nothing changes. There is the Sunday worship service, and then the shakedown at the Wednesday night prayer meetings. The same things happen, week after week. I think it would be difficult to penetrate such regimented activities because nothing changes. But if they seriously try to go global, everything changes. This is how we penetrate their organization. For want of a better term, Joel, you are a computer geek. If Hartsell wants

Rapture Ministries to go global, and we know he does, he will require the services of someone like you. What if we find a subtle way to make it known to Hartsell that right here, in his own backyard, is someone who can make Rapture global in a few weeks."

Joel's eyes got as big as saucers. The wheels were turning. "Wow, Doc, I think you nailed it! Rapture is too tight to attack from the inside. But from the outside of Rapture, it should be easy. Hector had always told the Council that the best way to get close to and bring down a narcissistic bully always starts with stroking their ego."

Doc continued. "This will be like a Hollywood production. Someone needs to sell Reverend Hartsell on an outfit which can create a Rapture website. This is the ticket to worldwide exposure. Then we can have DVDs made showing the type of stuff he uses in his Wednesday night prayer meetings. You know, climb the ladder by donating to Rapture, so he can feed and clothe the people of the world. We can send them love gifts for different levels of donations. Hartsell will be blinded by dollar signs."

Joel's wheels were still turning, silently, but at high speed. He was getting ideas of his own. "You know, Doc, these services do not come cheap. To do the production right, a highly professional job, designed to generate donations of say one hundred million dollars, may require Rapture to spend...say five million dollars."

3

BLOODY BASEBALL BAT

Martha was intrigued by the cold case given to her by Yolanda. The first officer to arrive at the convenience store had a brief preliminary report. It stated that on Wednesday, March 26, 1980, the local police were summoned to a mom and pop style grocery store. It was 10:55 PM when the police arrived. Inside the store they found a hysterical middle-aged Greek woman and two black teen-aged boys. Behind the counter there was an old man, presumably the woman's father, who was beaten to death. The cash register was open, but it appeared that no money was taken. The man was lying on his side, and there was a bloodied baseball bat on the counter next to the register. The poor man's head had been caved in, and there were brains and blood spattered everywhere. The area was cordoned off by the police, and "Do Not Cross" tape was draped over the entrance. The two boys were taken to the local police precinct for questioning and the investigation began.

Thankfully, the formal investigation was much more detailed. The hysterical woman, Helena, was, in fact, the daughter of the victim. She told the police that on Wednesdays the store closed at midnight. Many nights, like this one, business slowed to a crawl after 10:00 PM so she would often retire to the back room and watch television until closing. She and her father would then lock the store and walk around the back of the building to their upstairs apartment.

When she heard her father yell, Helena knew that it was close to 11:00 PM because the program she was watching on television was ending. Her father yelling to her was not unusual, so she chose to ignore him until her program was over. Helena then heard a crashing sound and became concerned. She called the police as her father had taught her to do, and then hid for a few moments until she heard the sirens. When Helena opened the door which separated the back room from the store, she saw her father on the floor with the two boys standing over him. The cash register drawer was open, and one of the boys, the taller of the two, held the bloodied bat in his hand. This was all Helena had to offer

The two boys were apparently not close friends, but knew each other casually from living in the same apartment building. The taller, older boy was Bernard Jones. Everyone had always called him Bubba because he was tall for his age and he was fifty pounds overweight. When this incident took place, Bubba was seventeen years old. He was six feet two inches tall and weighed two hundred pounds. Roddy Jackson, on the other hand, was a beanpole. He was fifteen years old and was five feet six inches tall and weighed only one hundred and five pounds.

As required by police protocol, the two boys were separated for interrogation. About an hour later, it was determined that their stories were identical. Except for one thing.

Roddy had three dollars which he said he had earned babysitting a neighbor's child. Like all normal fifteen year old boys, the money was burning a hole in his pocket. He decided to go out and purchase a cold drink and some potato chips. Roddy met Bubba on the sidewalk in front of the apartment building. Roddy liked hanging around with Bubba, especially at 10:30 at night. Roddy was always a little skittish and Bubba's impressive size made him feel a lot safer. So, if Bubba would accompany him to the convenience store, Roddy would buy him a drink and chips as well. Bubba did not get to two hundred pounds by saying no to potato chips, so off they went.

A few minutes later, they had their drinks and chips and were tee-heeing as they looked through the girly magazines. Roddy decided he might want a different kind of soft drink, so he walked alone back to the cooler. As Roddy was trying to make his choice, he heard the old man who owned the store yelling in Greek. Roddy told the police that he laughed because he thought that the old man had caught Bubba eyeballing the centerfolds again. But then Roddy heard struggling, a thud, and then a crash, like a shelf falling down. He decided on his original soft drink, and he proceeded to the checkout counter. There he saw blood everywhere, the crumpled body of the old man, and Bubba standing at the counter holding a baseball bat with blood all over it. Bubba had dropped his chips and just stood there with the "deer in the headlights" look on his face. A moment later, Roddy heard police sirens and a woman came screaming from the rear of the store. This was all that Roddy could offer the police, except that he did not believe Bubba could have killed that man. Bubba was big, but he couldn't hurt anyone.

Bubba's story was the same as Roddy's until the part where the old man started yelling. Bubba also thought that the store owner was yelling at him for looking at the naked women in the magazine. Bubba said that he quickly threw down the magazine. Bubba then walked to the checkout, and turned to look at the door because the little bell on it was ringing. Only instead of someone coming into the store, Bubba saw a man running away, quickly disappearing into the night. Bubba thought that the man had forgotten his baseball bat which was on the counter. He picked up the bat and was about to run after him, but he stopped and froze when he saw the old man's body. It was then that Bubba heard the sirens and the woman came screaming from behind him. Clearly Martha thought, Bubba was not the sharpest knife in the drawer, but that did not make him a killer.

It was easy for Martha to understand why the jury found it so easy to convict these boys. They were seen by both the old man's daughter and the police as they stormed into the front door of the store. The cash register was open, and there stood Bubba, bat in hand. And Bubba did not have a nickel in his pocket to buy a drink and chips. No one paid much attention to Bubba's story about the man running out of the store.

This was originally not an FBI case. Yolanda had been in the police precinct on other business when the boys were brought in and arrested sixteen years ago. She found it incredulous that these two boys could commit murder. Martha remembered Yolanda telling her about the community's demand for swift justice.

A few aspects of the case bothered Martha. Why did Bubba have absolutely no history of violence of any kind? There was not even a record of his having a fight in school. Also, when the boys were searched, the police found no weapons, not even a jackknife. People that have robbery or killing on their mind usually carry a weapon. The search of the boys also produced three dollars from Roddy's pocket. Why would they steal if Roddy had enough money to pay for everything? Lastly, if the boys committed this crime, why

68

didn't they take the money from the register, or why didn't they make an attempt to run away? Things just did not add up. And then, of course, there were Yolanda's screaming instincts.

Martha wanted to interview Bubba and Roddy herself. She called Folsom Prison in Sacramento and made the necessary arrangements to visit both Roddy Jackson and Bernard (Bubba) Jones. She then called the Evidence Division of the San Francisco Police Department to locate any old evidence of the convenience store crime scene. Whereas old evidence should be stored indefinitely, it was amazing how things had a tendency to disappear. And poor storage conditions including things like heat and humidity extremes could compromise the integrity of old evidence. Martha was not hopeful, but it was worth trying. In any case, she wanted to give them the whole day to locate any evidence. It frequently took that long to find anything.

4

THE SLOW MOVING LINE AND THE CLIFF

Hector decided to drive to the Wednesday evening prayer service separately from Judge Lamar and his wife Colleen. He did this for two reasons. First, he decided that the Rapture elders and parishioners should not get the idea that he and the judge knew each other. This could work to the Council's advantage for future activities. Secondly, it was his mother's birthday. After driving to Reverend Hartsell's two homes and taking a few pictures for the Council, Hector was taking her out to dinner. It was a shame to have to end such a nice day by getting browbeaten by the elders at the Wednesday evening prayer service, but it had to be done.

Hector ended his landscaping work at 2:00 PM on Wednesday. His mother was dressed and ready to go when Hector walked in. He showered and grabbed his camera and binoculars along with the addresses Yolanda had given him for Reverend Hartsell's two homes. A short time later, Hector and Rosa were parked across the street from Reverend Hartsell's two story colonial home. There were no cars in the driveway or parked in the street in front of the house. The house appeared empty. Hector took a few pictures, but there really was not much to see. He and Rosa sat and watched the house for twenty minutes. No one went by the windows, and Hector became convinced that no one was there. Emboldened by his curiosity, he walked up the porch steps and rang the doorbell. He probably should have expected it, but was nonetheless surprised to hear the doorbell chime the first few bars

70

of *Rapture O' My Soul*. No one was home. Through the window, Hector could see that the home was modestly appointed and comfortable. It was exactly what most people would expect if they visited their clergyman. The next door neighbor was mowing his lawn, so Hector decided to push his luck. He went up to the neighbor and introduced himself. "Excuse me, sir," Hector waited for the man to stop. The neighbor killed the engine and removed his earplugs. Hector continued, "Hi, I am Rick from Tisdale Plumbing. I was asked to come by the house next door and check the hot water tank. Do you know when they might return?"

"Return?" said the neighbor, "I have not seen anyone there in months. How could they possibly know there is a problem with the hot water? Some kid mows their lawn, but he is the only one I have seen."

Hector asked, "Well, do you have a phone number or some way I can get in touch with them?"

The neighbor added, "Look, I was at work when they moved in about nine months ago. Since then, I have never laid eyes on them or anyone else either in or outside that house. I think my wife said he was a minister or something, but I don't know."

Hector motioned toward the house. "OK, thanks for stopping to speak with me. I'll take a walk around back just in case they might have left me a note. Thanks."

The neighbor replaced his earplugs and started the mower. He managed half of a wave and drove away.

Hector put up his first finger in the air showing Rosa that he would be right back, and he walked to the back of the house. Again, there was nothing remarkable to be seen. Hector returned to his car. He headed out of town toward the second house owned by Reverend Hartsell. He had previously written down directions from a city map he kept in the truck he used for landscaping. After another hour of driving and quiet conversation with his mother, Hector was on the road where Reverend Hartsell lived. This was a beautiful mountainous area, and sparsely populated. Each home up here appeared to have its own access road from the street Hector was driving on. The road was winding as the elevation increased, and every quarter mile or so, there was a clearing which made it possible to look down upon the last two or three homes he passed. Hector hoped this would continue once he passed Reverend Hartsell's home. After about ten more minutes driving uphill, they found what they had been looking for. The ornate mailbox said only "Hartsell" and appeared to stand sentry in front of the massive iron gate. The three foot golden initials "TH" were affixed to the front of the gate doors. Hector noticed a camera pod on a pole adjacent to the gate, as well as an intercom and speaker which obviously was used by visitors and delivery people to alert the owners to their presence outside the gate. Not today, Hector thought to himself, not with my mother. He kept driving up the winding hill, and just like before, the trees opened up, and he was looking down upon the palatial mansion of Reverend Thomas Hartsell. Hector parked his car on the far side of the road where it could not be seen from below, and he grabbed his binoculars and camera from the backseat. Once again, he promised his mother that he would be right back. Hector crossed the road and found a comfortable position alongside a large tree. Reconnaissance. For a moment,

Hector was a Navy SEAL again. This was another of life's ironies. When he was a SEAL reconnaissance was his least favorite activity, yet now it blessed him with fond memories.

Hector first used the binoculars to quickly look over the estate. Wow, he thought to himself, talk about occupying the catbird seat. He had a tremendous advantage from here. He could survey the entire property without being seen. This was not just a house, this was an estate rivaling Joel's home in Tanglewood Hills. There was a large swimming pool and hot tub next to a covered patio area. Once again, the golden "TH" was painted on the bottom of the pool. Hector estimated the house to be between fifteen and twenty thousand square feet. The detached garage looked as though it could accommodate four cars. Unlike Hartsell's first house, there were several signs of activity here. Sprinklers were watering the lawn, and he could hear the sound of a weed whacker coming from the other side of the house. Hector liked the circular gravel driveway in the front of the house. A late model black Cadillac was parked there, and a dark blue Buick Roadmaster was parked a car length behind it. Hector laughed to himself when he saw the *RAPTURE* license plate on the Cadillac. What is it with these guys and their vanity license plates? He heard several people laughing, and moved the binoculars in that direction. Two men Hector recognized as church elders from Rapture were coming out of the house, and behind them were three scantily clad women in tow. Obviously quite inebriated, they were laughing and falling all over the place. As the men proceeded to help the girls get into the backseat of the Buick, Reverend Hartsell came out of the house in a bathrobe and yelled to the driver. He gave them an admonition reminding them to be ready for prayer meetings in a few hours.

The last woman to get into the car yelled back to Reverend Hartsell, "You gonna give them a little laying on of the hands like you did us Tommy?" Again they all laughed. The Buick sped off and Reverend Hartsell returned to the house. Hector took several pictures and noted that the property could be easily accessed by going down the hill. The front gate only denied entry to the house from the main road. Rosa was patiently waiting when Hector returned to the car. Now it was time to focus on his mother's birthday. He took her to a very exclusive Mexican restaurant. San Francisco is home to thousands of Mexican-Americans, and restaurants like this one are very popular.

The hallmark characteristic of Hector's life was its simplicity. He was totally unpretentious. What you saw him as, was exactly what he was. Hector's parents, Juan and Rosa Martinez, were all about family, and this was passed on to their two sons. Probably being in a strange country when they raised their family had a lot to do with the strong bonds between them and their sons. Not knowing about American traditions, the Martinez family had a tendency to stay home while they marveled at their new countrymen who always seemed to be running around and going places. Juan, Hector's father, was the one who took the initiative in the family. He was honest, ambitious, and could work all day long. If a landscaping client was in a hurry to get a job done, Juan was happy to work extra hours. But for Juan, it was never about the money. Hector remembered his father always asking clients, "How may I help you?" and he meant it. Hector's sincerity came from his father. Never one to complicate things by weighing all of the options, there was simply what was right, and what was not. Life was that simple to Juan. And now, it is the same way for Hector.

After Juan died a year ago, there was never any question how things would change. Hector was now the man of the house, so he stepped up and became the provider. There was no whining about "his needs" or how he was being inconvenienced. Juan's landscaping clients never even noticed a difference. Hector had worked with his father ever since he retired from the Navy SEALs. He loved the fresh air and working outside. He also found independence in working for himself. He was not the kind of man who could punch a timecard or sit in front of a computer. Yet, the thing which defined Hector more than anything else, was being a Navy SEAL. It wasn't about the killing or the prestige of having been one of a handful of sailors special enough to wear the trident. It was about doing the right thing and standing up for those unable to fight for themselves. Hector hated bullies. He, also, hated handouts. If someone was deep in a hole, Hector wasn't about to throw them a rope and pull them out. No, that was not what he was all about. Hector preferred giving them a ladder so they could have the dignity of climbing out of the hole themselves. People had to seize their own initiative. Hector saw his role as leveling the playing field, so that everyone had the same chance at life.

Hector was given the chance to become a Navy SEAL because his commanding officer, Lieutenant Commander Michael Gibson, saw something special in him. The proudest moment in his life was the day his father, with tears running down his cheeks, saw the Navy SEAL trident pinned to his son's chest. Hector experienced the one thing all men covet. Hector saw that he was worthy in his father's eyes.

Following Rosa's birthday dinner, Hector slipped the waiter an extra ten dollars to put a sparkler in a large wedge of her favorite

75

coconut cake. Hector enjoyed spending several hours with his mother. He made her feel special, and indeed she was. They sat for a while after dinner and had coffee while they reminisced about Juan and how much he was missed both as a husband and a father.

Hector never spoke to anyone of this, but he visualized death as a long line and a cliff. The atmosphere was a dark, moonless, Halloween-type night with the wind providing a chill that went right to the bones. All the characters in this visualization had ashen faces and moved in slow zombie-like steps. All living persons were in a line approaching the cliff and awaiting their turn to go over and into the abyss. Whenever someone died, he visualized everyone in the line moving up one space, one step closer to the cliff. Everyone silently moved one step forward toward the end of their life. It was all unavoidable, life coming full circle. The only thing was...you never knew exactly where your place in the line was.

The long line and the cliff had nothing to do with Hector's belief in God or salvation. This was merely one man's attempt to understand that which we cannot fathom. Juan had gone over the cliff a year ago. He was missed, but at times like this both Hector and Rosa felt he was still here.

"What say, mom?" Hector smiled. "Are you ready for a prayer meeting?"

Rosa knew it was time to go. "I guess," she said.

Hector paid the check and left a generous tip. He took his mother's arm and walked her to the car. Twenty minutes later, they entered the halls of Rapture Ministries. As expected, they were greeted by the same elders whom Hector had seen leaving

Reverend Hartsell's home less than three hours earlier. Hector and his mother knew that they would be separated, so they put on their smiley faces and accepted it. He never saw the judge or his wife Colleen. They must have been in other groups, but Hector did see Lamar's car in the parking lot.

A little over an hour later, Hector and Rosa waited in the parking lot for Judge Laningham and Colleen. After a few minutes, they came out of the building.

"Hey, Judge," said Hector. "You look like you'd like to slap the crap out of somebody."

The judge laughed. "Is it that obvious? I feel so badly for those folks. All they want to do is the right thing, and Hartsell's goons are relentless." He abruptly changed the subject. "Hey, let's go somewhere for a drink. I think we all need one." He looked at Rosa and smiled. "And I hear that someone is a birthday girl."

"Done," said Hector. "The faster that I can get away from this place, the better I will like it." Hector and his mother followed the judge to a small out-of-the-way place which had a lot of atmosphere, but not a lot of people. They spoke of the prayer meetings. Their experiences were similar, and they agreed that these meetings were designed for a single purpose...to raise money. Hector told the judge of his travels to Reverend Hartsell's two homes. After a few moments, they changed subjects, and for the remainder of the evening, Hector amused everyone telling the tales of his escapades as a Navy SEAL.

5

TRAGEDY IN OREGON

Agent Danno Lockwood received the call that Del Reese's truck had been spotted. A gas station attendant saw Del at the pump. The attendant's boss was the one who took the call from the FBI, and he left a note on the cash register alerting all of his employees to watch for the red pickup truck and its two occupants. The gas station attendant said that the truck left the station about ten minutes ago. He did not notice if there was a passenger or not. The truck headed north on Route 5.

Agent Danno had been following the movement of the truck on a map. Each time Del Reese used his credit card, a red dot was added to the map. So far, it appeared that Del's wife and friends were correct. Del was in Oregon. The red dots continued north along Route 5. The question was, where would the red dots stop? Del had to know that the police would be looking for Amy, and he, also, had to know that he would be the primary suspect. So why then, was he taking his time?

Danno was not at all concerned that Del would hurt Amy. He, therefore, concluded that patience was best at this point. Once Del stopped using the credit card, this would be a clear indication that he may have reached his final destination.

Alicia Reese was sitting by the phone. She had been there for days. Agent Lockwood had promised to keep her informed every time he learned anything new. He also asked Alicia to be ready to leave with him at a moment's notice once Delano and Amy had been found. Years of experience had taught Danno that a loved one can defuse a bad situation faster than a cop every time.

The plan which Danno planned to follow was textbook. Once the subject was located and his presence confirmed, the FBI and local authorities would surround the location, making escape impossible. Then the negotiations started. The kidnapper was always assumed to have a gun. Of course, they already knew that Del was a hunter and that he had taken his weapons with him when Alicia asked him to leave their house. Even though Danno believed that Del did not look upon his daughter as a hostage, the FBI had no choice but to negotiate as though she was one. No matter how you looked at the situation, Amy was abducted against her will. Usually, the first few hours into a negotiation could predict the outcome. Good endings usually came quickly. Bad endings sometimes took several days. And then, of course, there were any number of complications which could alter negotiations, such as whether or not the kidnappers had food and water; whether either the abductor or the hostages had any medical issues; the physical layout of the building; and any demands which might be made by the kidnapper.

Two hours after the gas station attendant called, they got a break. A clerk at a small grocery store about one hundred miles north of the last gas station called the local police. The clerk handled the situation perfectly. He recognized both Del and Amy from the descriptions provided by the authorities. In addition, he feigned looking at the weather outside, when in fact he was looking for a red pickup truck with California license plates. This, too, he verified. Without being overly obvious, he tried to find out where they were headed. However, his attempts at conversation went nowhere. Del and Amy were too focused on their shopping. When Danno asked what they purchased, the clerk practically gave them an itemized list, and then he provided the police exactly what they needed. He told the police that Del, in addition to several other items, bought milk, hamburger, cheese, macaroni salad, and ice cream, but no ice. This meant that either Del already had a cooler with ice, or that he intended to stay somewhere very nearby. Since Del had not purchased perishable items thus far on this trip, the police and the FBI both surmised that Del was very close to his final destination.

Danno called Alicia, informing her that he was on his way to pick her up. As per his earlier instructions, she already had an overnight bag packed. Within forty-five minutes, they, along with another FBI agent, were in a helicopter on their way to Oregon and the area where Del and Amy were last seen. The local police had already been asked to identify any possible rental cottages or hunting cabins where they might stay. Danno guessed that ice cream would begin to melt in half an hour, so a circle with a thirty mile radius sounded about right. The good news was that there were not a lot of side roads up here, and they could use the helicopter to search the designated area until dark. The bad news was that the forest often created a canopy making it nearly impossible to see anything underneath the trees.

Hours later, after refueling once at a small airport, the helicopter finally landed in a field where the local police were waiting with a car for Danno and the others. Two local policemen, knowledgeable with the area, took to the air in the helicopter to scour the landscape looking for the red truck. Forty-five minutes later, Danno received a call from the helicopter pilot. They spotted a red Ford pickup truck with California license plate KEG0606. The truck was outside of a hunting cabin about twelve miles from where the helicopter had dropped off Agent Danno and the others.

The policeman in charge of the local officers had already called for backup, and within an hour, everyone was ready to go. Danno, also, requested an ambulance. He hoped that it would not be needed, but since the location was so remote, having it close- by made sense. The police silently and slowly drove along the access road which led to the cabin. They stopped well short of being in sight of the building and blocked the road. Quickly and silently, the police surrounded the cabin. Alicia was made to wait in a police car with a policewoman, well out of view of the activity. The guns, helmets, bullet-proof vests, and the static on the police radio, all contributed to the backdrop of an already surreal and frightening situation. Alicia put her face in her hands and tried to hide from the reality of the scene playing out before her. Her husband and her little girl were just a few feet from a dozen men with guns trained on the small building. The policewoman did her best to console Alicia.

Everything seemed to happen in slow motion. Agent Danno was crouched behind the red truck, and he waited for verification that everyone was in place around the cabin. Danno looked at the policeman in front of him. He did not know these men and he had no idea how they might react. Minutes before, Danno had given them all final instructions before they fanned out, completely encircling the small building. It was just beginning to get dark, Danno liked to think of it as the gloaming, and figures could be seen passing back and forth in front of lights in the cabin.

81

Finally everything was set. Agent Danno took one last look around and stood up with the bullhorn. Danno spoke slowly, "Delano Reese, this is the FBI. You are completely surrounded. We know that you have your daughter Amy with you, and her mother is here with us. Please send Amy out and we will talk. No one wants to hurt you. We will give you a few minutes. In five minutes, I will speak with you again."

Inside the cabin, Del and Amy were startled by the bullhorn and the loud voice. They sat quietly together on the sofa. Five minutes later, Danno summoned Del again. Danno requested that first Amy be sent out alone. Following this, they wanted Del to come out without any weapons, and with his hands held high in the air. Minutes later the cabin's porch light was turned on and the door opened. Amy walked out and slowly descended from the porch, down the steps, to the sidewalk. Danno motioned Amy toward him, but Amy turned around as though she were waiting for her father to join her. Since Amy was now safely out of the cabin, all eyes were focused on Del as he stepped out from the shadows into the light. As instructed, his hands were high in the air.

By this time, knowing that Amy was safe and out of the building, with Del about to surrender, the policewoman led Alicia toward her daughter. Once she saw Amy, Alicia yelled out to her. "Amy," she shrieked! Amy recognized her mother's voice, spun around, and bolted toward her.

Del saw his daughter run and he yelled out to her, "Amy wait." As he did this, Del dropped his right hand and reached toward his hip.

"NO!" Screamed Danno and he started to duck. All hell broke loose. A hail of bullets cut Del down, and he was dead before his body reached the porch floor. He was shot eight times. The scene was terrible. Alicia and Amy were both hysterical, and Amy broke away from her mother and ran to her father's body. Del had fallen on his back, and his right hand was still pinned behind his body.

"I thought he was going for a gun," said the young policeman who fired first. Of course, once one shot was fired, the other policemen instinctively fired in support.

"Yeah," thought Danno to himself, "so much for good endings coming quickly in hostage negotiating."

The policewoman pulled Amy and Alicia back away from the scene. Danno rolled Del's body onto its side. His hand was still clutching an envelope which Danno carefully pulled from his fingers. The envelope said "Happy Birthday Amy."

The policewoman had moved to position herself between Amy and the cabin where the bleeding, contorted body of her father was in full view. Another policeman had come to help direct Amy and Alicia into a squad car, and the ambulance, with its orange and red lights on, backed toward the sidewalk. Danno put the envelope in his pocket.

Two days after Delano Reese was killed, Danno submitted his report to Yolanda. Nearly all of the information in the report had been supplied by Amy. Several days ago, Del picked his daughter up after school and took her away because he had no choice. He had been trying desperately to turn his life around. Del had quit drinking, and he had made arrangements to move north with his brother Rick while he looked for a new job. He wanted Amy to know that he still loved her and Alicia, and that he was sorry for the way he had acted since he lost his job. Del had planned to get re-established once he found a job, and he was then going to send for his girls to join him. Del explained to Amy that starting over would take some time, so he wanted to be with her a while before he left. Amy said that she never felt threatened or in danger. She knew her mother would be upset, but Amy knew that this was the only way that she and her father could spend time together. Besides, her father had promised to drive her back to Forestport after a few days together in the cabin. Del had been killed trying to give his daughter a birthday card. Del knew that he would not be around for Amy's birthday since he was moving to his brother's house. The card told Amy how much Del loved her, and that he promised to return to pick her and Alicia up as soon as he was able to find a job. The card contained an inexpensive heart-shaped locket.

Yes, a man takes it much differently than a woman when he loses his job. And now all Amy has are her memories and recurring nightmares about a cabin, a park, and a green swing.

6

FOLSOM PRISON

It took Agent Martha Green a little over an hour and a half to drive the one hundred miles between Santa Molina and Folsom Prison in Sacramento. She had never seen the inside of a prison, and she was not exactly looking forward to the experience. She parked her car in the visitor's lot, removed her gun, and locked it in the trunk. As Martha walked through the first of several gates, she looked up at the walls. The silhouette of the massive structure against the morning sky, seen through the spiraling rolls of concertina wire, gave her an ominous feeling. Instinctively, Martha reached for the security of her gun only to be reminded that she had left it in the car.

Martha and several people entering through the prison's visitor's gate were ushered into a large waiting area. One by one, each of the visitors was walked through a metal detector. They were then patted down and any belongings were thoroughly searched. They were then taken to a second large waiting area. Here sat inmates' family members, friends, and attorneys. This was not a happy place, and there were no smiles or small talk such as you might experience in the waiting room of a doctor or dentist. It sometimes took a few minutes to locate the inmate, and the rate at which the guards worked indicated that customer service was not a high priority here. After ten minutes Martha was taken to a long corridor which had a whole series of doors. The guard opened the fourth door on the right and held it for Martha. The guard explained that visitors were allowed to speak to inmates for twenty minutes. Since Agent Green was here to see two inmates, after twenty minutes with Bernard Jones, she was to remain here, and Roddy Jackson would then be brought in, again for twenty minutes. Finally, the guard warned Martha against making any sexually explicit gestures, raising her voice, or riling the inmates in any way. Agent Green did not appreciate being spoken to like this, but she nodded in agreement. The guard was just doing his job. Martha thought that the miserable attitude of these guards made the folks at the Department of Motor Vehicles look like party animals.

Bernard (Bubba) Jones was not at all what Martha had expected. She expected an angry, pissed off young black man with a chip on his shoulder and an attitude to match. Instead, she found a very polite and respectful, shy, and beaten down young man. Everything was "Yes, ma'am," or "No, ma'am." Martha explained that, at the request of her boss, she was reviewing some old cases, and she merely had a few questions.

Bubba had sixteen years to become angry, but all that Martha could detect was fear and hopelessness. She asked Bubba to walk her through the events of that horrific night many years ago. After all these years Bubba told the exact same story. Nothing had changed. She decided to try to focus on the one area which the police had ignored, the man Bubba saw run from the store. Bubba thought that the man had left his baseball bat on the counter and left without it. He picked up the bat and was going to run after the man when he saw the blood and the old man dead on the floor. Bubba added that he didn't even know that the bat belonged to the store owner until the trial. He said that the old man's daughter testified that he kept it under the counter for protection. The poor

86

old man was killed with his own weapon. Martha's time with Bernard was nearly done. She thanked him for his time, and just like Yolanda, she came to the conclusion that there was simply no way Bubba could have killed the store owner.

Five minutes later, Roddy Jackson was brought in. Roddy was no longer a frightened young man. He appeared to have taken full advantage of Folsom's weight lifting program. Roddy looked as if he had muscles on his muscles. Somehow it made no sense to Martha that he had a package of non-filtered cigarettes rolled up in his sleeve. Unlike Bubba, Roddy did have an attitude. It was unusual that someone as young as Roddy would have been tried and convicted as an adult and given such a long sentence. Yolanda had told Martha that this happened because the crime was so heinous and because the community was so outraged. Yolanda, also, told her that if this crime had happened one hundred years ago, both boys would have been lynched.

Martha asked the same questions of Roddy, and once again, the story never changed. But what a difference in HOW the stories were told. Bubba's delivery was slow and remorseful. It was clear that he knew that he had been in the wrong place at a very bad time. Roddy was no longer the introverted, skinny little guy Yolanda described. He was assertive and at times he bordered on belligerent. Before Martha left, Roddy gave her one more thing to think about. Roddy said that he believed Bubba would not last much longer. Bubba refused help, and over the years, became more and more despondent.

Martha thanked Roddy for meeting with her. She could not wait to get back outside. Martha did not expect that her visit with the two young men would be a joyous event, yet she could not have anticipated just how depressing it would be. Once she got back to her car, she took her gun from the trunk, dropped it on the seat next to her, and drove away. She recalled having seen several old black and white movies in which the bad guy, a gangster type, is cornered by the police in a hopeless situation. Martha always pictured Spencer Tracy as the cop and James Cagney as the villain. The police, of course, request that the bad guy throw down his weapon and come out with his hands up. Invariably, the cornered villain refuses to give up stating that he prefers death to returning to prison. Until today, until her visit to Folsom Prison, she had never understood this death wish. If you could begin with despair and absolute hopelessness, and then paint it with desolation and depression, you might begin to understand incarceration.

Agent Green had an hour and a half to try to shake off the effect her visit to the prison had on her. She had often heard people speak of their greatest fears. Things like spiders, snakes, mice, and fear of the dark always came up. Martha thought that if people could visit a prison, incarceration would certainly become "numero uno." The thought of having every single positive thing in your life taken away in a single moment was beyond her comprehension. Your love, your spirit, your confidence, your pride, your dignity, your privacy, your ambition, and the freedom to make your own decisions...all taken away the moment the door slams shut behind you. The reason that prisons are nicknamed "the slammer" is because of the symbolism associated with the door slamming shut. Everything good in your life is gone forever once you hear that sound. And even if you complete your sentence and are released, it does not matter. The prison follows you wherever you go. The rest of your life becomes black and white, the color is gone. There is a taint about you. People treat you differently, and getting a decent job becomes almost impossible. Martha found everything about prison absolutely horrifying.

Something was bothering Martha. In both the police report, and the conversation with Bubba, it was stated that the bloody baseball bat was left on the counter. It had to have been left there by whoever killed the store owner. But the bat belonged to the old man. So how did the killer get it? There had to have been a struggle and the killer wrestled it away from the old man who undoubtedly was trying to protect himself with the bat.

Martha's next stop was the Evidence Division of the San Francisco Police Department. She tried not to get her hopes up. Sixteen years was a long time, long enough for things to disappear or become contaminated beyond being of any value. Yet now Martha shared Yolanda's mental image of Bubba's heartrending face.

The policeman stationed at the evidence cage was pleasant enough. He recalled Martha's request for the old evidence, but he was not sure if his technicians had processed it yet. He excused himself and went to a back room. Ten minutes later, he returned with a large box. The box had a label which identified the date and the case number. Martha signed a receipt and thanked the policeman. She was so excited that they found this evidence, she wanted to rip open the box right there. However, as an expert in the collection and processing of evidence, she knew better.

An hour later, after a quick lunch at her desk, Martha claimed a large empty table in the evidence processing room. She put on a mask and gloves and carefully opened the box. There were separate labeled brown paper bags containing the clothes of Bernard Jones, Roddy Jackson, and the victim, Adamos Lazopoulos. There was a file of photographs of the crime scene, as well as police interviews and various police reports. Finally, in the bottom of the box, was the bloody baseball bat which killed the old man.

Martha started with Roddy Jackson's clothes. She carefully separated the shirt, blue jeans, socks and shoes. The visual inspection showed nothing. She pulled to herself a large magnifying glass which was movable and suspended from the ceiling with a series of pulleys and wires. Slowly she rotated the clothes under the magnifying glass for closer inspection. Martha found some hairs which she removed using tweezers, and she transferred them to a new evidence bag labeled *Roddy Jackson*. Martha worked on Roddy's clothes for about an hour. Nothing remarkable caught her attention, but one could never tell what all the hairs and fibers and stains might reveal when they were scrutinized in greater detail by the technicians. Next Martha inspected Bernard Joneses' clothes. Again she found random hair and fiber samples scattered throughout the clothes. It appeared to Martha that Bubba's clothes were not washed as often as Roddy's. Sometimes the absence of evidence could tell an investigator as much as the presence of it, and this was a perfect example. Where was the blood? Old man Lazopoulos was hit in the head with the baseball bat with such force that his blood and brains were splattered all over the area behind the counter where he stood. This was corroborated by police testimony as well as dozens of photographs. The total absence of blood spatter on Bubba's clothes was virtually impossible, unless, of course, he was not the killer.

Finally, the last bag of clothes belonging to Adamos Lazopoulos was examined. Unlike Bubba's clothes, finding blood on these clothes was not a problem. His shirt, pants, shoes, socks, and the apron he wore, were all covered in dried blood. In addition, there were all kinds of hair and unknown fibers embedded in the dried blood. The amount of evidence which Martha was able to remove from the old man's clothes was much greater than that from either of the boy's clothes. At this point, most of what she removed was unidentifiable. Certainly a lot of the material would be old tissue from the victim, but it had to be examined anyway. Mr. Lazopoulos' clothes were a treasure trove of evidence. Martha knew that if this evidence had been collected by today's standards and procedures, there would be no way that all of this material would have been left behind. Oh well...one man's trove is another man's treasure.

At last came the baseball bat. The macabre side of Martha wondered if it had ever been used to hit a home run. Since the bat was in a transparent bag, Martha decided not to open it just yet. She held the ends of the bat through the bag and slowly rotated it under the magnifying glass. She thought it best not to take any chances with contamination. Since all of the evidence was sixteen years old, this could be the last time it was examined. Although this was not a crime scene, Martha was still hopeful that this evidence would "talk to her" nonetheless.

7

A "HECTORISM"

The two weeks since the previous Council meeting passed quickly. All of the Council members had a very busy two weeks, except Judge Lamar Laningham. He had not told anyone, but he had not felt well in months. Three months ago he fought a cold and a nagging cough had persisted since that time. The judge's best friend and Council colleague, Dr. Jerry Woodson, had an associate, a Dr. Procter, who liked to say that "getting old was not for the faint of heart." Not wanting to alarm his wife Colleen, Lamar made an appointment with his family physician without telling her. The appointment was for three days from now, and since he had been feeling this way for months, a few more days would not matter.

True to form, Hector was the last Council member to arrive. The judge had never figured out if Hector's habitual tardiness was unintentional, or if he just liked to make a grand entrance. No matter, once Hector entered the Laningham's study, took his appointed seat at the round table, and flashed those pearly whites, all was forgiven. Like his father, Hector's occupation as a landscaper added tan to his Latino skin hue. This made the contrast to his perfectly white teeth all the more striking. When Hector smiled at you, it was impossible not to smile back.

Judge Laningham raised each of his hands about eight inches from the table with his palms facing the others. "OK, folks, we have a lot to go over, so let us begin." He continued, "Colleen, Hector, his mother Rosa, and I all went to the Rapture Ministries' Wednesday evening prayer services. Hector was absolutely correct. These meetings are nothing but shakedowns. I understand the mission of evangelizing. Ever since Christ's original disciples, there have been spirit-filled Christians who spread the good news of Christ and salvation to the four corners of the earth. And they often do this at great peril to themselves. Over the centuries and still today, these well-meaning people are sometimes murdered for their belief. Thank God for such people. Then there are those like Reverend Hartsell. Their greed and insatiable desires drive them to become the most contemptible type of men. Like those who enter and loot stores and homes following natural disasters, they are devoid of morals or conscience. Unfortunately, Rapture Ministries is run by such people. When we were getting out of our car last Wednesday evening, we saw elderly people who had to be picked up in Rapture buses because they could not afford their own cars. Wouldn't you think that these people would be spared the extortion? They were not. The humiliation that these people were made to feel because they did not give more money was deplorable. Hector, can you share with us the photographs you took of Reverend Hartsell's humble homes?"

"Sure," Hector answered. He opened a small envelope and sent around the table pictures of the small colonial house which he had visited first. Hector added, "This is the home which Reverend Hartsell calls his primary residence in the church bulletin." Once again he passed the pictures to his right. "The church bulletin states that Reverend Hartsell is pleased to meet with parishioners in this, his home, but by appointment only. This is not because he is busy, this is because he is never there. He is here." Hector took several more photographs from the envelope and again passed them around. Hector noted the wide-eyed reaction of each Council member. "And while I was there, I also saw this." Hector removed the last two photographs and passed them around as before. "Three well-oiled floozies came out of the house with two elders a few hours before the Wednesday night prayer meetings. Reverend Hartsell was there as well. Obviously, on his declared salary from Rapture, the good reverend could not afford to pay the interest on the mortgage let alone the entire mortgage payment. A multimillion dollar mansion built on the money extorted from the poor. The closest this guy can get to a conscience is the first three letters. He is a 'c-o-n' who has made a 's-c-i-e-n-c-e' out of cheating the poor." The pictures had made their way around the table back to Hector, and he returned them to the envelope.

The judge looked at Yolanda. "What about the Rapture Ministries' finances? Were you able to discover anything?"

Yolanda opened a folder in front of her. "First let us talk about the money going in. To say that the recordkeeping is slipshod is a huge understatement. The records are nonexistent. Most churches recognize the problems which can come when handling large sums of money, so they create a built-in system of checks and balances. Two or more people count the money taken from the collection, and records are kept and given to either the elders, or more often, a special finance committee. Several people are typically involved, and the pastor or minister is never included. To avoid any impropriety, most clergy members avoid getting involved with money. In Rapture Ministries, the opposite is the case. Reverend Hartsell and the elders appear to be the only ones who handle the money. And once again, if you look at the attendance

94

records compared to the amount of money allegedly donated, there seem to be some serious discrepancies. For example, if we look at the Sunday prior to when Lamar and Colleen went with Hector and his mother, you will see what I mean. The bulletin states that the attendance that week was seven hundred and eighty-four people. Yet the bulletin also states that the collection was $2206. Seriously? This equates to an average donation of $2.81 per person. The way that the reverend hammers everyone about tithing and giving, I would conservatively expect that thirty percent of his people tithe. If they are tithing based on fifty thousand dollars each per year, and the rest of the congregation can only manage a mere ten dollar donation each per week, this amounts to about thirty thousand dollars per week. And since he claims donations of two thousand dollars, he pockets about twenty-eight thousand dollars weekly. And THAT, gentlemen, translates to nearly a million and a half dollars per year in tax-free unreported income. And we have not yet included anything from the Wednesday evening services which must be substantial based on the Wall of Attainment. None of this, of course, makes it into the church bulletin. My guess is that he pockets over two million dollars a year."

Yolanda gave the Council a moment to think about what she had spoken thus far. She continued. "There are eight Rapture Ministries' supported charities and overseas missions listed in the bulletin. Six of those appear to be bogus. I can find no records of them anywhere. I was able to locate and contact the other two charities. One never heard of Rapture Ministries, and the second said that Rapture donated one thousand dollars a year ago to help feed relief victims, but the check bounced. This means that all of the money collected on Wednesday nights is pocketed. Who knows

95

how much that brings in?" Yolanda hesitated. She appeared to be collecting her thoughts. "As far as the illegality of this is concerned, we have a problem. There are no contracts, nothing in writing. These people give of their own freewill. Yes, I recognize the extorting and cajoling which goes on, but a good lawyer would make a joke of our allegations. Besides, we have all seen the Sunday morning preachers who get caught fleecing the public for millions, or they get caught visiting prostitutes or sodomizing the choirboys. They get their hands slapped and maybe even do a little jail time. Then, a couple of years later, they ask forgiveness in a public forum, shed a few crocodile tears, tout their repentance, and then they jump right back into the game and start all over again, bigger and better. This business is just too lucrative. And what about the people that support them the second time around? Forgiveness is one thing, but stupidity is another. It is my opinion that going after Reverend Hartsell through legal channels would be a huge waste of time. He could get a fancy lawyer who would tie this up in the courts for years, and as I mentioned, he may only end up with a fine and a slap on the wrist with a promise to play nice. No, I believe we should expose him for exactly what he is, a low-life bottom feeder. As far as the public goes, after that...*caveat emptor*." Yolanda closed her file.

Judge Laningham turned his hands palms upward and held them out toward Dr. Woodson and Joel Harris. "Gentlemen," he said. "Do we have a plan?"

"I believe we do," offered Dr. Woodson. "Joel and I believe that once again, a 'Hectorism' is in order. We need to stroke Reverend Hartsell's ego and his ambitions big time. If someone such as myself were to attend a Wednesday night prayer meeting and make a record-breaking donation, I bet a personal audience with 'King' Thomas Hartsell could be arranged. At such a meeting, I would praise the good work he is accomplishing through Rapture Ministries and reinforce the need for him to go global. Why, just think of the good work he could do if his message was proclaimed across the entire nation, or even worldwide! I could speak of DVDs and Rapture websites and build my aspirations to a crescendo, just like his Sunday sermons Hector has described. And then I could casually mention my friend, the famous Hollywood production specialist. This friend could easily make Rapture's dream of going global a reality. He has done it many times! I could throw in an example of his work to whet his appetite. Let me turn this over to Joel since he is the expert."

Joel smiled and took a moment to organize his thoughts. "My company has the people to make this happen. If there are areas unfamiliar to us, we have connections everywhere. Obviously, we will use a fictitious company. We can create a temporary dummy website in case he decides to check us out. But we intend to give him so much to do before our production deadlines, that he won't have much time for anything else.

At my company, HOT Software, whenever we come out with a new product, we bombard the market with advertising, free sample downloads, and mailers to our loyal customers. Essentially, we are creating the demand for our product.

With Hartsell I see it happening something like this. As Dr. Woodson suggested, I think we could show him an example of something which has been immensely successful and made someone very wealthy. Once he is able to visualize Rapture

Ministries in the light of a Hollywood production with himself as the star of the show, he will not be able to resist making such a presentation for Rapture. I could have someone film Reverend Hartsell extolling the work of Rapture in one of his sermons. We could work in the choir and take some flattering pictures of the church. Hartsell's own Wednesday night movies highlighting the work abroad would be helpful. Since this is now May 1996, maybe we could challenge the nation to raise enough money to end starvation and maybe a particular disease such as AIDS by the end of the century. Hartsell will need a striking website, which we can create. My people will make a complimenting DVD introducing Reverend Hartsell and Rapture Ministries to the nation and the world. And then, once all of these things are in place, we bait the hook. We tell Hartsell that everything is in place to go global. For, say five million dollars, we can launch Rapture Ministries worldwide. He will expect hundreds of millions of dollars to pour in from everywhere. Once we have his money, we give him a taste of Council justice."

Judge Laningham smiled. "Nice work. Let's meet again next week. Jerry, you and Joel refine your plan and find places for Yolanda, Hector, and myself to help you."

8

RETIREMENT

Monday morning, Judge Laningham arrived at his physician's office fifteen minutes early. Dr. May had been Lamar's physician for many years, and since the judge had always been fortunate enough to stay in reasonably good health, yearly checkups had pretty much defined their relationship. The nurse called for Lamar and led him to the next waiting room. The nurse weighed him and took his blood pressure, and indicated that both were good. She then asked the judge a series of questions, most of which were unrelated to the reason why he was there. Finally, she was satisfied. The nurse thanked Lamar and told him that Dr. May would be right with him. The judge had never been bothered by the fact that his doctor was a woman. To spare both of them embarrassment, he chose to have his prostate checked elsewhere. He questioned the wisdom of this decision since Dr. May had delicate little hands, while his proctologist looked like a mountain man and had fingers like sausages. Thank God for Kentucky (KY) jelly!

Ten minutes later, Dr. May tapped lightly on the waiting room door and walked in, already absorbed in reading Lamar's chart. "Hi, judge, what brings you here? I know it's not time for your physical."

"Hi, Dr. May. About three months ago, I had a cold. It took me about a week to get over it, but I still have this nagging cough, and sometimes I find it difficult to catch my breath. But mostly Doc,

I haven't got any energy. I don't seem to have the ambition to do anything."

Dr. May took her stethoscope from her lab coat and started putting in her ear buds. "OK, let me listen to your lungs. Take slow, deep breaths." The doctor slowly and methodically moved the instrument to several locations on both the front and back of Lamar's chest. Finally, she spoke. "I hear a little congestion, but it is the wheezing I am concerned about. I want you to give me a sputum sample, and I am sending you to the hospital for chest X-rays. You can get dressed, and I will call you later, after I speak with radiology."

The judge went to the hospital to have his chest X-rays as ordered by Dr. May. By the time he was done, it was nearly noon. As he was driving home, he wondered if his retiring had been such a good idea. Before he retired, Lamar remembered how much he had hated his alarm clock. While he was working, he never woke without it. Yet now that he is able to sleep as long as he desires, the judge finds that he often wakes earlier than he used to when he required the clock. His friends, who had retired before him, predicted that he would love retirement. They also warned Lamar that the first year or so would seem strange, but give it time, and he and Colleen would grow into retirement and learn to love it. A lot of things were indeed strange. Sitting on the porch on a Tuesday morning watching the neighborhood awaken and go to work was weird. Going grocery shopping in the morning when hardly anyone else was in the store was wonderful. There were no lines at the deli counter, and you could browse without having to dodge other people's shopping carts. Yet, the best part was the instant checkout. During his first month into retirement, around 9:00 AM each morning, his dog would lay curled up with his head on his paws and roll his eyes up to peer at Lamar. He thought that perhaps the dog was wondering why he was still around and not gone like he used to be. Lamar looked at his dog and told him that it was Saturday.

Lamar missed his many friends and co-workers at the courthouse, but he most assuredly did not miss sitting on the bench. It seemed to him that throughout the years, people had grown more cruel and less sensitive to the feelings of others. He remembered that thirty years ago, if you were driving down the road and came upon a pedestrian in your path, you would slow down, and the pedestrian would hurry to get out of the way. Today, the driver goes right to the horn, and the pedestrian gives a condescending look or throws the middle finger salute as they make the driver wait for them to get out of the road. Also, in past years, there were not as many excuses for breaking the law. If you committed a crime and got caught, you admitted your wrongdoing and accepted your punishment. End of story. Now, every crime has a mitigating factor attached to it. Child abuse results from parents who received spankings when they were children. People who are addicted to drugs are unable to deal with the stress or the reality of everyday life like the rest of us. Thieves and murderers are only reacting to the injustice society has dealt them. Today all of the criminals are victims. The reasons defense attorneys postulate why their clients should not be held accountable for their crimes are limited only by their imaginations. We hear things like, "the drug I was taking for my depression made me axe murder my family," or "I mowed down my classmates in school with an assault rifle because I played too many video games," or "I sued the manufacturer of my kitchen stove because they failed to warn me against putting grocery bags on hot burners, and my house burned down. Insurance? No, I didn't have any." No, Judge Laningham did not miss the insanity.

Now, well into retirement, Lamar also had a lot of time to think about Council activities, and he had come to believe that what it had accomplished represented some of the best work of his life. The Council was old school. Right and wrong were not vacillating principles which can be re-tooled to fit new circumstances. Interpreting the law is not like painting on a canvas where the artist's manipulations could change what we perceive to be the truth of what we see. No, thought Judge Lamar Laningham, the Council's undertakings were more pure than "modern" justice doled out by the courts. When the Council acted, there was no plea bargaining. There was no "quid pro quo." There was no "nolo contendere." No compromising was necessary to achieve a guilty verdict. Ironically, although the Council's mission was the delivery of justice, the Council hardly ever defined or administered the justice. Following Council interventions, it was invariably the miscreants themselves or their victims who ultimately decided how justice would be served.

When he walked through the door, Lamar could smell the chili which Colleen had made for lunch. His wife did not ask her husband where he had been all morning, nor did Lamar offer an explanation. After lunch, exhausted, the judge laid on the couch in his study and fell asleep while watching investigative reporters and pundits speculating on the depth of involvement of the President and the first lady, both lawyers, in the Whitewater scandal.

9

THE CATACOMB

Martha Green was thrilled with the results which were delivered to her from her technicians. She was told that after sixteen years, the evidence had been remarkably preserved. It looked as though it had been collected yesterday. The sealed paper bags in which the evidence had been stored, together with the temperature, humidity, and the absence of damaging light, created near-perfect storage conditions for the preservation of the evidence. Nothing surprising or of substantive value was found in the hair, fibers, or other specimens taken from the clothes of either Bernard Jones or Roddy Jackson. However, the clothes of the victim, Adamos Lazopoulos, were an entirely different story. His socks, shoes, and pants were found to contain his own blood, skin, hair, and brain matter. Of course, this was expected. But on his shirt and his apron, there was found the blood and the hair of a second person. Martha was right, there had been a struggle, and by the look of the evidence, Mr. Lazopoulos put up quite a fight before he was killed. He drew blood, and the hairs found were consistent with two people wrestling. Finally, there was the bloody baseball bat. The only blood, hair, and tissue recovered from the bat all belonged to the old man. However, three distinct fingerprints were found. One fingerprint, of course, belonged to the owner of the bat, Adamos Lazopoulos. The second fingerprint matched that of Bubba Jones who had admitted to having picked the bat up off the counter on the night of the killing. The third fingerprint belonged to someone else. Martha was willing to bet that the third fingerprint belonged to the unidentified man whose hairs were found on the apron.

Martha was cautiously optimistic. Nothing found in the evidence could prove that Bubba did or did not kill the store owner. Sixteen years ago, Bubba was truthful with the police.

His honesty about picking up the bat explained his fingerprints there. Yet what the police made no attempt to explain was the total absence of blood on Bubba's clothes. The forensic lab technician took the initiative to create DNA profiles on various samples of the evidence which Martha had provided, but these DNA maps would take a few weeks to create.

This was a frustrating part of Agent Green's job. Once evidence was collected and processed, some of the tests such as the creation of DNA profiles could be painfully slow. What made it worse was that active cases always received priority status. Cold cases were pushed to the back of the "to do" list. Martha knew she would have some extra time, so she decided to pay Agent Danno Lockwood a visit.

Martha had two reasons for wanting to speak with Agent Danno. First, Martha wanted to extend her condolences for how the situation in Oregon turned out. She clearly remembered Danno's reluctance to use the standard FBI protocol in the Delano Reese case. Yes, in the technical sense, it was a kidnapping, but Danno was able to understand Del's frustration and his desire to spend time with his daughter Amy. Del's death was unnecessary and painful beyond words. Sometimes, people have a tendency to forget that policemen and policewomen have families, too. Martha just wanted to make sure that Danno was OK. She spoke quietly with him for a few moments, and she came to believe that he was dealing with the tragedy as best as he could. Clearly his heart was breaking for Amy and Alicia. Agent Lockwood had no idea what, if anything, was happening with the local policeman who took the first shot at Del without first seeing a weapon. Like every other aspect of this case, he tried to put it out of his mind. Nothing good could come from any of it.

The second reason Martha wanted to see Agent Danno was to surreptitiously find out where he lived as a teenager. He mentioned previously that his sister had been raped and brutalized thirty years ago by an unknown assailant. The rapist was never caught. It was an incredible longshot, but the DNA had been so well preserved in the Adamos Lazopoulos case that she felt Darlene Lockwood's case also deserved another look. Of course, this assumed that the rape took place in the San Francisco area, and that the evidence was still available and of forensic value. Agent Green wasn't about to get Danno's hopes up, so she got the information she needed, and then she changed the subject.

Thirty minutes later, Agent Martha Green was back at her desk searching her computer for any information on a Darlene Lockwood. Danno told her that he was attending high school in this area when the incident took place, so she used a reference range of from 1966 to 1969. The computer searched for a few moments, then "Bingo", a hit. The rape took place on March 13th of 1968. Since there would be little point researching the case any further without first determining if there was any evidence, Martha decided to visit the evidence room first. She took down the case number, date, and victim identification. Agent Green wanted to handle this case as discretely as possible, so she did not call the evidence room first. The drive from Santa Molina to San Francisco would take only a few minutes, so she left a message with Ruth, Yolanda's secretary, stating that she could be reached by phone, and walked to her car.

When Martha was selected to enter special training to become a cold case investigator for the FBI, she received a warning. She was told that as soon as it became common knowledge that the Santa Molina FBI division had a cold case investigator, the office would be deluged with requests to open old cases. Just wait and see, they said. Everyone's son, husband, boyfriend, and father were wrongfully convicted. Sadly, too often it was true. Past histories of criminal activity, racial or ethnic prejudice, profiling, and a host of other reprehensible motives led attorneys and juries to sometimes mold the evidence to fit the crime and the defendant. Cases destined to be reinvestigated had to be based on merit. The evidence leading Martha Green to open and re-examine an old case should be at least as good as that which supported the conviction.

The drive to the Evidence Division gave Agent Green time to ponder the overwhelming responsibility of a juror. The twelve men and women who sat through trials and deliberated over testimony, as well as the best efforts of prosecuting and defense attorneys, are the backbone of America's judicial system. The enormous responsibility delegated to these individuals is greater than most people will face in a lifetime. Then why is jury duty considered by most to be an annoyance and a waste of time? Yes, it is inconvenient to leave your home or your job to have to sit through hours of testimony. But, what about the responsibility of having to determine the guilt or the innocence of the accused? Their freedom or even their life may be at stake. It would seem that the weight of having to make such a decision would give us pause. In 1957 a movie was released which gave us a glimpse into a jury room during deliberations in a murder trial. *12 Angry Men* depicts men of different backgrounds and temperaments arguing back and forth in an attempt to come to a unanimous verdict. The story takes place on an extremely hot summer day in a very small jury room. The sweltering heat makes tempers flare. None of the actual trial was shown in the movie, but bits and pieces of testimony and evidence are revealed as the jurors discuss the case. Emotions and prejudice sway the group of men back and forth. Everyone wants to go home and get on with their lives, yet after each vote, there are one or two holdouts who vote for acquittal.

Before juries are dismissed from the courtroom, judges instruct them in various nuances of the possible verdicts. They are told that if they possess reasonable doubt about the defendant's guilt, they must acquit him.

The advances in technology we possess today can clearly place a person at a crime scene. Fingerprints and samples containing DNA can remove any reasonable doubt.

Martha's life was evidence based. She knew that without today's technology, if she had been a member of a jury years ago, it would have been difficult for her to send someone to their death.

Agent Green was happy to see Sergeant Edgecomb, the friendly policeman who had helped her previously. Quietly, she explained to him that she wanted to examine any evidence in the 1968 rape of Agent Daniel Lockwood's sister. Not knowing if she would find anything of any value, she wanted to spare Agent Lockwood any further anguish by not telling him what she was doing. Martha asked Sergeant Edgecomb to handle her request personally. He nodded in agreement. However, there was a problem. All evidence from cases before 1975 had been relocated to a building a few blocks away. The policeman pressed on a console in front of him and spoke into a microphone. He asked one of his technicians to please come forward and sit in the cage until he returned. Officer Edgecomb led Martha out a back door. There was a modified golf cart there which was used to shuttle between the two buildings using the alleyway in the back. The trip took about one minute. The second building had no markings or anything identifying it as a police or storage building. The officer entered a combination into the keypad which gave him access to the interior of the building. He turned on the lights and Martha was surprised to see that the building looked as large as an airplane hangar. There were floor to ceiling cages as far as she could see, and the continuity of the cages was broken into a series of individual cells which Agent Green estimated were about twenty feet wide. Martha told Sergeant Edgecomb that this must be what Noah's Ark must have looked like on the inside.

The officer smiled. "Yeah, but I bet this smells a whole lot better."

There were rows upon rows of individual cages, each having its own keypad. The Sergeant explained that a lot of evidence had disappeared over the years, so when a sprinkler system was added, the department had both buildings wired with camera surveillance and keypad entry. Agent Green got a cold chill thinking about what a sprinkler system could do to pristine evidence. The officer told Martha that as soon as the exterior keypad is activated, the cameras come on. Of course each evidence officer has their own four digit combination, so they know who has entered the building as well as the individual cell. As a final precaution, there is a table near the entryway. All evidence containers are bar-coded. A camera mounted on the table must scan all evidence bar codes as well as the officer's ID badge. If this is not done, an alarm goes off as soon as the door is opened.

Sergeant Edgecomb quickly walked two rows over to the right. "1968 should be down here," he yelled knowing that Agent Green had fallen behind.

Martha was absolutely overwhelmed. There were rows upon rows, cells after cells, each packed floor to ceiling with shelves crammed with thousands of boxes, both large and small. Most of the boxes appeared similar, about the size printer paper is sold in, and each box had preprinted areas for the evidence people to fill out, including the case number, name, and date, along with an area for miscellaneous comments. Every box also had a bar code. All of the boxes were taped shut, and several had post-it notes attached. Martha noted that in the corridor, between the cages there were randomly placed staircases on wheels like the ones used in warehouse stores to retrieve items which are too high to reach.

As an evidence specialist, Agent Green felt that this must be what it was like when they first opened King Tut's tomb. Where do you start? Martha's imagination was running wild thinking what kinds of secrets these boxes held. There were likely murder weapons, ranging from the typical firearms and kitchen knives, to the more imaginative stiletto-heeled shoes and fireplace pokers. Martha always said that evidence talked to her. She imagined that if all of these boxes could be opened simultaneously, the din of the evidence speaking to her would be more than a person could bear.

Agent Green continued to lag behind the policeman. She was awe-struck by the number of boxes. She laughed to herself thinking that just south of here, in an evidence room just like this one, in Los Angeles, there was an evidence box in the 1994 aisle which contained a glove that screamed in a munchkin-like voice "if it doesn't fit, you must acquit," and laughed hysterically. Agent Green shook herself back to reality...well almost. She remembered, as a child, her parents took her to an animal shelter to pick out a puppy. As she and her parents walked down rows of cages, all of the dogs and cats pawed at the doors begging "pick me, oh please...pick me." Martha felt like a hero when she chose her puppy, and yet she also felt terrible having let down those other poor creatures. All of this evidence was having a similar effect on her. But she could take only one box. "Pick me, pick me."

"Here we go," shouted Sergeant Edgecomb. It felt like cold water waking her. He waited for her to catch up. "If there is anything, it should be in here," he said.

Agent Green waited for him to work his way through the dozens of boxes in this cell. Even though this building was reasonably well lighted, the shelves were so high that the flow of light was kept localized, giving the building the feel of a catacomb.

Sergeant Edgecomb looked up and scratched his head under his hat. "Looks like we will need the wheels," he said. "Why do we always seem to need the wheels?"

Martha held the door open for the officer as he retreated from the cell back into the corridor. Thankfully, one of the moveable staircases was only about thirty feet away. She pulled the door open wider, and the policeman pushed the stairs inside. He

110

went about three-quarters of the way up the stairs and pulled up his glasses to squint at the writing on the boxes.

"Ahhh,"he said and removed a box from the shelf. Before he had come all the way down the stairs, he checked the box one more time. Once again, Agent Green held the door open as the sergeant returned the moveable staircase to the corridor. He shut the door behind him and together they went back the way they had come. At the table next to the door, Sergeant Edgecomb removed his ID badge and held it up to the camera. He was about to do the same thing with the evidence box when Martha stopped him. She pointed to the upper right corner of the box where it said '1 of 2.' She asked, "Does this mean what I think it does?"

Once again the sergeant lifted his glasses and squinted toward where she had pointed. "Oops," he said. "It sure does. At least we discovered it before we left. Wait here." He went back to the cage where he got the first box and pushed the stairs inside. Sure enough, at the back of the shelf was box "2 of 2." The sergeant replaced the staircase and was back with Martha in moments.

"Sorry Agent Green," he said. "Now let's try this again." He passed his badge, and then the two boxes in front of the camera. He then looked at Martha and pointed to her ID badge. "Do you mind?" he asked.

Martha came out of a trance. She had been thinking about what she might find in the two boxes. "Oh, sure." She looked a little embarrassed. She held her ID badge up to the camera.

Sergeant Edgecomb picked up the boxes and they headed toward the door. "I like this system," he said. "In addition to the

111

paperwork we have yet to fill out, everything removed from this building has been visually recorded. If the paperwork somehow got lost, and I died tonight, they would know who has this stuff."

Martha got cute. "Please don't die tonight or I will be the one making out all the paperwork tomorrow." They both laughed. "Sergeant, why didn't I have to go on camera the last time when I took evidence from the other building?"

Officer Edgecomb answered, "You were on camera, you just didn't realize it."

In moments, they were back at the evidence cage in the first building. The technician returned to the back room and the sergeant began filling out the paperwork. As he was doing so, Martha took notice of the cameras she had not seen during her previous visit.

Once again, Martha thanked Officer Edgecomb for his help in retrieving old evidence. She promised to return it as quickly as possible, and they both realized that they would be seeing a lot of each other in the future. He wished Martha luck on this, her second cold case. She knew she would need it. As before, Agent Green could hardly wait to view the contents of the two boxes in her hands.

CHAPTER THREE

1

ETHAN COLE LANINGHAM

"What's up Lamar?" Colleen Laningham was standing over her husband as he slowly came out of a deep sleep on his study sofa. Colleen had turned off the television, and she stood over the judge holding up a cordless phone so he could see it. Lamar felt like a child about to get scolded by an irate mother who had just learned of her son's transgressions. He blinked at his wife and rubbed his eyes as he struggled to understand what was happening.

Colleen held the phone out. "Dr. May's office just called and said that you were there this morning. The nurse also said that they had received the X-rays from the hospital. Dr. May has left the office for the rest of the day because of some emergency, but she would like to see you tomorrow at 2:00 PM. Would you like to include your wife in this? Please tell me what is going on."

Lamar struggled to sit up and braced himself with his left arm. "You worry too much," he said, "and that is why I didn't tell you that I was going to see Dr. May. Remember a few months ago when I had a cold? I am still coughing. Occasionally I get short of breath, and I feel exhausted most of the time. That's all, I promise. I didn't want you to make a fuss. If it will make you feel any better, you can come with me tomorrow, OK?"

Lamar managed a smile in an unsuccessful attempt to placate his wife, but she saw right through it.

"No, Lamar, it is not OK, but you can bet that I will be there." Colleen turned and walked from his study with an air of determination, yet clearly upset.

Lamar and Colleen had been married for twenty-seven years. They had one son together, Ethan Cole, two years after they were married. Like his father, Ethan had laser-like focus, and he excelled at everything he attempted. He was the salutatorian of his high school class, and although Judge Laningham wanted Ethan to go to college, the boy was headstrong and determined to be a soldier. Ethan enlisted in the Marines a month after he graduated high school. Lamar and Colleen were disappointed, but they kept it to themselves. Even so, Colleen had to admit that her blood would pump a little faster every time she passed in front of the television and saw the picture of Ethan, game face on, in his Marine dress blues. Lamar and his wife's feelings were not rooted in a disdain of the military. Both were strong patriots. They were parents, and there was a lot of trouble throughout the world. The United States had assumed the role as the world's police, and the Soviet Union was teetering and soon to collapse under the weight of its own debt. All of the nations possessing nuclear capabilities had been flexing their muscles. Alliances were made and others were broken. Yet one thing had become abundantly clear. If any of the hot spots escalated to dangerous levels, we would likely be involved. Had their son gone to college, the Laninghams felt that he would have been safe from harm. A year and a half into his enlistment, Ethan, along with six other Marines, were killed in a night exercise when two helicopters collided in flight. All that worry that Lamar and

Colleen had kept to themselves was released in a torrent of tears. A normal funeral is difficult enough, but a military funeral, with all its tradition, can rip your heart out. The playing of Taps, the folding and presentation of the American flag to the soldier's mother, and the rifle salute are beautiful and stirring to watch, but when they bury your loved one, everything is on a different level.

The first year was by far the most difficult for the Laninghams. Colleen would frequently and without notice just break down and cry, when she would hear Taps played in a movie, see a funeral, or watch a mother playing with her son. Thankfully her episodes of depression became fewer and fewer until they finally seemed to disappear. Any mother who has lost a child knows better. The wound has not healed, and the tears have been covered over with scar tissue, preventing their release. There is a natural order to things in the world. Spring follows winter, dawn follows the dark, peace follows war, and old people die and babies are born. When children die before their parents, the natural order is violated. Parents know this and sometimes manifest that knowledge with guilt, distrust, and depression. Relationships and sometimes entire families can be torn asunder. There is no assuaging of grief or the emptiness we are left to feel. At a time when people need love and support the most, it is too often rejected. The reason for the rejection is a defense mechanism built into each of us. Why would we give love another chance to live within us only to have it ripped from us again?

For Lamar the first year without Ethan was a little different than what his wife experienced. He would come across a wrench which Ethan had left somewhere, or find a note in his son's handwriting used as a bookmark. Perhaps he would come across the baseball cards Ethan loved to collect as a boy. For Lamar, it was the personal things, things which his son had touched or had loved that affected him most.

Lamar and Colleen Laningham had somehow been fortunate enough to survive the dark days following the death of their only child. Their relationship had changed, however. The passion had gone, and they did just what it took to survive from one day to the next. It was not clear to either of them how they had changed, or when it happened. Nonetheless, they both silently acknowledged that they were not the same people they used to be. It has been said that misery loves company. This, of course means that no one wants to suffer alone. Lamar preferred to think of it as misery finding solace being with others who have experienced a common heart-rending loss.

Lamar and Dr. Jerry Woodson decided to form the Council about three years after Ethan's death. They had philosophically discussed the merits of such an organization many times over the years. Normally, such talk followed several glasses of merlot or brandy when ideas were pliant and inhibitions were few. The judge and his doctor friend had, in fact, solved many of the world's great problems while in a pleasant state of inebriation. However, like all barroom meetings of the mind, the ideas disappear directly proportional to the dissipating effects of the inebriant.

Lamar sometimes wondered if Ethan's death had somehow affected him in a way which made the creation of the Council more urgent. His concept of time had certainly taken on a new dimension. Ethan had his entire life in front of him when he was killed. Marriage, the love of a family, a civilian career, a home, and

116

all of the other blessings we so often take for granted would never be his. God gave the Laningham's son only twenty years of life on this earth. Ethan was not even given enough time to prepare for life, let alone experience it. Yes, time acquired a new meaning for Lamar since Ethan's death. There simply wasn't enough of it.

And, what of the work Ethan had so looked forward to accomplishing? Work now left undone. Somehow, Lamar had passed to his son a sense of duty and honor. Unlike the countless troubled souls who had stood before Judge Laningham awaiting sentencing, Ethan did not believe that the world owed him a living. Quite the contrary. Lamar's son believed that he wasn't owed anything. Joining the Marines was his way of paying his dues. Ethan felt compelled to earn his own way. The Laninghams were wealthy. College tuition, a car, or anything else, were never issues. Honor and respect were things which Ethan's father and all his money could not buy.

In many ways, Hector reminded the judge of his son. Both were jovial and carefree on the surface. Yet inside, they shared a spirit of duty, love of country, and an abiding need to take care of those who were unable to fend for themselves. Lamar guessed that the last part, Ethan inherited from his mother. Perhaps the judge, through the Council, was unconsciously trying to carry on the work which his son was never given the chance to start. Certainly they shared the same ideals.

Lamar also wondered what Colleen thought of the Council's activities. He never discussed what went on behind closed doors in his study when the Council convened. But his wife was no fool either. A few years back, when the Council was in its inception,

Lamar told Colleen that he was having his old friend Jerry and a few others over to discuss issues of mutual concern with respect to law enforcement and the judicial system. He never mentioned that the main topic of discussion would be the failings of this branch of the government. Jerry's presence in the Laningham home would come as no surprise to Lamar's wife regardless of what was going on. Jerry was something of a fixture in the Laningham home. Yolanda's presence wouldn't come as a surprise either. Colleen knew her socially, from times when the court and the cops co-mingled at fundraisers, charity events, picnics, and Christmas parties. Colleen also knew that her husband respected Yolanda's work as Santa Molina's FBI director.

Colleen never asked about Hector Martinez or Joel Harris. They were much younger than the other three Council members. Of course, Colleen knew their jobs as a landscaper and computer geek had absolutely nothing to do with law enforcement or the judicial system. Yet she never asked the obvious questions about their participation in the Council. "Don't ask, don't tell" worked for Lamar, so he left well enough alone.

The judge's thoughts returned to the present. Lamar felt sorry for not including Colleen in his decision to go to the doctor. After Ethan's death, they only had each other, and he should have known better. He would never shut her out again, whether or not he was inclined to do so.

2

DNA

Agent Martha Green carefully examined the contents of the two evidence boxes of the 1968 rape of Darlene Lockwood. One box contained Darlene's clothes, and the second box contained the bedding. The police indicated that Darlene was raped in her home while her parents were attending a basketball game in which her brother Daniel was playing. Whoever assaulted Darlene didn't seem to care that she was a child. There were several blood, hair, and skin deposits found in the sheets. Once again, Martha carefully removed the samples and transferred them to new paper bags labeled **Lockwood, Darlene: bedding** and **Lockwood, Darlene: clothing**. She closed the evidence boxes and re-taped them as she had received them. The two boxes, along with the other one from the Lazopoulos case could now be prepared to return to Sergeant Edgecomb. However, she first wanted to replace the samples which she had given the DNA technicians for processing. Since this could take several days, Agent Green locked the three boxes in her office closet for safekeeping.

Aria Heaton had been processing DNA samples for nearly six years. She was very good at her job and everyone knew it, but she could not be rushed. Her work, and the conviction rate which resulted from it, were legendary. Aria had not yet begun to process the DNA from either case Agent Green had given her. Martha requested that Aria reverse the order of the cases and do the Lockwood case first. She reasoned that since there were fewer samples in the Lockwood case, it would take less time to complete the DNA profiling.   Besides, Bubba and Roddy were not going anywhere.

Aria Heaton knew that the quality of her work depended on how well the evidence was collected.   At a minimum, gloves had to be worn when picking up evidence.   She remembered a case a few years back which took place in Hollywood.   The case had become a classic example of what NOT to do in a crime scene.   A voluptuous twenty-three year old starlet was found strangled in her townhouse.   This beauty was unmarried and had a reputation as someone who had numerous gentlemen callers.   News of her death spread quickly throughout the police department.   She had been found in the nude, lying in a position which highlighted her natural assets.   Apparently, the evidence people in the police department were the last ones notified.   By the time they arrived and sealed off the area, no less than fifteen sets of fingerprints of Hollywood policemen became part of the official crime scene.   Once a crime scene has been contaminated in this way, it doesn't much matter how good the evidence may be.   A good defense lawyer would easily be able to refute just about anything presented because the crime scene had been repeatedly violated.

Aria had been working as an FBI technician for nearly ten years.   Before DNA, the vast majority of her work involved dusting for fingerprints, analyzing blood, and looking at hair, fibers, and tissue samples under a microscope.   All of these functions are still vital today, in 1996, but improvements in technology have relegated their importance to more of a supportive role, the scales having tipped dramatically.   Up until about ten years ago, interrogation detectives were responsible for solving the majority of cases.

Fingerprints could sometimes place a suspect at a crime scene, especially if the murder was impromptu. Spontaneous killings resulting from anger or lust typically yielded more fingerprints than a crime scene where premeditation was involved. A husband coming home early and finding his wife in a compromising position with the pool boy does not think to put on gloves or wipe down incriminating evidence. Thinking about one's actions is not a hallmark feature of a crime of passion.

Premeditated murder is a different story. The murderer plans the crime, including the weapon of choice, the location of the crime, his escape, and his alibi. The murderer knows to wear gloves and manipulate the crime scene in an effort to divert suspicion away from himself.

Crimes of passion are normally much easier for police detectives to solve. Motive is often obvious, and there always seems to be plenty of evidence left behind linking the murderer to the crime. And sometimes the killer even confesses! The suspect is really a nice person who is simply in the wrong place at a bad time and pushed beyond their limits. For whatever reason, they became enraged and did a very stupid thing. Now, full of regret and contrition, they confess their crime to the authorities.

Before technological advances including the use of DNA evidence, the interrogation experts were the ones who frequently solved the big cases. In cases involving premeditation, the murderer usually wore gloves and left little evidence behind. It was up to these detectives to discern plausible motive, means, and opportunity, along with any circumstantial evidence to link the suspect to the crime. The jury then had to be convinced of the suspect's guilt.

Agent Martha Green and technician Aria Heaton's positions of importance had been significantly elevated within the last decade. Thus, prior to 1985, without fingerprint evidence connecting a suspect to a crime, interrogation was perhaps the most important ingredient in crime solving. Evidence was used in a supportive role. Today, however, the roles have reversed. Evidence is of paramount importance, and interrogation, while still of great importance, may no longer be considered the backbone of crime solving.

While it is relatively easy to exit a crime scene without leaving fingerprints, it is much more difficult to commit a crime such as homicide without having deposited DNA evidence. Sources of DNA include saliva, blood, skin cells, semen, hair, and sweat. Any of these sources may be found in clothing, bedding, carpeting, bathroom items such as dental floss, hairbrushes, facial tissues, washcloths, or toothbrushes. And if the assailant has had any contact with the victim such as during sex or a struggle, DNA evidence is normally plentiful.

With the single exception of identical twins, no two people share the same DNA. Once evidence containing DNA has been collected as part of an investigation, with respect to any suspect, there are three possible conclusions: inclusion, exclusion, and inconclusive. Inclusion results when the suspect's DNA matches the profile of DNA taken from the crime scene. In other words, he or she cannot be excluded as the source of the DNA. If a suspect's skin cells are matched with the skin cells from the fingernails of the victim, he or she is conclusively the source of the DNA. Conversely, an exclusion results when a suspect's DNA does not match any of the DNA evidence from the crime scene. The suspect is excluded as the source of the DNA found in the samples of evidence. It is important to remember that exclusion is not synonymous with innocence. For example, a suspect may have left several DNA samples at a rape scene which, of course, includes him as a suspect. But if he wore a condom, there would be no semen to conclusively identify the suspect as the rapist.

Inconclusive results occur when samples of DNA evidence can neither include or exclude an individual as the source of the biological evidence. For example, if a woman has consensual sex with one or more men, and is later raped, it cannot be conclusive that the semen found belonged to the rapist. Yet if the rape took place in a different location, and the rapist's DNA was found there, he could be conclusively linked to the scene of the crime. Other factors which may contribute to inconclusive results include poor quality DNA or insufficient amounts of DNA samples.

The FBI as well as state and local law enforcement agencies were quick to realize the revolutionary changes which were taking place in forensic technology. The FBI created the Combined DNA Index System (CODIS). DNA samples are stored in the mammoth database and can be utilized in two ways. A suspect's DNA can be entered via the Offender Index to see if they can be tied to a particular place where the evidence had been collected. Secondly, if DNA evidence had been removed from a crime scene and there are no suspects, the DNA sample can be entered into the CODIS Forensic Index to see if there are any matches in the system. In addition to the FBI database, each state has its own laws which define the circumstances in which criminals must have their DNA entered into the FBI database. Finally, some states even go so far as making it mandatory for all convicted felons to have their DNA entered into the national database. Martha Green was used to having evidence "talk" to her. She was soon to hear evidence speak with life-altering ramifications.

SHELDON AND JESSICA LORTZ

It had already been one week since the Council last met in Judge Laningham's study. Yolanda, Hector, and Joel sat at the round table waiting for Lamar and Dr. Woodson. Colleen Laningham came into the study and explained that her husband and the doctor would join them in a few moments. They needed to speak alone in the kitchen. She offered the group refreshments from the bar and then disappeared, closing the sliding pocket style doors on her way out.

After the Tuesday follow-up appointment with Dr. May, the judge and Colleen returned home, and after lengthy discussions and mulling over the various treatment options available, they agreed to ask their friend, Dr. Woodson for a second opinion. To accomplish this, the doctor was asked to come to the Council meeting an hour before the others.

Joel and Dr. Woodson had formulated a plan to expose Reverend Thomas Hartsell and Rapture Ministries as frauds, and in typical Council fashion, they would seek the reverend's help in making this happen. After the judge and Dr. Woodson returned to the study, the doctor outlined the plan.

"Since Judge Laningham and his wife, Colleen, along with Hector and his mother, have already attended both Sunday services and Wednesday evening prayer meetings, they are the logical choice to begin the Council's ruse. The judge and Colleen will endear themselves to Reverend Hartsell by making a whopping donation to Rapture Ministry supported charities. This will obviously get the attention of Hartsell and the elders. The Laninghams, using false identities, of course, will then seek a private audience with the reverend. The size of their Wednesday night donation will pretty much guarantee such a meeting. He will undoubtedly want to meet the source of such funds. Lamar and Colleen, posing as Professor Sheldon and Jessica Lortz, a retired couple from Chicago, are newcomers to Rapture. They will applaud the wonderful work which Rapture is doing throughout the world and drop not so subtle hints that future donations will be forthcoming. When the judge senses that the time is right, he brings up Rapture Ministries going global. Lamar (Sheldon) mentions that his nephew, played by Joel, is a Hollywood production specialist who has the know-how and the experience to put Reverend Hartsell on a worldwide stage." Dr. Woodson pointed to his chest. "I will be Joel's senior production editor. My job will be running around giving orders and creating diversions whenever necessary. We need to make Hartsell believe that this Hollywood crew is extremely busy and very successful so that the whole production can be done within two weeks."

Judge Laningham interrupted. "What about Hector and Yolanda?"

"Hector's mom," continued Dr. Woodson, "if she is willing and able to play a part in this, is about to receive a multimillion dollar inheritance. Her bachelor brother has just died and left her a fortune, and she just doesn't know what to do with all that money. Yolanda's role is supportive. She too will attend Rapture events and cultivate friendships as we need them. Using the resources

126

available to her, she can also help us create false identities and anything else we might need."

This was the way Council actions normally developed. Once a problem was brought before the Council, the merits of taking or not taking action were debated among the five members. Sometimes it was clear from the beginning that Council intervention was necessary. At other times, it was felt that law enforcement agencies could better handle the situation, and the Council backed away. Commonly, by the time this group became involved, law enforcement and/or the judicial system had already unsuccessfully dealt with the problem. Reverend Hartsell and Rapture Ministries, however, were somewhat unique. Since no crime had been committed, the police had no reason to investigate the reverend or the church. Milking money from people, including the poor, may be shameful, but it was not illegal. Members gave donations to Rapture of their own volition. The ONLY way this shakedown could be stopped was through Council involvement.

Thirty six hours after the Council meeting, the judge and Colleen were preparing to go to Rapture in the Round. They dressed without speaking and were rehearsing in their minds the roles which they were about to assume. When Lamar and Colleen first attended Rapture a week ago, they had already introduced themselves as Professor Sheldon Lortz and his wife Jessica. The last thing in the world they wanted was for Hartsell to know their real names or how much they were worth. The judge didn't mind assuming a false identity, and it did not bother him playing the role as Professor Lortz. What he DID mind was missing services at his own church. Lamar and Colleen had been members of their church in Santa Molina for many years, and attending on Sundays had become a pleasurable ritual.

The drive from Santa Molina to San Francisco was not a long one, and it was actually quite scenic. Very few people knew it, but Lamar had a romantic side to his personality. He was able to identify sights, sounds, and especially smells with events in his distant past. Certain smells triggered his memory to remind him of days long ago. A few times a year, like today, the air smelled sweeter than it normally does. The smell is incredibly fresh and makes you want to breathe deeply. This smell reminded him of a time when he was young. His parents had rented a cabin high in the mountains in early summer. He was lying in a hammock, gently swinging, probably thinking about girls or football. The air smelled exactly as it does today.

The smell of leaves in the fall was, also, a favorite which triggered memories. Lamar remembered being a teenager when he and his friends loved riding their bicycles at full speed into piles of leaves which homeowners had raked into the road. The smell of leaves also reminded Lamar of a time long ago when he and a friend were walking to school. A garbage truck back then required two employees, one to drive the truck, and one to dump the garbage cans into the back of the truck. The vehicle was very large and had a compactor built in, and after five or six cans were emptied, the man in the rear would activate the compactor and it would squeeze the trash and move it toward the front of the truck. There was no way the driver could know when the guy in the back was done dumping cans, so they worked out a system of communication. When the man in the rear of the truck was done dumping cans, he climbed onto the rear of the truck and loudly whistled. This signaled the driver to pull ahead to the next set of cans. Lamar's ability to whistle was well known, so one day, while the man in the rear of the truck was returning the empty cans to the curbside, Lamar whistled as loudly as he could. The driver of the truck pulled away while the man in the back chased after him, all the while waving his arms and screaming obscenities. Lamar and his friend laughed all the way to school. Yes, something as simple as the smell of leaves brought Lamar back to memories of long ago. A "closet" romantic, he wondered if other people associated smells or songs with past events in their lives.

A dog in the road brought Lamar back to the present. He decided to rehearse their pretend roles with Colleen one more time. "OK, Colleen, I will run through this again. I am Sheldon Lortz, a retired professor of constitutional law. I should have no trouble faking my way through that. You are my wife, Jessica, and we moved from Chicago to San Francisco to escape the winter weather and the crime. We have no children and are doing our best trying to settle into retirement.

Colleen answered, "I've got it Lamar, but honestly, I don't think they care about us or our past."

He looked at Colleen. "I bet that will change after Wednesday night." He turned the car into the Rapture parking lot. Many cars were already parked there, although the service was not scheduled to start for another fifteen minutes. On the way into the church, Lamar and Colleen went out of their way to be friendly with everyone, especially the elders. Lamar, normally a reserved, modest man felt like he was running for office. Surely his face would hurt tomorrow.

The church service and sermon were much like the last one. The songs changed but the message stayed the same. After the service, the judge and Colleen, (as Sheldon and Jessica Lortz), promised to come to the Wednesday evening prayer meeting.

4

TWENTY THOUSAND

The Wednesday following the Sunday service at Rapture in the Round would be Judge Lamar Laningham's acting debut. He and Colleen had already pretended to be Professor Sheldon and Jessica Lortz for several weeks at Rapture. However, taking someone's name was a lot different than assuming their persona. Lamar hoped that Colleen was correct when she predicted that the Rapture folks were only interested in the Lortzes' donation, not their history.

The Council's deception in helping Rapture Ministries going global would happen quickly. The plan was to hit Thomas Hartsell very hard and very fast. Dr. Woodson and Joel would masquerade as a big time Hollywood crew that was between jobs. They would express a willingness to help Hartsell, but the production had to happen immediately and strictly on their terms. Many demands would be placed on Hartsell and the elders. Absolute compliance with all requests would be a prerequisite, otherwise Rapture could look elsewhere and hire someone else. Adolf Hitler's Minister of Propaganda, Josef Goebbels is commonly credited as having said: *"The bigger the lie, the more people will believe it."* Judge Laningham and the other Council members were counting on the validity of that statement. The entire Council mission was predicated in Hartsell's believing that Rapture could go onto the worldwide stage in only a few weeks. Everyone hoped that the reverend's greed would consume him. The Hollywood production crew would descend on Rapture Ministries in blitzkrieg-like fashion and keep them so busy that they would not have time to think.

"Good evening, Professor Lortz." The smiling elder bowed respectfully and held the door open. "And a good evening to you as well, Mrs. Lortz."

"Thank you, Jesse," replied the judge. He always thought that wearing name tags was corny, but since he did not know the elder's name, it served its purpose. Once they reached the Sunday school classrooms, Lamar was directed one way and Colleen to a different room. The judge was pleasantly surprised to see that he had been assigned to the same room as Hector...misery loves company. Hector was using the name Tomas Zapata and his mother was Lolita Zapata. Luckily, till now no one had asked their names. The two Council members acknowledged each other with their eyes, but said nothing. The Sunday school classroom contained perhaps twenty chairs in two rows arranged in a semicircle which faced the teacher's desk. Behind the desk was a portable metal cart on wheels which had three shelves. A large screen television took up the entire top shelf and a video cassette recorder was below on the second shelf.

At about 7:05 PM, once it appeared that all prayer group participants had arrived, one of the elders entered the classroom and closed the door behind him.

"Good evening everyone, I am Elder Marcus Billings. I hope everyone is well this evening. Are there any newcomers with us this evening?" Elder Marcus paused a moment and scanned the group. An elderly woman in the second row next to Judge Laningham, obviously apprehensive, slowly raised her hand.

132

"Wonderful," said Elder Billings. "Can I ask you your name?"

"Thelma Kwecien," she replied, although she could barely be heard. "I came with my husband, but the man in the hall made us separate and now I don't know where he is." Thelma was clearly very agitated and confused. Both Lamar and Hector felt badly for her, but could do nothing.

In an obvious attempt to change the subject, Mr. Billings added, "Mrs. Kwecien, we are all delighted to welcome you to our Rapture family. This is going to be a special evening tonight. Rapture Ministries is going to share with all of you some of the good work which we are hoping to accomplish in Mozambique." He paused, put his hands together, and bowed. "But first, please join with me in prayer." Elder Billings expressed his thanks for the people attending the meeting and for the opportunity that Rapture Ministries had been given in helping the poor people in third world countries such as Mozambique. He added that all of the people of the world are brothers and sisters and that God expects...no, He requires that we do everything within our power to help those less fortunate than ourselves. In a very convincing show of humility, Marcus Billings described the poor country in southeastern Africa and the goals of Rapture's missionary program there. When he finished outlining what Rapture intended to do in Mozambique, he turned on the video cassette recorder. Before he started the presentation, Marcus turned and slowly looked at each of the people in the classroom. Although he was measuring them, he deliberately made eye contact with each person. Nearly pleading, and in a breaking voice, he implored, "As we look at this documentary, search your own heart and ask what YOU can do to help these suffering children of God. Remember...these are

133

your...OUR brothers and sisters. We are blessed to be able to share our abundant resources with them. If one of the children in this film was your son or daughter, or your grandchild, wouldn't you want someone to help them? Please, keep these things in mind as we face the challenge before us." Elder Marcus started the film and turned the light off. He sat in a chair by the door. Hector wondered if the elder sat there to be polite or possibly to discourage anyone from trying to leave, and then he experienced an epiphany! He realized the real reason for separating couples and family members into different classrooms. How could someone like Thelma Kwecien possibly leave when she had no idea where her husband was? This gave new meaning to the term "captive audience." Also, instead of donating money as a couple or as a family, by separating them, once the extortion began, they would all likely empty their pockets. Rapture would get twice as much.

The video presentation lasted about twenty minutes. As expected, it depicted a small village in Mozambique which had been ravaged by war, disease, drought, and now starvation. Mothers were shown holding their children who were obviously dying. All of the children in the village were severely emaciated and this made their eyes appear larger than normal. These children fixated on the camera and ripped your heart out with those haunting stares. Flies were everywhere and the entire situation appeared hopeless. Everyone in the room had seen films just like this one numerous times on weekend television infomercials. Lamar and Hector were both silently seething knowing that while the deplorable conditions shown in the film were real, Rapture Ministries had no intention of sending them a dime. Places around the world like the village in Mozambique desperately needed help. Yet Reverend Hartsell and his elders played upon the emotions and goodwill of their parishioners to raise thousands of dollars, and then they kept the money for themselves.

Elder Billings turned on the lights and returned to the front of the classroom. Much like Reverend Hartsell did in his sermons, Marcus addressed the prayer meeting participants using a carefully arranged delivery which included a variety of inflections in his speech. He started very solemn, almost pitiful, as he described the deplorable conditions in which these unfortunate people had to exist. Then slowly his voice gained confidence and became louder and more forceful as he introduced hope into the lives of the villagers. "Please help," Marcus pleaded. "Don't let one more child die." His voice grew louder still. "Think of the money you and I waste each day while these poor souls are starving." And then he rebuked the group as he slowly moved from one person to another with his collection basket. "Don't jeopardize YOUR salvation because you choose not to help." He then went to the next person. "When YOU say your prayers tonight, will your conscience be clear in the knowledge that you did everything possible to help our brothers and sisters?" Everyone was putting money in the basket. Judge Laningham was worried about Thelma Kwecien. Her turn to be singled out by Elder Billings was approaching and she was trembling anticipating the confrontation. Thelma obviously had little to give, but this did not matter to the elders. The judge had seen them in action before and they showed no mercy. Lamar thought of Hector's Aunt Francisca and her friends Stella and Anita. How could they endure this browbeating week after week? Finally Elder Billings stood directly over Thelma.

"Do YOU have children Mrs. Kwecien? How would YOU feel if no one helped them? Have YOUR children ever gone to bed hungry, so hungry that they did not have the strength to cry?" Marcus thrust the basket toward Thelma and she started visibly shaking as she reached for her purse.

"I would be honored to donate twenty thousand dollars," said the judge. The silence was deafening. Elder Billings turned to face Professor Lortz. Thelma was immediately dismissed although she was now as wide-eyed as everyone else in the classroom.

The tone in the elder's voice changed from that of a bully to someone experiencing disbelief. No one had ever donated an amount even close to that figure. Elder Marcus Billings required confirmation to what he had just heard. "Professor Lortz, did you indeed say twenty thousand dollars?" There was still no sound or movement from any of the others in the classroom. Like people following the ball in a tennis match, all eyes went back and forth between Elder Billings and the professor.

Lamar answered, "Yes, I did say twenty thousand dollars. I believe that it would be a good start in helping those poor folks in Africa. My wife Jessica and I are proud to be part of such a worthy project."

Hector and Lamar had, of course, known all along of the plan to give this large donation, yet actually hearing the words still carried somewhat of a shock. As he sat and listened to Elder Marcus bully the people in the room, Hector got more and more angry at Rapture and he began to lose focus on their goal. Thankfully, the professor's pledge seemed to satisfy the elder. The shakedown ended and Hector's anger abated. The prayer meeting ended and Judge Laningham (Professor Sheldon Lortz) remained behind with the elder. Lamar was purposely delaying writing the check until Colleen joined them.

Yolanda had a unique business relationship with a San Francisco bank which allowed her to do just about anything she wished. A letter sent directly from the Director of the FBI gave this authority to Agent Yolanda Tubbs, director of the Santa Molina division. The federal government would guarantee all account transactions. Of course, the intent was to use these fictitious accounts for FBI, not Council business. Only the president and vice president of the bank were allowed access to these accounts, so a teller would be able to see that the record existed, but they could not view details or bring these statements up on their computer screen. These accounts were designed to be used in situations where the FBI had to quickly create an identity and have access to large amounts of cash. Following the last Council meeting, Yolanda created the Professor Sheldon and Jessica Lortz account. The bank had their check printer "overnight" a single checkbook to the bank. Only "Sheldon and Jessica Lortz" was printed on the checks. There was no address or phone number listed per client request. Yolanda specified that the check numbers begin with 2075. A new account starting with check number 001 might raise eyebrows. Once the checks arrived, Yolanda deposited twenty thousand and five dollars, supplied by the judge, into the new account. With the money in the Lortz account everything was ready.

Colleen entered the classroom as her husband, the professor, began writing the check to Rapture. Professor Lortz introduced his wife to Marcus and explained to her that he was making a donation to help Rapture with the Mozambique Mission Fund.

"Oh please," interrupted Marcus, "make the check out to Rapture only. We will funnel the donation through regular church funds. Normally our donations are received in cash." He smiled politely.

"Jessica Lortz" came to play. "Oh, that is so nice Sheldon!" She turned to the elder. "You know, Sheldon and I have traveled and done everything we wanted to do. We have been blessed in our lives, and since we have no children or close family to leave our money to, when we find a worthy cause, it pleases us to help. Rapture seems like such a help to people in need."

Elder Marcus Billings smiled as Lamar continued to stall finishing the check. "We will certainly put the money to good use," said Marcus. He took one of Colleen's hands and held it in his own. "You folks are wonderful."

Mrs. Lortz added in a meek voice, "Do you think that there is any way we could give this check to Reverend Hartsell ourselves? He seems like such a nice young man."

Professor Lortz, nearly done writing the check, looked up. "Why Jessica what a lovely idea."

There was a phone on the wall next to the door and Elder Billings went to it and punched in a few numbers. He spoke softly so Mr. and Mrs. Lortz could not hear him. As quickly as he went to the phone he returned to them. "Reverend Hartsell is on his way here right now. He is thrilled with your generosity and he would very much like to meet you."

Less than two minutes had gone by when Reverend Hartsell stormed into the classroom. He had a huge smile and he stuck out his hand to shake hands with the professor and his wife.

Elder Billings jumped in. "Professor and Mrs. Lortz, this is Reverend Thomas Hartsell."

Sheldon said, "We are delighted to finally meet you. Jessica and I are enthralled with Rapture's outreach programs around the world and we are honored to help support them."

Reverend Hartsell bowed slightly. "It is because of the generosity of people such as yourselves that our programs are a success. We only wish that we could do more. There are so many people in need all over the world."

The professor asked, "Then why don't you? We have been listening to you speak of expanding Rapture Ministries on a global scale, and Jessica and I have been excited waiting for this to happen. Just think about the help you would be able to provide with hundreds of millions of dollars pouring in from all over the world? With all those people in such need of help, what could be holding you back?" All right thought Lamar, the hook was placed. When he mentioned hundreds of millions of dollars he could practically hear Hartsell salivating. Now, let's reel in this bottom feeder. "My nephew is a Hollywood production specialist and he could surely help you with this. You know that shopping network on television which sells jewelry to people at home? P.J. did that. He told me that this network did over three hundred million dollars in sales last year. I bet he could help Rapture go worldwide."

If Reverend Hartsell attempted to conceal his excitement, he failed miserably. He asked the professor "Could you contact your nephew on our behalf? This could be exactly what we have been looking for."

Professor Lortz handed the check to Reverend Hartsell. "Jessica or I will call P.J. and get back to you. I'll warn you, he is a very busy man and he does not like to sit still. Many find him difficult to work with because he insists on things being done his way. Once he gets involved, the job gets done right. His services do not come cheap, but they are the best. Once he is finished, he never gets complaints. Give me a number where he can reach you and I will ask him to call you."

Reverend Hartsell was uncharacteristically speechless. First a twenty thousand dollar donation, and now perhaps the possibility of Rapture Ministries getting worldwide exposure. Again he held out his hand to Professor Lortz. "Thank you, sir. Rapture Ministries is indebted to you. I very much look forward to hearing from your nephew."

Professor and Mrs. Lortz rose and headed out of the classroom. Elder Billings held the door open for them. Simultaneously, both Judge Laningham and Thomas Hartsell smiled thinking "what a sucker" about each other.

ZENITH PRODUCTIONS

Martha Green was at her desk when she received the call from her DNA specialist. She learned that using the evidence collected from the Darlene Lockwood evidence boxes, they were able to create two separate DNA profiles. Martha wanted to hear this directly from the technician, so she turned off her computer and headed down the hall to the lab. Lucy Mazzarella and Aria Heaton were waiting for her.

Aria discussed what they had discovered. "I went through the bedding and Lucy did the girl's clothing. From the sheets I was able to extract several long cranial hairs. We found two different X chromosomes in these hairs and the same in the blood samples from the sheets, so these samples are from a female, presumably Darlene Lockwood. Lucy also found hair samples and ancient semen stains."

Lucy took over. "The hair samples which I found proved to be excellent specimens. These hairs were clearly from a different person, and the DNA profile showed a Y chromosome meaning the hairs came from a male. Lastly, the DNA profile from the hair is the same as that from the semen."

"So," Aria said, "we conclude that there were both a man and a woman at the crime scene, and we have DNA profiles on each. We realize how stupid this sounds. It is a rape case...of course there were a man and a woman present. However, we just analyze the evidence. Interpretation is left to the detectives and the lawyers." Martha expressed her gratitude for their good work and returned to her office.

Looking at the evidence from this case nearly thirty years after the crime proved to be more beneficial than it did when the evidence was originally collected. It now appeared possible that modern forensic technology may be able to solve very old crimes. There were two other things which could potentially be in their favor. The first was that rape was one of those crimes which tended to be repeated. The act of rape was a statement. Through this act of brutality, the rapist was able to demonstrate his power over the victim. Low self-esteem, shyness, disfigurement, an overbearing mother, and poor social skills are but a few of the manifestations the rapist may be trying to overcome. He feels the overpowering need to show the world, or perhaps just convince himself, that he is able to confront and defeat the source of his fear. Unfortunately, any gratification he may have experienced from his act of savagery is short-lived and he is compelled to satisfy the need again and again.

The second thing, a hope to which Agent Green was now desperately clinging, was CODIS. If the man who raped Darlene Lockwood left evidence at yet another crime scene, a DNA match could possibly help establish patterns to his crimes. Often the victims have something in common such as shopping at the same stores or going to the same school. Any commonalities could develop a lead in this very old case.

As it turned out, FBI Agent Martha Green was only a few hours away from solving the crime which had been unsolved since

Daniel Lockwood was in high school. After she entered the DNA profile of the male evidence samples into the Offender Index of the CODIS system, Martha waited forty-five minutes until she got her first match. The DNA profile matched positively to that of a Raymond Howard. While the search continued for possible additional matches, Martha decided to use her time finding out whatever she could about Mr. Howard. It was now 4:00 PM on a lovely Friday evening. Most people were looking forward to going home to begin their weekend. However, Agent Green was, piece by piece, putting together a puzzle which had left a hole in the lives of several people, including her friend who worked downstairs. Many FBI agents like Martha were tenacious. Once they were "on the scent," they were relentless. Agent Green called home and explained to her boyfriend that she might be very late. He had already started dinner, yet he knew any attempt to dissuade her would be a waste of time.

This same Friday evening, on the other side of town, Dr. Jerry Woodson, Joel Harris, and Judge Lamar Laningham were deep into their plot to bring ruination to the dream of Reverend Thomas Hartsell. The judge had asked Jerry and Joel to come to the Council meeting early so he could learn about what was going to take place tomorrow, Saturday morning, at Rapture Ministries.

Judge Laningham, posing as Professor Sheldon Lortz, promised to contact his nephew, P.J. Mustav (Joel Harris), and ask him to, in turn, contact Reverend Hartsell regarding the possibility of a campaign to give Rapture Ministries a worldwide stage. P.J. called the reverend on Thursday morning, the day following the prayer meeting. P.J.'s production company, Zenith Productions, had been hired by a New York City publishing firm and had to leave in fifteen days. Zenith had a window of only two weeks to devote to Hartsell's project. Otherwise Rapture Ministries would probably have to wait a minimum of nine months till Zenith returned to the west coast. Reverend Hartsell expressed concern about the feasibility of going worldwide in only two weeks.

Joel was nervously pacing around the judge's study as he described his conversation with the reverend. He picked up random items from the judge's bookshelves and studied them as he spoke. He was one of those people who thought best while he fidgeted and moved around to the annoyance of those with him. He picked up a baseball signed by Willie Mays and replaced it after a moment. "What is this?" he asked and held up a stone which looked like green quartz.

The judge was trying to be patient. "Colleen and I found that in Hawaii on our honeymoon. It is a memento. How did you answer Hartsell?"

Joel continued his inspection of the shelves. "Oh, I told him that Zenith could absolutely have Rapture up and running worldwide in only two weeks. I told him that this was an opportune time because all of the television networks were in the process of ending their normal programming for the summer and they were hungry for new opportunities to fill their time slots. However, I cautioned him that in order to get a project of this magnitude done in two weeks, I demanded absolute control and total cooperation from his staff and parishioners." Joel came across a pipe rack which held six pipes and a vessel for tobacco. He removed the top of the container and smelled the pleasant aroma of the old tobacco residue. "Lamar I didn't know that you were a smoker?" he exclaimed.

The judge's patience was wearing thin with Joel's nervous pacing around the room. "I used to smoke a pipe, but that was a long time ago. A bowl of tobacco was one of my greatest pleasures, especially while I was reading. However, my doctor and a nagging wife eventually wore me down so I quit several years ago. That's one bad habit which I truly miss. I hope that I will enjoy a good pipe again in heaven one day along with potato chips, brandy, and chocolate cake, none of which you will presently find in the Laningham home." He coughed remembering the pleasure of the smoke tickling the back of his throat.

Finally, Joel turned and joined them at his place at the Council table. "Thomas Hartsell is no fool, and he is street-smart. Given time, I have no doubts that he will be able to see through our little deception. Dr. Woodson and I are banking on the fact that his greed will overpower his common sense and his curiosity. Just in case, however, we plan to keep him so busy that he won't have time to think. We will give him cookies, you know, tantalizing samples of what we have created for him at intervals throughout the two weeks. This will serve to reinforce the idea that his dream is rapidly coming to fruition. My people are creating a phony website with state of the art graphics. Believe me, in addition to their technical skills, if my employees share one thing in abundance it is imagination. We have created an awesome Zenith Productions website in case someone tries to check us out. This website lists an e-mail address and phone contact site which are routed through my home office." It was clear to the judge and Dr. Woodson that Joel was pleased to use his resources to help the Council. "Dr.

Woodson, who is Woodrow Dennison, my senior production editor, and I together created an imaginary reference which we may speak of when discussing the success of Zenith Productions. A little over a year ago, the jewelry channel contacted us to launch their station and make their products known to consumers across the nation. Last year their sales were over three million dollars."

Dr. Woodson gave Joel a rest. "Joel's workers are in the process of creating a tremendous website for Rapture Ministries. You should see it." Dr. Woodson was, also, very excited. "The homepage shows Reverend Hartsell on the altar looking to the sky with his hands high in the air. The choir is elevated behind him in a semicircle, and above the choir is a massive pipe organ. The toolbar directs the user to a variety of Rapture services including Rapture information, missions, and a listing of outreach programs. Of course, all visitors to the website are encouraged to leave their contact information including their e-mail address and phone number. There is a special feature for making donations including...are you ready for this? Yes, Joel created a sidebar which allows you to 'climb the ladder' in donations. Once you reach a designated level in contributions, you even get to see your name magically appear in lights on the website's Wall of Attainment. As an added incentive to give, every time a donor hits the 'submit' button after filling out their credit card information, they hear the choir sing *Rapture O' My Soul*. Finally, there is a section describing 'Love Gifts' where, for specified donation levels you can receive books, DVDs, or even an autographed picture of Reverend Thomas Hartsell."

Once again Joel spoke. "We have designated 'G' day as the target date to go global. Until this date, seventeen days from now, nothing goes live except for testing purposes."

Hector and Yolanda entered the Laningham study and sat around the table with the other Council members. With help from Dr. Woodson and Joel, the judge brought them up to date.

Hector's assignment was to continue taking his mother to both Sunday services and Wednesday evening prayer meetings at Rapture. At the next Wednesday meeting, Rosa (Lolita Zapata) was to drop a not so subtle hint that she was soon to inherit a monstrous inheritance from her brother's estate. Lolita is not sure exactly how much her brother was worth, but the lawyers have indicated it would be millions. Hector was amused as he explained how excited his mother was to be taking part in this charade. Rosa was aware that her son and some of his friends were attempting to expose Reverend Hartsell as a fraud. She was infuriated to learn what had happened to her sister-in-law Francisca and her two friends at Rapture, and she was delighted when Hector asked her to play a part in bringing him down. "Besides," said Hector, "she says this is the most fun she has had since well before dad died."

Rosa was a simple woman. She radiated humility in how she spoke and how she lived. Her modest home was paid for and her only bills were her monthly utility bills, food, and church donations. Everyone knew that Hartsell and the elders would be incessant in their attempts to separate Lolita from her inheritance. And now they would need it to help pay Zenith Productions.

Yolanda's role in the Council's mission was still unclear. Joel suggested that she would be helpful assuming a role as perhaps a

147

secretary to P.J. and Woodrow from back in Hollywood or as some sort of liaison between Hollywood and the Zenith crew in the field. Council experience had shown that having someone in the shadows whose identity was unknown was always a good idea.

6

SHY RAYMOND

Saturday morning Dr. Woodson rented a car from the airport. It didn't seem like a good idea to begin the deception by getting caught with local license plates which could be traced. Besides, P.J. and Woodrow were supposed to have flown from Los Angeles to San Francisco, so they would have had to rent a car. Dr. Woodson rented the car using the fake ID which Yolanda had supplied to both him and Joel. He picked up Joel earlier and they used the short drive to create a simple game plan to follow once they met Thomas Hartsell. They had to act arrogant, in charge, and supremely confident in their roles as a Hollywood production crew. Hartsell had to be made to believe that Rapture Ministries would start raking in millions of dollars in two weeks. There was no room for compromise and Hartsell and his minions had to comply with everything which was asked of them. In a nutshell, P.J. and Woodrow were attempting to con a con.

Dr. Woodson pulled into the Rapture Ministries parking lot. There were only five or six cars there since it was Saturday. P.J. and Woodrow hurried up the steps to Rapture's administration building, and at the top of the stairs they were greeted by Elder Jesse Carter.

"Hello, I am Elder Jesse Carter. I presume you are the gentlemen from Hollywood?" He smiled and extended his hand toward Joel.

"Yes," said P.J., "and we are obviously giving up a lovely Saturday to be here, so if you don't mind, can we get on with this? Where is Heartsmell?"

"Hartsell sir, his name is Reverend Thomas Hartsell."

"Whatever," answered P.J.

Elder Jesse was clearly upset. He was not used to being on the receiving end of intimidation. "Come this way, sir." He opened the door and led P.J. and Woodrow down a corridor to a door which said **Rapture Ministries**, and underneath, **Reverend Thomas Hartsell**. Elder Jesse knocked politely and opened the door. Hartsell got up from behind his desk and motioned for his guests to join him around a small conference table.

"Gentlemen, I am Reverend Hartsell of Rapture Ministries. I have been looking forward to meeting you." They shook hands.

"I am P.J. Mustav, President of Zenith Productions, and this is Woodrow Dennison, my senior production editor." P.J. made no attempt to conceal his using hand sanitizer which he rubbed into his hands. "We have come a long way and have precious little time to accomplish a great deal of work, so let us dispense with all of the usual preliminary nonsense and get down to why we are here."

Reverend Hartsell was somewhat taken aback by the direct way which P.J. presented himself. The reverend, himself was more used to softening up his prey before he swooped in for the kill.

"Well, yes sir," said Hartsell. "We are hoping to work with your production company to give our church, Rapture, worldwide exposure. We are looking to help feed, clothe, and spread the word of God to all nations of the world."

P.J. cut Reverend Hartsell off in the middle of a thought. "Excuse me, Mr. Hartsell, but we need to get a few things straight up front. I don't need you, you need me. You will not be working WITH my company. We will NOT be having discussions, and we will NOT become friends. Personally I find friends very overrated. You have indicated to me what you want done, and I am here to do it. We have only two weeks to accomplish what we need to do, so there is no time for discussions or chit chat. What I need is for your people, whoever they are, to do exactly what I say, when I say it. If I instruct them to paint the church black, then it had better be black the next time I come here. Should I tell you to have the choir sing country western songs, then you'd better buy some cowboy hats. Look...you are going to pay me a lot of money, and you will give me half of it up front. So the first time someone challenges me or tries to tell me how to do my job, I walk. I am the best at what I do precisely because I answer to no one. Believe me when I tell you that I had to learn that lesson the hard way. Let's be frank, shall we? You are looking to bring in a lot of money in donations from all over the world. Now the watch on your wrist, which I believe is a Tourbillon, and the rings on your fingers, tell me that you like nice things. I could not care less. And while we are at it, I don't care if you feed the poor or sell them used car parts. Once my people and I leave here, you will be bringing in a ton of money from all over the globe, probably more than you are able to fathom. What you do with it is your business. I make no apologies for being so blunt, and I don't care if you approve of me or my methods. As I said, having friends is overrated. Here's the deal. I want five million dollars, and

I do not take checks. Two and a half million Monday morning and the balance once we are ready to go live in two weeks. Remember, we are leaving for a big job in New York City two weeks from Monday. Everything must be completed by then. I am staying in town tonight and I can be reached at this number." P.J. handed Reverend Hartsell his card created by his company. "You have until tonight to make up your mind. Should you want us to continue, I will be in church tomorrow. I will need to see just how much work needs to be done." P.J. and Woodrow stood up and headed toward the door which Jesse opened for them.

Reverend Hartsell was speechless. Normally, he was the one who controlled the conversation. Dr. Woodson was a psychiatrist. He knew how Hartsell operated, and it was he who instructed Joel how to take the control from Hartsell. On the way back to the car Dr. Woodson said, "Well played, sir. I must confess that you even pissed me off. Now we come to the real battle, Reverend Hartsell's ego versus his greed." It took Dr. Woodson and Joel twenty minutes to drive to their San Francisco hotel. Before they had been in the room ten minutes, Joel's phone rang.

"This is Reverend Hartsell. We have a deal. I will have your money for you on Monday as you requested. Church is at 10:00 AM tomorrow."

"See you then," answered Joel and he hung up the phone. He turned to Dr. Woodson. "Greed won...what a surprise," he said.

While Joel and Dr. Woodson were relaxing in their hotel room, Agent Martha Green was at home preparing a report for Yolanda. She put together the story of rapist Raymond Howard. Martha wanted Yolanda to have the information and let her decide how to present it to Daniel Lockwood. After all, Martha was the new "guy."

Raymond Howard had raped four young girls before he got caught. Darlene Lockwood had been his first victim. Extremely shy and antisocial, Raymond avoided people whenever he was able to. He was a janitor in the Ferndale High School which was attended by Daniel and Darlene Lockwood. It was ironic that Raymond's personality disorder was the reason he worked at the school. Russell Wells, the school superintendent did all of the hiring and firing, and he had a soft spot in his heart for people with disabilities. Until Raymond, Mr. Wells had never had any trouble with anyone he had hired.

The head custodian of the school gave Raymond all of the responsibility for the south end of the high school which included the cafeteria and about ten classrooms. There were two shifts of janitorial workers at Ferndale. Four janitors worked from 7:00 AM until 3:00 PM. Three more worked from 3:00 PM until 11:00 PM. Among the janitorial staff, the preferred shift was the later one. Except for the occasional after school activity such as basketball or football games, the second shift janitors had much more freedom. Their boss did not care how they got their assigned tasks completed as long as they WERE completed. So if there was a basketball game, the janitors would clean classrooms while the boys or girls trashed the gymnasium and the locker rooms. Then, once the kids left the building, the men would deal with the mess in peace. A few members of the janitorial crew actually became quite adroit at being able to tell if Ferndale had won or had lost the games by the condition in which the locker rooms were found. The majority of the janitors couldn't care less who had won or lost. Although this was the preferred shift, after   school activities were thought to be a pain.   Normally these activities, such as practice for the sports teams or intermural activities, were done by 5:00 PM.   The little darlings had to be home for supper and homework. Only the actual games were later, from 7:00 PM until about 9:00 PM.

Hence, aside from the home games, the second shift janitors had it made. They could create their own schedules in terms of how they got their work done. They could play music, take frequent smoke breaks, have dinner whenever they chose, or hone their skills in talking dirty to each other.   The more friendly janitors even worked together. Double-teaming each other's assigned work areas made the shift more pleasant and the time went by faster.

None of these freedoms were an option for the day shift janitorial workers.   They were under constant scrutiny of the teachers and the students. The day janitors were warned to keep a respectable distance from the kids, yet they were expected to be cordial. At times maintaining civility could be difficult because high school students could be very cruel. A few years back someone thought that it would be a good idea to incorporate developmentally disabled students into the mainstream student body. They would play sports together and attend the same classes. The idea, of course, was a lofty one. The slower students would be given a taste of "normalcy" and this would in turn increase their self-esteem.   Everyone would be accepting of each other and everything would be sunshine and rainbows. Unfortunately, in the real world things are not that easy.

A small percentage of students are just cruel, while others demand attention and are perfectly willing to get it at the expense of others.

The cruel kids are easier to understand. They likely learned to behave this way from their parents. In a house full of mean people, the meanest one is the alpha dog. This of course spills over into all social relationships, and by picking on the less fortunate, the cruel student feels superior.

The attention-craving students are the more difficult to understand. There are many reasons people seek attention, but unlike their cruel counterparts, it is not their intention to harm anyone. These are the class clowns. Unable to get attention by excelling in sports or academics, they rely on humor. Unfortunately, humor is nearly always realized at the expense of another. There can sometimes be a fine line between humor and cruelty.

Raymond Howard knew well the games played by the cruel students and the attention seekers. An introvert when he was in high school, Raymond was frequently the target of jokes and bullying. To him, high school was intolerable as a student, and to his dismay, he has found himself in the same environment as a working adult.

Cleaning the classrooms in his assigned area was not a problem for Ray. He quickly learned the "rhythm" of the classes. Classrooms were used in a staggered fashion. At any given time seven of Ray's ten classrooms would be in use. He could clean the other three. Teachers would often stay behind after the rooms emptied of students to grade papers or prepare for their next class. The teachers were always nice to Ray. Some even helped him clean.

155

An hour later, different classrooms would empty and he would start all over again.

Unfortunately, lunchtime in the cafeteria was a different story. Since there were so many students, two separate lunch times had to be created. Each group had forty-five minutes to go through the food line and eat. Naturally, Ray had to be there the entire time to attempt to keep up with the mess created. Only twice were there actual food fights, because the punishments lasted much longer than the fun.

Normally the messes resulted from giddy teenagers laughing and letting off steam outside the confines of structured classrooms. They were just kids having fun and being young. Unfortunately, the bullies and the attention seekers also required noontime sustenance. Once a new school year began it became clear within a week who the new troublemakers were and throughout their four years in high school, they never changed. The seniors graduated and left to create havoc elsewhere while a new freshman class sired more of the same.

The large lunchtime audience seemed to enhance the creativity of the little deviates. One would think that there would be a finite number of ways which food could be shoved into the various cranial orifices. Yet every year the "bar" was raised. Several of the children were merciless in their treatment of Raymond. They knew he was helpless to defend himself lest he would lose his job, and this just made everything worse. The lunch line workers watched in horror as the children continued to abuse Raymond Howard. Finally, the cafeteria employees demanded that Raymond be removed from cafeteria duty. His area of responsibility changed

156

from the cafeteria to the gymnasium. The gym, of course, was adjacent to the girl's locker room, the holy of holies for a man who fantasizes about young girls.

CHAPTER FOUR

1

SUNDAY MORNING

As the judge and Colleen prepared themselves for their Sunday morning trek to Rapture Ministries, Lamar found comfort in the fact that this Council mission would be over in two weeks. He would then be able to attend his own church and get some needed rest. Since his appointment with Dr. May he began taking "power naps." Another stupid expression, he thought. The reason he sought naps was a lack of power, and normally when he woke from his naps, he still had no power to do anything.

Two weeks ago Dr. May told Judge Laningham that his coughing and wheezing had nothing at all to do with the cold he had a month ago. He has non-small cell lung cancer (NSCLC). The X-rays, CAT scans and myriad of other tests he had been forced to endure, determined that the cancer had progressed to Stage IV. Essentially this was a death sentence because it meant that the cancer had already metastasized to other organs in his body, and treatment, except for comfort measures, was next to useless. All of this was confirmed by his long-time friend Dr. Woodson. Almost no one who has Stage IV NSCLC survives beyond a year or two. Although the cancer is normally slow growing, it can very suddenly, and without notice, change to wildly aggressive. Dr. May was honest with Lamar and Colleen and gave them no false hopes. She emphasized that the decision was theirs regarding possible treatment options. As their friend, she made it clear that her preference would be quality over quantity. What good would two additional months of life afford if they were spent retching and staring at your wiggly shadow in the bottom of the toilet?

Most people would have said that Colleen took the bad news remarkably well. She was able to ask the right questions of the oncologists, and she was able to give Lamar whatever support he required. Together, the Laninghams agreed that they would do nothing until the pain came. They were told that Lamar would experience increasing fatigue and loss of appetite. The wheezing, coughing, and shortness of breath had already taken up residence in his chest.

Judge Laningham had always been his own man. Colleen would do whatever it took to continue following his wishes whatever they might be. He decided against any treatment. Colleen supported the decision. Lamar, also, asked that no one except Jerry Woodson be told of his cancer. He did not want to be pitied or treated differently. He, also, wanted to continue Council activities as long as he was able. Again, Colleen gave her full support of this as well. Lamar had never gone into detail about the Council's affairs and she never asked. For over two years Lamar and his four friends had been meeting in his study. She knew that they were not playing poker. Colleen never felt the desire to learn about the Council. She only knew that the last two years were the happiest in Lamar's life since they were forced to deal with the death of their son. Yes, she would support his continued participation in the Council. At least he would have a distraction from his cancer and still have purpose. Everything would stay the same until the pain came.

Until Reverend Hartsell and Rapture Ministries came along, Colleen had never been asked to join Council activities. Now, however, Lamar thought that it would appear more realistic if his wife continued to accompany him when he attended Rapture on Sundays and Wednesday evenings. Colleen had already witnessed Hartsell's extortion of his parishioners, many of whom were poor. Lamar told Colleen how the Council planned to disrupt his fraudulent activity. Like Rosa Martinez, Colleen found it rather exciting. Unknown to Lamar, she felt the more important reason for her participation was to stay close to her husband. Colleen took one final look in the mirror, fixed her hair, and they were ready to go.

Hector and Rosa were also preparing themselves for a morning at Rapture in the Round. This morning Lolita Zapata was to plant a seed. She intended to let it "slip" to one of the elders that following the inheritance she would receive from her brother's estate, she was soon to become a wealthy woman. Her son Tomas would be at her side as always.

The real stars at Rapture this Sunday morning would be Joel (P.J. Mustav) and his production editor Woodrow Dennison (Dr. Woodson). They intended to attract as much attention to themselves as possible. Zenith Productions was there to help Rapture acquire a worldwide following, and they wanted everyone to know it. This morning they wanted the Rapture congregation to be brought to a heightened state of excitement. Dr. Woodson believed that if everyone was a part of the charade, the Council's job would be easier and more credible.

All of the Council's members except Yolanda would be at Rapture this morning. It was hoped that the deception today would initiate the ruse which would ultimately bring an end to Hartsell and his extortion. Planning and executing deception on this level would test everyone's nerves. However, Reverend Thomas Hartsell was far more agitated than any of the Council members. After all, he had to come up with two and a half million dollars in just over twenty-four hours. The reverend's stomach was in a knot as he showered and dressed for church. He had nearly a million dollars of the church's funds in the bank. Thankfully, he had also been using mission donations to make large payments on the mortgage principal of his six million dollar estate. He should be able to tap into the equity of both his home and the church building to come up with the money he would require tomorrow afternoon. He remembered the twenty thousand dollar donation from Professor Lortz. This could be a good start for the final payment he would require in two weeks. He wondered if that old fool Lortz had any more cash he could squeeze out of him. Over and over he worked the numbers until his head hurt. There was simply no way he could think of to come up with the money for the final payment. He would meet to discuss this with the elders. They would just have to work harder to raise the required funds. And what if he could not come up with the money? He had two weeks to figure it out.

Thomas Hartsell and his elders loved their lavish lifestyle. After church on Sundays and the prayer meetings on Wednesdays, they would lovingly transport the money collected from the parishioners to the Hartsell mansion where, like pirates, they would count their plunder. This was always the best part of their day. Thomas, Marcus, and Jesse were like brothers. They did everything together. Often on Sunday afternoons they would collectively fly to Las Vegas and live like kings until Wednesday when they would have to return for the prayer meetings.

The triad had been together for many years. At thirty-four, Thomas was the undisputed leader of the pack. Growing up in a large city like Chicago can be rough. Unlike small towns where everyone knows everyone else as well as their business, cities like Chicago tend to swallow up people and it becomes easy to get lost. To make matters worse, when Thomas and his two friends were roaming the streets of Chicago, the specter of civil rights was raging all across the nation.

Growing up fatherless had become an epidemic in large cities. Many argued that generous welfare benefits discouraged able-bodied people from looking for employment as well as providing an incentive for women, black and white, to continue having children without any husbands. Others felt that we as a society owed the poor reparations for opportunities denied to them. Affirmative Action, an executive order signed in March of 1961 by President Kennedy, was but one of many attempts to ameliorate social injustice as he perceived it in the sixties.

Our social programs were a conundrum which were, and still are debated in barbershops and all the way up to the floor in congress. Perhaps the clash between the lavish social giveaway programs versus societal responsibility through work and moral discipline was best illustrated in the legendary philosophical debates between J. Edgar Hoover and the Kennedy brothers. While not the first clash between liberal and conservative values, few such battles have had such far-reaching consequences.

J. Edgar Hoover spent his entire life fighting crime. In May of 1924, at the age of twenty-nine, he became the first Director of the Federal Bureau of Investigation (FBI). Hoover brought to this office and to the entire organization an *esprit de corps* which included a strict code of conduct. His simple but uncompromising values included morality, decency, loyalty, hard work, and a love of God and country. Hoover truly believed that aspiring to these values was what made individuals and, in turn, middle class society, the backbone of the nation, great. This was our strength as a nation. Conversely, a rejection of these values would rip the heart out of America and eventually lead to its demise. J. Edgar believed that the gangsters and criminals whom he chased all his life embodied the rejection of American middle class values. They chose not to work and they exhibited a lack of discipline in all areas of their lives. Hoover later came to believe the same thing of civil rights activists and communists. The ethos we chose for ourselves would define us both individually and collectively as a nation. Adherence to the American ethic would virtually guarantee any man or woman success in life. Further, the level of success which anyone could achieve was in direct proportion to their degree of commitment to these social mores.

After J. Edgar Hoover served as Director of the FBI for nearly forty years, along came the Kennedy brothers. Born into wealth from dubious origins, these upper class Harvard-educated boys had their hearts set on social change in America. Although elected by the narrowest of margins, President Kennedy and his younger brother Robert, appointed Attorney General, viewed their victory as a referendum for change. Elected in 1961, the Kennedy years in the White House marked the beginning of the tumultuous sixties. Hippies, long hair, marijuana, the Beatles, free love, antiwar and civil rights demonstrations, and a relaxation in discipline were all an integral part of a new generation which J. Edgar Hoover could not abide and would not embrace.

Hoover thought that America was being torn apart right in front of him, on HIS watch. He saw the Kennedy brothers and Martin Luther King as arrogant, rebellious upstarts lacking in moral fiber and discipline. Instead of helping to mend the nation, he viewed them as part of the problem. Numerous extramarital affairs and alliances with Hollywood and organized crime figures were illustrative of their moral decrepitude. The Kennedy brothers thought that dumping tons of money into social programs would lower the crime rate and combat prejudice. It did not.

Just as America was wrestling with a myriad of social issues including social inequality and social prejudice, Thomas, Marcus, and Jesse were roaming the streets of Chicago. They didn't care about antipoverty programs or job training. They certainly did not care about pride in their country or moral values. They never had fathers to give them guidance or serve as role models. These three boys banded together for survival and they continued together until they were caught in their credit card scheme and sent to Leavenworth for a decade.

Thomas Hartsell was no fool. He knew he would get another chance at life once he was paroled. While the other inmates at Leavenworth lifted weights or played basketball, he studied and schemed. Thomas wanted to control people. He needed to know how to make people do what HE wanted them to do. Then, of course, he needed to learn how he could profit from this talent. One day in his cell, to take a break from his reading, young Thomas Hartsell decided to watch television. He watched a Sunday morning television evangelist and was amazed at how the preacher was able to use his voice and his words to mesmerize his audience. By using his body language and changing inflections in his voice, the pastor was emotionally manipulating the congregation. Yet the best part was during the collection. Thomas had never seen the inside of a church and he was unable to understand why these people, hundreds of them, were willingly giving all their money to this man. He had finally found his calling. Thomas Hartsell threw himself into his new obsession and he was delighted to learn that "preaching" perfectly complimented the skills he had taught himself in learning to control people. Hartsell used the remainder of his incarceration watching and studying the television evangelists and honing his skills. He promised Marcus and Jesse a new career, only this time, instead of taking money from people; Thomas had found a way in which they would want to give it to him willingly.

The three young men were eventually released from prison. They all returned to Chicago and for a time, to satisfy parole requirements, they had to stay in the area and report periodically to a parole officer. They started small and opened a little church in an abandoned store. The three would travel the streets going door to door seeking people in need of salvation. To their amazement, people came to their "church" in droves, and just like on television, they willingly parted with their cash. They didn't make a lot of money because the church was in a poor neighborhood. Yet this gave Thomas, Marcus, and Jesse time to satisfy their parole

165

requirements, and they were able to refine their skills in manipulation. A year later, they had all managed to stay out of trouble and they set their sights on someplace warm and sunny where no one knew them and they could seek a larger more affluent congregation to fleece. Chicago was delighted to see them go, and the three were off to San Francisco. In addition to satisfying their desires for a warmer climate, Thomas Hartsell knew from his prison readings that Jim Jones had much success in San Francisco evangelizing affluent people before he lost his mind and moved to Guyana.

2

LOLITA'S NEW CLOTHES

Professor and Mrs. Lortz were the first of the Council members to enter the church. It was a beautiful Sunday morning and both the judge and Colleen hoped to get to enjoy the remainder of the day after church. Elder Marcus Billings greeted them and held the door open for them. Colleen wondered how many of the twenty thousand dollars from their donation had found their way into Elder Billings' pocket. Not knowing what theatrics Joel and Dr. Woodson may have planned for today, Lamar thought that today's service might be fun.

Moments later Hector and his mother entered Rapture in the Round. Hector spotted Lamar and Colleen. He was too far away to speak with them, but he wanted to be able to see the Lortzes when Reverend Hartsell announced their donation to the congregation. There were only a few minutes remaining until the service was scheduled to start when a loud disruption from above them caught everyone's attention.

"Hey, get out of here!" screamed the organist. He was clearly upset that two men had joined him in the tiny area above the altar.

"Relax pal, why don't you just go back to diddling on your organ. We're just here checking the view and the lighting." Dr. Woodson pretended to nearly fall from the balcony and was grabbed by his belt from behind by Joel. Having received the

167

desired attention, they exited the organist's area which was only designed for one person.

A few moments later, having regained his composure, the organist resumed playing as the choir came in and assumed their usual semicircular position on the elevated platform behind the altar. A few seconds after the last choir member was in position, the organist changed songs. The choir director motioned for the congregation to stand and as the choir members swayed back and forth in unison, the people sang with them. On the wall behind the altar, between the choir and the organ, there were two large screens which scrolled the words of the song. The two screens were angled so that they were visible to all seats. After the opening song, a church member approached the altar and invited the parishioners to join her in prayer. During this time, both the choir and the congregation remained standing. Following the prayer there were two more songs. At the conclusion of the second song, Elder Jesse Carter went to the pulpit near the altar. Realizing that this was a departure from the normal order of service protocol, the congregation began whispering, trying to figure out what was happening.

"Excuse me brothers and sisters. I realize that my being up here at this time is not what you are used to, but Reverend Hartsell has asked me to make an important announcement."

Everyone was now talking even louder as they speculated about what might be going on. Elder Carter held up his hands in an effort to silence the crowd. His gesture worked and in seconds everything was quiet. "Rapture Ministries has truly been blessed. You have all heard us speak of taking Rapture's message to the world. Today that dream starts to become a reality. We are fortunate to have two men with us this morning who are production specialists from Hollywood. Reverend Hartsell will introduce them to you. These two men from Zenith Productions will give us a worldwide audience in two weeks."

For a moment the congregation was still, and as Elder Carter's message began to be understood, there was suddenly an eruption of applause. Many stood and raised their arms. "Amens" and "Hallelujahs" were offered by others. Elder Jesse allowed everyone to bask in the grandeur of the moment. From a remote television screen Reverend Hartsell was able to view the congregation's splendid response. Again Jesse raised his arms for quiet.

"Reverend Hartsell has opened our church to these folks from Hollywood and has allowed them to make any changes necessary to transform Rapture in the Round to the magnificence required to take our message to the world. We have designated Monday, June 17th as **G Day**. This is the day we go global. This is only two weeks from tomorrow, and it will come fast. We will erect a banner to count down the number of days left. The reverend has asked that you cooperate with these folks and assist them in their work. Finally, we will likely have projects requiring assistance, so we may ask for volunteers from the congregation. Thank you." Again the parishioners responded with raucous applause.

The organist and the choir led everyone in two more songs and right on cue, at the height of the moment, Reverend Hartsell was raised up from below to the altar. He danced and swayed with the choir to the final verse of the song, and as everything slowly calmed, he approached the pulpit.

Reverend Hartsell began his message describing his path to the present and how he felt led to become a pastor. He neglected to mention that the journey started in cell number 103 of C Block in the Leavenworth Penitentiary, a medium security prison in Kansas. He was now living his destiny. Once he received the revelation to take Rapture's message across the globe, he knew a way would be provided. Of course the poor people of the world were mentioned and how it was Rapture's responsibility to care for them. He asked P.J. Mustav and Woodrow Dennison to stand. When he explained that these two men and Zenith Productions were beginning work tomorrow, the church again responded with acclamation. Finally he got to the point. He thanked the congregation for all of the support that they had given Rapture and its missions until now. However, they were now turning a corner in the ministry and Reverend Hartsell was compelled to ask them to dig even deeper into their pockets. Help was on the way. In two weeks, the entire world would come to help. He told them that he was refinancing his own home to help and he hoped his example would inspire others to do the same.

Instead of waiting until the end of the service, the reverend decided that this would be a good time to use the Lortzes' donation as an inspiring example. "Brothers and sisters, I don't mean to embarrass these kind folks, but they exemplify exactly what I am talking about. Will Professor and Mrs. Lortz please stand up?"

Lamar and Colleen knew this was coming yet that knowledge didn't seem to lessen the impact. They were playing roles in a drama which they hoped would have a happy ending...not for Hartsell and his sycophants...but for the poor devils who were being picked clean thinking they were doing good work helping the needy. The hypocrisy of it all washed over the Laninghams as they stood to receive their adulation.

Reverend Hartsell spotted the Lortzes. "Brothers and sisters, the professor and his wife retired and moved here from Chicago. No wonder I feel a connection with them...I moved here from Chicago as well. It was our good fortune, no, I believe that it was a guiding hand that brought them to Rapture."

Lamar thought to himself that if he was twenty years younger, he'd give Hartsell a guided hand of his own.

Hartsell continued, "these wonderful folks were so moved by our work in Mozambique that they made a donation, the likes of which has never been seen at Rapture, to support the mission. Talk about 'climbing the ladder.' Brothers and sisters, the Lortzes have climbed the ladder and stepped off onto Mt. Everest. Decorum would dictate that I not reveal the amount of their generous donation to our mission fund." Reverend Hartsell gave a lengthy pause which produced its intended effect. Meanwhile Sheldon and Jessica had their heads down hoping it would soon be over.

Hartsell slowly looked over the parishioners. "This morning, decorum be damned. The good people of Rapture need to know what real giving looks like." He pointed to Mr. and Mrs. Lortz. "These are not rich people, they are caring people. The professor saw a need and he stepped up to the plate. Twenty thousand dollars was what they donated." The congregation let out a collective sigh. Again Hartsell paused for effect. Now he yelled,

"THAT'S RIGHT, TWENTY THOUSAND DOLLARS!" The entire church body stood to give Sheldon and Jessica Lortz a rousing applause. They, also, heard many "amens" and "hallelujahs." Reverend Hartsell took a handkerchief from his breast pocket and slowly wiped his eyes even though there were no tears. He pretended to cry and he introduced a little sobbing type inflection into his voice.

Suddenly Judge Laningham was taken with a bout of uncontrollable coughing. Because they were standing, he and Colleen drew everyone's attention including that of Reverend Hartsell, who took a bottle of water he kept on the pulpit and passed it to the professor. After a few sips of water the coughing stopped. Exhausted and embarrassed, Lamar and Colleen sat down.

"I know what you mean, Brother Lortz, I too am choked up," said Hartsell. "Ladies and gentlemen, brothers and sisters, we have come to a crossroad. I know where Professor and Mrs. Lortz stand, but I need to know where YOU stand! Let's help these people. Let's take a stand against poverty and sickness. Let's help ALL of God's children. Show the Lortzes they are not alone. Give till it hurts. No...better yet...give till it feels good."

The organist took the cue and the choir stood. *Rapture O' My Soul* sounded better than ever. Joel and Dr. Woodson were standing in the back and they were impressed. Reverend Hartsell raised his hands and stopped the music and the singing just a moment after it had started. He motioned for Elder Carter to come to him. Reverend Hartsell whispered in the elder's ear, and this made the elder smile and run down the aisle toward P.J. and Woodrow. Hartsell pointed to the elder. "Forgive me brothers and sisters. I have been remiss in neglecting to introduce you to P.J.

Mustav and Woodrow Dennison. These fine gentlemen and Zenith Productions are here to take Rapture's message to the world." The elder brought the two guests up to the altar. The music started again and the choir with new energy came down from their raised platform. In seconds, the choir, Reverend Hartsell, Elder Carter, P.J., and Woodrow were all locking elbows and dancing with the choir members all around the altar. Everyone in the congregation, including the Laninghams and the Martinezes loved the celebration.

The collection of church donations took longer than usual. The choir director always monitored the passing of the collection baskets and coordinated the end of the singing to coincide with the end of the collection. This morning was unusual. The choir had to sing two extra verses of *Rapture O' My Soul* before the baskets were returned to the altar. It appeared that the reverend had done his job well and the parishioners were revisiting their wallets and purses. The doxology was sung and following a few brief announcements, Reverend Hartsell reminded everyone of the importance in attending the prayer meetings on Wednesday. The crowd was dismissed.

On the way out of the church, Hector intentionally separated himself from, and lagged behind his mother. Elder Marcus Billings addressed Rosa. "Why, good morning Lolita. You look different but very nice today."

This was exactly what Rosa wanted to hear. Trying her best to appear both flattered and shy, Rosa responded. "How nice of you to notice. I had my hair done and I bought some new clothes. My brother has just died and we had to go to the services and meet with his lawyers. He never had time for a family but he was quite wealthy. My son and I were his only family so he left his entire estate to us. Honestly, what would someone my age do with all that money? Maybe I could give a donation to the mission fund."

Elder Billings morphed into a caring and sympathetic comforter. "I am so sorry to hear about your brother. We have an excellent lawyer on retainer with Rapture. If we can help you with the inheritance of course we would be happy to, at your convenience. You should have legal representation at a time like this. Do you have any idea how large his estate may have been?"

Lolita put her hand up to whisper into the elder's ear. "Millions" was all she needed to say.

3

FERNDALE

Monday morning Agent Martha Green was about as excited as she could get. Since Friday afternoon she had spent nearly all of her waking hours learning about Raymond Howard. She prepared a report and was ready to deliver it as soon as Yolanda was ready. Ruth, Yolanda's secretary, told Martha that since it was Monday, the boss first wanted to catch up on weekend activities. Ruth promised that Yolanda would soon be available. In the meantime, Martha went to the DNA lab.

Aria Heaton had not come to work yet. Her daughter had been sick, so Aria phoned the lab and said that she would be late. Lucy Mazzarella had already been preparing to delve into the samples of evidence provided by Martha. There were pieces of tissue and hair samples from the clothes of Bernard (Bubba) Jones, Roddy Jackson, and Adamos Lazopoulos. Lucy already knew that Martha's greatest interest would be in the DNA profiles produced from the store owner's clothes. For this reason Lucy was preparing to process them first. Martha would have to wait to see what the evidence revealed, but her antennae were already screaming in anticipation that the DNA profile from the mysterious third person would be from the same person that left the unidentified third set of fingerprints on the bloody baseball bat. Martha thanked Lucy for her good work.

"Don't thank me," said Lucy. "Thank whoever collected the evidence. After all these years following the assault of Danno Lockwood's sister, the evidence has told us the identity of her attacker."

Agent Green's pager started beeping. The number shown on the pager display was that of Ruth, Yolanda's secretary. Apparently they were ready to see her.

Ruth's door was open. "Yolanda is ready for you. Go right in."

Yolanda was dunking a teabag up and down in her cup when Martha walked into her office. Once she looked up and saw Martha, file in hand, she held the teabag over the wastebasket and dropped it. "Good morning Martha, would you like some tea?"

Martha moved forward to the chair facing the front of Yolanda's desk. "No thanks, I already had coffee."

Yolanda sat and motioned for Martha to do the same. "What's on your mind this morning?"

Martha appeared anxious. "Well, first of all, thank you for allowing me to move the Lockwood case in front of the Jones/Jackson case. The DNA people agreed that since there was so much less evidence, it would be much quicker to process and finish. This turned out to be true and I now have the results." Martha handed the folder labeled DARLENE LOCKWOOD to Yolanda.

While Yolanda began reviewing the contents of the folder, she looked up at Martha and said, "Please summarize this for me. There is a lot here."

"Sure," Martha replied. "First of all, we've got the man who raped Darlene. What I mean is that he is already incarcerated. Allow me to start at the beginning."

Martha settled into the chair and crossed one leg over the other. She closed her eyes in an effort to remove all distractions so she could better concentrate as she recounted the story. "You will remember that I was impressed with Agent Daniel Lockwood when I did my initial rotation a few weeks ago. He told me of his sister's unsolved rape many years ago and he complained that no serious effort was put forth by the police to find out who did it. As you know, Daniel, or Danno as he likes to be called, had absolutely no idea of my intentions to look into his sister's case. In the first place, I felt that it might be a good opportunity to get my feet wet, so to speak. I had no idea if I would be able to find anything helpful. After all, the rape happened twenty-eight years ago. The Lockwood case plus the convenience store homicide which you assigned to me would provide me with the opportunities needed to expose me to the people and places I would need to know to properly do my job. Both cases proved to be helpful. Sergeant Edgecomb from the evidence division gave me a tour of the cages where everything is kept, and I now have seen some of the old evidence processed. By the way, both Aria and Lucy are remarkable."

Martha returned to the Lockwood case. "Anyway, in addition to Darlene's DNA, they found samples from a male. They created a profile and I ran it through CODIS, the national DNA database. We had a positive match with a Raymond Howard. This Mr. Howard was a janitor at the Ferndale High School where the Lockwood kids attended. A short time prior to the rape, Raymond was given a change in his work responsibilities. Raymond was a

177

little slow and an extreme introvert. The kids picked on him relentlessly and eventually the cafeteria staff felt so badly for him that they made his boss transfer him to a different assignment. No one knew that Raymond had sexual issues until he started spending an extraordinary amount of time cleaning the girls' locker room. He received a few warnings and for a time everything calmed down. He knew the schedules of the varsity and junior varsity sports teams which were posted in the gym, and of course he knew the kids that were on the teams, since they practiced all the time."

"Everything I am telling you came from what he told the police after he was arrested. He was pretty much caught in the act, so he could not deny what he had done. Anyway, I believe that Darlene Lockwood was his first victim, even though he was never tied to it. Remember, this was before DNA was used as a tool in solving crimes. Her brother Daniel was playing in a basketball game when Darlene was assaulted. This was in the police report. Raymond was known to sometimes go to school games on his own time. He knew which parents went to the games and which did not. He also knew which players had sisters who did not attend the games with their parents. From here it was relatively simple. The games started at 7:00 PM, so he would drive to the home of his victim and park somewhere where he could watch the parents when they left for the game. He explained to the investigator that if only one parent left, or if both parents and the daughter left to go to the game, he would simply drive home. If only the parents got into the car, he would watch the house. Should a light be turned on, or if he could see a television on, he would prepare to enter the home. He also told the police that if he saw no movement he would sometimes call and hang up if anyone answered. Should a young girl answer, he would likely enter the house. Of course, he knew to wear a ski mask and gloves. He also carried a knife and a roll of duct tape."

Yolanda was no longer paying attention to the file. She drank her tea and listened as Martha continued her story.

"Raymond Howard's second victim, Tammy McKesson, was actually the first rape he was charged with. The scenario was very similar to the Lockwood case. Tammy's parents and her younger sister left for her brother's basketball game and in their haste the front door was left unlocked. Tammy had planned to have a girlfriend come over so they could work on a school project together. Raymond just walked in the front door and went to Tammy's room. She was watching television and never heard Raymond enter the house. Tammy's girlfriend said that she had tried to call before going over, but since there was no answer, she assumed that Tammy changed her mind and had gone to the game with her parents. Shortly after 9:00 PM, when Tammy's parents returned home, they found their daughter still taped to the bed. Since Raymond had turned off the lights, Tammy was unable to provide a description or any helpful information. Later, during his confession to the police, Raymond said that after he raped Tammy he felt both scared and exhilarated at what he had done."

Martha went on, "A month went by after he assaulted Tammy. Raymond Howard was beginning to gain confidence, and he was becoming a little more imaginative. His third victim, Rachel Gallese, actually went to a different high school, Greenbriar, on the other side of town. The Greenbriar girls' varsity basketball team had come to Ferndale for a game. Following the game, Raymond heard Rachel talking with one of the boys. She told the boy that her brother's team would be playing Ferndale in two weeks. Since Rachel left her game with her parents, Raymond figured that her parents would likely accompany their son to his game as well. The rest was easy. The schedule on the gymnasium door told Raymond when the Greenbriar boys would be coming to Ferndale. Also, tonight's basketball program provided him with Rachel's last name. He found her address in the telephone book and there was only one Gallese. As he had always done before his assaults, on the day of the game, he parked across the street from the Gallese home an hour before the game. At 6:15 PM Rachel's parents left in their car. Raymond told the investigator that from his car he could see Rachel dancing in her room with earphones on. The side door to the garage had been left open so Raymond entered the garage and then the house through the kitchen. The remainder of the Gallese's supper was still on the kitchen counter. Raymond helped himself to a nice piece of pot roast and some mashed potatoes before heading upstairs for his dessert. He told the police that Rachel was too frightened to resist much, so he let her keep her earphones on. As usual, he left with her still taped to her bedposts."

Martha paused, took a deep breath, and continued, "Marcia Bolton was Raymond's fourth and final victim. He was gaining more confidence and was not as cautious. Unknown to Raymond, the police had noticed the pattern. However, for some reason they did not include the rape of Darlene Lockwood with the other two girls. Yet the police felt compelled to warn the parents of both the boys and girls basketball teams. The coaches of Ferndale and the schools they played against were asked to speak with the parents and warn them against leaving girls home alone."

Yolanda was impressed with Agent Green's narrative. She asked Martha, "You put this all together yourself?"

"Yes," Martha answered. "My boyfriend wasn't very pleased, but I worked on it most of the weekend."

"What about the fourth victim?" Yolanda was anxious to hear how the story ended.

"I think you may like this part, Yolanda." Agent Green shook out her hair and sat forward in her chair.

"By the time Raymond Howard got to Marcia Bolton, basketball season had ended and boys' varsity wrestling was underway. Not being one to discriminate based on the sport or the season, Raymond was ready to continue his reign of terror. He sat in his car in front of the Bolton home and ate his takeout hamburger and fries. At 6:45 PM Raymond saw Marcia's mother and father get into their car and leave. As always, he sat quietly until he saw movement in the house. Since only one room had the light on, it had to be Marcia's room. The front door and the side door to the garage were both found to be locked. The rear door was also locked, but offered little resistance when Raymond was able to force it open by pushing a putty knife between the latch bolt and the strike plate. Slowly he made his way in the dark through the downstairs of the house. The street lights and the digital blue lights from the kitchen appliances provided just enough light to allow Raymond to slowly make his way to the stairs. He paused at the bottom of the stairs to listen. All he could hear was music emanating from where he saw the light. He knew it must be Marcia's room. Thanks for young girls and their music thought Raymond. Now it wouldn't matter if the stairs squeaked or not. He quickly made his way up the stairs to Marcia's room. The door was ajar and he was delighted to observe Marcia in her underwear painting her toenails. As Raymond moved into the room, his shadow cast on the wall in front of her caused her to turn and face him. Marcia screamed and he grabbed her wrists. She screamed again as Raymond said to her, 'Screaming won't help you.'

'It already has,' said a man's voice behind him. Raymond felt cold metal on his neck and heard the click of the hammer being cocked on what he guessed was a shotgun.

Raymond later learned that the man he had seen getting into the car with Marcia's mother was actually Marcia's older brother who was home from college. Her father had been sleeping in his bedroom across from Marcia's room when he heard the first scream."

Agent Green paused and looked at Yolanda. "The rest is history as they say. Raymond Howard turned out to be one of those criminals who actually possessed a conscience. He may not have had the ability to harness his sexual appetite, but he never meant to harm the girls. Raymond told the police everything they wanted to know about the rapes of Tammy and Rachel and of the failed assault on Marcia. Everything was explained in the greatest detail. Yet he never mentioned Darlene Lockwood."

Yolanda was still processing all of this information when Agent Green interrupted her.

"Now comes the hard part," said Martha. "What do we do with this information? Danno is under the impression that the creep that raped his sister was never caught. Yet Raymond has been serving time for nearly twenty six years. Surely Danno has the right to know everything we have learned. His sister is now married and has a family. Do we want her to have to relive this after all these years? Since Raymond has been punished, should we just let this be?"

Yolanda closed the file. She stood and looked at Martha. "My dear, what you did with an old pair of bed sheets and underwear is nothing short of remarkable. Unfortunately, this is not my call to make. I will let you know how this turns out." She pushed a button on her telephone. "Ruth," said Yolanda. "Get Agent Lockwood in here." She dismissed Martha with her gratitude.

4

PREPARATIONS FOR G DAY

At exactly the same time that Yolanda was summoning Danno to her office, several miles away, Reverend Hartsell was sitting down across the desk from the President of the Golden Gate Savings Bank. Reverend Hartsell was a preferred customer, he was treated like a VIP in the bank. After all, the reverend had three mortgages at this bank as well as a savings account which totaled slightly over one million dollars. Reverend Hartsell carefully explained why he needed two and one-half million dollars today and how after a few weeks, he would surely replace what he borrowed with a much larger sum of money. After that, a constant flow of cash would be coming into the bank.

The bank president and Thomas Hartsell were much more alike than either cared to admit. The good reverend shamelessly took money from his parishioners and kept it for his own use. He and his accomplices took extravagant vacations, bought custom made designer suits and expensive jewelry, and paid down the principal of Reverend Hartsell's six million dollar estate. All from well-intended church donations.

The bank president, on the other hand, had thirty employees who all together made about the same amount of money which he took home per year. All of the tellers, loan officers, and security people were made to dutifully smile at customers and treat them like royalty. The bank's motto was "to us you are family." Yet the bank president lived on one side of the tracks while his employees and nearly all of his clientele lived on the other. To show his gratitude the president gave his employees a nice Christmas party and Thanksgiving turkeys (purchased in quantity at a big discount). Nice, but it was just too reminiscent of Ebenezer Scrooge and Bob Cratchit from *A Christmas Carol.* Technically, the ways in which the bank president and Thomas Hartsell got their money were not illegal, but both required audacity and a character which was devoid of conscience.

The bank president was no fool. Reverend Hartsell came into the bank after church services and prayer meetings to deposit money into his personal accounts. The Rapture Ministries accounts were in the bank as well. However, there were never any checks made out to charities or missions. The bank president knew exactly what was going on at Rapture because he and Reverend Hartsell shared a symbiotic relationship. Each flourished with the help of the other. Today it was the reverend that was playing nice. He needed cooperation. Hartsell knew he was cutting it close asking for such a large amount of his mortgage equity. But the bank president had a large appetite as well and Reverend Hartsell walked away from the bank with his two and one-half million dollars, leaving the bare minimum required on the mortgages. Carrying such a large amount of cash didn't bother him since he was used to transporting large sums of money.

P.J. Mustav, Woodrow Dennison, and Elders Carter and Billings were already at work in Rapture in the Round when Reverend Hartsell arrived.

"I have your money." Hartsell put the large gym bag on the floor in front of Joel. "Where would you like to count it?"

Joel motioned for Dr. Woodson to take the bag. "We have no time for that. They will count it at the bank. We rented a temporary safe deposit box in a bank near our hotel. Woodrow, please take this to the bank. Have them wire two million to Hollywood, and we'll keep the rest here in the bank."

Hartsell offered, "Let me send one of the elders with him."

Joel raised his voice and looked directly at the reverend. "I said that we have no time for this! I need you and the elders to pay strict attention to my instructions and take notes. We have no time for frivolous activity." Joel looked at Dr. Woodson and dropped his voice back to normal. "I will walk Hartsell and the elders through our list of recommendations. Hurry back and don't forget to pick up the fabric when you return."

Dr. Woodson hurried away with the bag of money. He had made arrangements to bring it to Judge Laningham and Hector who were already waiting in a store parking lot four blocks away.

Back at the church, P.J. was going through a list of changes which he wanted made to the sanctuary. "First of all, we are going to film the service next Sunday. This will be an integral part of your website and DVD presentations as well as the commercials advertising your upcoming television presentations. Woodrow has been all over the inside of the church and has decided to film from two separate locations. He will put one tripod up where the organist sits, and we will need to have a platform erected there." Joel pointed to an area near the back of the church. "He wants it about five feet off of the ground. While the primary focus will be on Reverend Hartsell, Woodrow, also, wants to pan the audience to capture their enthusiasm and support for him. Watching the service yesterday was very helpful since we were able to see the order of things, but just to be on the safe side, I would like one of the elders to stay with Woodrow this Sunday. By shadowing Woodrow, he will be able to cue him when it will be time to change cameras."

Elder Carter was taking notes as P.J. gave instructions. Reverend Hartsell kept looking over Carter's shoulder making sure that he didn't miss anything.

P.J. asked, "Do you have a list of all of your parishioners?"

Hartsell answered, "Most of them, yes, but it's over in my office. I can send Marcus..."

P.J. cut him off. "No, that won't be necessary. Between now and Sunday I need you to call each of them. They all need to know that we will be filming the service on Sunday. It would be nice if everyone could arrive a few minutes early. Once they have all taken their seats we will shuffle them around. We want the beautiful people up front. The last thing we want is some nasty looking camel face in the front row stealing the show, or some clown with a big mustard stain on his shirt grinning like the Cheshire Cat. We only have one take so it has to be right. Oh, and I need you to give everyone some rules. Once they realize they are going to be on television, everyone does outlandish things to become more visible to the camera. Please make it clear to everyone that if anyone violates these rules, they can either go home or sit in the back where they will not be seen. Everyone wants to be on TV, I get that, but Woodrow and I have done things like this many times and we know how people react. It must be made abundantly clear that if our rules are not followed, the guilty will be relegated to the back rows."

P.J. pointed to Elder Carter's notepad to stress the importance of writing down his recommendations. "No one is to wear loud colors or anything gaudy. The focus is on YOU." P.J. pointed to Hartsell. "I don't want to see any loud reds or canary yellows, no tie-dye shirts. No floral patterns or giant sunflowers. Nothing in print on the shirts, no *I am with Stupid* shirts, and I really don't care if grandma gave you the tie with the big fish on it for Christmas. Stress earth tones or attire appropriate for a funeral. No 'Mr. T.' kind of jewelry. No earrings which a cockatoo could perch on. Am I making myself clear? Tell the ladies to leave their Kentucky Derby hats home. No lapel pins and no Elton John sunglasses. And lastly, I want no babies. I know they are cute and cuddly, but they puke and they cry. This would ruin our production. Keep them in the nursery."

Woodrow returned through the front door carrying a large box which he set down in the aisle. He looked at P.J., Hartsell and the elders. "Where are we?"

"I just gave them the 'do nots' for the parishioners," said P.J., "and they were shown the placement positions of the two video cameras."

"OK." Woodrow pointed at the two angled television screens above the altar. "Those have got to go. Taking a video of a video never works. If the parishioners need them for the words to the songs, move them to where we won't see them." He walked to the aisle and opened the box which he had placed there a moment

188

ago. "I am sure that you are familiar with 'green screen productions' which are used in Hollywood movies all the time. Basically, it is a backdrop behind a central character...in this case Reverend Hartsell. Using the green screen, while he is delivering his sermon, we can project videos onto the screen behind him. We can make it appear that he is giving his sermon from the Grand Canyon, the bottom of the ocean, Paris, or even from the surface of the moon. Productions of this magnitude are all about the special effects."

Dr. Woodson could tell by Reverend Hartsell's expression that he was buying the entire scam. His emphasis that Hartsell was the main focus of the production was all it took...stroking the ego as Hector liked to say. He looked at the elders. "Now, boys, please pay attention. What I want you to do is this." He removed some of the green fabric and held it out to them. "This is green screen material. The color isn't anything to write home about, but don't worry. We can project anything we want onto it in the studio, so this color will never actually be seen. We need this fabric draped on the wall behind the altar from the balcony all the way down to the floor. In addition, it must cover the entire floor of the altar, anywhere that Reverend Hartsell might walk. Keep it as tight and free of wrinkles as you can."

P.J. took over giving instructions. "The congregation has to realize the limited amount of time we have until **G Day** when we flip the switch and go global. Sometimes large corporations use banners which count down the days remaining to a target date of some upcoming event. These banners are surprisingly effective, so we will have one made. After the green screen is in place we can suspend such a banner to remind everyone how little time we have left. Of course, it will not be visible in the production."

P.J. continued. "Yesterday the choir was impressive. Make sure they practice the songs they will be singing on Sunday, and have them also practice their swaying in unison. Everyone will like that. The color of their robes is awful. The bright blue with the gold trim makes the service look like a high school graduation ceremony without the cardboard hats and tassels. Let's go with something classier...more regal. I would like to see perhaps a soft gold color with scarlet accents. See what you can find by next week. Reverend Hartsell, I would like you in a light tan or beige suit. With a pastel yellow shirt and scarlet tie to match the robe accents, you will look sensational."

P.J.'s instructions were coming to an end. "I realize that I have given you a lot to accomplish by this Sunday. Woodrow and I are returning to Hollywood this afternoon. We will be working on two things: using some of the money you have given us, we are trying to lock in air times on some of the major television networks. I think that a number of fifteen minute infomercials will serve your needs. And the second task is the creation of a website which will blow you away! Woodrow and I will be at the Wednesday night prayer meetings. The films showing the deplorable living conditions and the sick and needy children will be helpful to us in making DVDs which will be available from your website. Any questions, gentlemen?"

Reverend Hartsell and the elders were overwhelmed, but no one said a word.

"OK then," said P.J. He and Woodrow left the building.

Several minutes went by before the reverend and his elders said anything. They were used to getting involved in projects for the church, but nothing quite like this. The reason the Council thought it best to keep them so busy was to distract them. Hartsell was a con artist and given the opportunity, he could likely figure out what was going on. Hopefully, they would soon be able to remove any doubt he might have using a little technological magic provided by HOT Software.

Hartsell and his elders reviewed the list of instructions and divided up the tasks. Hartsell would contact all of his parishioners and inform them of Sunday's dress code and what was to be expected during the church service. He, also, used all these phone calls as an opportunity to strongly urge all parishioners to show their support for worldwide outreach by attending the Wednesday night prayer meetings. He hadn't yet had the chance to speak with Marcus and Jesse regarding the need to squeeze even harder for larger mission donations. He would, also, somehow have to find the time to call his tailor to be fitted for a beige suit.

Marcus was told to contact the choir director and attempt to find new robes as P.J. had described. Then they would have to be altered to fit each of the choir members. Somehow, all of this had to be completed in less than one week. Jesse was given the job of making Rapture in the Round ready for filming. He had to remove the two television screens, find a way to affix the green screen behind the altar, and erect a platform from which Woodrow could pan the congregation next Sunday. P.J. was returning on Wednesday to inspect their progress.

191

Agent Daniel Lockwood reported to Yolanda's office as requested. He listened intently as she reiterated the story of Raymond Howard and the evidence which provided conclusive proof that it was he who assaulted Darlene many years ago. Danno asked what had prompted reopening the case. Yolanda explained that although it was Agent Martha Green's idea, she fully supported it. Yolanda told Danno that his display of compassion in the Delano Reese shooting made an impression on Martha, so she wanted to test her skills and see if they could work to heal an old wound and perhaps provide some closure for a nice guy.

Yolanda made it clear to Danno that whatever happened from this point forward would be left up to him. It was to be his decision if Darlene was to be notified. Raymond Howard was a few years from finishing a thirty year sentence. He had essentially been incarcerated since Darlene and Danno finished high school. He was no longer a young man.

Yolanda gave Danno a sad look. It had clearly been difficult for him to hear this story. She asked him, "Do you know what you will do?"

Agent Lockwood was trying to make sense of the mixed emotions he was attempting to process. He knew that regardless what his feelings might be, Darlene was the important thing. He looked at Yolanda. "The man has been punished. I cannot speak for my sister, but she is a kind, forgiving person, much more so than I am. When the time is right, I will tell her. Right now she is in a good place in her life and I am not about to screw that up. Raymond Howard already messed her up. Giving her this information will not unring that bell. It has taken Darlene twenty-eight years to find her way back to happiness."

5

HELP FROM HOT SOFTWARE

Ever since Martha's presentation of the Darlene Lockwood cold case investigation, Yolanda was enthralled thinking about the possibilities which this DNA technology brought to the crime solving arena. Agent Green was able to solve an ancient crime practically from her computer. It was fortunate that the old evidence was still available and, also, that it had not been contaminated. Yolanda had an idea. It was an incredible longshot, much like the two cases Agent Green had been working on. She wondered if like Hollywood deaths, good things, also, came in three's. But what the Hell, she thought...*nothing ventured, nothing gained*. She made three phone calls. The first was to her FBI counterpart in Detroit. Her second phone call was to Agent Green. Yolanda requested that she come to her office in half an hour. The FBI director's third call was to her friend Judge Lamar Laningham.

Approximately thirty minutes later, Ruth announced to Yolanda that Martha Green was waiting.

"Send her in Ruth. Thank you." Yolanda straightened her desk.

Martha sat in the same chair she occupied earlier. She waited to see why she had been called to the boss's office and decided it was likely for a status report on the convenience store murder case.

"Agent Green," began Yolanda. "Since your investigation of the Lockwood case, I have not been able to concentrate on anything else. By the way, Danno was very appreciative of everything you did. He was surprised and I think touched that you thought to look into Darlene's old evidence. He didn't give me the impression that he was going to share the information with Darlene, at least not yet. He did say that it afforded him some closure. Anyway, I know that your focus will now be on the store homicide, but I wanted to give you something else to start thinking about. There is a seventeen year old unsolved triple murder which I really know very little about. It concerns a close personal friend. We are now attempting to determine if any of the old crime scene evidence is still around."

Martha interrupted. "I can do that for you. I can just call Sergeant Edgecomb and..."

"Not this time," interrupted Yolanda. "How would you feel about a road trip?"

The confusion on Martha's face made her boss back off. "There is no point in going into any details now, so wait until more information becomes available. Just like the two cases you have been working on, everything depends on the quality of the old evidence. Should the evidence be gone or compromised, there is no point in going any further. When do you think the girls in the DNA lab will have anything for us?"

"Perhaps we will have something tomorrow. Let's keep our fingers crossed until then. When I have anything at all, I promise to contact you."

Yolanda asked Martha, "Didn't you go to Folsom Prison to interview the boys?"

"Yes, Yolanda, I went about a week ago. That place has given me nightmares about jail cells and concertina wire. Bubba made my heart bleed. There is no way that kid could hurt anyone. He was pitiful. However, Roddy did not evoke any sympathy from me. He was arrogant and had a huge chip on his shoulder. He even tried playing the race card on me saying that the only reason he was in jail was because he was black. Anyway, nothing new was learned. Hey, why wasn't there more done by the police to find out about the guy Bubba saw running from the store?"

Yolanda raised her eyebrows. "I believe, Agent Green, that they felt they already had their man." Yolanda rose from her desk signifying that the conversation had come to an end. "Thanks, Martha, I look forward to hearing from you. Once again, kudos on the Darlene Lockwood case."

After they left Rapture in the Round earlier in the day, Dr. Woodson returned to the VA hospital to check on a few of his patients and Joel went to HOT Software to speak with one of his computer software specialists.

A little over a year ago, after his friend Judge Laningham retired, Jerry Woodson was prompted to wonder if he should also consider retirement. Financially, he was certainly able to consider quitting, yet, he still enjoyed going to work. He knew that before Lamar retired, he had become frustrated because he felt that the legal system had become so befouled with corruption that he was beginning to question his effectiveness as a judge. For Lamar, that made retirement an easy question. Yet, Dr. Woodson continued to believe that he, himself, was still making a difference in people's lives. Granted, he was a hospice care physician, so any difference he made came at the end of their lives. Dr. Woodson entered the lives of patients and their families when the countdown to death was a certainty. In Hector's vision of death, these patients would be at the head of the long line overlooking the edge of the cliff and staring down into the abyss. By definition, hospice care meant that the patient was expected to live less than six months.

In years past patients with terminal illnesses would often linger for months in a hospital or nursing home until they died. The costs for this kind of care were catastrophic to families and insurance companies. And what did the dying patient get for all that money? Clean sheets, food that resembled flavored cardboard, a remote control with limited channel selections, and a roommate who likely snored. This end-of-life scenario was nobody's fault. People did the best they could. There were just no alternatives available. Finally, someone realized that ninety-five percent of people preferred to die at home surrounded by loved ones and familiar surroundings. It took a while, but health professionals came to realize that with a little support, terminally ill patients could reasonably be managed at home. Almost overnight, specialized pharmacy, nursing, respiratory, and pain services became available. Patients and their families were happier, much needed hospital and nursing home beds became available, insurance companies were saving millions of dollars, and the nature of death changed. Instead of the impersonal surroundings of an institution, patients were allowed to pass from this life with peace and dignity.

Sometimes, as expected, these patient's conditions could change quickly. They sometimes required brief hospitalization and

Dr. Woodson would be required to modify treatment or make dosing adjustments to their medications. He would always try to get his patients back home as quickly as practicable. The hospice service had been a part of the Santa Molina Veterans Hospital for nine years. In terms of patient care, Dr. Woodson believed that the hospice program was superior to most others. The VA medical center was a teaching hospital and, as such, had affiliations with no less than three San Francisco medical schools. Residents could volunteer to do a hospital rotation under Dr. Woodson's hospice care service. Whenever Dr. Woodson was required to participate in Council activities, other physicians in the oncology or general medicine services would cover for him along with the residents.

Dr. Woodson had become accustomed to dealing with death. Since most of his patients were not known to him personally, remaining detached from them was not a problem. Yet, as much as he tried to avoid it, he bonded with several of his patients. This was difficult for Dr. Woodson. He believed that when you loved someone and they were very near death, there is a faint voice within you that tells you that it is time to let go. Perhaps this is a defense mechanism trying to protect you from hurt. Or it could be a warning telling you of danger, like the buzzer when you don't buckle your seatbelt.

All of Dr. Woodson's training and experience with impending death could not help him prepare himself for Lamar's death. Hospice care teaches that death is a part of life's cycle and should be accepted as such. Yet, Jerry pictured life without Lamar like wearing only one shoe. You could function, yet it just didn't feel right. He dismissed thoughts of Lamar from his mind. He would deal with it later.

When Joel returned to HOT Software, he sought the assistance of one of his computer design specialists to help create a Rapture Ministries webpage. In the middle of the screen, of course, would be Reverend Hartsell and behind him, the choir. Joel asked his employee, Michael Cavanaugh, to enhance the blue and gold robes of the choir. Michael was given photographs taken at the previous Sunday service by Dr. Woodson. Michael possessed a world-class imagination, and he loved projects like this. Joel knew from experience that all he had to do was give Mike a rough idea what he wanted and then sit back and enjoy the ride. Another good thing about Mike was that he didn't ask questions. He was well paid to create things and he had a sense of satisfaction knowing he was the very best.

Joel explained to Mike that he wanted to create a fake webpage that would blow Reverend Hartsell away. In about thirty hours he wanted to be able to show the webpage to the Rapture people. Mike was told about the placement of the green screen and how, once **G Day** came, the entire website would undergo an immediate transformation. Mike immediately got the idea and repeated it back to Joel.

"OK, so you want a state-of-the-art webpage created so this phony Reverend Hartsell will believe that in two weeks it will go live worldwide." Mike smiled. "You want the website to have all of the high-tech bells and whistles. Then, if I understand you, once you turn it over to him, everything changes to the webpage from hell."

Joel smiled as well. "Exactly. Mike I knew you were the right man for the job. I am sorry that I can only give you forty-eight hours."

Mike sat back in his chair and laced his fingers together behind his head and stared up at the ceiling marshalling his thoughts. "Two days should be plenty of time."

Joel had already started away from Mike when he stopped and turned around. "Oh, and one more thing, when I return on Thursday, I will bring you some videos, cassette tapes I think. We will be using those in a similar fashion."

6

UNABOMBER

It was Tuesday, June 4, 1996. Yolanda had been at her desk about an hour when she received the call. A policeman from the evidence division in Detroit, an equivalent to Sergeant Edgecomb, acted like an absolute jerk. Yesterday, as per protocol and common courtesy, FBI Director Yolanda Tubbs placed a phone call to FBI Director Avery Resque of the Detroit bureau. Whenever it becomes necessary to work or investigate on another officer's turf, it is a simple courtesy to inform your counterpart of your intentions. More often than not such gestures in human decency result in cooperation at all levels. If Yolanda had called the Detroit police herself, which she had every right to do, she would have bypassed her Detroit FBI counterpart, effectively cutting him out of the loop. Yolanda had been around long enough to realize that by virtue of an unwritten but long accepted code of conduct, this simply was not the way in which things were done. After all, she knew how she would feel if a Detroit FBI agent was found sniffing around in Santa Molina. No, professional decorum dictates that Director Tubbs should personally contact Director Avery Resque, explain her intentions and what she hoped to accomplish in Avery's backyard. Then, as a way of reciprocating the professional courtesy, the Detroit FBI Director would do whatever it took to make the request happen. In this case it meant that Avery would personally place the phone call FOR Yolanda and make her requests for any old evidence which may or may not be available from the Harris family triple murder case. From this point, it would be professionally acceptable to either have Detroit Evidence call Avery back, and he would then, in turn, call Yolanda. OR, it was Director Resque's prerogative to ask the Detroit police to contact the Santa Molina FBI director with the results from the search for the old evidence. It was all about professional courtesy. Once competing law enforcement agencies were on the same page, cooperation normally ensued. Normally, but not always.

Following Yolanda's request, Director Avery Resque phoned the Detroit Evidence Division. He requested that THEY call Yolanda back in Santa Molina. This was when the spirit of cooperation broke down. The Detroit officer who took the call from Director Avery was perfectly willing to help in any way. However, the policeman he passed the assignment to did not share the same enthusiasm. Three boxes of evidence were located. As instructed, the officer called Yolanda, and then everything went "South." He asked Yolanda if there wasn't enough crime to solve in California thus making her feel the need to look into Detroit's business. Then the officer asked why the FBI, a federal law enforcement agency, was interfering with a local crime? He asked Yolanda if she thought the FBI could do the job better than the Detroit police? Yolanda had neither the time nor the inclination to listen to this abuse. She told him "thank you" and hung up.

Most police agencies work very well together. As an FBI agent, Yolanda and her people have often worked with local or state police. On other occasions the FBI worked in association with Alcohol, Tobacco, and Firearms (ATF), the Drug Enforcement Agency (DEA), the Internal Revenue Service (IRS), postal inspectors, federal marshals, the National Security Agency (NSA), the Texas Rangers, and even the Secret Service and the Central Intelligence Agency

(CIA). Sometimes a single law enforcement agency has the sole responsibility in the investigation of a crime. Other times, multiple agencies become involved. Yolanda remembered being grateful to not have been involved in two very recent FBI investigations which required the cooperation of multiple law enforcement agencies.

The first was an FBI designated investigation from the beginning. Yolanda remembered being home babysitting her one year old grandson Warren when she first heard the news. She was changing little Warren's diaper on the floor in the living room. The television was on and the network interrupted whatever program had been on for *Breaking News*. Someone had detonated a truck filled with explosives in front of the Murrah Federal Building in Oklahoma City. Since the building was federal property and was home to offices of the FBI, ATF, and DEA, it was immediately clear that the Federal Bureau of Investigation would be the vanguard in a host of law enforcement agencies tasked to find out who was responsible for the explosion. Yolanda remembered April 19, 1995, very well. She held her grandson especially close knowing that the Murrah Building also had a daycare facility which had been full of children when the explosion took place.

The second example Yolanda thought of was that of an ongoing investigation. Less than two months ago, on April 3, 1996, FBI agents had just arrested Theodore "Ted" Kaczynski, the alleged Unabomber in his tiny cabin near Lincoln, Montana. The near twenty year campaign of terror of the Unabomber started in May of 1978 and had been, without doubt, one of the most costly crime investigations in United States history. Yolanda remembered the confusion and the political jockeying that surrounded this case until the FBI finally took full possession of the responsibility for the investigation. In the beginning the first bomb victim was a police officer at Northwestern University in Evanston, Illinois. Hence, the immediate responsibility belonged to the campus police and the Evanston Police Department. The second victim, also from Northwestern University, was targeted almost exactly a year later in May of 1979. At this time, since the bombs were sent through the mail, the U.S. Postal Inspectors were the lead investigating agency. However, this quickly changed. Six months following the second explosion at Northwestern, an airplane in midflight between Chicago and Washington, D.C. was forced to land due to smoke in the cabin. A bomb was found in the cargo hold of the plane with a nonfunctioning timing mechanism within the explosive device. Had the timing mechanism worked, everyone aboard would have been killed. Retrieval of the evidence changed the investigation in two dramatic ways. First, since airplanes fly between states, the crime became a federal one prompting the FBI to assume the major responsibility of the case. Both the ATF and the U.S. Postal Inspection Service also played important roles. Secondly the perpetrator of these bombings was given a name by the FBI task force. The man they hunted, a **UN**iversity and **A**irline **BOM**ber became forever known as the Unabomber.

Apprehending the Unabomber proved to be a formidable task. From his remote ten foot by twelve foot cabin which had neither running water nor electricity, he was able to elude hundreds of law enforcement officers, forensic experts, explosive analysts, profilers, and investigative reporters for seventeen long years. Yet Theodore Kaczynski was no ordinary criminal. He was determined to have a genius level IQ in grammar school. His IQ score of 167 defined him as exceptionally gifted. Young Ted was allowed to skip the sixth grade, and although his brilliance was unquestioned, he was the victim of bullying and he had underdeveloped social skills. Later, Ted was also allowed to bypass the eleventh grade, and in 1958, he entered Harvard University at the age of sixteen.

Kaczynski's brilliance was further demonstrated at Harvard where he continued to excel in mathematics. However, a most bizarre thing happened to young Theodore while he attended Harvard. Somehow he became a participant in a personality study designed by a Dr. Murray, a leading expert in conducting stress interviews. Ted and the other study participants were forced to endure lengthy psychological stress tests apparently devised to test the limits of what they could mentally tolerate. All subjects were hooked up to scientific monitoring devices while they were bombarded by devastating personal attacks on everything in their lives which they defined as important. Exactly what such a dehumanizing and torturous study had hoped to accomplish was unclear. It was also unknown what, if any, lasting effect this study may have had on Ted Kaczynski.

Ted graduated from Harvard when he was only twenty years old, and he then entered a graduate program in mathematics at the University of Michigan. He was legendary in his ambition and his intellect. He was not one for "letting his hair down," and no one ever remembered seeing him at a Michigan Wolverine football game yelling "Go Blue!" A few years later, Kaczynski had earned a PhD in mathematics. His thesis, called *Boundary Functions* was rumored to be so esoteric that only a handful of people in the world could comprehend its meaning.

The end of Dr. Kaczynski's short, albeit brilliant, association with academia was soon to follow. After becoming the youngest professor ever hired at the University of California, Berkley, he resigned without explanation after two years.

Ted moved back in with his parents following his resignation from Berkley and two years later, in 1971, he built and moved into his tiny cabin where he ultimately became a recluse. Perhaps loneliness and his intellectual musings pushed Ted Kaczynski over the edge. He, by his own admission, became consumed in his reading and he rejected technological advances and wanted them stopped. Between 1978 and 1995, he mailed sixteen bombs which resulted in three deaths and injuries to twenty-three others. Ted made sport of his activities by including false clues in the bombs designed to mislead investigators. He also sent letters containing his demands and his manifesto to the larger newspapers and to law enforcement. Were it not for his brother and sister-in-law recognizing his style of writing, it is conceivable that he might never have been caught.

Yolanda's memories of the hunt for Ted Kaczynski and his connection to San Francisco were still vivid in her mind and the whole story was rekindled because of the crap she received from the cop in the Detroit evidence room. There are many reasons why policemen refuse to cooperate with other investigators outside of their own agency. Some officers worry that outside agencies will do a better job. Others, like the officer Yolanda spoke with, are just jerks. Their lives are unfulfilled and they are miserable, so they pass along their displeasure to everyone around them. However, perhaps the greatest obstacle in the way of cooperation among competing agencies is affectionately known as a "pissing contest."

High profile cases can bring fierce competition among different police agencies. Whoever is responsible for apprehending and convicting so great a prize as the Unabomber would be an instant celebrity. There would be promotions, countless interviews, talk shows, book deals, movie rights, and the endless adulation and appreciation from a grateful nation. So what would be the incentive for one police agency to help another as they begin to close in on capturing such a villain?

Once Ted Kaczynski was in custody, the police retraced his life back to his childhood. Learning about someone's past not only provides insight as to why they chose deviant behavior, but it frequently sheds light on past crimes for which they may have been responsible. Ted Kaczynski was discovered to have lived in the San Francisco region from 1967 to 1969. This was the same time period in which the infamous Zodiac killer was the most prolific in his killing spree. Yolanda had just joined the FBI back in 1968, and she well remembered the rivalry and the intense competition among various law enforcement agencies to catch this person who was responsible for terrorizing an entire city for years. In letters to the police and newspapers, the Zodiac killer claimed to have shot and stabbed to death thirty-seven people, and he has never been caught. Police investigators, reporters, and police profilers touted the similarities between the Zodiac killer and the Unabomber. Both were highly intelligent, and both amused themselves taunting the police and newspapers with letters promising more homicides if their writings were not published and their demands were not met. Most important of all, was the fact that they inhabited the same area during those crucial two years. Many thought Kaczynski was the Zodiac killer. No pressure there, thought Yolanda. If in fact they were the same person, whoever caught such a criminal would undoubtedly be hailed as the greatest detective in history!

Early in her career, FBI Agent Yolanda Tubbs witnessed the jealousies between competing police agencies and she hated it. Today she had no patience for the offensive evidence cop in Detroit. She stood at her desk and pressed the button on her telephone which connected her to Ruth.

Ruth answered, "Hey boss, what can I do for you?"

Yolanda looked at the name she had written down. "Ruth, once again would you get me Director Avery Resque from Detroit?"

"Sure." Ruth was able to sense the agitation in her boss's voice. A few minutes later Ruth was again calling Yolanda. "Director Resque is on line two."

"Thank you Ruth." Yolanda left her telephone on speakerphone and pushed the second button.

"Avery?" Yolanda asked.

"Hello again, Yolanda," The director said. "Were you able to find what you were looking for?"

"Well both yes and no," Yolanda answered. "I was told that there were three boxes of old crime scene evidence, but whether or not any of it has any value remains to be seen. However, I need a favor from you. The local cop I spoke with in 'evidence' is giving me a bad time. I don't think he likes FBI agents, and he doesn't want to play nice. He felt that since it was a local crime, the Detroit cops should retain jurisdiction. When I mentioned that the crime had never been solved, he asked me if I thought that the FBI would do a better job than the Detroit police. So instead of allowing him to evoke my wrath any further, I backed off. I had concerns that if he and I got into a pissing contest, some of the evidence might disappear, if you know what I mean."

Agent Avery replied, "Yeah, I know exactly what you mean. We watched YOUR O.J. Simpson trial last year. Talk about your evidence screw ups and interdepartmental pissing contests. What would you like me to do?"

Yolanda realized that she asked for that one. "Touche`, Avery, you're correct on the O.J. Simpson trial. I need you to flex your muscles. Get a court order from a federal judge and subpoena all three boxes of evidence from the 1980 Harris murder case. Don't leave without them. Then have your people properly prepare them and send them to me by overnight delivery. I have a great evidence team who insists on going through everything themselves. Please go to the evidence room unannounced so nothing comes up missing. If you run into the same jerk I did, handle it any way you want. Avery, this is for a personal friend of mine that I am trying to help. I really appreciate this."

The Detroit FBI Director was happy to comply with Yolanda's requests. "No problem, Yolanda. I'll call you once the evidence is on its way." He hung up.

Yolanda seemed satisfied. She called Judge Laningham without going through Ruth. She told him of Agent Green and her DNA technicians and of the good work they had done. She believed that if anyone could solve the murders of Joel's parents and sister,

Martha Green would be the one. They agreed to keep the information to themselves until they knew more.

7

JEWELS

Joel had a few of his employees erect an inexpensive plastic banner to hang on the green screen which was intended to remind the parishioners how little time there was until **G Day**. Two small wood furring strips were painted the same color as the green screen. Tacked on the strips were the white letters:

14 DAYS TO G DAY

RAPTURE IN THE ROUND

Mike Cavanaugh continued working on the Rapture Ministries webpage and was sure that it would be completed by Wednesday afternoon. Joel had the graphics people create stationery with the logos of the three major television networks which they knew Reverend Hartsell would recognize. Judge Laningham was using his legal talents in preparing three separate contracts for each of the television stations. Each of these contracts would then be typed onto the appropriate stationery.

Both Dr. Woodson and Judge Laningham owned fancy video cameras with tripods which would be used in filming the service on Sunday. The judge had Colleen pick the loudest dress she dared to wear next Sunday so that they would get sent back to the rear of the church. Unfortunately Lamar owned no ties with large mouthed bass on them. Hector borrowed a large hat from a neighbor for his mother to wear. At first she was reluctant, but after she tried it on,

Hector laughed so hard that she couldn't say no. Little by little, all of the lies were falling into place.

Today after lunch Yolanda received a call from Martha Green. She had some results from the evidence in the convenience store murder. As expected, the store owner's clothing was replete with the DNA of an unknown person. Both Bubba and Roddy were positively excluded as the source of the DNA.

Because Agent Martha Green preferred going to Yolanda with answers, not questions, she ran the DNA profile through the CODIS Forensic Index. A positive match was found for a Julius Bennett. Since Julius, alias Jewels, was a repeat offender, Martha was able to bring up his photograph, a complete rap sheet, and best of all, a copy of his fingerprints. The fingerprints proved to be an exact match to those found on the bloody baseball bat which killed the store owner. Yolanda was ecstatic and she wanted to move fast. She instructed Aria and Lucy to work with Martha in creating an airtight presentation to give to a judge in order to procure a warrant for the arrest of Julius Bennett. Yolanda then instructed Agents Danno Lockwood and Adam Franklin to drop whatever they were doing and come to her office. Within minutes, Adam and Danno were sitting across from Yolanda hearing the story of the convenience store murder which took place sixteen years ago. She then brought them back to the present telling them, that on a hunch, she'd asked Martha to look for DNA in the old evidence since she could not believe Bubba was a murderer. Without saying anything, Danno thought of what Agent Green had done with his sister's old case.

Yolanda dismissed both agents with instructions to begin the search for Julius Bennett. She would call them as soon as she had the warrant for his arrest.

Two hours later, warrant in hand, they were all on their way out the door. Agent Franklin had learned from Julius's income tax records, which he filed only three months ago, that he was currently employed at a carwash which was about six miles away. Before the warrant was ready, Adam sent Agent Beverly Walker with a picture of Julius to go and get a car washed to see if he was working. Julius was wiping cars down using a chamois outside the wash area. Agent Walker drove her car through the carwash and then parked across the street. She called Adam and told him that Julius was here. Adam instructed Beverly to stay put and keep an eye on him till they got there.

The plan was for Yolanda and Adam to drive through the carwash while Danno and Martha would block any escape from the street. It all went like clockwork. After their car was washed, Adam drove to the area where Julius was working to have the car dried. As Yolanda and Adam got out of the car, Danno and Martha pulled their vehicle between the street and Julius. Agent Beverly Walker was there as well. Adam and Martha had their guns drawn. Yolanda showed Julius her badge and the warrant for his arrest. She said, "Julius Bennett, I have a warrant issued by the State of California for your arrest."

Julius, in an arrogant tone, said "For what, I didn't do nothin'."

Yolanda held up the warrant. "For the 1980 murder of Adamos Lazopoulos."

213

"Who's that?" Julius was confused.

Martha answered him. "He is the store owner you beat to death with his own baseball bat. He is the old man YOU killed while two innocent boys have been sitting in Folsom Prison sixteen years for YOUR crime."

Danno put handcuffs on Julius. Martha whispered in Yolanda's ear. Everyone heard Martha say, "Please, just this once?" Martha stared at Yolanda.

Obviously embarrassed, Yolanda exclaimed, "Oh, alright."

Martha got a big smile on her face, turned, and said "BOOK EM' DANNO!" Everyone including Yolanda had to laugh. Everyone, that is, except Julius "Jewels" Bennett.

On the way back to the office, Agent Lockwood explained to Julius how he had been linked to the murder of the convenience store owner after all these years. Julius remained incredulous.

Julius Bennett was being booked and Yolanda, Martha, and Danno sat in Yolanda's office and shared in the jubilation which they all felt. There were only a few hours left before quitting time. Unable to concentrate on anything else, Martha asked Yolanda if she could leave early. She was anxious to drive to Folsom Prison and bring Bubba and Roddy the good news. Yolanda acquiesced and Martha hurried out the office door. She was halfway to the stairs when Danno called out to her.

"Wait, Martha I am going with you," Danno yelled. "I'll drive."

Five minutes into the drive they were still celebrating overdue justice. The traffic along Route 80 Northeast was light. Danno could tell how eager Martha was to get there. He looked at her and said, "What the hell, it's not like anyone is going to give me a speeding ticket." He put the flashing red bubble light on the dashboard and pushed the gas pedal down. He did not use the siren.

Danno used the ride to take the opportunity to properly thank Martha for her efforts in solving his sister's rape. He had not yet had the chance to speak with Darlene, but when the time was right, he would do so. Danno and Martha spent the remainder of the ride bonding on a personal level. They were both unpretentious, and neither felt threatened in the other's presence. About a mile before reaching the prison, Danno turned off the bubble light and resumed the legal speed limit.

Somehow entering the prison felt different to Martha this time. It wasn't familiarity, you could never get used to this place. It was Danno. He gave Martha a feeling of security. He, also, made the time go by faster. The last time she was here, Martha remembered having the time to study everything around her as she waited. The visit this time seemed to pass more quickly.

The Folsom Prison rules for inmate visitation stipulated only one visitor at a time. Danno agreed to wait where he was.

The prison guards were able to locate Roddy first. Martha explained the DNA profiling and the apprehension of Julius Bennett. Of course this meant that Roddy could look forward to being set free in the near future. Yet Roddy's demeanor never changed. Martha got the impression that he accepted a life behind bars as his

215

destiny. She asked him to remain hopeful and think about being released.

Bubba's reaction was completely different. He spoke in almost a whisper, as though speaking aloud would jinx what he was being told, or that if the guards heard, they would prevent his release. After all, the guards controlled every other aspect of his life. Three times Bubba asked Martha to explain the DNA profiling and how it proved that he and Roddy were innocent of the old man's murder. After three attempts in the simplest terms, Martha was sure that Bubba still didn't get it. He asked Martha that if this DNA guy said that he didn't kill the old man, why couldn't he go home to his grandmother now? She tried to make Bubba understand that there first had to be a trial. Agent Green began to wonder if coming to see the boys had been such a good idea. As with Roddy, Martha tried to convince Bubba to remain optimistic. She promised to keep him informed of their progress. Martha left Bubba in a worse state than she found him when she arrived half an hour ago. On her way out she was reminded of Roddy's premonition during her last visit. He warned her that Bubba couldn't last much longer. Hang on big guy, she thought, hang on.

T. GATOR, "THE TOUCHDOWN MAKER"

Wednesday came quickly for Joel and Dr. Woodson. The doctor had to work at the hospital until early afternoon and he promised to meet Joel at HOT Software at 2:30 PM.

Joel met Mike Cavanaugh at 10:00 AM. As promised, the demo website was nearly finished. Mike was not yet done, but he was close enough that he could share it with Joel. The webpage opened with a picture of Reverend Hartsell in the middle of one of his sermons. Atta boy, thought Joel to himself, stroke that ego. It was a flattering picture and the reverend looked fit and perfectly manicured in his custom made suit. Not a hair was out of place. Behind him was the choir. As instructed, Mike enhanced the color of the choir robes to make them look hideous. Reverend Hartsell would be made to understand that this webpage was only put together for demonstration purposes. Following the Sunday service, images from the videotape which Woodrow was making would be used to create the final webpage. Reverend Hartsell in his new suit as well as the choir in their new robes would be featured. In the meantime, the demonstration webpage would serve to whet Reverend Hartsell's appetite for his upcoming global experience.

A series of dropdown boxes were along the top of the webpage. From left to right, the boxes were: About Us, Staff, Rapture in the Round, Missions, and Donations. The "About Us" box gave a brief history of the church, a mission statement, and contact information. The "Staff" dropdown box would show several pictures of Reverend Thomas Hartsell, the elders, and the choir director. All of these pictures would be taken by Woodrow on Sunday. The "Rapture in the Round" dropdown box was a series of flattering photographs of the church, both inside and out. Included were photographs taken during the Sunday services as well as the Wednesday evening prayer meetings. The "Missions" dropdown box showed starving and sickly children from various countries which Rapture Ministries purportedly was supporting with massive donations from people of goodwill. There were, also, some "before and after" photographs which clearly illustrated what fat donations could accomplish. Mike was most proud of the "Donations" dropdown box which he knew would be the most important one to Reverend Hartsell. Since this was the box which would generate the donations, this was where Mike spent a majority of his time and creativity. A special feature demonstrated a cartoon man climbing a ladder. Each donation which a person contributed would make the little man climb higher up the ladder. The magic number at the top of the ladder was ten thousand dollars. Once this figure was reached in donations, angelic voices sang *Rapture O' My Soul*, and the person's name was added to the website's Wall of Attainment for the world to see. Books and DVDs could be purchased as love gifts. Of course, checks and all major credit cards were accepted. Those who could not make large donations were encouraged to arrange automatic monthly deductions from their credit cards. Joel was impressed. He asked Mike how things would change on **G Day**.

"I am still working on that. You just get me the things I ask for and I will make the magic happen. Come by at the end of the day and I will have the demo for you."

Hector was concerned about his mother. He knew that because she had mentioned getting a multi-million dollar inheritance, the elders would be all over her to get their hands on it. The pressure would be intense and Hector wanted to be sure she would be able to handle it.

When Reverend Hartsell gave P.J. Mustav the two and a half million dollars, Woodrow brought it to Lamar and Hector who were waiting a few blocks away. Before putting the money in his study safe, Lamar paid himself back the twenty thousand dollars which he had "donated" the week before at the prayer meeting. Lamar then withdrew another twenty-five thousand dollars for tonight's donations. Finally, he removed another thirty thousand dollars which Hector would hold for now. Ultimately, the thirty thousand dollars would be evenly divided and returned to Hector's Aunt Francisca and her friends Stella and Anita. This left a total of two million four hundred twenty-five thousand dollars which Lamar put in his safe.

Lamar had previously asked Yolanda to make two new dummy checking accounts in addition to the one she had already created for Professor and Mrs. Lortz. Using the money he returned to the safe, he instructed Yolanda to deposit ten thousand dollars into the Lortz account, another ten thousand dollars into an account for Tamayra Wilson. Tonight Yolanda would be assuming the identity of Tamayra. She borrowed the name from an old friend she trained with during her days at Quantico, Virginia. The final five thousand dollars would be deposited into a fake checking account for Tomas Zapata since Hector would also be making a donation tonight.

Yolanda was very excited and could hardly wait to go to Rapture Ministries' Wednesday night prayer meeting. Until now, she had only been a background player in the Council's mission to take down Reverend Hartsell. Tonight she would get to participate and even make a donation. How exciting! She was to assume the role of Tamayra Wilson, a recently widowed wife of an ex-football great T. Gator "the touchdown maker" Wilson. A fictitious gridiron hero, Tamayra would say that her late husband was the best at scoring both on and off the field.

At 6:45 PM cars started filling the Rapture parking lot. Everyone anticipated a larger than normal crowd because of the anticipation of **G Day**. All five Council members, as well as Colleen Laningham and Rosa Martinez, would be present. Indeed, it was a rare occasion when all five Council members were "working" at the same time.

Professor Lortz and his wife Jessica were separated into different classrooms as were Tomas and Lolita Zapata. Yolanda (Tamayra Wilson) found herself with Hector's mother (Lolita) and Judge Laningham (Professor Sheldon Lortz).

Elders Marcus Billings and Jesse Carter, along with two other elders, each took one of the four classrooms. As they were starting the video cassette tape in Jesse's classroom, the same thing was taking place in the other three rooms. This was, in fact, a large group for a Wednesday night.

P.J. Mustav and Woodrow Dennison went directly to Reverend Hartsell's office. They had a lot to go over this evening. First they covered the contracts with the television networks. Among the three networks, they told Reverend Hartsell, that he and

Rapture Ministries would be seen in twenty-three countries, all fifty states in the United States, and they estimated that fully one-third of the world's population would be able to tune in to his program. They tried to select time slots between 6:00 and 10:00 PM on weekends when it was estimated that they would have the largest target audience. The programming fees for the first month had already been paid assuming, of course, that Reverend Hartsell signed the three contracts. After that, Rapture would be taking in enough in donations to easily continue the contracts. From week to week the Sunday services would be videotaped and sent to the television networks. For special occasions, such as, missions week and Christmas, there was, also, the capacity for live broadcasts. As he spoke to Hartsell, P.J. had been referring to notes he was reading from, and he made sure that the reverend could see the TV network logos which were recognizable by everyone. P.J. asked a series of questions which were necessary for the contracts such as the "official doing business as" name of Rapture, its complete address, the name of Rapture's bank, and some disclosures giving these stations exclusive programming rights. P.J. said that the contracts were pretty standard issue and he wondered if Hartsell wanted anything added to them.

Hartsell suggested, "I probably should show them to our lawyers."

"There is no time," replied P.J. "We will barely make production schedules as it is. Should we have to stop everything because of lawyers, we will be unable to meet our deadlines. Have you ever seen lawyers get anything done on time? My God, I could have built my home faster than it took to close on it. Besides, this is why you have Woodrow and me. We know how to make things happen, and we have been through this many times. So, unless you have any objections, we will 'overnight' these contracts to the stations and have them back for you to sign in about a week." Before Hartsell could even react, P.J. closed the folder and said, "OK, we still have a lot to cover, so before we inspect the church, let's take a quick look at the demonstration webpage. While Hartsell looked over P.J.'s shoulder at his laptop, Joel quickly navigated through all of the features. The reverend agreed that the choir robes did not look good and he scribbled a note to check with Elder Marcus to see about getting new ones by Sunday. While P.J. continued demonstrating the webpage, Woodrow was observing the reverend's response. As expected, Hartsell was most pleased with the "donations" dropdown box. He made P.J. make the little man climb the ladder twice and grinned from ear to ear when it played *Rapture O' My Soul* after reaching the ten thousand dollar goal. P.J. reminded him that photographs of the staff would be taken by Woodrow on Sunday.

"OK," said Woodrow. "I need to see what has been done in the church." The three men left the administration building and headed toward Rapture in the Round. Once inside, Woodrow noted that the platform for videotaping had been completed to his specifications. As instructed, it appeared to be about five feet from the floor. Access was provided using a stepladder. Further down the aisle, Woodrow noted that the two large TV screens had been removed and had been inconspicuously placed in the corners of the room. It would be difficult to see them from the back of the church, but it was the best they could do. The green screen had been draped down the wall but was not yet on the floor. Reverend Hartsell explained that with all of the walking around that had been

222

going on, they were afraid that it might get ripped, so they elected to wait until Saturday to put it down.

"Oh, I almost forgot," said P.J. He said that he would be right back and he ran out of the church. He was back in a moment with the two furring strips and white lettering which would be the countdown to **G Day**. "Have your people attach these to the green screen before Sunday."

P.J. asked Reverend Hartsell, "Have you called all of your parishioners and told them what we expect of them on Sunday?"

"Not everyone yet," said Hartsell. "There are a lot of people, and almost everyone works during the time I have been making the calls. I will keep at it, but you have given us an awful lot to do in a short time."

P.J. continued to keep the pressure up. "How are you coming with the choir robes?"

Hartsell was obviously flustered. "Honestly I don't know, but while we were in the office, I made a note to remind myself to check with Elder Marcus about it. I delegated the task to him."

"Excellent," said P.J., "and while you're at it, make a note to get your new suit as well. Now let's go see if we can use your cassette tapes for the missionary work."

During the time the three men were discussing the webpage and the modifications to the interior of the church, the elders were performing their usual Wednesday night rants and shaking down their parishioners. Thanks to a little preplanning by the Council and funds graciously provided by Thomas Hartsell, the elders were to find this a most productive evening. Professor Lortz donated another ten thousand dollars, Tomas Zapata, Lolita's son, donated five thousand dollars, and an attractive middle-aged black woman who possessed an air of authority, gave an astonishing ten thousand dollars. Normally, when there are big dollar donations such as these, the elders had a tendency to lighten up on the other folks. This was part of the Council's plan. In addition, it was felt that new donors showing a willingness to donate serious amounts of cash would act as another distraction to Hartsell and his elders.

Elder Jesse seemed to be smitten by the new black woman with the deep pockets. Originally, Jesse had intended to corner Lolita Zapata and pressure her about her inheritance, but as is true with all men, there is a certain order in which things must be satisfied. Lolita didn't make the cut this evening.

"Hello, I am Elder Jesse Carter. I don't recall having seen you here before. May I ask your name?"

Yolanda did the cutesy thing with her eyelashes like Betty Boop used to do in the cartoons. "You haven't, and you may," she said. "My name is Tamayra Wilson." Tamayra started laughing and she put her hand over her mouth in a wantonly gesture.

"Did I say something funny?" Elder Jesse asked.

"No, no" said Tamayra. "I was just wondering...if your name was Barry...would they call you 'elderberry?'" Again she laughed.

"I suppose so," he answered, but Tamayra's attempt at humor was clearly lost on Jesse.

She continued, "I am a newcomer to the church, although I am from San Francisco, at least until my husband was traded to Miami."

"So you're married?" Jesse's disappointment was obvious.

"Was," said Yolanda. "His work took us to Miami. That is, if you call a stupid game work. He was a football hero. You must have heard of T. Gator 'the touchdown maker' haven't you?"

"Sorry, I am not a sports follower." Jesse said.

Yolanda breathed a sigh of relief. "Yeah well, the move to Miami turned out to be worth about one hundred million dollars, so we learned to like it real fast." Might as well get right to the point thought Yolanda. "Gator died last year in a boating accident. He was drunk and no one noticed that he fell off the boat."

"Weren't you with him?" asked Jesse.

She answered, "We lived separate lives. He used to tell me that he liked to score both at home and away. Thank God, I stayed married to him." She held up her fingers full of diamonds. "Imagine that, Florida is full of gators, and I had the only one that couldn't swim." Once again, her attempt at humor was lost on Elder Carter. He was thinking about the diamonds. "Well, Jesse, it's been fun, but I have to go."

"I sure hope I run into you again," said Jesse.

Yolanda, now thinking as an FBI agent answered, "Oh, I wouldn't be all that surprised if our paths should cross again Mr. Carter."

By the time P.J., Woodrow, and Reverend Hartsell got back to the administration building where both Hartsell's office and the Sunday school classrooms were located, nearly everyone had already left. Elder Jesse was walking Yolanda to the door. The elder stopped to introduce her.

"Reverend, allow me to introduce a new parishioner and donor to our mission. This is Tamayra..."

The reverend cut off Jesse so quickly and so dramatically that everyone was standing agape as he spoke, "Did you speak with Lolita as I instructed?"

Elder Jesse looked wounded to be spoken to like this in front of Tamayra who he was clearly trying to impress. "Well no, I was speaking with Miss Wilson and I guess Lolita slipped out the door."

Hartsell was fuming. "Slipped out the door? I doubt you would have noticed if she would have slipped out of the window."

Yolanda pretended to feel bad for Jesse. She put her hand on his forearm. Turning to the reverend, she said, "You must be 'Irreverent' Hartsell. Let's not be rude."

Hartsell came to the realization that he had been out of line. He took a step backward, bowed slightly and apologized, but only to her. "I am sorry Miss Wilson, I WAS rude. We are under a lot of pressure and I require help in getting things done. Jesse, I need you to collect all of the mission cassette tapes right now and bring them to my office for Mr. Dennison."

"Yes, sir." Elder Jesse remembered his place and hurried off to the classrooms. Yolanda interpreted the look she received from

Hartsell to mean that not only was he the boss, but that Yolanda's flirtatious behavior was directed at the wrong man. Within five minutes Jesse returned with the mission video cassette tapes.

Hector was truly amazed that Elder Jesse did not put the squeeze on Lolita about her inheritance. Rosa did not know Yolanda, and Hector was amused at his mother's description of her.

His mother said, "You know, Hector, the judge, I mean Professor Lortz, said he and his wife wanted to donate another ten thousand dollars and Elder Jesse was very nice to him. After he had the judge's check, he went to this very attractive black woman. She was dressed like she just got off the bus from Fifth Avenue, and she had enough jewelry to set off a metal detector. Anyway, she introduced herself as some football player's wife, and she, too, gave Elder Jesse a ten thousand dollar donation. Where do these people get all of this money? All of a sudden it was like there was no one else in the room. I was next in line after this woman, but he never saw me. Not a word. Jesse was infatuated like a high school kid. We all left and I nearly tripped over his tongue trying to get by."

Rosa's description made Hector chuckle as he thought of Jesse and Yolanda. He wondered if the Council might use this relationship to their advantage.

CHAPTER FIVE

1

NEW ROBES

Yolanda was still thinking of the last evening's entertainment at Rapture when Ruth walked into her office and said, "Avery Resque called quite late last night and left a message for you. He said that he was involved with a homicide investigation and never had an opportunity to get back with you. He was able to secure the evidence you requested and his people have sent it to us. They expect it will be here sometime tomorrow."

"Thank you Ruth. Anything else?"

"Yeah," said Ruth. "Martha would like a moment when you get a chance."

"OK, Ruth." Yolanda thought for a moment. "Tell her to come by in fifteen minutes."

Judge Laningham was tired after last night's prayer meeting. He hated being exhausted all of the time. He wondered how the others made out at Rapture. Lamar smiled at the thought of Yolanda playing a vamp. Now THAT would have been fun to watch, but before he cornered Yolanda, Jesse made sure that all of the others in the classroom were gone. He wondered how Jesse would have looked if he realized that his attempts to seduce Tamayra

Wilson were actually being directed at Yolanda Tubbs, Director of the Santa Molina Federal Bureau of Investigation.

Lamar knew that Hector and his mother were a bust. To a man, including Yolanda, all Council members believed that one of the elders, or even Hartsell himself would be all over Lolita pressuring her about the inheritance money. A second opportunity for this would come on Sunday.

The judge's greatest concern was for the safety of Joel and Jerry. For sure, they had the most difficult parts to play in this ruse. They had to be right in the face of Hartsell and the elders all of the time. So far, it appeared that they believed Zenith Productions was going to make them rich. As far as the judge knew, no one had checked on the validity of Zenith, P.J., or Woodrow. They HAD to keep them busy. Colleen called to Lamar from the kitchen. Since his fatal diagnosis, Colleen has made bacon for him several mornings. Before NSCLC, the fancy acronym for his particular type of lung cancer, finding bacon in the Laningham house was about as likely as finding garlic in a vampire's coffin. Colleen knew her husband craved bacon, real bacon, but she never bought it...too many nitrates. Lamar had always been amused by the games people play. Not wanting to blame the dietary changes on his terminal diagnosis, Colleen told him the bacon was on sale and snuck it back into the Laningham menu. He appreciated her compassion and pretended not to notice the change. Damn the nitrates! Bring on the bacon!

Before Lamar was able to taste his bacon, Agent Martha Green was in Yolanda's office.

Yolanda rose from her chair and motioned for Martha to sit. "Has Danno forgiven you for your *Hawaii Five O* reference? I have to admit, it was funny."

"Yes, it was. Who would think you could have fun while making an arrest for murder? This is actually what brings me to why I am here. You will remember that after the Julius Bennett arrest, Danno and I drove to Folsom Prison to tell the boys the good news. The reaction, especially from Bubba, was disconcerting. The whole DNA thing was beyond his comprehension. When I told him that we were able to prove that he did not kill the store owner, he thought that I came to bring him home. He could not understand why he couldn't just walk out the door and go home. I am worried about him. Is there any way the courts can fast-track this thing and get him out of prison quickly? Also, I will go to his old neighborhood and poke around. If I can find some of his family, they could be a big support to him right now."

Yolanda touched the fingers of each of her hands together and tapped her lips in thought. "This is outside my area of expertise. We catch em' and the courts take it from there. However, I have a personal friend who is a judge. Let me see what he thinks about this. Bubba has a good point. If we can prove he is innocent, he and Roddy should be released posthaste. Checking for family is a good idea. You do that and let's talk again on Monday. Thanks."

Yolanda waited until Martha was gone and she closed her door and dialed Judge Laningham. He picked up the phone on the second ring. "Hi, Yolanda, Elder Jesse was quite taken with you last evening. I wish I could have been there to watch the hustle.

Colleen and I are about to sit down to breakfast. What can I do for you?"

Yolanda got right to the point. "First, are we having a Council meeting tomorrow? Since I am a player now, I would like an update on what everyone else is doing."

The judge answered, "As a matter of fact, I was going to call everyone. Let's make it here at the usual 7:00 PM. What else can I do for you?"

Yolanda explained how her new agent had proven that two young men had been wrongfully imprisoned for sixteen years for a crime that they did not commit. She asked Lamar how the courts might fast-track this case to set these two young men free again.

Lamar was impressed with Agent Martha Green's feelings for justice. "Wow, Yolanda, she sounds like one of us, a potential Council member perhaps? Something to think about." He neglected to mention that a vacancy would soon be created. Lamar promised to go personally to the courthouse to see if he could exert his influence on behalf of the two young men. Tomorrow, he would share with her, anything he learned.

"One more thing judge," Yolanda offered. "Agent Martha Green, the one you spoke so fondly of, the same investigator who broke this case, will be receiving three boxes of evidence from Detroit. The boxes contain all that remains from the murders of Joel's parents and sister. After it has been processed, I will let you know what, if anything, we have found."

Lamar sat at the kitchen table. "OK, thanks." He turned off the phone and reveled in the smell of bacon.

One hour later, Lamar called Jerry, Joel, and Hector and told them of tomorrow's Council meeting.

While Lamar was calling the Council members, Reverend Hartsell was sitting at his desk fuming. He was frustrated because he was unable to reach very many members of his congregation to tell them what they could and could not wear to the Sunday service. He thought such menial tasks were beneath him yet he felt he could not entrust the work to others. While he had a personal secretary who was not hired for her secretarial skills, he only had her handle things like preparing the bulletins or making sure the janitorial requirements were taken care of properly. At times like this, he wished he could delegate more but he simply did not trust the people around him. A few minutes earlier, he came across the note reminding him to check on the choir robes. He asked his secretary to find Elder Marcus and send him to his office. Hartsell quickly became convinced that calling his congregation was not working. He and the elders would just have to come back and make the calls in the evening when everyone was home from work. What a chore! He tried to stay focused on the big picture. This was what he laid awake nights thinking about in cell number 103 on C Block in the Leavenworth Penitentiary. He had no less than two weeks to wait until his dreams would come true. And today he would be getting a new suit. Last Monday, after first meeting with P.J. and Woodrow, he phoned his tailor and told him what he needed. He glanced at his watch. There were only two more hours to wait until his appointment for the fitting. Reverend Hartsell went back to making more phone calls to church members. After three unsuccessful attempts, he was interrupted by Elder Marcus.

"Reverend Hartsell, your secretary sent for me?"

Hartsell pointed to a chair. "Marcus, sit down. These phone calls are killing me. No one is home. Listen, how are you and the choir director doing in securing the new choir robes by Sunday?"

Marcus answered. "We are cutting it extremely close boss. We found a vendor who is able to provide the colors you asked for, but in order to get them to us by Saturday afternoon, they were forced to halt production on whatever they had been working on. The robes are being created as we speak. Since we are in such a rush, they charged us an extra fifty dollars per robe. We used the current robes and ordered the same sizes from them. They suggested that we have a seamstress stand by just in case. The director has asked for choir practice on Saturday evening, so we hired two seamstresses to be here, and one by one we will pull the choir members from practice to have them measured for any necessary alterations. Of course, the alterations will have to be completed Saturday evening in order for us to be ready on Sunday morning. This will cost us a lot before we are done."

Hartsell became even more frustrated. "Marcus, please keep an eye on this and let me know right away if there are any problems. By the way, find Jesse. The three of us will have to stay late tonight to finish these calls. We'll get pizza."

Marcus left Reverend Hartsell quite bewildered. There was so much to do and only two days until the Sunday service. He had not even prepared a sermon. He tried making two more calls. No one was home. He began wondering, why five million dollars? For only two weeks work? Granted he should be receiving thousands of donations once they go global, but five million dollars? He thought he had better look deeper into Zenith Productions and P.J. Mustav. Hartsell made a mental note to do just that. However, right now he was going to get a new suit.

2

GOTH GIRL

It was a spectacular Friday morning. The air was crisp and clean and there was a slight chill in the wind which Martha found invigorating. The week had been a very productive one and it sapped the strength from her. Martha looked forward to the weekend so she could rest and recharge. Besides, she had been neglecting her boyfriend. He had been patient with her and she promised him that she would not bring work home with her this weekend.

Martha checked in at her office, and since everything was relatively quiet, she decided to visit Bubba's old neighborhood. The original police report and arrest record provided Bubba's old address as well as that of the convenience store where the old man had been murdered. Agent Green told Ruth where she was headed, and she grabbed the police report on her way out.

Twenty minutes later, Martha was approaching her destination. She was struck by the number of chain link fences. There were fences around buildings, around small parks, and encircling parking lots. Somehow, it was unclear to Martha if these fences were intended to keep the inhabitants in or the visitors out. However, one thing was clear beyond question. Bubba and Roddy had merely exchanged one fenced environment for another. She slowed her vehicle to a crawl trying to envision what this street might have looked like sixteen years ago. Martha decided that since the numerous tenement structures probably dated back to the 1960s, little could have changed. There were fenced in lots used as makeshift basketball courts, and everything was painted in graffiti. Much of it was quite good, especially the giant bubble lettering. The presence of street gangs was reflected in the spray-painted territorial warnings of those misguided adolescents. Perhaps we are not so different from animals after all, Martha mused. Instead of marking our territories with scents from glands or urine, we use acrylic enamel.

Here and there Martha saw a few signs that optimists had passed by. Fresh coats of paint on doors or posters inviting neighbors to block meetings were seen. Mostly, however, there was just brick, asphalt, broken glass, and litter. Grass and trees were conspicuously absent. Finally Martha found Bubba's address which she had written in her notebook. The massive brick structure reminded Agent Green of Folsom Prison. There were no coils of concertina wire or series of locked gates, yet she felt the same foreboding feeling knowing she had to go in there. She wished Danno was with her.

Martha parked her car and made sure that her service revolver was in place before she got out. Bubba's address was 304. There was an open vestibule which led to a series of ground floor apartments. Martha, also, noted two elevators which had been out of service for so long that there were "Vote for Jimmy Carter" bumper stickers ON TOP of the "Out of Order" signs. Next to the elevators was a door indicating a stairwell. She took a deep breath and summoned her courage, much like the first time she ventured off the highest diving board when she was in high school. She pushed open the door and headed up the stairs. When Martha arrived at the third floor, she pushed it open and stepped into a dimly lighted corridor. The hallway was littered with baby strollers, bicycles, and trash receptacles.

"Hey baby, you lost?" The voice behind her was a deep baritone.

Agent Green spun around quickly and immediately knew that this man posed no threat to her. If lust was on his mind, it was for liquor and cigarettes, not her. "I am looking for apartment number 304," she said.

"Second door on the right, I think." He appeared to teeter and belched.

Martha gave him a hurried, "Thanks." and moved on. She noted that some of the doors did not have room numbers, but thankfully the one she was seeking did, and she knocked loudly. After a few moments, a feeble sounding voice from the other side of the door was heard.

"Who is it?" said the voice.

I am Agent Martha Green from the FBI, and I would like to speak with Mrs. Jones, the grandmother of Bernard Jones."

Once again the voice was heard but the door remained closed. "There ain't no Jones here. I have lived here for six years, and there ain't no Jones here."

Martha spoke to the door. "Mrs. Jones would have lived here about sixteen years ago. Do you know where she may have moved?"

The "door" answered, "Look, I don't know any Jones. Ask next door at 306. She has lived here twenty years. Maybe she can help you. Her name is Mrs. Cleveland."

Martha wondered what the face behind the voice might look like. "Thank you," she said. One door down the hall Martha again knocked. This time she heard a man's gruff sounding voice. "What do you want?" the man asked.

"I am FBI Agent Martha Green, and I am looking for information regarding a Mrs. Jones. She would have lived next door in Apartment 304 about sixteen years ago."

"There ain't no Joneses here." He yelled to someone else in the apartment. "Baby you know any Joneses?"

Martha heard a woman say, "Get out the way you old fool." The door opened as far as the chain would allow. The old woman continued, "Sorry, honey. There used to be a Mrs. Jones next door, but she died about six years ago."

Martha asked, "Did she have any other family?"

"Come in honey, there's rats in the hallway. Idiots leave their trash out there and they get into it."

The interior of the apartment was better lighted than the hallway, but not by much. Martha sat and explained the story about Bubba and the circumstances which were allowing him to be released from prison. Mrs. Cleveland became very sad. She recalled Bubba's arrest and his being sent to jail. She said that everyone knew Bubba could never hurt anyone. His grandmother had taken care of him ever since his mother died from an overdose

238

of heroin. Mrs. Cleveland was teary. "Most folks thought that boy was so 'slow' cause his momma always liked the needle. When dat boy went to jail, his grandma just cried and cried. Folsom was so far away she couldn't visit him. She got no car. Anyway, she died of a broken heart. She loved dat boy and she worried 'bout what would become of him." Mrs. Cleveland looked up at Martha. "You might as well leave him in jail. At least someone is lookin' after him. He ain't got no family, and he can't live in the outside world. It will kill him. What a shame."

Martha thanked Mrs. Cleveland. She had hoped to find family for Bubba, but there was none. Now she was unsure if she was delivering justice or merely throwing Bubba to the wolves. She began the day with such optimism and enthusiasm thinking about Bubba and Roddy being set free. Now it has been suggested that setting them free may do more harm than good.

Before returning to the office, Martha wanted to visit the scene of the crime. The ancient convenience store was still there. The front windows were cracked and had tape on them. Abandoned many years ago, fixing the store was beyond hopeless. She stepped close and cupped her hands over her eyes to peer inside. All of the shelves had been overturned by vandals years ago with miscellaneous garbage strewn everywhere. Then she saw what she was looking for, the counter where Bubba had picked up the baseball bat. Agent Green experienced a very cold chill travel up her spine to the nape of her neck. How sad. Why don't they tear down these useless structures?

Reverend Hartsell and the elders were exhausted. They stayed at Rapture until 11:30 PM, calling parishioners about the

239

rules of attire for Sunday. The three men working in concert actually had good success in reaching most of the congregation. After the hour ride back to his estate, Reverend Hartsell decided to relax until 1:00 PM at which time he was supposed to pick up his suit. This was the first time he'd had a few minutes to himself since becoming involved with Zenith Productions. P.J. and Woodrow had kept him so busy that he had no time to think about anything. He decided to start writing his sermon for Sunday. Thomas Hartsell remembered a sermon he had watched in his cell just a few years back in Leavenworth. He remembered the pastor telling a story about a hidden treasure and the man who had lost it. This man was distraught trying to remember where he had hidden the treasure. Since yesterday, Hartsell had been distraught thinking about his "treasure" which he willingly handed over to P.J. He was becoming determined that he would not pay him the balance of what he had promised.

Lamar Laningham had not been in the Santa Molina Courthouse in many months. At Yolanda's request, he went to see if there was any way he could expedite the release of Bubba and Roddy from prison. Lamar spoke with Judge Dawson, the man who had been assigned the boys' case. He told Lamar that he had been given wrongful imprisonment cases several times in past years.

Judge Dawson said that extenuating circumstances such as Bubba's deteriorating mental status could sometimes provide leverage and hasten an inmate's release. He alluded to a recent crime boss who was released after many years in prison due to a terminal illness. However, Judge Dawson explained that the public wanted the satisfaction of having someone in prison for the crime. Unfortunately, it didn't seem to matter so much who was being punished as long as someone was incarcerated. The faster Julius Bennett was behind bars, the quicker the two boys could be released. Judge Dawson thought for a moment and then Lamar thought he saw a twinkle in his eye.

Judge Dawson began. "Here's the deal, Lamar. Whenever a horrific crime like this store murder happens, there is great public outrage and everyone wants the death penalty. This crime, however, happened sixteen years ago. The public doesn't even remember the crime. If we can simply switch the occupants of the cell, no one will ever take notice. Here's my plan. If we can pressure this Julius Bennett into believing that there is an outcry for the death penalty, we may have a chance. We have to get Bennett to admit to killing the old man. He must be convinced that the DNA evidence is so overwhelming and so compelling that a jury trial would surely result in his being electrocuted. We need to convince him that a deal is in his best interest. We offer him a one-time only opportunity to spare his life. Instead of going through the anguish of a long jury trial which will send him to the 'chair,' if he spares the taxpayers a fortune in court costs, then we, in exchange, will take the death penalty off the table. It's a win/win situation. If all of these things can be done, this matter can end quickly."

Judge Dawson folded his arms and held them to his chest. "In the meantime, I will push the extenuating circumstances of the boy's worsening depression as well. Check with me in a few days and I will have a much better idea of how things are proceeding."

Lamar was grateful and drove home to take a nap before tonight's Council meeting.

Martha was unable to work her way through her sullen feelings for Bubba. She wondered if the prison officials would consider putting him on a "suicide watch." She, also, wondered if anyone in Folsom even cared should he attempt to end his life. Once back at her office, she shared with Yolanda her disappointment at finding no family members for Bubba. All she could do now was wait on the mercy of the court. Martha hoped that Yolanda's judge friend could help.

Martha spent the next few hours in her office checking and then double-checking all of the information that proved Julius Bennett killed Adamos Lazopoulos. Submitting probable cause evidence to a judge in order to secure an arrest warrant was one thing. Proving DNA evidence to a jury was quite another. And then, of course, there is the small matter of a defense attorney who will do everything possible to introduce doubt.

Martha desperately needed a change in venue. She opted to have lunch in a small Greenwich Village-looking restaurant around the corner from her office. This place always seemed to cheer her up. She loved to "people watch" and this place was a magnet to the unusual. The cuisine offered only the basics for lunch, but the food was good and the prices were reasonable. Martha ordered a chicken salad sandwich, a pickle, and a glass of milk. As always, the restaurant was crowded, but she was lucky and fast enough to spot a couple vacating a small table next to the window which overlooked the street. The table was cleared quickly. She was two bites into her sandwich when a Goth dressed young woman asked Martha if she could share the table.

"Sure, sit down," answered Agent Green. She was reminded that her parents always taught her to be tolerant in the ways of others. However, Clint Eastwood movies had taught her a few things as well...one of which, from *Dirty Harry,* was "A man's got to know his limitations." Well, one of Martha's limitations just joined her for lunch. Jet black hair and clothes to match, she seemed to be a pretty girl. Leather and chiffon were just the start to this young girl's ensemble. Both her nose and her left ear were pierced, and a small delicate chain was draped between them. Black lipstick and mascara, with a black cross, completed the total absence of any color. Every fiber in the girl's being was screaming "LOOK AT ME," while every fiber in Martha was just screaming.

Martha was still wearing her lanyard and identification badge which clearly showed she was an FBI agent, so naturally this young girl asked her, "Do you work for the FBI?"

Martha tried to be polite. "Yes, I work with the DNA lab."

Goth began eating her salad. "Cool...maybe you can answer a question which has been bothering me for a long time?"

"I'll do my best," replied Martha.

"OK, well our body's cells die and are regenerated, right? I mean, like our skin cells die and we get new ones. Our blood cells die and we make more in a few days, right?"

Martha had no idea where this could possibly be going. "Yes, that is correct."

"OK, then, is it fair to assume that within a few weeks or even a month, ALL of our body's cells have been replaced, yes?"

"Yes, that sounds reasonable," agreed Martha.

"OK," said Goth, "then how could you arrest me for something which happened a month ago? Cell-wise, I am a completely different person. Not a single cell in my body was there a month ago when the crime took place? Or how is it possible for me to remember something which happened a year ago when all of my memory cells have been exchanged for new ones?"

Martha had to admit that she was stymied. She was unable to answer and decided to take the coward's way out. She said, "You know, young lady, I learned about that in college, but all those memory cells have passed away, and I cannot remember." It bothered Martha to have been bested by Miss Goth, so before any more questions were asked, she thought it best to leave.

Agent Green was still pondering the Goth girl's question when she returned to her desk. Someone had left her a note stating that she had a package in the mailroom. Ten minutes later, she was looking at three boxes marked as evidence which were postmarked from Detroit. The clerk told her that although they were addressed to Director Tubbs, she was instructed to give them to her. Martha remembered the conversation with Yolanda...something about an old murder in Detroit and a friend of Yolanda's. Agent Green thought for a moment and decided that this stuff, whatever it was, could wait until Monday. She wasn't about to risk another lost weekend. Her boyfriend didn't deserve that.

Lamar sat in his study waiting for the others to join him. He wondered how many more meetings there would be at the round table. He smiled to himself as he recalled the camaraderie which began and was nurtured around this piece of furniture. The friendship alone was worth the creation of the Council. Yet there was so much more. Sometimes Lamar felt like a dinosaur. In his waning days on the bench, he sometimes felt alone. Were honor, honesty, and the rule of law now vestiges of a society which, because of greed had rejected and abandoned the very principles which have made this country great? Is it that we don't remember our greatness, or do we just close our eyes to it because we are ashamed to have left a legacy of compromise and second-best to our progeny?

All of the Council's members shared the judge's lamentations for the direction in which our nation was headed. They, also, shared his gratification that through Council activities, they were able to take a stand and make a difference. Lamar realized that he was not alone. He felt fortunate to have joined with others like himself who chose to draw a line in the sand and say "NO, not on my watch!"

Yolanda asked to meet with Lamar before the other Council members arrived for two reasons. First, she wanted to let him know that evidence from Detroit had arrived at the Santa Molina bureau. Within a few days she hoped they would know if there was any chance of solving the Harris family murders. Yolanda and the judge were the only Council members aware of what they were doing. There would be no point in stirring up the old rage which still lived within Joel if the evidence provided nothing.

The second reason Yolanda wanted to speak with Judge Laningham concerned Bubba and Roddy. Lamar explained what would be necessary to avert a trial which could last months. He told Yolanda of his conversation with Judge Dawson and all of the "ifs."

245

IF they could convince Julius Bennett that the DNA evidence against him was absolutely irrefutable; and IF they could convince Julius that he would be facing the death penalty; and IF they could convince him that exchanging a guilty plea for life in prison was his best deal, then it could work. Lamar hoped he would know the answer in a few days.

Within a few minutes the remaining Council members arrived. This evening Yolanda, alias Tamayra Wilson, was the star of the show. Everyone wanted to know about her role as the sassy ex-football player's wife. Prior to last Wednesday evening, Yolanda had been used to performing Council activities from the shadows. She clearly loved her role as Tamayra, and like a little-leaguer who hit his first home run, re-telling the story never gets old.

After ten minutes of laughing, the Council got down to serious work. The judge made sure that Dr. Woodson was prepared to take still photographs of the Rapture staff on Sunday. Dr. Woodson said he was prepared for both the still photographs and the videos from the two locations. The cameras and tripods were already in his car. Joel would run around giving orders and playing the director of the production. Yolanda was pretending to be away in Chicago at a charity auction. She was relishing her role as the naughty lady with all the money and a fondness for Elder Jesse and Reverend Hartsell. Hector and his mother would be banished from view because of her big hat. The Laninghams likewise, would be made to sit in the rear of the church for wearing loud colors.

The judge was satisfied. "OK, everyone, we have done a good job getting ready for Sunday. This means we have to keep Hartsell and his boys busy for one more week. Any ideas?"

The Council adjourned having created a series of diversions to keep Hartsell and the elders busy and off balance for one more week. Before leaving, Joel asked Hector if he could return to Hartsell's mansion one more time and take some still photographs emphasizing its' opulence.

3

JACK DANIELS, NEAT

Saturday morning Reverend Hartsell slept in late. He was still tired and could have stayed in bed another hour or two, but he had to go to Rapture to meet Jesse and Marcus for a final walk-through before the Sunday service. He stumbled through the motions of a shower and breakfast and gradually felt his strength return. Thomas was on the road by 10:00 AM and he expected to be at Rapture in an hour.

Jesse and Marcus were already busy working when Reverend Hartsell arrived. Marcus had received several boxes of choir robes which recently arrived by express delivery. He had set up card tables and folding chairs adjacent to the altar area where the seamstresses could work while the choir practiced. On one large table he began separating the robes by sizes. Reverend Hartsell and Marcus had to agree that P.J.'s choice of colors was superb. The soft, almost pastel, gold of the robes was very rich looking and the scarlet sashes and accents were stunning. The organist and choir director's colors were opposite. Their robes were scarlet with accenting gold sashes. The choir was scheduled to practice from 4:00 PM until 6:00 PM. Elder Jesse had tacked down carpeting on the videotaping platform to make it quieter. He decided to wait until the choir was done practicing and then he and Marcus could tack the green screen material to the floor in the altar area.

248

Reverend Hartsell went to his office. He still had not reached everyone in the congregation and he wanted to try one final time. He had attempted about six calls when his mind started to wander. To take a break he went to his car and returned carrying a box containing several reams of green printing paper which he had purchased. His secretary was off for the weekend, so he opened the drawer of the copy machine and removed all of the white paper, replacing it with the green paper. He opened the lid of the copier and very carefully lined up one hundred dollar bills, face down on the glass. He tried one test copy. The machine spit out a sheet of green paper containing four facsimiles of one hundred dollar bills. He compared the printer copy to a real bill. Not bad, he thought. The thickness of the paper was close. He had brought with him a bank stack of one hundred dollar bills. One stack contained one hundred bills totaling ten thousand dollars, which was indicated on the band which wrapped the bills.

It took Reverend Hartsell a while, but he methodically copied and cut out one hundred of the counterfeit bills. He compared the thickness of the ten thousand dollar stack of real money to the stack made on the copy machine. The printer paper was thicker than real money, so after some experimenting, Hartsell determined that if five of the fake bills were removed from the stack, the thickness of the real and fake money stacks were virtually identical. He made a note that each stack required a real bill on the top and bottom with ninety-three fake copies sandwiched in between. He made nine hundred and fifty additional sheets and hid them in his office. On his way back to the copier, which was in the anteroom where his secretary worked, he heard a knock on the door. Thinking it was

Marcus or Jesse, he yelled, "Come in." The door opened and Reverend Hartsell stood amazed. In walked Tamayra Wilson.

"Why Tamayra, what brings you here on a Saturday?" Reverend Hartsell was taken aback by the surprise visit and he nearly forgot what he was doing.

Yolanda pretended to seem disinterested in her surroundings as she strutted around the office, but she did notice the odd box of green paper and the four one hundred dollar bills on the copying machine.

Tamayra Wilson was a woman who knew what she wanted and she knew how to get what she wanted. She was direct and she did not mince words. "You are a man, and I am a woman, what do YOU think brings me here? I have to be at the airport in a few hours, and I need a drink. Reverends DO drink don't they?" Tamayra asked the question as though the answer was already obvious to her.

Hartsell seemed desperate to find a way to take control of the conversation, but Tamayra was unwilling to relinquish it. "Um, yes some reverends drink. The airport, are you leaving?"

"I am going to the airport because that's where the planes are. Of course, I am leaving. Honestly, do you always waste time like this when you talk with people? Why don't you gather up that money you were copying and take a lady out for a drink."

Having been caught copying money, Reverend Hartsell was totally embarrassed, so much so, that he didn't attempt an explanation. He quickly scooped up the money, stuffed it into his pocket, and closed the copier without replacing the white paper. Hartsell stepped into his office, put the box of paper behind his desk, and grabbed his keys. As the reverend and Tamayra walked down the Rapture administration building steps toward his car, Elder Jesse was coming out of the church. Jesse stopped cold when he recognized Tamayra, but she was too occupied to have seen him in front of the church. Jesse was crestfallen.

Reverend Hartsell took Tamayra to an out of the way restaurant. He had been there several times with his secretary as well as the wives of a few of his parishioners. He knew it would be quiet and that they would not be interrupted.

Trying to break the ice with his new lady friend, Hartsell began. "So, where are you going?"

"Chicago. They are having a fund raising event for charity at which they will be auctioning off some sports memorabilia. They asked me to donate some things from Gator, so I said I would bring them."

"Yes, Jesse told me that your husband was killed in a boating accident. I am sorry."

"Thank you," responded Tamayra, "but I really don't believe you are sorry."

Hartsell was direct. "You know, Tamayra, I have never met anyone quite like you. Do you always say exactly what is on your mind?"

Yolanda knew she was getting to him. "I try to. The last I knew, the shortest distance between two points was a straight line.

251

Look, I know it's a bit on the rough side and it ruffles a lot of feathers, especially among women, but I believe it is more honest. When someone wants something, they should just say so instead of playing all the games. I know what you want from me. I just haven't made up my mind if I am going to let you have it. It seems to me that people generally tell others what they think they WANT to hear. It's all a game."

Hartsell was becoming interested. "OK, Miss Wilson, let's be honest. Why are we here? I thought you were interested in Jesse."

Tamayra cut him off. "Oh, please, do I really strike you as someone who is willing to accept second-string? I can't believe I used a football colloquialism." She paused. "Actually I was a bit dishonest, but I needed bait. I dropped ten grand on some dumb-ass mission which I know neither of us cares about because I knew it would attract YOUR attention. Is that direct enough for you? Jesse merely expedited my effort. I may have been born at night, but it wasn't last night. I know clothes and I know jewelry." She held up her hand full of rings. "You don't wear the kind of bling you boys wear on a preacher's salary."

The waitress finally came to the table. Tamayra looked up and said, "Jack Daniels, neat."

Hartsell followed, "I'll have a Manhattan." The waitress said nothing and backed away.

"You don't strike me as a man who would want to be a preacher," observed Tamayra, "at least not the kind of preacher I was brought up knowing. But we all have to do something, so if this gig brings you what you need, go for it. I got lucky. The star running

252

back took a liking to me in college. I knew a good thing when I had it, and I knew how to keep him coming back for more. We were smashed one night in Vegas and thought it would be fun to get married. All the ladies loved him and he couldn't help loving them right back, lots of them. He didn't even pretend to hide his dalliances, and it nearly cost him our marriage. Some dogs just gotta run free. He provided well for me…in several ways. That man knew his way around the bedroom. Thankfully, I hung in there. So now, I own the castle, complete with all of the amenities." Tamayra looked at her watch. "Oh my, I should get to the airport. Can you bring me back to Rapture? My trunk has a bunch of footballs and jerseys which have to be checked in before I can board."

On the way back to the Rapture parking lot Tamayra told Hartsell, "I'll call you in a few days when I get back from Chicago. Then I want to hear YOUR story preacher man."

He shut her car door for her and thought it ironic that where she was headed was exactly where his "story" started. He looked around the parking lot, and except for his car, the lot was now empty. It was just as well, he thought to himself, since he had to get home and finish his sermon.

4

THE PROMISED LAND

The anticipation of the Sunday morning service at Rapture Ministries could not have been greater. All of the parishioners knew the service was being filmed for broadcast all over the world. Hartsell and the elders had completed a grueling week preparing both the church and the congregation for filming. The Council had done their best in preparing to destroy Hartsell and bring down the Rapture empire.

P.J. Mustav and Woodrow Dennison had asked Reverend Hartsell and the elders to arrive early on Sunday and to have the congregation do the same. When P.J. and Woodrow arrived at 8:15 AM, there were already several cars in the Rapture parking lot. Each of them hoisted a video camera onto their shoulder. The cameras had already been fastened to the tripods and were ready to film. Once in the church, they were unable to put the first camera on the platform since the stepladder was missing. They leaned the tripod against the platform and headed toward the balcony where the pipe organ was located. The stairs were very narrow. Dr. Woodson was a spry sixty-three year old, but he went slowly to avoid an accident. Both men were delighted to see that the fidgety organist hadn't arrived up there yet. Last Sunday when they climbed up into the organ loft, they thought that their presence up there would give the little man a heart attack. After they set the tripod in place, Joel and Dr. Woodson took a moment to look down over the balcony. They could see why the stepladder had been missing. Elders Jesse and Marcus were attempting to change the white numbers on the countdown to **G Day** banner. As Marcus was attempting to secure the stepladder, Jesse was poking fun at Reverend Hartsell. Jesse assumed Hartsell's deep baritone voice and struggled up the ladder saying "Lookie boss, I is climbing da ladder." They were actually quite funny. Jesse stretched, balanced and put the "8" onto the small hook.

8 DAYS TO G DAY

RAPTURE IN THE ROUND

Jesse was laughing as he came down the ladder. All of a sudden, P.J. and Woodrow's attention was drawn to the front row of seats. An old lady was pummeling a younger woman in the head with her purse. The younger woman was pleading for her to stop. Elder Marcus heard the commotion and ran to separate them. The old lady would not give any ground. She explained to Marcus that she had come to Rapture an hour early just so she could get a front row seat to be in the video. She put her gloves on the seat to lay claim to it and went to the ladies' room to check her hair and lipstick. When she returned, the young lady was in her seat.

P.J. laughed and said to Woodrow, "Oh boy, this is going to be fun." They carefully made their way down the treacherous stairs.

Elder Jesse had just finished returning the stepladder to its place next to the video platform. Woodrow asked Jesse to find Reverend Hartsell, all of the elders, the organist, and the choir director and deliver them posthaste to the front of the church, near the Wall of Attainment, for photographs. One by one as they arrived, Woodrow photographed them. When he photographed

255

Marcus, Woodrow learned that all of the alterations to the choir robes had been successfully completed. The robes had been returned to Rapture late last night and they were now ironed and hanging in the choir's dressing room. Woodrow looked at his watch which indicated 8:40 AM.

P.J. had been busy in the front rows of the church instructing people where to sit. Many were clearly upset having this young man telling them what to do and where to sit. One woman told P.J. that she has always sat where she was and wouldn't move for anyone except Reverend Hartsell himself. P.J. dispatched Marcus to quickly locate and return with Reverend Hartsell before everything got totally out of control. Within minutes, Reverend Hartsell, clearly annoyed at having been interrupted, addressed the congregation. He held up his hands to quiet the parishioners and get their attention. "Brothers and sisters!" He paused until it became quiet. "I apologize to you for the inconvenience, but I called each of you to tell you this would happen. This man," he motioned toward P.J., "He is a Hollywood production specialist who makes his living doing this. Please, give him your attention and sit where he directs you." Reverend Hartsell looked around and was clearly frustrated. So many people did not comply with his dress code instructions. Just as P.J. had predicted. "Look at you," said Hartsell. "Why Mrs. Lortz, that dress would glow in the dark. Tommy Pendergast, you don't need sunglasses in here. Lolita Zapata, I've never seen you wear a hat so large. Please folks, this is a special day for Rapture Ministries...for all of us." He turned and pointed to the countdown banner. "Only eight days to go, PLEASE." He put his palms together imploring them to cooperate. The reverend then hurried off to get ready for his sermon. The remainder of the first ten rows was filled in by P.J. with "beautiful people" who correctly followed the dress code. Behind them, it didn't matter what they wore. P.J. dismissed Elder Marcus who had been designated to stay with Woodrow during the filming. P.J. waited until he saw Woodrow, in place with a thumbs-up, on the platform. He looked at his watch and then up to the organist. All was ready. He took one last look around, pointed to the organist and slowly backed away as music filled the church.

P.J. had found a wonderful place to hide where he could observe the service. The corridor from where the choir entered was out of view of the cameras, yet two steps back into this corridor, he could see nearly everything. As the choir members filed by him, P.J. watched the crowd's reaction. There was a hush as the choir took their place on the raised platform behind the altar. The choir looked stunning and they knew it. They swayed back and forth in unison a little better than usual, and their voices seemed more powerful than before. Even the organist got into the glory of the moment, adding several delightful flourishes between verses. P.J. and Woodrow were both smiling at their creation. This place was rockin'! From his vantage point, one thing Joel could not appreciate was just how hideous the green screen appeared behind the choir.

This morning a new twist had been added to the church service. After the choir had finished two songs, the choir director turned around and addressed the congregation.

"Good morning, my brothers and sisters. This is a wonderful day at Rapture in the Round. Please turn and shake hands with your neighbor and tell them that you love them." She paused and waited about two minutes, and then she winked at the organist. The music, the gyrating, and the singing started again. Two more songs and the congregation was primed for the reverend.

Marcus cued Woodrow to come down from the position on the platform, and to make his way to the organ loft since Reverend Hartsell would be up soon. Moments later, he made his way up the steps to assume his position alongside the organist. Once again the organist gave Woodrow that hateful gaze for violating HIS space. Woodrow could not resist the temptation. He puckered his lips like a kiss and said in a taunting fashion, "Ha ha, daddy said I could play up here."

Each verse became louder than the previous one, the choir became more animated, and finally, when the organ music and the singing reached the simultaneous crescendo, Reverend Thomas Hartsell was lifted out of nowhere onto his stage. His arms were held high and he quickly moved down the choir line kissing the ladies and shaking hands with or high-fiving the men. Clearly enjoying the moment, he whispered in the choir director's ear who, in turn, signaled the organist to play one more verse. The congregation was reaching a fever pitch when, from underneath the pulpit, Reverend Hartsell produced a long sash, or more appropriate for this reverend, a "stole." The stole was scarlet and matched both his tie and the accents on the choir robes perfectly. Reverend Hartsell's new suit looked exquisite. Everything was magnificent.

Woodrow's vantage point was awesome. He was able to pan from the choir to the reverend to the parishioners in fluid-like motion. After putting his stole around his neck, Reverend Hartsell worked the crowd like the master showman he was. He raised his hands to the sky, he pointed to parishioners (the beautiful ones), and he danced with the choir. "Amens" and "Hallelujahs" were heard everywhere until the singing stopped.

Reverend Hartsell slowly moved to the pulpit. "Brothers and sisters of Rapture Ministries...brothers and sisters around the world, today is a glorious day. Hand in hand, we are about to embark on a new journey together. Everyone join hands my brethren."

Woodrow caught it all. The choir joined hands and everyone in the congregation did as well. Woodrow called this a "camera moment." Once again, Woodrow could not resist the temptation to piss off the organist. He held his hand out to the organist who got wide-eyed and promptly sat on both of his hands and turned up his "hate stare" a notch. Woodrow bit his lower lip in disappointment. What was it that made him so enjoy pissing off this weasel?

Reverend Hartsell compared Rapture's new journey to that of Moses leading his people to the Promised Land. Clearly the reverend was addressing his new worldwide audience. He chastised those who were lazy or reluctant to join him. Most of all he scorned those who did not share their abundant gifts with their brothers and sisters in need. On and on he went, always coming back to inclusion and to giving. This really wasn't much different from his other sermons, but now he invited those from around the world to join Rapture in this new journey. Of course, the journey would begin in one week and Reverend Thomas Hartsell was both honored and compelled to lead the way. He concluded his sermon with an emotional plea. His voice was quivering and he wiped his eyes as he implored the congregation and those at home to raise their hands if they were willing to take the journey beside him. Of course, everyone raised their hands. Woodrow zeroed in on the more emotional responses for his film.

On cue, the choir director nodded to the organist as the music and singing of *Rapture O' My Soul* filled the building. People emptied their pockets as the collection baskets were passed. Before the song was over Reverend Hartsell motioned for the choir director to stop. Everyone became still.

All eyes were focused on the reverend. "Brothers and sisters, it just struck me. If we are going on our journey together as you have just indicated, it is best that we travel light. Leave EVERYTHING behind. Everything we need will be provided for us. I want those with the collection baskets to work your way forward again. Let's give these good folks an opportunity to leave EVERYTHING behind. Amen." The music and the singing and the giving started again and *Rapture O' My Soul* was sung louder than ever.

As always, Reverend Hartsell ended the service with announcements and an invitation to participate in the upcoming Wednesday evening prayer meeting. As was customary, he singled out those who had "climbed the ladder" and those who had been added to the Wall of Attainment. The doxology was sung and the good people of Rapture were dismissed.

Following the service, P.J. and Woodrow congratulated Reverend Hartsell on a job well done. They promised to return Tuesday to show him the completed webpage.

5

VENUS

Monday morning Judge Dawson checked in on the status of Julius Bennett. It came as no surprise to the judge that Mr. Bennett could not afford a lawyer and was assigned a public defender. Public defenders were assigned on a rotating basis and Julius had drawn the services of a Bradley Hightower. Judge Dawson summoned Mr. Hightower and a representative from the prosecutor's office. The three men sat in agreement that if an impartial DNA expert would validate the finding of the FBI lab, then the two innocent men should be released from Folsom Prison with all possible speed. The judge also noted that Bernard's depression was worsening and cautioned the attorneys that should anything happen to him while he was wrongfully imprisoned, the state would likely face a huge lawsuit. Besides, noted the judge, since the state has already borne the trial costs, did they really want to put the taxpayers through this again?

Bradley Hightower asked, "OK, so if the DNA evidence is irrefutable, and he still won't admit to the crime, then what?"

Judge Dawson was adamant. "Look, the only thing that is certain is that Julius Bennett killed the store owner, and two innocent men are now doing hard time for HIS crime. All these years Julius Bennett has enjoyed being a free man." Judge Dawson fixed his stare on Bradley Hightower. "You can tell Mr. Bennett that he is finally going to have to pay for his transgressions. Make him

261

understand that the only way he can avert the death penalty is through an admission of guilt. He has until noon tomorrow. After that, he will most assuredly die by electrocution, and I will do everything I can to make it happen. Tell him, also, that if Bernard Jones dies, I will find a way to charge him with that as well." Judge Dawson stood. "Good day gentlemen. Mr. Hightower, I will hear from you by noon tomorrow." Once the two attorneys left his chamber, Judge Dawson phoned Lamar Laningham to tell him he would have an answer by noon the following day. Lamar, in turn, called Yolanda who also told Agent Martha Green.

Reverend Thomas Hartsell lay in bed staring up at the ceiling. Next to him was a sleeping twenty year old impressionable young woman who, the day before, had been captivated by the reverend's Sunday performance. She thought he had been filled with the spirit. Last night he did his best to fill her with spirits. She became putty in his hands. She was hardly a challenge to his skills of persuasion. He convinced her to do a lot of things most choir members never think about. Unmentionable things which bring guilt and shame once the liquor wears off. Worst of all, if she knew, these things would make her mother crazy with anger. Especially since her mother was Rapture's choir director. None of this concerned Reverend Hartsell. He was thinking how great the Sunday service turned out yesterday. Everything played out to perfection. P.J. and Woodrow had done their jobs well. He couldn't wait to view the new webpage and the DVD being created by Zenith Productions. He bet he looked great in his new suit with the scarlet stole. A month from now his life would likely be much different. If all went as planned, Rapture should start receiving millions of dollars in donations. His mind wandered, thinking of the possibilities. Perhaps after a few years of global donations, he would finally be able to divorce himself from Rapture and the elders and live the life he deserved.

The lovely young girl next to Reverend Hartsell started to waken. Her name was Venus and she was as beautiful as her namesake. Venus rubbed her eyes and appeared as though she had no idea where she was. She screamed when she saw that Reverend Hartsell was naked and she half gasped and half screamed realizing that she too wore no clothes.

"Oh, no, did we?" She stood covering herself with a sheet. Venus was still struggling to understand how she came to be here.

Hartsell boasted, "We sure did...more than once. You learned a few tricks you can share with your boyfriends." He laughed and pointed to the marks he left on her neck. "You might want to cover those with makeup." There were other marks covered by the sheets which Venus had yet to discover.

"How could you? You raped me. I would never have...I had only one drink."

"Actually you had several drinks." The clonazepam he slipped into the first one made the rest easy. "And please, don't say that you were raped. You are of age to make your own decisions, and if I am not mistaken, that is YOUR car in the driveway meaning you CHOSE to drive here last evening. Speaking of last night, those sounds you were making didn't sound like protestations. It is amazing that I did not get calls from the neighbors. Maybe with all the squealing, they thought I was watching *Deliverance* on television."

"You said we were only going to have one drink and that you wanted to celebrate Sunday's service. Why can't I remember anything? My momma must be worried sick."

Hartsell showed Venus no mercy. "Oh, we did celebrate...several times." He gave her a devious grin. "Telling your mother wouldn't be the best idea either. Especially since she, also, gave a command performance in the very bed you just got up from."

Venus stood aghast, as in shock. Holding the sheet to cover herself, she scurried around picking up her clothes. From the bathroom she heard Hartsell laughing as she dressed. Venus threw up in the driveway and was on her way home in five minutes.

Agent Martha Green took a few minutes to speak with Yolanda before turning the three boxes of evidence over to Aria and Lucy. It was always helpful to have as much information as possible about the crime when inspecting the evidence. Yolanda did not provide much help. Was it because she did not know more, or because she was unwilling to divulge what she knew? Martha decided it was probably the former since the boxes were from Detroit and the fact that they dated back to 1980.

Agent Green wheeled the three boxes on a stainless steel cart from her office to the DNA lab. Aria knew she was coming and she knew that the contents of the three boxes were somehow of importance to the boss. A large examination table had already been cleaned and sterilized in anticipation of receipt of the evidence. The three boxes were all marked "1980 Harris." In addition they were labeled: Box #1/3 Tim and Sally; Box # 2/3 Kate; and Box # 3/3

Miscellaneous. At one end of the table, Aria opened Box # 1/3, and at the far end of the table, Lucy opened Box# 2/3.

"Holy crap!" Aria looked at a variety of clothing which looked as though it had been steeped in blood. Very slowly the clothes were separated from each other. After ten minutes it became clear that there were two complete sets of clothing belonging to an adult male and female. Years ago, after a crime scene had been "cleared," and all of the evidence had been examined, it was frequently saved in case there were questions during court questioning. The collection and preservation of such evidence had not yet evolved to the standards mandated by current protocol. Hence, local authorities developed their own ways of handling evidence. Sometimes it was destroyed. Some localities separated clothing when multiple homicides were found. Other times, victim's clothing items were looked at, then thrown all together into a single box.

Like every other part of crime solving, evidence collection and preservation became a science in itself. Through trial and error, the best ways to process and protect things from a crime scene were developed. Papers were presented, lectures were given, and books were written delineating the best ways to probe and safeguard a crime scene. Years ago, dozens of photographs were always taken at crime scenes. They were a staple of investigative work. Photographs are still important today, but they have been relegated to more of a supportive role. Today science has created many ways to study various aspects of death. There is a teaching facility in Knoxville, Tennessee, which has become known as a "body farm." Donated corpses are left exposed to the elements in a variety of ways so that effects of decomposition can be studied.

Bodies are buried, left on top of the ground, submersed in water, or frozen. Knowing how the elements alter the rate of body decomposition has been helpful in determining the time and circumstances of death. Another of the more "glamorous" fields of study available to detectives is forensic entomology. A corpse left in the open becomes food as well as home for a variety of insects and arthropods. Studying the life stages in the development of these bugs has proven useful in understanding the rate of decomposition of the decaying corpse.

Aria and Lucy were not involved in decomposition. Their specialty concerned the retrieval and identification of foreign materials left at a crime scene. Martha knew that her presence was a distraction, so she left the two women to painstakingly go through the boxes to see what secrets, if any, they might reveal.

As Aria and Lucy were beginning their search for evidence and DNA samples, Mike Cavanaugh at HOT Software began reviewing the two films and the photographs taken yesterday at Rapture in the Round. In addition, at Joel's request, Yolanda provided Mike with the police mug shots of Hartsell, Marcus, and Jesse taken a few years back in Chicago. Her FBI files located these pictures when she searched their arrest records several weeks ago.

About two weeks ago, Joel and Dr. Woodson explained to Mike exactly what they wanted him to create. Essentially, he had to produce a "before and after" webpage and DVD. The "before" of each would be what they wanted Reverend Hartsell to see, the things which Rapture would be sending out to the world. They would reflect the glory of Rapture and provide the source from which donations would pour in from all over the world to be used in the service of mankind.

The "after" webpage and DVD were another matter.

When Venus arrived home Monday, she had to get ready for her college classes. She had a 2:00 PM class in American literature. As expected, her mother was furious that she was gone all night. Venus lied and told her mother that she had fallen asleep at a girlfriend's home and awakened when it was too late to call home. She showered and pretended to study in an effort to avoid confrontation with her mother. Ever since her parents' divorce, Venus's mother never remarried and she became overprotective to a degree which made Venus feel smothered. In the meantime, she was still trying to process how she could have possibly ended up last evening naked in bed with Reverend Hartsell. Why couldn't she remember anything? She prayed she would not become pregnant. As disappointed as she was to have learned that her mother had slept with Hartsell, Venus knew that her mother would be absolutely livid if she found out where her daughter was last night. Everyone knew Venus's mother's temper was legendary.

6

ADMISSION

Reverend Hartsell woke at 8:30 AM. It looked like it was going to be another glorious day. He was hoping it would be a good day for him as well. P.J. Mustav promised to meet him with the nearly finished Rapture Ministries webpage. Once people around the world viewed the Rapture broadcasts on television, they were directed to the webpage for more information on the ministry, free DVDs, and, of course, donation instructions. All major credit cards were accepted as were checks, money orders, automatic deductions and cash. There were even instructions and an online form to make Rapture the beneficiary of a person's estate.

If the television broadcasts were the bait, the webpage was undoubtedly the hook. P.J. had promised a state-of-the-art piece of work and the reverend could not wait to see it. Hartsell realized that he had never taken the time to count the money from last Sunday's collection. Normally, this was a ritual performed on Sunday evenings with Marcus and Jesse. Typically, they would go out to dinner on Sunday afternoon and then, depending on the season, watch either sports or movies in Reverend Hartsell's theater room. Later they would count their plunder and have a few drinks. However, this past Sunday afternoon, the reverend made it known that he would be entertaining a lady friend and he wanted to be alone with her. He didn't say who the lady was, and Jesse, not knowing that Tamayra had gone to Chicago, was fuming inside. He had seen the reverend and Tamayra leaving Rapture last Saturday afternoon, so Jesse naturally assumed she was the lady Hartsell was taking to his home.

A false shelf on Reverend Hartsell's bookcase opened to expose his wall safe. He smiled to himself remembering the extra pass of the collection basket he had requested during the service. He was about ten minutes into counting the money when his telephone rang. It was Tamayra and she would be returning from Chicago tomorrow afternoon. She wondered if the reverend would be willing to take her out for dinner tomorrow, prior to the Wednesday prayer meeting. Of course, he would. They agreed to meet at 5:00 PM at the same restaurant where they previously had drinks. Reverend Hartsell always interpreted receiving calls FROM a woman to mean only one thing. He made a note to change the bed sheets and make sure he had Jack Daniels. He knew he already had a full bottle of clonazepam. Wow, he thought, this WAS a good day. He had a sure thing for tomorrow night, and he had already reached the average amount from a Sunday collection, and there was a substantial amount yet to count. This would be a very good day.

Aria and Lucy were making progress with the evidence boxes from Detroit. Box # 1/3 did not yield much. There was so much blood that it likely would have "washed" away anything which may have been of value. In the pocket of the man's pants Aria found an 1896 silver dollar. She thought to herself that if it had been a good luck coin, it clearly hadn't worked.

Box # 2/3 was the evidence removed from Kate's bedroom. It contained the bed sheets, nightclothes, and a pair of partially charred underwear likely belonging to a teenage girl. The panties were a style not typically worn by adults. The size was also consistent with an adolescent female. When Lucy unfolded the underwear, two distinct types of hair were found. The same two types were found in the sheets. Microscopic examination of the samples validated them as having come from two different people. The portion of the underwear opposite the burned part showed what could possibly have been old traces of semen.

Box # 3/3 had by far the least amount of evidence, yet Aria knew from experience that it could possibly be the one which provided the most leads. This box contained a paper bag with no less than twenty cigarette butts, a wad of what looked like old chewing gum, and one garden style work glove.

Aria decided to ignore box # 1/3, at least for now. Lucy continued to work with the contents of the second box while Aria redirected her efforts to the last of the three boxes. Hopefully, by the end of the day they would be able to begin creating DNA profiles from the scant evidence they had to work with.

Yesterday, after meeting with Judge Dawson and the prosecuting attorney, Bradley Hightower met briefly with his client, Julius Bennett. He explained that the judge ordered the DNA evidence be sent to an impartial private laboratory. Having already given Julius the options available to him, Bradley instructed Julius to begin thinking about what he wanted to do.

Bradley Hightower did not have much hope that Julius Bennett's DNA evidence would exclude him from having been at the convenience store crime scene. The judge convinced Bradley that via the FBI investigation, there was absolutely no doubt that his client had killed Adamos Lazopoulos. Just the same, as a defense attorney, it was Bradley's job to make sure of the facts. One hour ago, the DNA expert from the private laboratory confirmed beyond any doubt that the DNA of Julius Bennett was all over the store owner's apron. All of the facts and the damning evidence were presented and explained to Julius. He was made to understand that there was only one way in which his life would be spared; a signed statement by him admitting to the killing of the old man.

Julius Bennett weighed his options and alternatives, but in the end it came down to one simple question: live or die. He waited until the last possible moment, and then he reluctantly accepted the offer. A police stenographer, as well as a tape recorder, was brought in, and Julius recounted the old story to the best of his ability. He recalled the two boys in the store and the anger of the community and the haste with which the two boys were prosecuted and sentenced. Now, all that anger would be focused on him. The stark reality that his life was over gradually settled upon Julius. He put his hands over his face and wept.

As ordered, Bradley Hightower reported to Judge Dawson before noon. He gave Judge Dawson a copy of Julius's signed confession. Before dismissing the young defense attorney, Judge Dawson called a law clerk into his chamber and told him to immediately call Folsom Prison and begin the procedures to release Bernard Jones and Roddy Jackson. The judge insisted that the two men be released with all possible speed, and on his order, he demanded to know the release date.

Judge Dawson then called Lamar Laningham. During these phone calls, Bradley Hightower sat there silently and just watched. Apparently the judge was done making calls. The situation quelled, and the judge looked up at Bradley, surprised that he was still there.

Judge Dawson blinked a few times and then went to the door of his chamber and closed it. He moved toward Bradley and sat in a chair close to and opposite the young defense lawyer.

"Counselor, I know that you just graduated law school and have only been practicing a year or two, but what you were able to accomplish here today was a remarkable thing. You helped deliver swift and mighty justice and rectify a miscarriage of our judicial system which screamed for retribution. You know as well as I do that our jobs...hell even our lives are nothing but a series of compromises. We make deals with our wives, our kids, and at our jobs. Even what we eat is a succession of trade-offs. You have to sit through a chick flick tonight so that you can play golf tomorrow with the boys; you give up your dreams of having a sports car so you can have a family; and doughnuts reluctantly relinquish their position as one of your breakfast staples in favor of fat-free yogurt. Everything becomes a concession. Yet today son, with your help, we were able to pull off a win/win. Believe me, from where I sit, such a victory is more rare than a sighting of Bigfoot. Your client's life was spared, the taxpayers were saved from a lengthy and expensive trial, and most important of all, two young men who were wrongfully imprisoned for sixteen years will be set free. The State of California allows a maximum payment of $ 100.00 per day which can be paid to victims of wrongful imprisonment, so I will have to determine reasonable compensation." Judge Dawson offered his hand to Bradley. "Remember this day counselor because in our line of work, you get few of them like this. Thank you again."

Five minutes after Bradley Hightower left Judge Dawson's chamber, the law clerk returned and knocked on the door.

"Enter," said the judge.

"Judge, the Folsom Prison people just told me that if all of the paperwork is in order, the two men may be released one week from today. I am already working on it."

The judge smiled. He had one thing to do before he called Lamar with the good news. He went to his bookshelf and selected the *State of California Statutes on Payment for Wrongful Imprisonment.*

Before driving to Rapture to meet with Reverend Hartsell, Joel and Dr. Woodson previewed the final "before" webpage with Mike Cavanaugh. Both men were impressed. "That is why he gets the big bucks," Joel told the doctor as they got into his car.

After a few moments, Joel and Dr. Woodson were climbing the stairs of the Rapture administration building, and they proceeded directly to Reverend Hartsell's office. P.J. knocked on the door and from inside they heard laughing and Hartsell yelled, "Just a minute." P.J. and Woodrow exchanged quizzical looks as they heard sounds like the rearranging of furniture and hurried whispers coming from inside Hartsell's office. After what seemed like two minutes or so, the door opened and a woman, looking quite disheveled and embarrassed, passed between them. Her hair was a mess, her lipstick was smeared, and her blouse buttons were not lined up properly. Obviously Hartsell's secretary, she quickly sat at her desk and did her best to look busy.

"Come on in boys, I was just giving my secretary a little dictation."

"Well put, sir," said P.J. as he pointed to the bottom of the reverend's shirt which was protruding from the zipper of his pants. "It beats shorthand every time."

Reverend Hartsell excused himself and ducked into his office bathroom. He returned in a moment and anxiously asked P.J., "Do you have the final webpage?" He motioned for them to join him at his conference table.

With P.J. in the middle, the three men sat down and repositioned the chairs so they could all view P.J.'s presentation on his laptop computer. The laptop booted up quickly and in a few seconds they were looking at the Rapture Ministries' webpage. It looked beautiful. Reverend Hartsell, in his new suit, stood with his arms raised upward and behind him the backdrop changed from country to country. First, Hartsell was standing in front of Buckingham Palace and Big Ben, then it changed to the Great Wall of China, and then to the Taj Mahal, then to the Eiffel Tower, then to the Statue of Liberty, and then to the Roman Colosseum, and so on. All three men noticed that as the country changed, so did the writing on the screen, to the language of the country displayed. Once the countries stopped scrolling, the backdrop stopped at the altar of Rapture in the Round, showing the choir behind Hartsell in their new gold and scarlet robes. It was sensational! P.J. clicked on the "About Us" dropdown box. This opened to a menu showing the church's address, phone number and contact information. The Rapture mission statement and history of the church were, also, available options. The "Staff" dropdown box, as expected, showed flattering pictures of each staff member next to the Rapture Wall of Attainment. Clicking on the "Rapture in the Round" box started an automatic slideshow of beautiful images of the church, both inside and out, and of the congregation. Many emotional moments caught by Woodrow were added. They included congregation members shouting "hallelujahs," others where they were holding hands, and some where they were tearful. Woodrow, also, included many random photographs of smiling children and seniors, families and friends, all looking happy. All of the pictures had been enhanced and were much nicer than before. The "Missions" dropdown box was not quite finished. P.J. wanted to make it look more personal, and he wanted some pictures from the Wednesday evening prayer service. As before, several of Rapture's chosen missions were showcased. Aside from the pictures of himself, everyone knew that Reverend Hartsell's primary focus would be on the "Donations" dropdown box. Mike used the little man climbing the ladder again, only now the little man had Reverend Hartsell's face. Another new feature had been added. Clouds were now visible and the ladder led up into them. Each time little Hartsell advanced a rung upward, the angelic voices got a little louder and the clouds parted a little more. P.J. decided to ask Reverend Hartsell a ridiculous question. "Would you like to see what happens when he reaches ten thousand dollars in donations?"

"Oh, yes, please," said the reverend.

P.J. entered a ten thousand dollar donation. Little Hartsell slowly advanced up the ladder and the angels sang louder and louder and the clouds began separating. Finally, when the man reached the top rung, *Rapture O' My Soul* was sung by the angels and the clouds opened up. Rays of sunshine came down through the clouds and the little man sprouted wings and flew up into the clouds. The message was clear enough. For a ten thousand dollar donation, you get to go to heaven. Reverend Hartsell beamed with satisfaction.

"What about the television contracts?" Hartsell wanted to know.

P.J. told him, "We are expecting them any time now. Be prepared to sign them as soon as we get them. Of course, we will make sure you get copies."

"Is there anything else?" asked Reverend Hartsell.

"You may want to make some calls to your people to make sure we have a nice crowd here tomorrow. A packed Wednesday night prayer meeting will look good on the DVD Woodrow is producing."

Judge Laningham was ecstatic having received the welcome news from Judge Dawson. He passed along the news to Yolanda. Since it was now late in the day, Yolanda decided to wait until tomorrow to share the news with Martha.

7

OBSTACLES TO FREEDOM

Yolanda summoned Agent Green to her office the first thing on Wednesday morning.   Martha was told of Julius Bennett's admission to killing the store owner and of the scheduled release of Bubba and Roddy on Tuesday, June 18th.

Martha placed a call to the prison. She wanted someone to tell Bubba and Roddy that they would be freed in less than a week. She also instructed the prison official to give them unlimited telephone access for the next week to help them in the transition to the outside. Of course, Bubba had no one to call, but the police records indicated that Roddy had a lot of family in the area.

Reverend Hartsell told his housekeeper that he would be having company this evening when he returned from Rapture. He instructed her to change the sheets and he left her money with which to run out and purchase fresh flowers and a bottle of Jack Daniels. Reverend Hartsell decided to leave his home after lunch. He promised P.J. that he would call some of his parishioners and try to swell the attendance at tonight's prayer meeting. He should have plenty of time to get this done before his dinner date with Tamayra. One final thing weighed on his mind. A week ago he had asked Jesse to put pressure on Lolita for a large donation from her inheritance. Jesse had been so smitten with Tamayra that he totally ignored Lolita. There were only a few days left until he had to come up with money for Zenith Productions, so he decided that now he had better take care of it himself.

The "before" webpage which had been shown to Reverend Hartsell yesterday by Joel and Dr. Woodson was now history. Mike Cavanaugh thought it kind of a shame after all that work, since it was really quite nice. He had now been given three days to transform it into something which would contribute to Rapture's demise. Joel had given Mike a "blank check" to use the dark side of his imagination in any way he chose to accomplish his task. Experience had shown Joel that these were the conditions under which Mike produced his best work. The entire Council looked forward to seeing the results.

Lamar had an idea. Like Yolanda, he had been troubled by the fact that this Bernard (Bubba) Jones would soon be at the mercy of the outside world. He had no job, or any idea how to get one, no money, no marketable skills, and the world was now a lot different than the last time he was a part of it. Yolanda described Bubba to Lamar, based on Agent Green's description, as somewhat of a lost soul. She was convinced that he was too nice and too trusting, and she feared that he would be easy prey and taken advantage of by those who rule the streets. Throughout his entire life, Bubba had been looked after and cared for and told what to do. All that would come to an abrupt end next Tuesday. Lamar thought about the potential ramifications of his idea. It was a longshot, and perhaps unfair in some ways, but if it worked, all the risks will have been worth it. Lamar made the phone call.

Those that do "hard time" and, having completed their sentences, are ultimately released, face many obstacles. For a time, they must report to probation officers. They are given a rigid set of guidelines which, of course, are intended to keep them from associating with people or doing things which would be a bad influence and have a negative impact on their rehabilitation. Sometimes, probation officers check up on their clients in an attempt to keep them out of trouble. Yet, despite all of these efforts and rules, the rate of recidivism is very high.

In old western movies, after a prison inmate completed their sentence, they were set free and could do anything they wished. Typically, once they were out of jail, they moved far away where no one knew them. They started new lives in some out-of-the-way place and became respected citizens. Their sordid past was unknown to anyone. These old movies followed a common story line, so these former inmates were nearly always gunfighters. Although they always seemed to be looking over their shoulders, these characters seemed happy in their reclusive lives until either their honor was threatened or they were recognized by some drifter. Once again, in keeping with the script, the gunfighter would have to put his guns back on one final time to save the town. The gunfighter, of course, always won, and the town was invariably grateful and hailed him as their hero. His past was forgiven and the town welcomed him back into their lives. Sometimes he put his guns away and resumed his boring, but respectable life. More often, however, the gunfighter chose to move on for fear that his presence would attract other bad elements to the sleepy little town.

Unlike the movies, people released from prison are not allowed to disappear or start afresh. Their history of incarceration and past sins become an indelible part of their lives and follow them wherever they go. Most are forced to accept menial jobs because it is the only thing available to them. Regardless of ambition or skill levels, former inmates are held back because higher paying jobs are more competitive and the employers do not hire felons. Police agencies are also notified when parolees are released into their communities. When there is a crime committed, the ex-inmates are always the first ones questioned.

Yet, with all the obstacles they face trying to start their lives over, be they fair or not, the greatest impediment to a successful rehabilitation comes from within them. People coming out of prison, especially those who have completed lengthy sentences, leave incarceration as very different people. Not having had to make decisions for themselves for many years, something as mundane as going to the store or budgeting money for living expenses can be a formidable task. When to wake, when to sleep, when to eat, when to go outside, when to exercise, or even when to shower have all been determined by prison regulations. All choice is taken away and replaced with a regimented schedule which never changes. Many inmates actually learn to like the regimentation. Simple decision making becomes more than they are capable of handling, and returning to prison may be a relief to them. A great many former inmates actually commit crimes because they WANT the security of having all decisions made for them. Unlike the western movies, many are unable to easily assimilate back into their previous lives as free men.

Lamar and Yolanda thought of all these things and how, without serious intervention, Bubba would never be able to make it on his own. Aside from his cognitive limitations, his grandmother's death meant he was totally alone in the world. Bubba was being set up to fail.

Reverend Hartsell arrived at the restaurant first. Actually, Yolanda had been there waiting in her car until she saw the reverend enter the restaurant. She thought it would be a tease to be fashionably late. Five minutes later she went in and immediately saw Hartsell wave to her from the bar. Since he already had a Manhattan, he ordered a Jack Daniels be sent to their table.

"How was your trip to Chicago?" he asked her.

"Boring," Tamayra responded, "although I did see a good play. I met an old friend and we caught up on some things. We were great friends for a time in Miami. Her husband and Gator were teammates, and we stayed in touch after her husband was traded to Chicago. How was Sunday's service?"

Hartsell smiled. "It turned out very well. My sermon was upstaged because the service was being filmed. Prior to the service, there was bedlam in the front rows. Everyone wanted to be seen on TV. The choir was spectacular."

Dinner was ordered, and throughout the remainder of their time together, they continued to lie to each other about their pasts. The only difference was that Yolanda knew the truth about both of them. She was playing a role whereas Hartsell's entire life was a lie. Reverend Hartsell never mentioned ever being in either Chicago or Leavenworth.

After dinner, Hartsell asked Tamayra to join him at his home after the prayer meeting. She admitted being tempted, but she was tired from the flight and would save her decision until later in the evening.

While Hartsell and Tamayra were having dinner, Hector was parked on the road above Hartsell's mansion. He had been there for about two hours and was waiting until all the cars left Hartsell's house. He was there when Hartsell left earlier, but there was another car in the driveway which he didn't recognize. The car was old and obviously nothing that either the reverend or the elders would be seen driving, so Hector assumed it belonged to the hired help. Eventually he saw a woman dressed like a hotel maid come out of the house to smoke. An hour later she got into her car and left.

Hector quickly threw the binoculars in the trunk of his car. He tied a white rag to the driver's side door handle and made his way down the hill with his camera. Just in case, he rang the doorbell, but no one was in the house. The front door was locked, however, the sliding screen door leading to the pool was closed, but not locked. Hector worked quickly. Hartsell's massive living room was a good starting place. After that, he took pictures of the game room, the theater, the bar, Hartsell's master bedroom, and study. Hector noted that there were more sculptures than books, but the office was beautiful just the same. Hartsell's desk was worthy of occupying the Oval Office.

Hector was gone in less than fifteen minutes. Once he was in the car, he realized that if he hurried, he still had time to get to Rapture before the prayer meeting was over.

Once again Yolanda was in the same meeting room as Rosa. The room was crowded with several other parishioners. This time Elder Marcus was the moderator. As usual the film showcased the sick and the starving people in need of Rapture's help. Woodrow

Dennison was in a corner of the room trying to remain as unobtrusive as possible. He was taking videos of the classes to be used in the DVDs Mike Cavanaugh was creating. Marcus's pitch was much like Jesse's which Yolanda had experienced the week before. The film was over and Marcus had just started going from person to person with the collection basket when Reverend Hartsell quietly entered the classroom. He was obviously on a mission. Hartsell spotted Lolita and whispered into her ear and led her by the hand to the rear of the classroom. He sat with his back to the others, but if anyone in the class were to turn around, Lolita was clearly visible. Yolanda positioned her chair sideways so she could see the others and still monitor Rosa without being obvious. After Hartsell had been speaking with Lolita for about a minute, Hector slipped into the classroom and sat in the closest empty seat. He and Yolanda made eye contact and Hector winked. Yolanda expected this would be entertaining. She nodded her head slightly toward the rear of the room. Hector looked back to see Hartsell's back and his mother curled up in a submissive position. Hector looked concerned, but not alarmed. Lolita's voice got softer as Reverend Hartsell's became louder. He could be heard saying things like, "what about those starving children? Did you see their faces?" Later they heard, "while your lawyers are screwing around people are dying." Lolita began shaking. The classroom's focus was now on Hartsell's confrontation, not on Marcus.

Lolita told him, "I got a letter from the lawyers, and they said that these things take time."

"WHAT, you have a letter?" He ripped Lolita's purse away from her. "Let me see it." He started digging through her purse.

Hector sprang out of his chair and moved between Hartsell and his mother. He punched the reverend square on the jaw so hard that Hartsell was unconscious before he fell out of the chair and smashed his head on the floor. Tomas had come to his mother's rescue. He picked up her purse and pointed his finger at Marcus. "One step and you're next," warned Tomas. He took his mother by the arm and walked her out.

"Well, I can't beat that!" said Tamayra, and she also walked out. That ended the prayer meeting as well as any thoughts Hartsell may have had of putting clonazepam in Tamayra's Jack Daniels.

8

ADVANCE ON THE INHERITANCE

Once again Agent Green was summoned to Director Tubbs' office as soon as she arrived at work. Martha was extremely pleased to learn that Bubba was scheduled to be released next Tuesday. However, like Yolanda, her excitement was dampened in the knowledge that Bubba had no one to help him, nor any support system in place to help him succeed outside of prison. Yolanda spoke to Martha of her friend Hector who had expressed an interest in possibly helping Bubba. Hector was looking for an assistant to help him with his landscaping business. However, he first wanted to meet Bernard to see if they would be compatible. Director Tubbs took the liberty of having Hector come by to meet with Martha. Yolanda thought that it would be helpful to have Martha and Hector go and visit with Bubba prior to his release to gauge how he might react to working with Hector. Martha was pleased that someone had shown an interest in helping Bernard. Yolanda said that Hector would be in the office in about an hour. She asked Martha to call Folsom Prison and make the arrangements for her and Hector to visit with both Bernard and Roddy.

Reverend Hartsell felt as though he had been hit by a truck. His mouth throbbed and his teeth felt loose. In addition, the back of his head hurt and he could feel a huge welt. He consumed several drinks the night before, and although they may have put him on the fast-track to sleep, they were now contributing to the anguish he was feeling. Trying to replay yesterday's events in his mind was fuzzy. He recalled the wonderful Rapture Ministries' webpage and counting the money from last Sunday's collection. He had looked forward to a date with Tamayra. Next to him, the bed had not been slept in. The Wednesday evening prayer meeting came back to him. He had been speaking with Lolita when...yes that was it. Lolita's son Tomas hit him. That was the final thing...no wait. He remembered being in the backseat of his car, and Marcus helped him to get into the house and into his bed. Marcus made him drink two...three Manhattans?

Hartsell sat up. He dangled his feet over the side of his bed. He felt faint.

Agent Green went down the corridor from her office to the DNA lab. Aria felt confident that she and Lucy would have definitive information for Martha by the end of the day. Their preliminary tests revealed the DNA of no less than five people from the crime scene evidence, but whether this preliminary testing would yield usable DNA profiles remained to be seen.

Martha's pager beeped and displayed Ruth's telephone number. She used the lab phone to call Ruth and was told that Yolanda's friend Hector had arrived and was waiting in her office.

"Thanks, Ruth, I am on my way."

Director Tubbs was speaking and laughing with a young Latino man who seemed nearly as broad across the chest as he was tall. He turned to face Martha and she saw the biggest smile and the whitest teeth she had ever seen. He thrust his hand toward her.

"Hi, I am Hector Martinez, and I am traveling to Sacramento with you to meet Bernard Jones." Hector said it like they were going to an Oakland A's game, not a prison. Martha was unable to discern if his unwillingness to say "prison" was rooted in naiveté or in supreme confidence.

"Hello, I am Agent Martha Green. Have you ever been to a prison?" She became embarrassed realizing the question came out nothing like she meant it. "I am sorry, what I meant was..."

Hector cut her off. He and Yolanda looked at each other and burst out laughing. "I think I know what you meant," Hector continued, "but I did do seventeen years in the military if that counts. No apology necessary."

Wow, thought Agent Green to herself. There was nothing at all naïve about this man. He could possibly be the most confident man she had ever met.

Yolanda excused herself. "Look, I have a lot to do, and you two have an hour to get to know each other. Have fun."

"I'll drive," said Agent Green. We might as well put the gas on the government's tab." In ten minutes they were on Interstate 80 Northeast headed toward Sacramento. It did not take Martha long to explain how she became involved in the life of Bernard Jones. Yolanda had thrust the convenience store murder on her as sort of a test case. Martha had been assigned to the Santa Molina division of the FBI as a cold case investigator, and Yolanda wanted to see what she could do. Martha admitted to Hector that she had become personally attached to Bubba just from speaking with him.

She felt terrible for what had happened to him and she felt inclined to try and make things right.

"I guess that's where I come in," said Hector. "As a Navy SEAL, I developed kind of a kinship with making things right. As SEALs, we sometimes participated in large scale operations. Normally, we were sent in before an assault to identify targets or maybe to neutralize enemy defensive positions. Most of the time, however, the SEALs operated in small surgical clandestine operations against the world's bullies. These were not military leaders or organized opposition forces trying to overthrow their government. They were street thugs with very sophisticated weapons who operated exclusively for their own pleasure and profit."

Hector explained to Martha that a great preponderance of his operations as a SEAL were not part of wars. They were small missions, designed to rid the world of bullies and terrorists. Typically, they were small groups of bandits or pirates who wanted to satisfy their desires the easy way. If someone has something you want, you simply get a gun and take it. Villages were pillaged, women raped, and adolescent males were recruited by kidnapping, sometimes forced to kill their own parents as a show of loyalty. Most of the time, without their guns or posse, Hector believed bullies were cowards. Hector told Martha that he was unsure if the feeling was always there, or if it blossomed during his time as a SEAL, but Hector developed a soft spot for the "underdog." This was why he was here with Martha today. If Hector could help Bernard, and if Bernard was willing to work hard for the business, this just might work out.

Martha pulled into the now familiar Folsom Prison visitor's parking lot. Once inside the prison authorities explained that due to the circumstances regarding the pending release of the two men, special arrangements had been made. They were told that Bernard and Roddy had been given unlimited phone privileges. In addition, they were allowed outside their cells all day and were allowed to go outdoors whenever they wished. Today the "one visitor at a time" rule was waived, allowing Martha and Hector to visit together with each of the two men. After her first two visits here, it almost seemed to Martha that Folsom was trying to atone for its part in this travesty of justice. The words "wrongful imprisonment" were never spoken. Law enforcement and the judicial system got caught with their collective "pants down," and all of a sudden everyone was running around playing nice, as if to say, "It is not MY fault." Oddly though, the demeanor of the prison guards never changed. They knew what was happening, and yet they still spoke in single syllable monotones and looked at the visitors with those drawn, faraway, zombie-like stares. The guards also continued to appear that doing their jobs was a life-threatening inconvenience.

Roddy was brought in first. Since Hector had no business with him, he was only an observer. Martha explained to Roddy the details of his release and of the confession of Julius Bennett. Roddy demonstrated no joy or relief that he was being freed. Instead, he was angry. He reiterated his belief that the outcome of their trial was predetermined because he and Bubba were both black. Martha had to agree that it certainly appeared to be a contributing factor. Roddy had good reason to be angry. The best years of his life had been taken from him. He wanted to know how those that put him here were now going to make things right with him and

289

Bubba for what they had been forced to endure. Martha explained that sometimes states gave monetary compensation for wrongful imprisonment, but that would be up to Judge Dawson. What Martha did not explain was that accepting the state's offer of compensation required a signature which guaranteed that former inmates would not be able to hire an attorney to sue for ten times the amount they received.

While Martha understood Roddy's anger and feelings of betrayal, she pleaded with him to focus on his freedom. She warned him that being released with all this hostility would make his transition to the outside much more difficult. Nothing Martha said had any impact on Roddy. He was angry, and he was five days away from being released into the world that had rejected and imprisoned him. Once Roddy left the room, Hector looked at Martha and said, "I would give that man a wide berth. He is as nasty as a junkyard dog with an axe he has been grinding for sixteen years."

A few minutes later, Bernard Jones was brought in. As big as he was, he always appeared as though he was expecting to be punished for something. Some dogs have a sad, pleading look which is a dead giveaway that they chewed your new shoes or pooped on the carpet. Bubba had that look. Martha made the introductions, but Hector's presence clearly made Bernard more uneasy. Agent Green asked Bubba if he was aware that he was to be released from Folsom Prison next Tuesday. Bubba said that he had been told of his release, but since his grandmother had passed, he didn't know what he was supposed to do or where he would live.

Martha attempted to calm him. "Well, Bernard, this is why Hector is with me today. He has a small landscaping business, and he needs a strong helper. He mows lawns, trims bushes, and plants trees for people, things like that. Do you think you would like to try that?"

Bubba looked nervous. "I ain't never had no job before. I wouldn't know what to do. Where I growed up there weren't no grass or bushes. I don't know nothin' 'bout that."

Hector felt pity for Bernard. "Look, Bernard, I can really use your help. Don't worry about not knowing how to use the mower or anything else. I can teach you everything you need to know. I can pick you up each morning until you get your own driver's license. Martha and I can help set you up in a small apartment and help you get what you need. What do you think Bernard, can we help each other out?"

Bubba seemed incredulous. "You means a real job, like I gets paid fo? An you will finds me a place to live? Why would you do dis fo me?"

Hector gave Bubba that big smile. He was beginning to like this big guy. "Like I told you, Bernard, or would you prefer that I call you Bubba? I need your help, too. We can help each other. What do you think?"

"I likes to be called Bubba cause dat is what my grannie called me. Yes, I would likes a job and a place to live. I will work hard fo ya."

"Good," said Hector. I will come and pick you up on Tuesday.

Martha was pleased. She even thought she saw a trace of a smile as Bubba stood and was led out by a guard. On the way out Martha thanked Hector for what he did.

"Don't thank me, Martha. If that man can work half as hard as I think he can, I will make out just fine."

On the way back to Santa Molina, Martha and Hector brainstormed about how they could set Bubba up and help him succeed. They spoke of getting him an apartment and furnishing it to make him comfortable. Martha could take him grocery shopping and help him learn to cook simple meals. They both admitted that it was sort of exciting. Hector and Martha divided up the tasks needed to get Bubba started.

Dangling his feet over the side of the bed did nothing to ameliorate Reverend Hartsell's dizziness or his throbbing headache, so he laid back down and slept for two more hours. Sometime after 10:00 AM, he was startled awake when the phone started ringing on the nightstand next to him. The caller was persistent, and after six rings, to stop the noise, he answered it. "Hello, what is it?" he managed to say.

"Hello, Reverend Hartsell, this is Lolita Zapata. I am calling to apologize for my son's actions last night. He is very protective of me and he has a bad temper and he thought..."

"Never mind what HE thought, I should sue him."

"Oh dear...I only called to tell you that I called my brother's lawyers and they said that I could get an advance on my inheritance this Monday. I felt bad for you and wanted to help those poor children, and..."

Again Hartsell interrupted Lolita. He sat up in bed and forgot about his aches and pains. "How much are you getting?"

"I asked for two million dollars...I hope that's enough...those poor children." Lamar and Colleen Laningham were sitting with Rosa and coaching her through the phone conversation. Lamar listened on an extension phone and wrote responses for Rosa to say.

Hartsell continued, "Well, two million is good...why can't you get it all?"

"The lawyers were understanding, but as I told you before, they said that all aspects of my brother's estate had to be closed before all of the money can be released. They have to wait to make sure any liens are satisfied and so on. However, they felt that since the estate was so large, an advance of two million dollars would not be a problem."

"I appreciate what you did Lolita, but you should have pressured them for more. When can you get me the two million?"

"Sometime on Monday. Maybe earlier if you and my son can drive to the lawyers?"

Hartsell's pain returned. "No, no. Monday will be fine. Thank you." Hartsell hung up the phone and then made the earliest appointment possible with his dentist. He would see him tomorrow.

Lamar told Rosa, "Sounds like the reverend has had enough of your son for a while."

"Did I do alright?" asked Rosa.

"Honey, you convinced me." Lamar smiled at Rosa. "You were wonderful. A few more days and this will all be over." Lamar and Colleen thanked Rosa and told her that her part in the ruse against Rapture was over except for one final thing. Lamar explained to Rosa that he had given Hector thirty thousand dollars from the money which Hartsell had given them. When this was all over, Rosa and Hector were to deliver the money to her sister-in-law Francisca, and her two friends, Stella and Anita, ten thousand dollars each. This money was intended to replace what Hartsell had extorted from them.

When Martha dropped Hector off in the FBI building parking lot, they had already developed a rough game plan of how they planned to help Bubba assimilate back into society. Before heading home, Hector planned to drop off the pictures of Hartsell's mansion to HOT Software.

Martha stopped by the DNA lab before going to her office. When she and Hector left for Folsom earlier in the day, Martha knew that Aria and Lucy were beginning to create the DNA profiles from the Detroit evidence. She was pleased to realize that they were now done. Tomorrow she would be able to determine if anything might be worth running through either the CODIS Offender Index or the Forensic Index. Martha had already experienced enough excitement for one day.

9

1896 SILVER DOLLAR

Martha Green began processing the DNA profiles from the Detroit evidence as soon as she arrived at work on Friday morning. Like Aria and Lucy, she knew that this information was, somehow, of great importance to her boss.

Just as Aria had told Martha previously, there were a total of five DNA profiles found. Of course, three of those profiles were from the victims; Tim, Sally, and Kate Harris. These profiles were removed from further investigation. Martha ran the final two DNA profiles through both the CODIS offender and forensic indexes to locate possible matches. Three hours later, Martha had a match. Tyler Hayes was found in the CODIS database as having been a convicted felon in the State of Michigan. Martha pulled up his file on her computer. Tyler Hayes had an impressive rap sheet, but not a lot of convictions. From his rap sheet, it appeared that he had been in and out of trouble since he was a teenager. Martha made notations for Yolanda that Tyler's DNA was taken from the cigarette butts in evidence box 3/3. The hair samples and old semen stain from the charred underwear in box 2/3 were from a different individual, but whoever they came from was not in the CODIS database.

Agent Green brought this information to Director Tubbs. She asked Yolanda if she wanted her to proceed further with the investigation and possibly contact Detroit.

"No, thank you, Agent Green. That will be all for now."

Somewhat bewildered at Yolanda's response, Martha left her office.

Hector's mother made a big breakfast. It wasn't so much that Rosa thought breakfast was the most important meal of the day. When she made large breakfasts, usually on Fridays, her son hung around and talked with her. Rosa enjoyed that.

Rosa told Hector of Lamar and Colleen's visit yesterday. She explained how they had asked her to place a call to Reverend Hartsell and promise him a lot of money. She was both relieved and a little sad that her part in the Rapture charade was at an end. Rosa also told Hector that she was excited to deliver all that money to Francisca and her two friends.

Hector told his mother of his trip with Agent Martha Green to Folsom Prison. He described Bubba and how he has spent half of his life in jail for a crime he did not commit. His mother looked sad as Hector described how everything seemed stacked against Bubba from the color of his skin to his mental deficiencies and the death of his grandmother. Hector planned to hire him to help him with the landscaping. Since his father's death, Hector had operated the business by himself. In addition to having help with the work, Hector was looking forward to the company Bubba would provide.

It was easy for Rosa to see that her son was drawn to Bernard Jones. All his life, he has had a soft spot in his heart for those who needed help. Hector was always the one who brought home stray dogs or birds with broken wings. Hector was also the one who played with the kids that the others rejected. He was always proud to be a fan of the underdog, but Rosa believed that it was those people who were drawn to her son, not the other way around. They could sense his kindness and his patience. Many times he protected them as well. Rosa recalled all the times her son had come home bleeding with his clothes torn and soiled. These were not from fights he instigated. They were always a result of Hector interceding between a bully and his victim.

"You like this Bubba, don't you son?"

"I do, Mom. I cannot ever recall seeing anyone so beaten down and with so little hope. He is not aggressive or dangerous. He is shy and scared of the world and everything in it. Honestly, Mom, I just think he wants someone to trust and to take care of him. This Tuesday may totally freak him out."

Rosa asked, "Why don't we let him stay in your brother's room, at least until he gets on his feet. You can teach him landscaping, and I can teach him how to cook and clean. If he stays here a while, he can save a little money to help him get on his feet. More importantly, maybe we can help him regain trust and show him that someone cares about him."

Hector now realized where his compassion came from. "Are you sure, Mom? This is a big decision."

"Absolutely, I think it will be fun. And you know, once you have been a mother, taking care of people kind of grows on you. We may not have a lot, but we have always been willing to share. You have always been a very good judge of character, and if you think Bubba is OK, than that's good enough for me. I will start getting his room ready."

Hector was blown away. Maybe this was why he never married. How could he improve upon her?

Reverend Hartsell's dental appointment was at 11:00 AM. Someone was kind enough to cancel a previously scheduled appointment, freeing up an hour for him to be seen.

"Damn," said Dr. Adam Shinebarger, "who hit you, Muhammad Ali? I can see you are hurting, so I want to get you numbed up before I inspect the damage." He administered two injections of lidocaine and said he would return in ten minutes. For a man of action like Reverend Hartsell, waiting in a dental chair for ten minutes seemed like an hour. Eventually, Dr. Shinebarger returned and looked into Hartsell's mouth.

"These three teeth are quite loose. There is always the possibility that you might lose them, but I think we will get lucky. I will splint them and check you again in two weeks. In the meantime, you can have no gum, taffy, or anything chewy. You know the drill. And stay away from whoever did this to you. One more hit like this one and your teeth will be lost." Dr. Shinebarger gave him a prescription for a narcotic analgesic which he promised would make him sleep. Hartsell had the prescription filled at the pharmacy next to the dental office.

Although he didn't feel like it, Reverend Hartsell had one more stop to make. He drove to the Golden Gate Savings Bank and asked for two hundred and fifty of the bands used to wrap ten thousand dollar stacks of one hundred dollar bills. The reverend's mouth was still numb, but the teller did his best to understand him and convince Hartsell that the bank would be happy to wrap the bills for him.

"Besides," the teller said, "the bank insists on removing the bands to count the money anyway," so Hartsell's wrapping the money would be counterproductive.

Reverend Hartsell's head and mouth still hurt. In addition, his mouth was still numb from the lidocaine, so when he spoke, he sounded like Elmer Fudd. His credibility suffered further from the steady trickle of spittle which ran down his chin onto his shirt. The bank teller did his best to remain professional, but he eventually lost control.

Hartsell said "Pweese donne laffe."

The teller laughed so hard that tears welled up in his eyes, and he started slapping the counter with the palm of his hand. A bank manager noticed the commotion and sent the still hysterical teller to the break room. Unlike the teller, this manager knew Hartsell was not one to trifle with. He handed the reverend a tissue and pointed to his own chin. Once again, sounding like he had a mouthful of cotton, Reverend Hartsell was slowly able to make the bank manager understand what he wanted. The manager went to a wall cabinet and gave Hartsell a large bundle of the ten thousand dollar bands. Furious at his treatment and being laughed at, Reverend Hartsell yelled "waaht hassouls," and stormed out of the bank. The bank manager was able to hurry to the break room before he, too, burst out laughing. He said to the teller, "Pweeze, wet me haab wat I assephor." They started all over again.

It was Friday, June 14th, and three days till **G Day**. The Council was meeting to make the final preparations for bringing down Thomas Hartsell and Rapture Ministries. Judge Laningham looked terrible. Clearly exhausted, his face betrayed his lack of sleep. To a few of the Council members at the round table, he also appeared thinner.

"We have a few subjects up for discussion this evening," Lamar said as he collected himself. "Forgive me, but I think I may be coming down with the flu. Dr. Woodson, would you and Joel bring us up to date on Rapture?"

"Sure," offered Dr. Woodson. "Joel and HOT Software are now putting the finishing touches on the new and improved versions of both the Rapture webpage and the DVDs. They should be a hoot. I only wish we could be there to witness his reaction, but then again, that might prove to be dangerous. By the way, speaking of dangerous, that is quite a right cross you have there Hector! Wednesday night he went off script and knocked Hartsell out cold."

"Sorry about that." Hector was tentative. "But she IS my mother, and Hartsell was getting physical with her."

"Sorry, hell," said Yolanda. "You did Tamayra a big favor. She was trying to figure a way to get out of going to that creep's house. We had dinner earlier, and he was persistent trying to get me to go to his house after the prayer meeting. I think maybe he was looking to give Tamayra a little donation of his own. Anyway, Hector, your right cross saved the day for me."

Dr. Woodson continued. "Saturday morning Joel and I deliver the bogus TV contracts for Reverend Hartsell's signature. We will tell him that we will copy them and "overnight" the originals to the three networks. Also, on Saturday, we will show Hartsell the 'before' DVD. He will be told we need it back to make him a thousand copies.

Joel added, "Then, on Monday, we pick up the money and give Hartsell the contracts, the webpage, and the DVDs. We already know that Hartsell is going to put counterfeit money with the real money. Yolanda caught the good reverend copying money in his office."

The Council members looked at each other to see if anyone else had anything to add. Lamar raised his left hand. "OK, then, if we are finished with Hartsell, the second issue I would like to bring up is one Yolanda and Hector are already familiar with." Judge Laningham stopped and experienced a coughing spasm. The coughs came from deep within him and shook his whole body. He coughed politely into a handkerchief. Dr. Woodson left the table for a moment and returned with a glass of water. The judge took a few sips of the water. It helped. He put the handkerchief on his lap. Only Dr. Woodson saw the streaks of blood on it. Lamar continued. "Yolanda has been blessed with a new cold case investigator. This investigator specializes in looking at old evidence using new technology. Using the DNA from old evidence, they were able to set free two men who were in jail for a murder they did not commit. In addition, the DNA from the old crime scene evidence was able to lead them to the killer. Yolanda, will you take it from here?"

"Glad to," she added. "As the judge pointed out, in addition to using this new technology to solve today's crimes, we are sometimes able to successfully revisit old crimes. Sometimes...not always. Yolanda reached into her pocket. She brought her closed hand up to the table. While her hand remained closed, she locked eyes with Joel and slid her hand across the table to him. She took her hand away exposing an 1896 silver dollar. All Council members' eyes were now fixed on Joel. The color drained from his face. Joel could hardly speak. He picked up the coin like it might break, and turned it over in his hands. "I...I haven't seen this since my father let me hold it."

Yolanda's voice became an apologetic whisper. "Joel, please forgive me. I had no right to do this without first obtaining your permission. Lamar and I spoke and decided to first ascertain whether or not the old evidence would produce any usable DNA. If we had found nothing, we would have dropped the whole thing. We requisitioned the old evidence from your family's crime scene. My DNA team was able to create one DNA profile and it was a match for a man who is now in the Ryan Correctional Facility in Detroit. This is where we left it Joel. We may not be successful and we will not proceed with this unless you want us to. What would you like us to do?"

Joel was still carefully inspecting the coin. He raised his head and his eyes were filled with tears.

CHAPTER SIX

1

COUNTING CASH

Reverend Hartsell slept in late again on Saturday morning. The pain pills from Dr. Shinebarger's prescription were a tremendous help in relieving his pain, but as the dentist had warned, they made him sleep. Hartsell was supposed to meet P.J. and Woodrow at his office at 1:00 PM, and then Jesse and Marcus were to meet him there at 3:00 PM. His head did not hurt anymore, and while his teeth hurt less, his mouth was still swollen. The reverend was sure he would be able to deliver his sermon tomorrow, but he would have to rely more on the wireless microphone since it would be a strain to shout.

Now that his pain was manageable, Reverend Hartsell could focus more on **G Day**, now only two days away. If the projections for donations were even close to expectations, within a year he should be rich beyond his wildest dreams. Reverend Hartsell fantasized about all that money and the wonderful things he would be able to buy himself. He thought how it might seem to people if he was enjoying a life of splendor, while asking "regular" folks from around the world to send him money. Hartsell came to the conclusion that it would be more prudent for him to squirrel away millions of dollars without detection until he could finally give up pretending to be a reverend. A Swiss bank account was what he needed!   As he showered, he came to the realization that he needed a game plan. He needed a concrete goal, a specific amount of money which would satisfy his needs and his dreams. Once that goal was reached, he would retire...perhaps on an island or in the French Riviera. He would go somewhere where beautiful women congregate. Oh, the women he would be able to attract! The hot water felt wonderful on his back.   After all those years he lay dreaming in cell number 103 on C block, everything was finally coming to fruition. He would start developing his "escape" plan soon. How wonderful that he was able to consider it at such a young age. He couldn't wait to rid himself of Jesse and Marcus. He looked at them as lead weights attached to a great bird. True, they had been together a long time, but he could see no reason to include them in his new life. After all, they contributed nothing except their loyalty all these years, and you cannot "spend" loyalty. Besides, he owed them nothing. He had taken care of them very well. Soon it would be time for him to shed the lead weights and soar to the heights where he belonged.

Brushing his teeth brought Reverend Hartsell back to the painful reality of the moment. In a few hours he would meet with P.J. and Woodrow to finalize everything. He could not believe that his dream was so close. In his bathrobe he opened the refrigerator looking for something soft. He wondered how you open a Swiss bank account.

Several miles away, Joel and Dr. Woodson were having Mike Cavanaugh walk them through the "before" DVD so they could show it to Hartsell. Judge Laningham purchased an expensive leather attaché case to put the three television contracts in when they were to be delivered to Hartsell to sign. Everything was ready.

Rosa spent a few hours removing personal items from her son Roberto's old bedroom, and she carefully wrapped each item and put them in large storage bins. Many of the items evoked pleasant memories of when her two boys were young and her husband was still alive. Rosa thought that removing these items would give Bernard the opportunity to personalize the room to his own liking. She also felt that removing Roberto's mementos might make their new guest feel like he was less of an intrusion into the lives of the Martinez family. Hector purchased an inexpensive television for the room as well as some t-shirts, underwear, and shorts which Bubba could wear. Finally, Hector purchased a variety of toiletries that Bubba would need and left them on top of the dresser.

Reverend Hartsell arrived at the Rapture office at 12:45 PM. Ten minutes later, P.J. and Woodrow arrived. Getting right down to business, P.J. unzipped the leather attaché case and removed the bogus television contracts. Each contract was written on expensive-looking paper bearing the recognizable logo of each network. Small yellow cellophane arrows were affixed to the places requiring Hartsell's signature.

"As you can see, everyone has already signed the contracts except you." P.J. pointed to the first of the cellophane arrows. "Woodrow is a notary public, so he can witness your signatures. Once you have completed signing the documents, we will reproduce them in their entirety and give you the copies." P.J. slid a pen toward Hartsell and waited till he and Woodrow had signed all of the papers. As each document was completed, P.J. quickly put them back into the leather case.

P.J. zipped up the leather case and directed his eyes on Hartsell. "As we previously explained to you, Zenith Productions has already paid for the first month of airtime for each of the three networks. Each of the individual networks will be contacting you, probably this next week, to make arrangements with Rapture to continue the process." P.J. was attempting to divert the subject away from the contracts. "With the amount of money we expect will be coming to you in all forms, from all over the world, make sure your security is in order. I suggest you run a background check on anyone who will be helping you with the money." P.J. allowed Hartsell a moment to fantasize. "OK, then, let's show you the DVD."

Woodrow removed the small disc from its plastic container, and P.J. inserted it into the laptop tray which then automatically disappeared back into the computer. In a few seconds the laptop booted up and Reverend Hartsell was shown with Rapture in the background. Just as it was shown in the webpage, one-by-one the countries of the world receiving the Rapture broadcast were shown behind him. Once this ended, Hartsell's voice was heard describing Rapture Ministries' crusade against sickness and famine around the world. Reverend Hartsell disappeared from the screen, and each of Rapture's chosen missions were shown, complete with the sad photos of the sick and the dying. The pitiful pictures, including Mozambique, continued from location to location. At the end, Reverend Hartsell, sitting at his desk, gave a heartfelt talk describing how it was everyone's responsibility to help. In an attempt to be more optimistic, he spoke of what a concerted worldwide effort could accomplish through donations in ameliorating the world's suffering. The DVD demonstrated what various levels of donations could bring in terms of relief. It suggested making a personal goal of climbing the donations ladder to reach the Wall of Attainment. Hartsell was pleased with the DVD. One could be sent to everyone who made a donation. More than anything else, Hartsell was anxious for the money to start coming in, and he could not wait to get started.

P.J. told him, "Everything is in place, and everything is done. Monday morning is less than two days away. Woodrow and I will meet you here at 9:00 AM on Monday. We will bring you the laptop with the webpage already on it, the DVDs, and the contracts. We have a 10:30 AM flight on Monday to New York City and we cannot miss it. Please have the two and a half million dollar balance you owe us ready so we can have a local bank wire it to Hollywood for us. Under no circumstances can we miss that flight. It has been a pleasure working with you." Both P.J. and Woodrow shook hands with Reverend Hartsell knowing that they only had to see him one more time.

Elders Jesse and Marcus met Hartsell at 3:00 PM in his office as they had been ordered. Hartsell explained to them that he had absolutely no intention of paying Zenith Productions another two and a half million dollars. He had a stack of five hundred one hundred dollar bills on his desk. From underneath his desk, he produced the sheets of counterfeit money he had made a week ago on the copy machine. Hartsell assigned Jesse the task of carefully cutting out the bogus bills while Marcus counted the bills and separated them into stacks of ninety-three bills each. Reverend Hartsell had purchased a very nice dark blue leather weekender carrying bag which, he determined, would nicely accommodate the cash. He carefully took the stacked piles which contained ninety-three counterfeit one hundred dollar bills. He added a real one hundred dollar bill on both the top and the bottom of each stack. Finally, he wrapped each completed stack with one of the bands he got from the bank which indicated TEN THOUSAND DOLLARS.

The work was both tedious and kind of silly for Marcus and Jesse. They felt like kids playing with pretend money. Reverend Hartsell, on the other hand, took it quite seriously. This little game of stacking and wrapping money was saving him two million four hundred and fifty thousand dollars. A nice start, he thought to himself. Adding this to the two million dollars Lolita would deliver to him on Monday would total nearly four and a half million dollars which would be a nice opening deposit for his Swiss bank account.

"How is your mouth, boss?" asked Marcus. Boy, that Tomas really nailed you the other night."

Incredulous, Jesse laughed. "You mean that little guy, Tomas did that to you?" He continued to laugh at Hartsell.

Being laughed at yesterday by a lowly bank teller, and now by his underling brought Reverend Hartsell to instant anger. Normally, Hartsell prided himself in being able to keep his emotions in check. However, the stress involved in getting to **G Day**, the larceny he was about to commit against Zenith Productions using counterfeit money, and two days of constant pain, culminated into instant fury. Jesse was caught totally unaware. Reverend Hartsell jumped to attention and instantly assumed a very threatening position directly over an already cowering Jesse. Hartsell clearly chose the former of the "fight or flight" choices when the adrenal glands pump epinephrine through the bloodstream. Extreme stress creates this endogenous reaction in the human body, and the secretion of the hormone prepares us to instantly attack or to flee

308

from the threatening stimulus. Hartsell's muscles were tensed, his fists were clenched, and he screamed at Jesse.

"You stupid idiot. All these years I have taken care of you and provided for you, and THIS is how you treat me? You haven't the brains or the ambition to do anything for yourself, and I take you under my wing and buy you nice things, and make your life comfortable, and THIS is how you repay me?"

Jesse had his arms covering his head in a defensive position preparing himself to be hit. Marcus backed away neither understanding the confrontation nor wanting any part of it.

"What did I do, boss?" Jesse was pleading and doing his best to comprehend what was happening. "I only meant that you are so much bigger than Tomas and it seemed funny that he could..."

Hartsell pointed to his jaw. "Oh, so you think that THIS is funny?" He slapped the top of Jesse's head quite hard. "Is this funny too? How come you are not laughing?"

Jesse could still not fathom a reason for Hartsell's wrath against him. "What did I do?" he yelled.

"What?" screamed Hartsell. "Well, first of all, two weeks ago, I gave you specific instructions to put some serious pressure on Lolita Zapata to get us some money from her inheritance, and did you follow my instructions? No, you did not. You, instead, chose to put the moves on Tamayra Wilson. Lolita walked out of the prayer meeting, and you never even talked to her. Did you honestly think that a woman like Tamayra could possibly be interested in YOU?" Hartsell was relentless. "She told me herself that you were second-string, and that she was buddying up to you to get to me. So because you let your one-eyed trouser-mouse do your thinking for you, I was forced to confront Lolita myself. Her son apparently took exception to my methods which I had to employ because of YOUR incompetence." Again he pointed to his jaw. "And this is what I got because of you. And the second thing you ruined for me was an evening with Tamayra. I was taking her home with me after the last prayer meeting. Apparently the sight of me out cold, bleeding on the floor dampened her desire. YOU caused that. Now get out of here before I give you a jaw like mine."

Jesse quickly got up and hurried out the door. Marcus resumed counting and stacking the counterfeit bills. All the screaming had an adverse effect on Reverend Hartsell's mouth and it started throbbing again. He and Marcus worked in silence until the 250 stacks were neatly arranged in the leather weekender bag.

2

WHAT'S THAT SMELL?

Jesse was unable to sleep more than a few hours on Saturday night. Following his castigation from Hartsell, he began drinking. He was hurt, humiliated, and worst of all, berated by someone to whom he had given years of loyal service and friendship. Jesse had been very fond of Tamayra, and he thought that his feelings had been reciprocated by her. It became clear to him why he had seen the two of them leaving Rapture in Reverend Hartsell's car last week. Still quite drunk, Jesse had to prepare for the Sunday service. After the browbeating he received yesterday, he dared not shirk from performing his responsibilities today. Jesse was able to shower without mishap, but as he was dressing, he stubbed his toe hard on the leg of his bed frame. He shouted all his favorite obscenities as he hopped around the room. Jesse called Marcus and asked him to pick him up. He told Marcus that he had been drinking all night after the fight with Hartsell and he was unable to drive.

Forty-five minutes later Marcus was at Jesse's door. Jesse looked disheveled, and his tie looked like a child had made the knot. Marcus was unable to convince Jesse that he should stay home. Jesse knew that not showing up at the service would evoke additional wrath from his boss. Jesse teetered and breathed stale alcohol on his friend as Marcus did his best to straighten his tie and make him appear presentable. On the way to Rapture, Marcus made Jesse promise to maintain a low profile and do only what was

311

absolutely necessary to get through the Sunday service. Jesse agreed and couldn't wait to return home to his bed.

The Rapture choir had their own bathrooms and changing rooms for both the men and the women. The women's room had a long line of toilet stalls, and a counter with four sinks and a mirror which ran along the entire counter. The choir included thirty women and getting their hair and makeup perfect could be an ordeal. This morning, Venus was touching up her makeup and listening to an eighteen year old friend of hers brag about how she had been invited to Reverend Hartsell's home to go swimming after church. To discourage her friend from making the same mistake she experienced with Hartsell, Venus described in very graphic terms what the reverend had done to her resulting in deep humiliation and shame. Venus told her friend how Hartsell had laughed at her and boasted that he had, also, slept with her mother in the same bed. She had been raped, and the only way it could have happened was Hartsell introducing something into her drink. She would NEVER have consented to such a thing. Venus begged her friend to not go to Hartsell's home. Venus added that the only reason she did not go to the authorities was because she was fearful of what her mother might do. The two girls left the bathroom still talking of Venus' horrific experience. The choir director flushed the toilet. She had been in the last bathroom stall, and she heard every word that her daughter Venus had said.

Jesse was still angry at Reverend Hartsell. He intended to do only what was expected of him and then return home to sleep. He had already put the bulletins in the front of the church and unlocked all the doors. He was now on his way to change the number on the "Countdown to G Day" banner. Jesse was still tipsy and he nearly dropped the stepladder. He was able to successfully position the stepladder directly underneath the banner, but he failed to spread the legs of the ladder to their full extension. He took the white number "1" from the box of countdown numbers and very slowly started up the ladder. Very carefully he removed and dropped the previous number to the floor. Jesse was thankful that this was the last time he would have to do this. He slowly stretched and tried to hook the "1" in the proper place. To be so high on the ladder and not have the ladder legs extended properly made everything very unstable. Once again, Jesse stubbed his already sore toe and he lost his balance. He thrust out his right hand in an attempt to balance himself, and in doing so, he accidently broke the "G" off the top line of the banner. The ladder tipped and he yelled "Oops" just as he was forced to jump from the ladder. This didn't help his sore toe, and he was suddenly overwhelmed with dizziness. Jesse was barely able to crawl under the choir platform before he violently expelled the contents of his stomach. The smell was so vile that it was about to make him heave again, so he backed up and sat for a few seconds. After a few moments, Jesse was able to collect himself. He picked up the stepladder and staggered away surprised at how much better he felt.

The Laninghams decided that it was in the best interest of the Council that they attend the Sunday service at Rapture one final time. Sheldon and Jessica Lortz entered the church for the last time. Should anything unexpected happen, at least someone from the Council would be there as a witness.

After a few minutes, the organist began playing and the choir came out. The choir took their places on the raised platform, but instead of swaying to the music, they gave each other disgusting looks trying to figure out the source of that repulsive smell. The choir slowly began singing, but several members did not join in since they were still fighting the ill effects of breathing in the repugnant odor.

A few people in the congregation started laughing and pointing toward the choir. They kept on pointing and whispering to those next to them, and within a few minutes, all of the parishioners were roaring with laughter. The disruption caused the organist to cease playing. At first the choir thought that THEY were being laughed at, but one of the choir members turned around and joined in the laughing. Soon all the choir members had their backs to the congregation and were staring up at the Rapture Countdown Banner. Jesse had accidently broken off the "G" from the top row of letters, but instead of falling from the banner, it became lodged with the lower letters making the banner read:

RAPTURE IN THE GROUND

In the back of the church, Jesse too, figured out the source of the disruption. He teetered, belched, and said another "Oops." After a few minutes and a good laugh, things calmed down and the choir sang as best they could still in the midst of the god-awful stench. After a few more songs, Reverend Hartsell was raised to the altar area. As usual, he acknowledged the congregation and made his way along the choir members. When he approached the choir director, she slapped him across the face so hard that through his wireless microphone, it was heard all through the church. Reverend Hartsell dropped to his knees and spit out two of the three teeth previously loosened by Hector.

"That's for me AND my daughter," said the choir director. She grabbed Venus by the hand and together they hurried from the church.

The congregation watched in horror as the service came to an abrupt end. No one had a clue as to the reasons why these things had taken place. Lamar and Colleen Laningham were glad that they decided to visit Rapture one final time. Since they weren't exactly sure why the countdown banner was like it was, or why the choir director hit Hartsell, they didn't know how to explain these things to the Council. Nonetheless, it was entertaining.

Marcus and Hartsell spent the rest of the evening trying to figure out how everything went so wrong. Hartsell understood the actions of the choir director, but he mistakenly thought that Venus told her mother what had happened between them.

Thankfully, the reverend still had some pain medication from Dr. Shinebarger's prescription. Tomorrow he would have to make another appointment with the dentist, but at least he would be able to get some relief until then.

Monday morning, Marcus and Reverend Hartsell were anxiously awaiting P.J. and Woodrow. At 8:55 AM they arrived carrying a large box. They were all smiles as they set the box on top of the conference table. P.J. said, "The box contains a laptop with the live webpage installed as before. We have added a few last minute enhancements which we know you will enjoy. We have included a case of the DVDs for you to begin sending out as you wish. Finally, the copies of the three television contracts with the networks are in the bottom of the box. We have left you contact information in case you have any questions." P.J. paused, "I know

315

you will be pleased with what we have done, and we have enjoyed working with you. I don't mean to be rude, but Woodrow and I have a plane to catch." Reverend Hartsell put the leather bag on his conference table. He zipped open the top and spread the bag open revealing stacks upon stacks of one hundred dollar bills.

"Thank you P.J. and Woodrow. You have made our dreams come true." Hartsell closed the bag, zippered it, and handed it to P.J. In about one minute, Joel and Dr. Woodson were driving away. Reverend Hartsell tried to smile. He said to Marcus, "Rapture Ministries is now a worldwide enterprise."

Marcus cut the packing tape with his jackknife. Joel purposely had the box taped to make it more difficult to open. The plan was for Joel to be long gone by the time they got the box opened. Inside the box, Reverend Hartsell found a second box with a DVD in a plastic sleeve on the outside. Obviously, this was the case of DVDs. Next Hartsell found the laptop. Marcus pulled up a chair and the reverend booted up the computer.

As before, Reverend Hartsell came up on the screen, and one-by-one, famous landmarks of different countries came up behind him. However, this time Hartsell morphed into a devil. The skin melted away from his face and hands being replaced with red scales. Two shiny black horns came out of his head, and his eyes became black and lifeless like those of a shark. His teeth became pointy and his nostrils grew wide and spewed smoke. The creature's body expanded ripping off the clothes. More scales covered the rest of his body, and he sprouted a long tail with an arrow shaped spike on the end which whipped back and forth. Once again, the pictures behind the Hartsell devil began scrolling;

316

only now they were pictures of Leavenworth prison, Hartsell's palatial mansion and Rapture in the Round. Every time the Hartsell devil reached upward, he was rained down upon with green bills and gold coins. Behind Hartsell, the choir began singing with voices which sounded like the munchkins from *The Wizard of Oz.* Their little voices sang *Capture O' My Dough* as the money kept coming down. Hartsell and Marcus stared at each other in disbelief.

"This must be some kind of a joke," said Hartsell. He clicked on the "About Us" dropdown box. The screen showed Reverend Hartsell and the Elders intimidating parishioners during the Wednesday evening prayer services. Reverend Hartsell was clearly shown ripping Lolita's purse from her and then Hector punching him in the face. The "Staff" dropdown box illustrated the Leavenworth mug shots of Hartsell, Marcus, and Jesse, complete with their rap sheets which detailed their crime histories. The "Missions" dropdown box scrolled through all of Rapture's chosen missions, and written underneath the screen showed the amount donated by Rapture to date. Of course, each was zero. Strategically inserted between each mission was one of the pictures which Hector had taken inside Hartsell's home. They were labeled as "Hartsell's theater room," "Hartsell's swimming pool," "Hartsell's game room," and so on. Hartsell slammed his fists on the conference table. "My home...how did they get pictures inside my home? If this is meant to be a joke, I do not find it funny." Finally, he clicked on the "Donations" dropdown box. The little Hartsell devil climbed the ladder and his little tail swished back and forth as he gnashed his pointy teeth and kept saying "gimme gimme." Each time he moved up a rung, the little angel's munchkin voice got louder and louder. At the top rung, the voice erupted into *Capture O' My Dough.*

"Try the DVD boss," suggested Marcus.

Hartsell became more and more angry. He ripped the DVD from the box and inserted it into the laptop's tray. Once again Reverend Hartsell's image came up, and it appeared as though he was on a hillside addressing a lot of people. Across the bottom of the screen, words moved right to left...*Watch Reverend Hartsell as he delivers the SERMON ON THE AMOUNT...Watch as he delivers his MEatitudes...*The picture changed to one of his house, and underneath it read...*Blessed is MY mansion.* Then the screen changed to a picture of the bag of money he gave to P.J. two weeks ago...*Blessed is MY money*, and so on. Hartsell slammed the cover closed on the laptop. "I will find those two who did this and I will kill them." He removed the television contracts from the bottom of the box. By this time nothing came as a surprise. He thumbed through the pages and they were nothing but gibberish. He saw things like "Rapture in the Round... hereinafter referred to as Ripoff in the Round," and "we agree to air this broadcast as soon as pigs can fly."

Reverend Hartsell's office door was open, but a member of the janitorial staff knocked on it anyway.

"WHAT DO YOU WANT?" screamed Hartsell.

The janitor took a step backward, clearly afraid. "I am very sorry, reverend, but some nice lady named Lolita said you would be waiting for this. He pushed the box into the office with his foot and ran away. An envelope was taped to the top of the box. He read the card.

"Roses are red, violets are blue.

318

Enjoy your cash, you dumb-ass old fool."

Love, Lolita

Hartsell was confused. He opened the box, and the janitor who delivered it, already quite a distance away, stopped abruptly. He could hear Reverend Hartsell's blood-curdling scream. Inside the box was two million three hundred and twenty five thousand dollars...in counterfeit one hundred dollar bills.

Hartsell was searching his brain. All of these events...all of these people had to be working together...but how, and more importantly, why? Slowly Thomas Hartsell came to the realization that he had been beaten at his own game. He had lost all of his cash, the equity in his two homes and the church, and he was nearly broke. Thomas Hartsell racked his brain trying to figure out who P.J. Mustav, Woodrow Dennison, Zenith Productions, and Lolita and Tomas Zapata really were. Considering his own motivations and priorities in life, he assumed that whoever did this to him did it for the money. That is, until the next day. On Tuesday morning, June 18th, 1996, Reverend Thomas Hartsell received a priority mail envelope. Inside the envelope was a very special thank you from the Mozambique mission for his generous donation of two million four hundred and seventy-five thousand dollars. This represented the balance of the money which Lamar was keeping in his safe plus an additional fifty thousand dollars from the top and bottom bills from each stack within the bag of counterfeit money. Hartsell sat and let the thank you letter fall to the floor. His money had vanished and now, so did any hopes of being able to recover it.

Tuesday morning Judge Dawson called Lamar Laningham to tell him of his decision to award both Bernard Jones and Roddy

319

Jackson with wrongful imprisonment compensation. Each was to receive two hundred and fifty thousand dollars. Lamar immediately forwarded the good news to Hector and Yolanda. The judge also requested a Council meeting at his home for the next Friday evening.

3

FULL CIRCLE

Bubba was excited to leave Folsom Prison. Hector was supposed to pick him up at noon. All of the belongings he cared to bring fit easily into a printer paper box which a guard had given him. A guard came to get him at 11:30 AM, and Bubba took one final look at what had been his home for the last sixteen years. The guard slammed the door to Bubba's cell. How many thousands of times had he heard that sound? Hard-time prisons have earned the nickname "slammer" because of that unique sound and the utter hopelessness associated with it. Bubba didn't yet know it, but that familiar metal-to-metal sound would haunt him in his dreams for years to come.

The final walk from his cell through the corridor connecting all of the cells was surreal for Bubba. Every single prisoner stood at their cell door as he passed. It was like a review of the troops when the President of the United States visits a military installation. Some of the inmates nodded as he passed, but most just stared at Bubba. They apparently just wanted to see what "freedom" looked like. It struck Bubba as odd that the first walk **to** his cell sixteen years ago, and his final walk **from** his cell today to freedom were backwards. Logic would dictate that entering prison would be a sad occasion. However, Bubba remembered that as he "passed in review" all those years back, the atmosphere was jovial. There were cheers and sexual taunts welcoming him to his new home. Now, on his way out, one would think it would be cause for celebration. Yet as

Bubba passed by, it was rather solemn. There were no smiles, no well-wishes or goodbyes.

As he was processed out, Bubba had to sign the necessary papers, but within a few moments, he could see the sky through the windows as he passed.

Hector had been waiting in a holding area for about fifteen minutes. Although there were dozens of chairs, he chose not to sit. He knew that it had to be a lot worse for Bubba, yet Hector could not help feeling anxious.

After what seemed like forever, and having passed through a whole series of locked steel doors, Bubba stood face-to-face with Hector. Hector gave him that famous smile and shook Bubba's hand for the first time.

From the moment he first got into Hector's car, it was like Bernard had passed through some crazy time warp where everything was now new and different. There were shapes and colors he had never seen except in books or magazines. In fact, after sixteen years pretty much everything WAS new. Bubba had only been in a car a few times in his life. His grandmother never owned one, and before he was sent to jail, most of his friends were too young to drive.

"Before we head home, allow me to have the honor of buying you your first cheeseburger and fries." Hector smiled, "I know that it would be MY first stop if I was away for a while."

To say that Bubba enjoyed his first "taste" of freedom would be an understatement. He made no attempt to hide his delight as he savored every morsel of his lunch. The remainder of the trip home was spent giving Bubba an idea of what was expected of him. Hector described his landscaping business and different aspects of the job. He also discussed the wrongful imprisonment compensation which Bernard was soon to receive from the State of California. Hector strongly suggested that Bubba open a savings account and deposit the money there until he became comfortable on the "outside." While that much money could be considered a blessing in helping him get started, it could also get Bubba into a lot of trouble. "Besides," Hector told him, "I will be paying you, remember?"

The time passed quickly, and when they pulled into Hector's driveway, he could see his mother, anxiously awaiting the arrival of their new guest. Rosa flashed the Martinez smile and held out both hands. "Hello, Bernard, I have been looking forward to meeting you. Welcome to my...our home."

Council meetings were seldom like this one. Everyone had a story to tell with respect to their role in the Rapture Ministries adventure. They knew that Hartsell must have tortured himself trying to determine exactly what had happened to his dream. Lamar described the dramatic irony in the Rapture countdown banner. Again, no one knew of Hartsell's adulterous behavior with either Venus or her mother, so the choir director's assault on Hartsell was a mystery to them. It was noteworthy that after learning what Hartsell had done with her daughter, the two women filed rape charges against Reverend Hartsell. The newspaper article indicated that three more yet unnamed young girls had come forward with similar allegations. When the police arrested Thomas Hartsell at his home, they found several videos taken of Hartsell

323

with the young girls as well as half a bottle of clonazepam on a shelf with the liquor bottles in his bar. The paper also said that although Hartsell could have been released on bail, he could not afford it, and thus far, no one had volunteered to pay it for him.

Hector was happy to report to the Council that Bernard Jones was doing very well adjusting to his new freedom. Granted, it had only been three days since he had been released, yet it was unmistakable how pleased he was to be free. Hector said that twice he had gotten up in the middle of the night to go to the bathroom and discovered that Bernard was not in his room. Looking all over for him the first night, Hector finally found him on the front porch. He asked Bubba if he was unable to sleep.

Bubba pointed up at the stars. "I haven't seen them since I was a kid." Hector understood, and left him alone.

Hector smiled at Yolanda. "You can tell Agent Martha Green not to worry about him. My mother treats him like royalty. She has taken up her fancy cooking again, and Bubba can't get enough. I honestly don't know which of them is benefiting more from the other's presence. Since Dad died, Mom and I have slowly settled into a routine. However, Bubba has now changed all that, and it has had a very positive effect on my Mom. Oh, and one more thing. She refuses to call him Bubba. She says that name was from his old life. Now he is either Bernard or Bernie." Lamar and Yolanda both appeared to be pleased.

Judge Lamar came to the real reason for the Council meeting. Joel had been given a week to decide whether or not he wanted to pursue following the DNA leads in his family's murders. It had been a very long time, and Joel had been told up front that there were no guarantees if the case was re-opened. Everyone knew Joel would want to follow the evidence, wherever it led them.

Lamar knew this would be Joel's response. That's what he would do as well. "OK, but before we continue, we should gather more information. Yolanda, I need you to find a way to make this a federal issue. If the FBI has jurisdiction in this case, we can utilize your people and your resources to our advantage. Let's do this. Yolanda, contact your people in Detroit and find out everything you can about the guy who was the DNA match. Once we have a complete profile on this guy, perhaps Yolanda and I can pay him a visit at his current penal residence. Let's plan to go see him next weekend."

Yolanda answered, "OK, I will clear my schedule. With respect to making this a federal issue, I don't think it should be a problem. Joel is now a resident of California, and the evidence has already crossed state lines. Also, since the case is so old, it shouldn't be contested, but if it is, I will remind Detroit that they have had sixteen years to solve this case already. Besides, WE are the DNA experts. Director Resque has already been very cooperative, and I am sure he will help us with anything we may require."

Lamar stood. "Joel, we will keep you informed of everything. Everyone, let's meet here again in two weeks. Let's see...that's Friday, July 5th.

4

TYLER HAYES

Judge Laningham boarded the plane with Yolanda early the following Friday morning. She had prepared a dossier on Tyler Hayes and had a second copy for Lamar to review during the five hour flight.

Tyler Hayes was currently finishing a sentence in the Ryan Correctional Facility for aggravated assault. He had attempted to collect a gambling debt using a tire iron. His rap sheet was not indicative of someone prone to violence, at least not before the assault which landed him in prison. He did not strike either Yolanda or Lamar as someone who would commit murder, yet stranger things have happened. For Joel's sake, they hoped that something substantive would be learned from this trip.

During the flight, the judge indicated how much he liked the approach suggested by Judge Dawson in interrogating Julius (Jewels) Bennett, so they decided to try it with Tyler Hayes. Old evidence from the Harris crime scene had been looked at using new DNA technology. Since Tyler was now serving time on a felony charge, Michigan state law stipulated that his DNA profile had to be entered into the federal CODIS database. From here it was easy. The DNA from the old crime scene was a conclusive match to Tyler's. Neither Yolanda nor Judge Laningham believed that Tyler murdered Joel's family, but he most certainly was there. More importantly, he knew who did it. Everything hinged on Tyler believing that HE was to be charged with rape and three counts of murder. This was the only leverage which they had to get to the real killer.

The original police report was of little value. The original detectives intuitively surmised that there were at least three perpetrators. The choice of robbing the Harris home appeared to have been a random act, but considering the crime rate of the area, they eventually got around to robbing just about everyone, some more than once. Since no fingerprints were found, they had obviously worn gloves. Nothing more could be gleaned from the old evidence. If they were going to uncover the killers of the Harris family, it could only come as a result of the successful interrogation of Tyler Hayes.

The Ryan Correctional Facility was a relatively new prison. Opened in 1991, even its outward appearance betrayed the fact that its original intent was not to incarcerate inmates. Instead, it was built by Daimler Chrysler as a storage building for cars and was later converted, to the dismay of people living in the area, to its present use.

Lamar Laningham and FBI Director Yolanda Tubbs were expected visitors, and they were able to successfully bypass most of the check-in procedures required by "regular" visitors. They were taken directly to a small conference room where inmates normally met with their attorneys and families. In about five minutes, Tyler Hayes was brought to them. His hands and feet were both shackled and connected by a chain which ran around his midsection. The ankle restraints made him walk with a pitiful shuffle. Tyler wore the required orange jumpsuit and his buzzed haircut looked recent. He sat opposite Yolanda and Lamar, and although he gave them a quizzical stare, he did not speak.

"Good afternoon, Mr. Hayes. I am FBI Director Yolanda Tubbs, and this is Judge Lamar Laningham. We have come a very long way today to share some information with you and hopefully solicit your cooperation in solving a very old crime. Long ago, sixteen years to be exact, on a hot summer night, you and two or more accomplices forced your way into the home of Tim and Sally Harris. While your intent was to rob them, we think things may have gotten carried away, and you slit their throats and then raped and killed their young daughter." Yolanda paused, both to measure Tyler's response as well as to give him a minute to bring forward some very old memories.

"You don't know what you're talking about. I don't know anything about any murders."

"Oh, but you WERE there Tyler," said Yolanda. "And you were kind enough to leave a little bit of yourself behind which we found and were able to match to you."

"What are you talking about, what was left behind?" Tyler was becoming agitated. Yolanda was getting to him and they both knew it.

"Your DNA, sir. It's a kind of photograph which is unique to you and proves you were there. Cigarette butts were found and collected from all over the crime scene. These were from cigarettes smoked by you. If I am not mistaken, you smoke non-filtered Camels." Yolanda shifted her eyes from Tyler's to the pack of cigarettes rolled up in the sleeve of his jumpsuit.

Tyler began shifting in his chair. "So what are you going to do, put me in jail?" He looked at Lamar who so far had said nothing. "Who are you people, and what do you want from me?"

Lamar took over. "You are here on a charge of aggravated assault and are scheduled to be released in a year or so. Director Tubbs and I will be here until 1:00 PM tomorrow. We then must return to California. Please listen carefully because we will return tomorrow to see you. We will be here at 11:30 AM. At that time you will have a decision to make. Simply put, your decision will be to cooperate with us or not. Look, we are going to figure this out with or without your help. Neither Agent Tubbs nor I believe that you killed the Harrises. But you WERE THERE, and you know who did it. If tomorrow you decide to cooperate with us, you will not be charged with murder, but as an unwilling participant in a robbery gone bad. Should you choose not to cooperate, you will be charged equally with the others when we find them." Lamar paused for effect. He tried to recall the look he gave quarterbacks as a linebacker back in high school. The look said "you're mine, and if you run, I will make it worse for you." Lamar continued. "Look, those people who were murdered were the entire family of a dear friend of ours. We will find whoever did this one way or another. The offer we gave you expires tomorrow at 11:30 AM. We will NOT make it again. Good day Mr. Hayes."

Yolanda and Lamar rose and walked out. Once they were out of earshot, Yolanda whispered to Lamar, "OK...let's see if he takes the bait."

Tyler was brought back to his cell. In one hour it would be scheduled time for inmates on B block to make phone calls to families and friends. Tyler had to get his thoughts straight before he made his phone call. He knew that the FBI lady and the judge were very serious. He also knew that his DNA left on the ancient cigarette butts definitely tied him to the Harris family murders. From conversations with other inmates, it was clear that there was no denying DNA evidence. Over and over he tried to think of a way out of this mess. There was none. Long ago on that summer night in Detroit, he and his cousin Marty Dehimer had been out looking for a good time. They became involved with Matt Dwyer. Neither of them had known Matt previously, and they could have no way of knowing he would involve them in killings. Tyler and Marty thought they were simply going to steal beer money. Tyler remembered running away after the killings. He hid in his home for three days waiting for the police to come. Matt was more bold. He told Tyler and Marty that he would never be caught because he was smarter than the police.

A guard came to Tyler's cell and asked if he wanted to call anyone.

"Yeah, thanks." Tyler was escorted to a wall of telephone cubicles. Each cubicle had one chair and a small counter to write on. Most of the other cubicles were already occupied by other inmates and Tyler had no way of knowing that the guard had purposely led him to this particular telephone cubicle because this was the one which the FBI had ordered bugged. Both the phone number and the conversation were recorded by order of the FBI.

Earlier in the week, Yolanda had called Detroit FBI Director Avery Resque and explained her intentions. It was Director Resque's idea to bug the prison phone. It was hoped that Tyler would attempt to call the other men who were with him that night to alert them to the new investigation.

"Marty...this is Tyler. Listen carefully. I have some very bad news...." Tyler explained to Marty that the FBI had re-opened the old investigation. The FBI lady who visited him had a personal connection with Joel Harris, the son of Tim and Sally who had been killed that night. Tyler explained the choice which he had been given: cooperate or become an accessory to a murder charge.

"Do they know about me?" Marty asked.

"No, but they will because I am going to tell them...I have to. Look Marty, I am due to get out of here in about a year. Cooperating with them will no doubt add more years to my sentence. You will also have to do some time. But I WILL NOT be executed or receive a life sentence for what that psycho did. They said that they know I was not involved in the killing."

Marty asked, "How can they know that? Maybe they think that I did it!" He sounded scared.

"They will know that you didn't do it because I will tell them that. I have no choice. And neither do you. The only way to get out of this is to tell the truth. You may as well turn yourself in because tomorrow I am going to tell them everything. Let Matt go to jail for what he did, but I am not going to be a part of it."

"Matt will kill us," said Marty.

"He won't if he is in jail, and I will put him there tomorrow."

Lamar and Yolanda were played the phone conversation from the jail between Tyler Hayes and his cousin Marty Dehimer. Director Resque was with them in a conference room of the Detroit FBI building. He pushed the button ending the recording. "Wow, folks, that was easy. Good call on bugging the prison phone if I do say so myself. Where would you like to go from here?"

Lamar interjected a thought. "It all starts with Tyler Hayes tomorrow. It sounds as though he is going to play ball. From what we have heard, it appears that two young men got hooked up with a very bad man. Let's listen to what Tyler tells us tomorrow. If he tells the whole story, let's give him an opportunity to have his cousin, this Marty guy, surrender to us. There is no way they won't serve time for their participation in this crime, but if everything goes our way, we can offer leniency. However, their stories must jibe, and they must tell us everything. This third man, Matt, is the one we are after.

Lamar spent a very restless night. He coughed up blood-streaked phlegm all night long. Drinking sips of water helped to slow the spasms allowing him to cat nap. Yet what he really needed was deep sleep...refreshing sleep. What bothered him the most ...apart from the exhaustion was the pain. Lamar had promised his wife, Colleen, that he would tell her once the pain commenced. Dr. Woodson told them together that the arrival of the pain signaled the beginning of the end. Thus far, he had been able to keep his secret from the other Council members, but soon, very soon, this would all change. Everything about his lung cancer thus far had been insidious. The arrival of symptoms reminded him of those movie trailers you see on TV which are meant to tease. At first, his coughing started as a throat-clearing process. The cough, like the trailer, was just a taste of what was to come. Hardly even bothersome at first, it progressed to spasms which soon became difficult to control. Now he was unable to stop them as he previously could. These coughs emanated from deep within him and made him shake violently. The bleeding came the same way. Hardly noticeable at first, he thought he likely ruptured a small vessel straining to stop coughing. Soon there were streaks of blood which he was easily able to hide from others. Now the blood was obvious. Copious amounts came frequently.

Finally, it was the pain's turn. The triad of lung cancer symptoms was complete. Just like the coughing and the blood, it was hardly noticeable at first. Lamar rationalized the pain as a response to the deep coughing. Soon the pain was there whether he was coughing or not. And now the pain became radiating. The core of the pain was always there, but with increasing frequency, it would "awaken" and send out bolts of searing electricity which he was unable to hide. The end was coming. Lamar knew it, and soon, so would everyone else. He decided that this would be his final Council mission. Somehow it seemed fitting that it would be to serve justice to one of the five.

Morning came, and with it were Lamar's constant companions; exhaustion, and more recently, pain. Later today he would return home and seek rest. He would then tell Colleen of his pain knowing the effect it would have on her, and he would visit Dr. May to get something to relieve it.

Lamar met Yolanda in the hotel restaurant for breakfast. They were hopeful that Tyler would cooperate and lead them to the maniac that killed the Harris family. Both Lamar and Yolanda tried to remain mindful of the fact this was about justice for Joel. Aside from finding the killer and bringing him to justice, they had to remain sensitive to their friend's feelings.

There really wasn't much to discuss in terms of a game plan. Everything had already been presented to Tyler. Whatever happened next would be up to him. It was Yolanda's idea that they not share the fact that they had eavesdropped on Tyler's phone conversation with Marty. This would help gauge his level of truthfulness with them. It, also, made no sense to broadcast the fact that prison phone calls were monitored.

Detroit FBI Director Avery Resque was very gracious and he lent Yolanda one of the agency's cars for their two days in his city. Saturday morning they arrived at the Ryan Correctional Facility at 11:00 AM. Once again, Tyler Hayes was promptly delivered to the conference room. Tyler wore the worried look of someone who was in an impossible situation, yet who was desperately attempting to find a way out.

"Good morning, Mr. Hayes," began Yolanda. "Judge Laningham and I have a plane to catch in a few hours, so we don't have a lot of time. We gave you a choice to make yesterday. You were involved in the murder. Are you to become an accomplice to a triple murder or an uninvolved accessory? It's your call."

Tyler was tentative. "If I tell you everything, how much time will I get?"

Lamar answered. "That will be determined by the judge. Between five and ten years will be added to your current sentence. Of course, your level of cooperation will have a direct bearing on our recommendations to the judge. I will tell you this; one lie, a single falsehood, or any attempt to deceive us, will result in removal of any recommendations for leniency from us. You have control over your destiny."

"OK, I will tell you everything I remember. It was a Friday night. I remember, because it was the start of the weekend. My cousin Marty and I were just out looking for a good time. You know, we wanted to get some beer and hang out. There was this guy who lived in our neighborhood, and he had a car and told us how we could score some easy cash."

"What was his name?" Yolanda was taking notes.

"Dwyer, Matt Dwyer. Anyway, he told us that he did this kind of thing all the time. He gave us gloves and told us not to take them off. We were to follow him and do exactly what he said. Matt told us that we were going to scare some folks, take their money, and leave. No one would get hurt, and we would get enough money for the whole weekend. So Marty and I went with Matt. We cruised around for a little while until Matt pulled into an alley and stopped. Matt got some duct tape from his trunk and we quietly walked down the alley until he said, 'this is it.' We went into a backyard and up onto the back porch of a small house. We knew that the people were home because we could hear them laughing and we could hear their television. The door was opened but the screen door was locked. Matt listened for a few minutes and then he took out his knife and cut the screen. He stuck his hand through the screen and unlocked the latch. The TV was loud and there was no way they could have heard us. Matt was in the living room and standing over the man and his wife with his knife before they had

335

time to react. The lady screamed at Matt and he told her to shut up because we only wanted their money and no one would get hurt. Matt made the man hold out his hands so that he could duct tape his wrists together. They had a daughter who heard her mother scream and ran downstairs. She was told that we were just looking for money. Matt made the girl wait while he finished taping her father's wrists and ankles. He then put tape over the man's mouth and his eyes. The same procedure was done to the man's wife. Matt told me to stay and watch over the parents while he ordered the girl to take him and Marty room to room looking for valuables. They looked through the downstairs first. I think they found some money hidden in the refrigerator. Next Matt ordered Marty and the girl to go upstairs. Once he heard them up there, he quietly slit the throats of both parents. I have never been so horrified in my life. Never have I seen so much blood. It was everywhere. And Matt did it as easy as you order ice cream! What he had done didn't faze him a bit. I would have run away right then except that I was afraid that Matt would have done the same thing to me. Besides, my cousin was still upstairs. Matt told me to stay where I was and keep a look out. I heard the girl scream, and a few minutes later, Matt and Marty came downstairs. I didn't need to ask. The look on Marty's face told me that he had, also, killed the girl. They took some stuff and we all ran out the back door to the car. Matt took us home, but not before we made him pull over so we both could puke our guts out. He laughed at us and called us rookies. When he dropped us off, he said that he would do the same thing to us if we said anything to anyone. We knew he meant it. And do you know what? Except for talking to Marty about it, I have never said a word."

Lamar asked Tyler a question which he already knew the answer to. "When was the last time you spoke with Marty?"

"Actually, I called him after you left yesterday. I told him that the cops were on to us and that I didn't want to get executed for what Matt did. He knows that I am telling you everything."

Yolanda thought for a moment. "OK, Tyler, here is what I want you to do."

5

SECRET DESIRES

Prior to returning home to Santa Molina, Yolanda met briefly with Director Resque to discuss strategy. They had every indication that Tyler was going to cooperate with them. Next, they wanted to question Marty Dehimer and determine the whereabouts of Matt Dwyer. Yolanda and Avery both agreed that if the stories of Tyler and Marty matched, and if they were forthcoming with all the details of the crime, then they would ask for leniency for both men. Yolanda asked that Marty be given a few days to turn himself in before Avery arrested him. In the meantime, Director Resque went all-out to locate Matt Dwyer.

Like every other city, large or small, Detroit was a city filled with people that had needs. While everyone shares the mundane needs of food, clothing, and shelter, some individuals have very special and secret desires which need to be satisfied. Large sums of money often changed hands, fulfilling the lustful cravings of those able to pay to be pleasured outside the realm of the ordinary. The rewards for those willing to satiate such covert desires could be substantial. Of course, discretion, secrecy, and customer satisfaction were tacit fundamentals of this dark trade.

Aside from "normal" prostitution, which is paying for sexual gratification in any number of ways, there are people who crave stimulation in ways which are light years away from what most people refer to as "kinky." Many of us would think of these acts as perversions or the antithesis of pleasure. Such activities may include, but are not limited to, pain, torture, humiliation, bondage, or even acts which conceivably could bring someone precipitously close to death. As unusual as it may be to find someone who enjoys such things, it is equally uncommon to find someone willing to accept remuneration to participate in or be the object of such unseemly activity. This is the basis upon which Matt Dwyer founded a specialty service. For a substantial fee, Matt has developed an ingenious way of bringing such people together.

Matt has created an extensive list of clients, as well as a stable of men, women, and, yes, even children, who are either willing or forced to cater to his client's cravings. Over recent years, Matt had, through trial and error, been able to improve upon the delivery of his unique service. Now his clients refer their friends to him, and the pleasure business is booming.

Several years ago Matt was actually a customer who paid for an evening's entertainment with a young woman named Jolene. During a brief intermission in the carnal phase of their relationship, Matt and his lovely seductress founded a fledgling business. Jolene described other customers with very unique desires which Matt and she could, using a little creativity, mutually satisfy. Matt and Jolene had complimenting talents and affiliations that could be used in combination to fulfill a not-so-public service. Matt had tremendous connections. He knew people who could provide illicit drugs, and others who could bring satisfaction to those well-paying customers desirous of things which are unspeakable in plain company. Matt also possessed business acumen as well as a delightful imagination which created the most interesting ways of keeping clients' dark desires from being discovered. Discretion and customer satisfaction had become hallmarks of Matt's service to his clients. He had many customers who had close friends or business associates who also partook of his services yet they remained unknown to each other. Many of Matt's patrons were wealthy and influential pillars of society. To have their sexual eccentricities made public would not only be embarrassing, but it would most assuredly cost them their positions as senators, judges, and corporate executives.

Jolene was still in her thirties and stunningly attractive. Unlike a lot of her friends, Jolene did not accidently stumble into her life of prostitution, nor was she forced into this sordid lifestyle by some pimp. No, Jolene knew exactly what she was doing the first time she chose to sell herself for money.

Jolene came from the poor side of town and she detested it. Her exceptional beauty as well as her physical attributes had made her an object of young men's desires since she was fifteen years old. Like so many young girls, at first, Jolene just liked to be liked. Giving of herself did not seem like a great price to pay to be with the boys who were football stars or drove nice cars. However, Jolene realized that after she had given these boys what they wanted, nothing changed. She was never asked to go to the movies or invited to their parties or their homes. She was from the other side of the tracks, and aside from a casual sexual dalliance, she was apparently expected to stay there. Jolene hated her life. School was not much help either, so once she turned eighteen, Jolene moved to downtown Detroit. It did not take her long to learn the ways of the street. She became a creature of the night. Jolene had one marketable asset, and no longer would she give it away. For two years she "worked" the higher class bars and nightclubs in the motor city. Everyone knew who she was and what she was selling, but no one ever attempted to stop her. After all, her exquisite looks brought in a lot of customers.

One night Matt decided to "trade-up." Jolene's services cost more than Matt was accustomed to paying, but she made it worth it. After a few hours of "doing business," Matt and Jolene were both staring at the ceiling and reflecting on their lives and their dreams. Matt was a good listener, and Jolene told him how she had come to be a lady of the evening. She hated being poor, and she despised being treated like an object of men's desires. Yet she knew that the key to her way out of that world was her beauty. When she was younger and still living at home with her parents, Jolene watched *Gone With the Wind* over and over. She marveled at Scarlett's tenacity and her audacious spirit. *"As God is my witness, they're not going to lick me. I'm going to live through this and when it's all over, I'll never be hungry again...If I have to lie, steal, cheat, or kill. As God is my witness, I'll never be hungry again."* Much like Scarlett, Jolene was willing to do whatever it took to survive. She was extraordinarily well paid for allowing men the temporary possession of something most of them could only fantasize about. To Jolene, this was an acceptable trade-off allowing her to escape the life she hated. She made a lot of friends with other working girls. Like other forms of employment, many of the girls spent a lot of time together when they were not working. Most of the girls enjoyed each other's company and some even lived together. To many like Jolene, having moved away from their homes, this became the closest thing to family that they knew. The girls would go to the movies and shop together, and they often had each other over for dinner. Mostly, however, they would commiserate with each other about the things they had to put up with just to make a living. However, there was one big difference between Jolene and the other girls. All of the other girls were paid only a small percentage of what they earned. Their pimps kept the lion's share of all the money. These pimps did not like Jolene's self-employment. She would have brought them big money because of her looks. Yet this was, also, the very reason she could freelance...she was so desirable that she needed no one to bring men to her. Some of the girls had "specialties" which did NOT necessarily indicate acts which they were especially good at performing. More often than not, specialties represented doing things which the others refused to do. This was where Jolene learned the limitations of each of her friends. She was astonished to learn of some of the things which the "johns" requested them to do, and she was equally surprised to learn of the exorbitant amounts of money paid for these services.

Matt and Jolene decided to combine their areas of expertise to create a very specialized way to cater to clients with unusual desires. Matt became responsible for finding the clients and collecting the money. He also determined the locations for each "encounter," and he would even supply any special equipment or "toys" as they were referred to, although most customers preferred to bring their own. Jolene's responsibility was finding the proper people, be they men or women, who were willing to perform these specialized services. The women Jolene contracted with kept their other jobs and used this as supplemental income. Very quickly Matt and Jolene had all the business they could handle. The police and investigative reporters would love to be privy to the secret lives and exotic lusts of their clientele. It is precisely for this reason that Matt created such an elaborate system to safeguard their secret pleasures. Clients would contact Matt on a special phone and describe the activity they desired as well as a time and any preferences with respect to a partner. Once a price was agreed upon, Matt would call Jolene and describe the type of "activity" that was required. She knew exactly which girls (or men) would be willing to perform such acts and when they were available. Once everything had been worked out, Matt would have the client picked up at a predetermined location and transported to any one of a dozen hotels or motels where he had special arrangements. Matt paid very well to safeguard the anonymity of his clients. All parties knew that although he paid well, if Matt's instructions were not followed to the letter, there would be hell to pay. Sometimes a hotel room would be rented for several hours. Rooms were chosen which were far from prying eyes and out of earshot from the other guests. Things could sometimes get loud, but more importantly, Matt insisted that his clients would not be seen. If the client was a very prominent person, which they often were, armed guards could be added as well as a back escape route with a car and a driver waiting. The hotel manager would never know who the client was, and Matt paid the managers more for a single night than they were normally paid in a week.

Such arrangements usually worked quite well, and all involved were happy. Matt, Jolene, and their employees all made a lot of money for the services they provided. The client had his (or her) cravings satisfied and his (or her) dark secret was kept safe.

During the years that Matt and Jolene had been providing services to their clients, only once did they experience trouble. The hotel manager who had been selected to host a Saturday night encounter got greedy and decided to do a little freelance work on

343

his own. Unknown to the client or to Matt, the hotel manager secretly videotaped the evening performance of one senior senator from Utah. The hotel manager made a copy of the tape and sent it forthwith to the senator along with a note demanding one million dollars for the original tape. The manager figured, and rightly so, that the conservative senator's constituents would take an interest in the tape. Their esteemed senator would be seen prancing around a hotel room wearing only a blonde wig, lipstick, an apron, and ruby red high heels while he tickled his gentlemen friend's unmentionables with a feather duster.

The senator went ballistic. He didn't mind so much paying the million dollars. After all, the taxpayers and his political contributors had very deep pockets. What the senator DID mind was paying Matt for a service and ultimate discretion which had been horribly compromised, and he phoned Matt to tell him so. Five days after receiving the video copy and extortion demand, the senator from Utah received a second package by overnight delivery. There was no return address but the package contained an unsigned apology along with the original video and the eyes of the hotel manager. Everyone, except the now deceased hotel manager, was happy. The senator maintained his anonymity and was allowed to continue practicing his fetish. And as a bonus, he now also enjoyed watching the tape late at night in his office while he attended to the state's business as well as his own. Matt and Jolene were happy since their business continued uninterrupted and they now enjoyed a new level of respect among their hotel managers.

Once they were back in Santa Molina, the judge was able to spend all day Saturday and Sunday resting. It helped, and by late Sunday afternoon, he felt much better. Lamar told his wife of the pain he was now experiencing, and after several phone calls, Colleen was able to track down Dr. May. Knowing that Lamar would eventually require stronger pain medication, she phoned in a prescription for a very potent analgesic.

The Wednesday following her return from Detroit, Yolanda received a call from Director Resque informing her that Marty Dehimer had turned himself into his local police precinct. Marty told them that the FBI was looking to question him about an old case.

Not wanting to waste what could likely be a final opportunity to solve the murder of Joel's family, Yolanda asked that Marty not be questioned until she flew back to Detroit. As added insurance, Yolanda called Agent Stephan Dakeslee and ordered him to clear his schedule. She knew that if anyone could squeeze the truth from a suspect, it was Agent Dakeslee. Marty Dehimer's testimony was especially important since he was the only eyewitness to what had been done to Joel's younger sister Kate. They had one chance and there was no room for error, including errors of omission.

Yolanda phoned Judge Laningham to tell him that Marty was now in custody and of her decision to have Agent Dakeslee accompany them this time back to Detroit. Lamar told Yolanda he had a head cold and was suffering from congestion. He saw no need to make the trip. Since she had Agent Dakeslee for company, Yolanda was fine with Lamar's decision.

Yolanda and Stephan boarded the plane for Detroit at 8:00 AM. This meant they would arrive about 10:00 AM, Detroit time. They would be ready for lunch when the motor city was finishing breakfast. During the flight, Yolanda had ample time to describe in detail every aspect of the case. She did not tell him of her friend Joel or her personal interest in the old case. Agent Dakeslee had plenty of time to formulate a series of questions for his suspect.

Once again the Detroit FBI director was very gracious. He sent a car to pick up agents Tubbs and Dakeslee and took them to the police precinct where Marty Dehimer was being held. The Detroit agent who chauffeured them around also monitored the interrogation from behind one-way glass, but he did not directly participate. This agent kept Director Resque informed of every step during the investigation. He knew of Yolanda's personal interest, and at least for now, he was content to play a supportive role.

Yolanda believed that Tyler Hayes had been forthright with her. At the end of her interview with him, she requested that Tyler contact his cousin Marty and make it clear that he was expected to turn himself into the police. They also requested that Marty make it known on the street that the old murder case was being reinvestigated. The FBI was hoping that Matt would learn of this and perhaps make the mistake of resurfacing from his dark world. They knew that his first act would be to silence Marty to keep him from telling the police what he knew. In the meantime, Marty was safe since he was in custody.

Agent Dakeslee slowly and methodically questioned Marty. The first half of the interview exactly matched Tyler's story, and since their phone conversations had been monitored, the FBI knew that the story had not been fabricated. However, the second half of the interrogation was what interested the FBI the most. Tyler had been left downstairs as a lookout while Matt and Marty went upstairs in the Harris home with Kate, the Harrises' young daughter.

Marty was left alone to tell the story in his own words. He almost seemed relieved to finally speak of the horror he had witnessed so long ago. Marty described how they had taken Kate's money and her brother's camera. Marty had already been upstairs when Matt slit the throats of Kate's parents. He was told that the objective was to steal their valuables and leave. When Matt pulled out the lamp cords and tied Kate's wrists to the bedposts, Marty said he first thought that Matt was just restraining her. Yet once Matt ripped off her clothes and raped Kate, Marty became paralyzed with fear. He said that Matt first stuffed her underpants into her mouth to keep her quiet while he raped her. When Matt had finished, he motioned for Marty to climb atop her as he had done. When Marty shook his head "no," he said that Matt laughed and then he slit Kate's throat. He then pulled the panties out of her mouth and stuffed them into her vagina. Matt lit a cigarette and then used the lighter to set the panties on fire. Marty said that he was shaking badly and was so scared that he remembered nothing more.

Agent Dakeslee requested a break in the interrogation. He and Yolanda left Marty alone and then went next door to speak with the Detroit FBI agent.

Yolanda looked at Stephan. "What do you think?"

"Well, I think that Marty has been carrying around a lot of guilt for a very long time. He knew we were after him, and he still turned himself in. I also believe he is scared that Matt may find him. Yolanda, I believe that Tyler and Marty got hooked up with a psychopath. It is my opinion that Marty gave us the complete truth as he remembers it. You and I traveled a long way to find out what we already knew. There is a very dangerous man roaming around

347

out there. Questioning this Matt Dwyer is an interrogator's dream. He is evil incarnate. The only thing I do not understand is why he let Tyler and Marty live. Matt is very smart. If he was otherwise, he could not have lasted this long. When they catch this guy, please bring me back to question him. Psychopaths are a rare breed. It would be like interrogating Jack the Ripper. However, if I were a betting man, it would be my guess that you are going to have to kill him. He thinks he is smarter and better than us, and he will never surrender."

ANTISOCIAL MATTHEW

It was Friday, July 5th. Judge Laningham was still not feeling well, so he promised to keep the Council meeting short.

Hector told the group that Bubba has been doing well. He was quickly learning the landscaping business and for obvious reasons, he loved being outdoors. Both Bubba and Roddy had received their checks from the State of California for wrongful imprisonment. Bernard followed Hector's prompting and deposited his money into the bank.

Dr. Woodson noted that since Rapture's **G Day**, the newspapers had been having daily articles delineating the evildoings of Thomas Hartsell. One investigative reporter was able to prove that Hartsell never attended any divinity college and was not an ordained clergyman. Another article indicated that it did not appear likely that Hartsell would be able to evade the multiple charges of rape which had been leveled against him. A substantial group of parishioners was attempting to initiate charges of fraud against Hartsell and Rapture Ministries because none of the money he extorted from them on Wednesday evenings was given to missions. One parishioner even ripped the Wall of Attainment glass case from the church wall as proof of donations made. The Golden Gate Savings Bank had started foreclosure proceedings against Hartsell's two homes as well as the church building. Elders Marcus and Jesse were never seen again. They'd both disappeared, but not before they took everything of any value from Rapture.

The judge and Yolanda shared with the Council what they had learned in Detroit. As the original police report had indicated, there were three men who entered the Harris home. While two were unwitting accomplices, all three murders, as well as the rape of Joel's sister, were all the acts of a single person. The two accomplices had cooperated with the police, and both were clearly afraid of retribution from the killer. The FBI Agent, Stephan Dakeslee, is convinced that the killer, who appears to be the very definition of a psychopath, is a very smart and a very dangerous person.

Yolanda added, "Detroit FBI Director Avery Resque has been very cooperative, and his people are now attempting to locate Mr. Dwyer. They believe that he operates a very lucrative business which provides wealthy clients with unorthodox sexual gratification. Both by necessity and design, he lives in a dark world which is far from public view. Tyler Hayes is in jail already, and his cousin Marty Dehimer, the second of the two accomplices, has quietly surrendered to the Detroit police. Before he turned himself in, we instructed Marty to put the word out on the street that the FBI was looking into these old murders and Matt's name was mentioned as a person of interest. We are hoping that this will make Matt surface and look to silence Marty. So far, there has been nothing."

Joel asked, "Don't Tyler and Marty know where to locate Matt Dwyer?"

"No," said Yolanda. "Apparently after the killings, they never saw each other again. Considering the ease with which he was able to kill, it is rather remarkable that he did not also kill Tyler and Marty. He doesn't seem like the kind of man to leave witnesses behind."

Hector offered, "How about we go to Detroit and flush him out ourselves?"

Yolanda was adamant. "Look, my colleague in Detroit has been very helpful thus far and I appreciate that. If we send in a bunch of civilians to do his work, how do you think he will react? Director Resque will find Matt Dwyer, and when he does, he will let me know. Until we hear something, we stay put."

Joel surprised everyone. "Look, none of us wants Matt Dwyer caught more than I do. I agree with Yolanda, let the Detroit people do their job."

The judge dismissed the Council. All agreed to wait to do anything until they received a response from the Detroit FBI. Hopefully, they would receive definitive information from them soon. Hector lagged behind the other Council members on the way out. As soon as everyone else had left, Hector asked Lamar, "Did you buy into any of that?"

"What do you mean, Hector?"

"Joel indicating a preference for letting the Detroit law enforcement people find Matt Dwyer. In the first place, the Detroit police have had over fifteen years to solve his family's murders. In the second place, if it were MY parents and sister, I wouldn't want anyone else doling out justice for me. Perhaps Joel has something else in mind. We should keep an eye on him just in case."

The judge began those deep coughs which made his entire frame quake. He took a few sips of water and slowly calmed down. "Summer colds are a bitch. Thank you, Hector. Once again, your intuitive knowledge of people has impressed me. What would we do without you? I will inform the others, and collectively we can keep an eye on Joel."

The next day, Joel went rock climbing with his HOT Software business partners, Ramon Ortise and Teddy Turner. The three had been friends since high school. After Joel moved to the Silicon Valley from Detroit, at his request, his two friends, also, moved to California and started HOT Software together. In no time they led the software game industry, and they all became very wealthy young men. They surrounded themselves with extremely talented, energetic, and imaginative people who kept their company in the vanguard of the computer game industry. Neither Ramon nor Teddy had any knowledge of the Council or where Joel disappeared to when Council activities required his participation. With the exception of HOT Software, Saturday rock climbing, and an occasional Friday or Saturday night on the town, the three friends led separate lives.

"Teddy," Joel asked, "does your younger brother still play our computer games?"

"Oh yeah," Teddy answered. "Zach is one of the family faithful, as are several of our younger cousins."

"Good. I want some feedback on a new game which is scheduled for release in a few months. Give me his address and phone number, and I will mail a few to him and the cousins in a day or two."

352

"Thanks Joel, he will like that. I will leave the information on your desk Monday morning."

Two hours and a few ounces of sweat later, the three young men returned to their separate vehicles and drove home.

Matt Dwyer learned from one of his street snitches that the police had been looking for him. At first, this meant nothing since all his life he had been doing things outside of the law. The police always seemed to want to talk with him about something. However, when his snitch mentioned that they sought him for questioning about three killings which happened sixteen years ago, Matt immediately wanted to know all of the details. He gave orders for the snitch to find the current location of a Martin "Marty" Dehimer. Matt saw no reason to panic just yet. However, it was always wise to stay a few steps ahead, if possible. He gave the informant a generous tip and insisted that he be told immediately of any further developments.

Matt still thought himself to be intellectually superior to law enforcement officials. After all, sixteen years after those killings and a few others since, he had never served one minute in jail. After all these years, what could possibly have happened prompting revisiting this old crime?

FBI Agent Dakeslee's assessment of Matthew Dwyer had been dead on. Dwyer was a walking poster child for the definition of the psychopathic or sociopathic personality disorder. All his life, Matthew had exhibited the classic triad of symptoms. Antisocial behavior, a complete lack of empathy, and bold actions had been hallmarks of his behavior throughout his entire life. Even as a young child in school, no one ever wanted to play with him. Matt was controlling and he flatly refused to share. He would rip toys from the hands of other children, and when they cried, he laughed. Teachers and other adults would often attempt to intervene, but to no avail. Authority figures meant nothing to him. Limits were established by his parents and teachers, but young Matthew was bold, and there were no such things as boundaries for HIM! One night Matt's mother threatened that if he wasn't in bed at the required 8:00 PM, he would not be allowed to accompany his classmates the next day on a special school outing. Most children come to realize that sometimes the punishment just isn't worth the crime. Not so for the psychopathic child. They insist on doing what they want regardless of rules, limitations, or the threat of consequences. Matt's parents tried to do the right things. They took him to child psychiatrists and worked with his teachers. Nothing helped. The fact that Matt was so intelligent only made things worse. He quickly learned that as a minor, he was, for all intents and purposes, "untouchable." Eventually Matt ran away from home. Other parents felt sorry for Matt and took him into their homes. Soon, however, their charity ended when Matt's behavior became so intolerable that they were forced to ask him to leave. Both sets of grandparents took their turn also, and they blamed Matt's parents for not being able to properly raise young Matthew. Actually, the truth was that they hated the parents for inconveniencing their own lives since they now inherited the responsibility for this adolescent social deviant. So, not only was Matt antisocial, but he also left havoc in his wake among all of those who tried to help him. All this continued because Matthew refused to follow the rules that everyone else had to live by. So Matthew continued to live on the street.

Tyler and Marty were horrified by the brazen behavior exhibited by Matt when he so effortlessly slit the throats of the Harris family. He showed no empathy for what he had done. In fact, he laughed.

Since that time long ago, Matthew Dwyer had come a long way. He found a way to exist outside of mainstream society where he could make his own rules. He and Jolene made a lot of money providing discrete services to those who could afford such things. On occasion, women got hurt. A few even died, but these were not the kind of people who were likely to be missed. Once again, there was no remorse. The military used the term "collateral damage" to define unintended death resulting from a related objective. Matthew viewed things in a similar fashion. Now that the police were making inquiries, Matt was unsure how much his life was threatened. He could only wait and see.

FLUSHING MATT

Joel stopped at the post office on his way to work on Wednesday morning and mailed the new computer game to Teddy Turner's younger brother. He had never returned to Detroit since his family was killed. Many times he wondered if things had changed there. Both Teddy and Ramon had gone back to Detroit for weddings and holiday visits, but they never made mention of any changes.

Imagining the killers of his family being brought to justice after all these years seemed surreal to Joel. It had taken him many years to put his anger behind him, and now he was welcoming the opportunity to reintroduce it back into his life. It was this anger and the injustice he felt that the killers of his parents and sister had never been caught, which, years back, had been the driving force behind Hector's introducing him to the Council. Since joining the Council, the injustice he experienced in his personal life had kind of melted into the background. Joel was now fighting back on his own terms. The Council had been instrumental in realigning the justice system on many levels. The bottom line, however, was that those who were able to successfully avoid being prosecuted within the judicial system were shown a different kind of justice which emanated from their own environment outside of law enforcement and the courts. Now the injustice was personalized, it had HIS name on it. Joel trusted that the Council would be successful. It always was. Judge Laningham and Yolanda had both instructed Joel to stay in the background during this mission. They feared that his personal involvement could affect his judgment. Did they really expect him to stand idly by on the sidelines while other Council members chased down the individuals responsible for the extinction of his family?

Later that same day, Yolanda received a phone call from Director Resque in Detroit. He told her that his agents had a lead on the whereabouts of Matthew Dwyer. It seemed that Mr. Dwyer and a very high end prostitute, known only as Jolene, ran an exclusive sex service for well-to-do clients with unusual appetites. The service was so specialized that Matt was rumored to have customers flown in from all over the country.

"How would you like us to proceed with this?" Director Resque asked. "I want to work with you to the degree that I am able to, but there will likely come a time when I will have to react without your knowledge. I have taken notice of your personal involvement in this case Yolanda, but it remains under my jurisdiction."

"Understood," said Yolanda. "Honestly, Avery, I would do the same thing. Your courtesy and cooperation thus far have been much appreciated. Really, though, I would handle it the same way. In the end, our only real concern is the apprehension and conviction of Matthew Dwyer. I do not want him to run free for another sixteen years. However, before we think about arresting this guy, I need to make sure he is the one we are looking for. We already have eyewitness testimony to a rape and three murders, but remember that this case is sixteen years old. And don't forget that one of our witnesses is already in jail. That never plays well to a jury. If we take Matt into custody and he makes bail or we have to release him for any reason, I can promise you that we will never see him again. He is both smart and audacious. We already know that he has no problem killing. But if we can use his DNA to irrevocably tie him to the crime scene, game over!

Here is what I propose...I realize it is not by the book, but we have to be extremely careful with this guy."

Over the next two days, the Council formulated a plan to help capture Matt Dwyer. The ideas were exchanged over the phone and discussed back and forth between Council members. Not knowing how Matt would respond, most scenarios were based on "what ifs." Predictably, the Detroit FBI was moving ahead very cautiously. The Council had experience with all kinds of people in rendering their form of unique justice to those miscreants who managed to evade punishment by the legal system. However, Matthew Dwyer's case was unlike previous experiences. He was a psychopath, someone who could kill and enjoy doing it. Matt believed he was smarter than the police and, unfortunately, thus far, he had been. There would only be one chance to get Matthew Dwyer, so there was no room for mistakes.

Judge Laningham grew weaker each day. His cough continued unabated, and he was now consistently bringing up blood. Dr. Woodson, who made his living dealing with end-of-life symptomology had spoken with Lamar and Colleen and given them his best professional guess that the judge has only a few months at best to live. With complete rest, it was possible to add only days to the inevitable. Both Colleen and Jerry attempted to get Lamar to end his participation in Council activities. Lamar agreed to do so, but only after this Detroit business had been completed, and he anticipated this would be very soon. Colleen and Jerry reluctantly agreed, but they made Lamar acquiesce to only participating as an observer, and they insisted that he inform the Council of this tonight.

At 6:45 PM the Council members began arriving at the Laningham home. Dr. Woodson was already there, and next came Yolanda and then Joel. As always, Hector arrived last, but he spoke first because he was obviously excited to give the Council an update on Bubba's progress. It quickly became clear that Hector had taken a very personal interest in helping Bernard Jones reclaim his life outside prison walls.

"Bubba hasn't been with us a month yet, and things have changed a lot. My mother is a whole new person. She and Bubba...I mean Bernard, watch game shows on television together, and she loves taking him shopping. All the clerks and cashiers yell to him like they are old pals. All the kids on the street think he is one of them, and last Saturday a gang of them stopped by the house. My Mom answered the door, and this little kid asked her if it would be alright for Bubba to come out and go to the park with them to play baseball. Sundays is movie day. Bernard says that his grandmother taught him that the Bible says not to work on Sundays. We have one of those theaters near us which shows six different movies. Well, Bubba does not seem to grasp the concept that you have to pay separately to see each one. He pays to see the first one, buys enough popcorn for a family of five, and he is gone for the rest of the day. He wanders from movie to movie all day long. I spoke to the manager regarding what Bubba's life has been like up till now. The movie manager was nearly moved to tears, and he instructed all of his employees to let Bernard stay in the theater on a single admission price as long as he wishes.

Bernard has also made tremendous headway in learning the landscaping business. He can now operate all of the equipment, and he requires almost no supervision. But the best part is that my customers love him. At first, his size intimidated some of the clients, but now he is getting their cats out of trees and carrying in their groceries."

Yolanda spoke up. "It is wonderful to hear that Bubba is doing so well. Unfortunately, his old companion Roddy Jackson did not fare as well. This morning my people informed me that he was found dead and penniless in a large suite in a Las Vegas hotel."

"Penniless, how can that be?" asked Hector. "Only a week ago, he and Bubba were each given two hundred and fifty thousand dollars."

Yolanda continued. "I guess if you want to go through a quarter of a million dollars in a day or two, Vegas is the place to do it. Witnesses said that Roddy was traveling with an entourage of seedy-looking home boys and hookers. They were throwing money around and partying pretty hard. No one cared. After all it IS Vegas. Anyway, long story short, he was found alone and stripped of anything of value. He died from a hot load of heroin. The needle was still in his arm." Yolanda shrugged her shoulders. "Sometimes freedom isn't free. Now, concerning our friends in Detroit, I received a call from Director Resque earlier today. His agents were able to bring in a hooker and squeeze her, figuratively of course, for information pertaining to Jolene, Matt Dwyer's partner. This hooker was one arrest away from doing hard time for possession, and since she was flying high when they brought her in, she had no choice but to cooperate. All they wanted from her was a way to get to Jolene, and then she had to keep her mouth shut. She told us that every Friday afternoon, Jolene frequents a particular beauty salon to 'get ready' for the weekend. Jolene may not practice her trade any longer, but the tradition of visiting the salon continues. Avery's men whisked Jolene away immediately after she left the salon. The FBI did not want to raise suspicion by making her miss her appointment.

At first, Jolene resisted any attempts at cooperation. She, too, had been no friend of the law. It was odd that while the services she performed for men were considered illegal, from time-to-time she was required to be handcuffed to her bedposts so the law enforcement officers could "examine the evidence" for themselves.

Once Jolene understood exactly why the FBI was seeking Matt, everything changed. She knew that Matt was brazen, and she had more than once been an eyewitness to his losing his legendary temper, but cold-blooded murder? The FBI agents made it very clear that if she cooperated, they wanted nothing from Jolene. Matt Dwyer was all that interested them, and they told her that no one need know that she had helped the police. The FBI wanted two things from Jolene. First, they needed her to surreptitiously acquire a sample of Matt's DNA. Secondly, if Matt's DNA matched the profile from the old crime scene, they would then ask her where Matthew Dwyer could be found. Jolene reluctantly agreed to help the FBI. She admitted to seeing Matt several times a week. They gave her a number to call once she had the sample of his DNA.

The Council agreed that they would likely get only one chance to nab Matt Dwyer. He was very smart, and he surely had enough money and connections to disappear forever if he wanted to. He hadn't taken the bait and did not surface to look for Marty Dehimer. Now, all the FBI's hopes depended on Jolene leading them to him.

Yolanda, Hector, and Dr. Woodson had formulated a relatively simple plan designed to force Matt to the surface while at the same time introducing each of them onto Matt's dark world in a plausible way. Once Jolene delivered a DNA sample, if it matched the crime scene DNA, they would set the plan into motion.

Judge Laningham stood to address the Council. "I believe, as I am sure we all do, that once this Jolene delivers us a DNA sample, it will match the profile which Yolanda's people have produced from the evidence. Once this happens, to the degree that we are allowed to, the Council will assist the Detroit FBI. This finds us in a place we are unaccustomed to operating from. Until now, the Council has operated independent of law enforcement. The justice we served up was our own creation designed to circumvent conventional means and methods. This is different. Yolanda's cold case investigator has used new technology to solve old cases like Bubba's and the murders of Joel's family. The police now have a decided advantage. Had this technology existed sixteen years ago, Matt Dwyer would be in jail now.

You will recall the original COUNCIL GROUND RULES. In section 3, it states that...'*all efforts will be made to operate within the law.*' This is what we will do. And since this case is now under FBI jurisdiction, Yolanda will be in charge. Please remember people,

362

we have always been about justice, not who delivers it. So if the FBI solves this case and Mr. Dwyer finally receives justice, our objectives will have been met." The judge paused. "My friends, it seems like yesterday we came together to create the Council. I regret to tell you that this will be the final Council meeting at the Laningham home. I have untreatable end stage lung cancer and have been informed by my friend Dr. Woodson that my life is now measured in weeks or months. Somehow it seems fitting that my final Council mission will be to help deliver justice to one of our own. Whether you continue the Council after I am gone, obviously, is up to you. Delivering Council justice has been the crowning achievement of my life. I love each of you for making this journey with me and I need you to know that I would not trade my Council memories for anything. The judge bowed gracefully to the group and walked from the library.

CHAPTER SEVEN

1

A MATCH OF OLD AND NEW

Monday morning, Yolanda was still reeling from Judge Laningham's words. She had all she could do to concentrate on both her job and the Matt Dwyer business. It took her two hours to catch up on the updates from her agents as well as the new things which came in over the weekend. When she was younger, Yolanda was known to inhabit her office on Saturdays or even Sundays. It took her a year or two to learn that attempts to keep her desk "clear" were nothing more than an exercise in futility. If she was to have a life of her own, things could wait till Monday. Finally, she was in a position to call Director Resque.

Yolanda was performing a balancing act and she knew it. The murders of Joel's family were officially FBI business...more specifically, Detroit FBI business. The Council had never before been relegated to the position as a back-up role, and being subordinate just wasn't their style. Avery Resque and Judge Laningham both had made it clear that this time, the Council had to "stand down."

Yolanda dialed Director Resque and received good news right away. Jolene had delivered a few DNA samples from Matt Dwyer in two plain envelopes to a grocery store one block from her apartment. Two days ago, at Matt's request, Jolene had ordered

Chinese take-out and brought it back to Matt's apartment. This was a working lunch as they were discussing upcoming client's appointments. Matt told Jolene of three clients' special "needs" as well as their preference in partners. Jolene listened attentively and made her recommendations as usual. She knew her girls as well as their limitations and what they would and would NOT do for money. She pretended to go to the bathroom, but instead she used tweezers to carefully remove six hairs from Matt's hairbrush and deposited them as she had been told in a plain paper envelope. She put the envelope in her bra and rejoined Matt to finish lunch in the kitchen. After a few minutes, Matt received a phone call and went into the bedroom for privacy. Once Jolene heard the door close, she again quickly used her tweezers to remove two cigarette butts from his ashtray. As before, she deposited them in a second clean paper envelope.

Once Matt and Jolene concluded the discussing of their clients' appointments, Jolene left. She stopped at a local coffee shop and then went directly to her apartment. She called the phone number given to her by the FBI and told them that she had the DNA samples which they instructed her to get from Matt Dwyer. The faceless monotone voice on the other end of the phone instructed Jolene to go to a grocery store one block from her home at precisely 1:00 PM. She would see a white book with a red football helmet on the cover at the far end of the check-out counter. Jolene was told to put her two envelopes inside the book and then leave the store.

Director Resque's DNA analyst created the profile and was in the process of faxing it to Director Tubbs. Pending the results from the DNA, Yolanda shared with Avery a plan to flush Matt Dwyer out of hiding and capture him. She noted that, in addition to herself, she wanted to include two civilians in the ruse, but she assured Director Resque that these two civilians would be long gone by the time Matthew Dwyer appeared on the scene. In addition, Yolanda assured him that she would be there and that if everything happened as planned, it would be virtually impossible for Matt to escape. Director Avery listened intently as Yolanda outlined her plan. The Detroit FBI director thought that her idea was ingenious, and he complimented his colleague on her imagination and her attention to detail.

"I see absolutely no reason why your plan should not work, but are you sure that YOU want such an active role to play? I am perfectly willing to have one of my female agents play your part."

"Oh no," said Yolanda. "I am very much looking forward to it. I will call you back as soon as we are able to compare your DNA profiles to ours." When she had finished talking with Avery Resque, Yolanda called Agent Martha Green. Agent Green was instructed to watch for the fax from Detroit, and once she received it, she was to immediately drop whatever she was doing and compare the two DNA profiles. Yolanda insisted on being told the results the minute they became available.

To no one's surprise, one hour later, Martha Green announced to Yolanda that the DNA samples from Detroit were an exact match to the DNA taken from the rape scene evidence of Kate Harris. Matthew Dwyer's hair and semen samples irrevocably proved that he was the one who raped Kate. No jury could disregard this fact.

Yolanda called Director Resque, and then she called Judge Laningham, Dr. Woodson, and Hector. Joel was not called.

2

HOTEL CARRETTO

The Council in Santa Molina and the Detroit FBI immediately began to work in concert. The first order of business for Detroit FBI Agent Mark "Moe" Mahoney was to contact Jolene. Director Resque designated Mark to run the case, and he and Yolanda were to maintain constant contact. Mark called Jolene and asked her to have Matt arrange an encounter between a new client and a middle aged black woman. Jolene was instructed to call Matt and tell him that she gave a new client his phone number. She indicated that the new client would call him and give him the details of his desired encounter. Jolene, of course, would recommend a girl...a girl provided by the FBI. Once the arrangements with the girl had been completed, Jolene's part in the ruse would end. Mark "Moe" Mahoney did a good job. He called Jolene and then sat back and waited.

Dr. Woodson called Matt Dwyer's "special" phone number. After three rings he answered. "Yes?" was all Matt said.

Dr. Woodson said, "Hello, this is Dr. Neal. I was told by a friend of mine that you can facilitate meetings between people with, shall we say, unorthodox sexual fantasies and partners who are willing to satisfy such fantasies?"

"Yes, I can make arrangements for such meetings to take place. Of course, I need to know exactly what you are looking for

368

and when this meeting will take place. And, just so we understand each other, these arrangements do not come cheap."

Dr. Woodson was a little uncomfortable describing the details even though everything was written down in front of him. "I am not concerned with the cost as much as I am with gratification. I am flying into Detroit for business on Saturday morning. Sometime in the afternoon, my business will conclude. Saturday evening, say 7:00 PM, I would like to be provided with a middle aged woman. I prefer black women. My predilection is sadomasochism. I role play as a southern plantation owner and the woman is my house slave. I will bring my own equipment. Are you able to provide this service for me?"

"That is what I do, sir. The cost is ten thousand dollars and you can have the woman and the room for the entire night if you wish." Matt asked, "Is this acceptable to you sir?"

Dr. Woodson continued, "Yes of course, but where…"

"Never mind where. That is my concern. I take care of all the details. You are to meet my driver in front of the Cadillac Hotel at precisely 7:00 PM. To make things easier to remember, a white Cadillac will be waiting there for you. The driver will be inside and he will take you to the location where the woman will be waiting for you. Bring only cash and give it to the driver. When you are done, phone the hotel's front desk. I will have my driver pick you up. Is there anything else you require?"

Dr. Woodson said, "No, I don't think so, except instead of you picking me up, can I have my valet follow us and take me back to our hotel?"

Matt answered, "Yes, as long as you don't mind him waiting in the lobby until you are done."

"No," said Dr. Woodson (Dr. Neal), that should be OK."

"Alright then, everything will be ready on Saturday at 7:00 PM. Have fun." The phone hung up.

Yolanda, Hector, and Dr. Woodson were all to take a plane Friday morning to Detroit. Judge Laningham insisted on going as well. Yolanda made him promise to stay in the hotel once the sting took place. Lamar agreed without hesitation. Given her husband's condition, Colleen was not in agreement about this trip to Detroit. He would only be gone 48 hours and he told his wife that he was playing no role in his final Council mission. Call it moral support, call it one last hurrah, call it a sad goodbye...Lamar just wanted to be there with his friends one last time. Colleen understood. She knew how much the Council meant to Lamar, but she still was not in favor of the trip. She insisted that Lamar leave her his complete itinerary and phone numbers where he could be reached. Lamar smiled and kissed his wife.

Joel was no fool. He knew that his Council friends had purposely kept information from him. It was obvious that the other Council members were soon to be headed for Detroit. He also knew that they would try to keep everything from him. He needed to find out their plans.

On Thursday morning, Joel called Yolanda's office at the FBI Building. Yolanda's secretary, Ruth, answered the phone.

"Director Tubbs' office, may I help you?"

"Yes, may I please speak with Director Tubbs?"

Ruth answered, "She went to the lab and should be back in a few minutes, can I help you?"

He realized that Yolanda was still here. "No, thanks, I will call her back." Joel hung up the phone.

On Friday morning, at 8:00 AM, before they would begin landscaping, Joel called the Martinez home which also served Martinez's Landscaping Service, to inquire about an estimate for some new bushes. A man answered. Joel knew that it had to be Bubba.

"I am sorry, sir, but the boss will be out of town until Monday."

BINGO! "OK, I will call back on Monday, thanks." They have left for Detroit! To be sure, Joel called the Laningham's house. Colleen answered. "Hello, Joel." She said. "Lamar left with the others this morning, and ..."

"I know, Colleen, and I am sorry to bother you, but this is an emergency. There has been a break-in at my home, and I need to speak with Lamar."

"I am sorry, Joel, are you all right?"

"Yes, I am fine. I was not at home when it happened. Do you know where Lamar is? Where can I call him?"

"He is on his way to Detroit. Wait a minute, yes here it is. He should arrive at about 2:30 PM. He is staying at the Carretto

Hotel and should be there by 3:00 PM. Call him there. I don't have his room number yet."

"Thank you, Colleen." Joel hung up and drove to the airport. In anticipation of having to move fast, several days ago, Joel packed a weekend carry-on bag with clothes and toiletries and kept it in his trunk.

Joel parked his car in the airport's short-term parking lot. He hurried to the Excelsior Airline ticket counter and learned that the next flight to Detroit, which was scheduled to leave in only one hour, was filled to capacity. However, several seats were still available on the subsequent flight which would leave in three hours. He purchased a ticket on the later flight and hurried to the gate. However, Joel did not go to the gate which HIS plane was scheduled to leave from. Instead, he intentionally went to the gate of the earlier flight. It appeared that most of the passengers were already there waiting to board. Joel went to the front of the seating area near the boarding ramp. He spoke loudly and with urgency in his voice. "Excuse me people. This plane to Detroit is full. There are no empty seats. It is absolutely imperative that I get to Detroit as quickly as possible. My wife just went into labor." Joel held up a ticket and waved it so all could see it. "I have a round trip ticket on the next flight to Detroit which is scheduled to leave three hours from now. If any of you will give me YOUR ticket, I will give you five hundred dollars cash and this ticket. Can anyone help me?" A young man, perhaps a college student, raised his hand. Together this young man and Joel approached the boarding podium. The airline employee had also heard Joel's plea. She was a recent mother herself, and she quickly did her magic and switched the seat assignments and printed new boarding passes for each. Joel thanked the airline employee as well as the young man who was delighted to be five hundred dollars richer.

One half hour later, Joel walked down the jet bridge and boarded the plane to Detroit. He had enough time to call his secretary at HOT Software and tell her that he would not be coming to work today. Once the plane reached its cruising altitude, Joel reclined his seat and closed his eyes. He knew he would be very busy during the next thirty-six hours and he needed to formulate a game plan.

Yolanda, the judge, Dr. Woodson, and Hector touched down in Detroit at 2:35 PM, local time. After retrieving their luggage from the baggage area, Hector said, "I'll get a taxi." Unexpectedly, a large black sedan, with a large antenna, which may as well have had POLICE CAR printed on the side, was waiting for them outside the baggage claim area. The same agent who picked up Yolanda the last time recognized her and called out, "Director Tubbs!"

"Forget the taxi, Hector, we have a ride." Once inside the car, Yolanda, who sat in the front seat next to the Detroit agent turned to thank him. "Once again, we are most appreciative for your tending to us. Director Resque is most thoughtful. But seriously, where we are going it is advisable that we arrive in a slightly more nondescript looking vehicle, like say...MAYBE A FIRE TRUCK!" Everyone laughed.

"Your point is noted," said the driver. "I will tell the boss that from here on, you folks will use cabs or rental cars."

Yolanda added, "Thank you, and that reminds me, will you be kind enough to drop off my friend Hector at the car rental area

373

so he can get us a car? We will need it tomorrow. And please wait so he can follow us to our hotel, the Carretto."

"Sure," said the driver, "but I really like the fire truck idea." Again they laughed as they pulled into the car rental building. Hector and Dr. Woodson got out.

"I might as well start getting used to you being my chauffeur," Said Dr.Woodson. It took fifteen minutes before Hector had a rental car, and only twenty minutes after that, Hector followed the FBI driver to the unloading area in front of the Carretto Hotel. Hector dropped off Dr. Woodson and the luggage and was fortunate to find a close parking spot in the hotel's lot. Everyone made their way to the lobby and Hector quickly caught up with the others. Dr. Woodson was the first to approach the hotel registration counter. He requested that he and the judge share a room. The inference was that since they had been lifelong friends, they would have a lot in common to talk about; and while this may have been true, everyone knew that Colleen had insisted that they stay together so the doctor could keep a close eye on her husband.

Hector looked at Yolanda with his famous smile as he threw her "butterfly kisses" with his eyelashes. He said, "I guess that leaves you and I to share a room, huh babe?"

Yolanda raised her eyebrows and peered at Hector over her glasses. "I am afraid you might hurt yourself. Besides, I need to conserve all of my sexual energy for tomorrow night." All four Council members laughed, but the poor registration clerk was clearly lost in the conversation.

"Separate rooms for me and Sparky please," Yolanda said to the desk clerk. The four agreed to make their way to their rooms and relax. They would meet each other again in the lobby at 6:00 PM for dinner.

3

EMILIO SCAVO

Two and a half hours after the Council members checked into the Carretto Hotel, Joel landed in Detroit. Having only his carry-on weekend bag, he quickly hailed a taxicab.

"One-oh-four South Madison Street, please." The driver started the meter and drove away without speaking.

"Are you also on duty tomorrow?" Joel asked the driver.

"Yup, noon until 9:00 PM, every day but Tuesdays. I gotta feed two kids and another one is on the way."

Joel looked at the driver's picture which was prominently displayed on the dashboard. It read Emilio Scavo. "Well, Emilio, how much do you average a day in tips?"

The driver, obviously interested, looked at Joel in his rearview mirror. "Probably a couple of hundred bucks, why?"

"Because Emilio, how about if I give you ten times that amount, two thousand dollars, above and beyond the amount on the meter. I want to exclusively own your services. You will be at my beck and call for the remainder of this shift, as well as your entire shift tomorrow, from noon until 9:00 PM, or longer if I need you."

"This sounds illegal." Said the driver.

"Absolutely not, Emilio. Four of my business associates are in town staying at the Carretto Hotel. One of them is leaking privileged information to one of my competitors, and I am trying to find out who it is."

"OK, if you are sure that there is nothing illegal. We start now?"

Joel reached into his wallet. He handed Emilio ten one hundred dollar bills. "Here is half. I will give you the rest when I dismiss you tomorrow."

Ten minutes later, Emilio parked alongside the curb in front of 104 South Madison St. The step back into time hit Joel like a sledgehammer. Outside the waiting taxicab, Joel stood in front of the Turner residence. He and Teddy had spent countless hours here doing all of the things adolescent boys do. He never thought he would see this house again. The porch had been rebuilt, treated lumber replacing the ancient wrought iron supports and railings. The windows and siding had also been updated, yet the old house remained unmistakable. Joel walked up the steps and rang the doorbell. He hardly recognized the young man who opened the door. The ice blue eyes were the same, otherwise he would have had no idea this was Teddy's younger brother. Now twenty-six, Gary Turner was only ten the last time Joel had seen him.

"Come in, Joel." Gary stood aside and Joel stepped into the house. The inside of the house was just as Joel remembered it. How many times had he and Teddy been scolded for running up and down those stairs?

"Hey, thanks for the games," Gary said. "Have a seat. My parents should be home soon."

"No, I really can't, Gary, I have a cab waiting." He motioned toward the front bay window where they could see the taxi in front of the house. The exhaust indicated that the cab was burning too much oil. "I mailed a package last week with the games and asked your parents to hold it for me till I got here. It has my name on it."

"Oh, yeah, I saw it on the kitchen counter. Hang on." Gary left the living room and returned in a few seconds with Joel's package. "Here ya go. Listen my parents are grateful for everything you have done for Teddy, and I know they would love to see you."

"Sorry, Gary, but I am on a tight schedule. Maybe I will be able to come back in a day or two. Please give them my best."

"I will," said Gary. Joel was already halfway down the steps with his package.

Back in the taxi, Joel told Emilio, "OK, one more stop before the hotel. Emilio, please find me a sporting goods store. I need some running shoes." Once again the driver waited with the meter running until Joel returned. "OK, please take me to the Carretto Hotel." Emilio noted that, in addition to a new green and white Michigan State Spartan baseball hat he was now wearing, the package his client brought from the sporting goods store couldn't be running shoes...unless they were possibly for a newborn. He said nothing.

Once they reached the hotel, Joel gave Emilio very specific instructions. "Remain parked in the hotel's parking area designated for taxicabs. No one will bother you if you keep the meter running. This cab is already taken and you are here waiting for your fare to return from the hotel. You will wait here until 9:00 PM tonight. If I do not require your services before then, you may go home. Regardless, come back here tomorrow at noon and do the same thing." Joel gave Emilio a handful of money. "This should satisfy the meter charges for both tonight and tomorrow. At the end of your shift tomorrow, I will give you the remaining thousand dollars which I promised you. Thank you." Joel took his two packages, as well as his weekend bag and exited the taxi. He pulled the brim of his baseball cap way down over his eyes so no one would recognize him. He quickly traversed the lobby to the registration desk. Joel asked for a room on the ground floor explaining to the clerk that he had severe acrophobia and that even changing a light bulb in a ceiling fixture made him dizzy. Of course, the real reason was so he could respond quickly if the other Council members were on the move. Joel asked the clerk, "Several of my friends are here for a retirement party for Dr. Jerry Woodson. Can you tell me if he or a Yolanda Tubbs, Hector Martinez, or Lamar Laningham have checked in yet?"

"Why, yes, I checked all of them in a few hours ago. They all went to their rooms, and as far as I know, they are still there." He picked up the desk phone. "I will call and tell them that you are here."

"No, no, don't do that. I want to surprise them." He gave the desk clerk a fifty dollar bill. "Please do NOT tell them I am here, but if they should come to the lobby, please call my room immediately and let me know."

379

The clerk slid the fifty dollar tip across the counter and into his pocket. "Very good, sir. I will do so."

At 6:00 PM Yolanda and Hector met in the lobby of the hotel. Minutes later, Lamar and Dr. Woodson joined them. Lamar told Hector and Yolanda that Colleen called to make sure that they all arrived safely. "She, also, said that Joel was looking for me...something about his house being broken into. She said that Joel would get back to me, but that he was fine. So far, I haven't heard back from him." Hector went to get the car while the others discussed dinner preferences and slowly made their way outside. The desk clerk rang Joel's room to tell him that his friends were leaving, probably going to dinner. Minutes later, Joel got into the taxi wearing a hooded sweatshirt. He had seen Yolanda getting into a blue Chevrolet and he told Emilio to follow that car without being obvious about it. Perhaps a mile and a half down the road, Hector pulled into the parking lot of a very nice looking restaurant.

"Nice restaurant," said Emilio. "I wish I could afford to bring my family here. Are you going in?"

"Not tonight."

Nearly two hours later, the four Council members came out of the restaurant. Lamar looked exhausted and Hector was scanning the street while cleaning his teeth with a toothpick. It was almost 8:00 PM, and Joel was reasonably sure that nothing more would happen this evening. He and Emilio stayed well behind Hector. This time Joel had the driver drop him off in front of the Carretto lobby. He gave Emilio another one hundred dollar bill. "Here...take your family to that restaurant...but don't do it tomorrow. Good night." Joel dismissed the taxi and hurried into the hotel. He was in his room before the others were even in the lobby. Joel knew that his Council friends had full stomachs, but he was famished. He carefully removed the 357 magnum Smith and Wesson revolver from the waist pocket of his sweatshirt and ordered a salad and a chicken sandwich from room service. He replaced his gun into the box in which he had mailed it to Teddy Turner's parents. The bullets he purchased at the sporting goods store he left in the revolver.

Dr. Woodson and Judge Laningham settled in for the evening. Lamar was tired and he knew tomorrow would be a long day. He and Jerry turned on the history channel, and Lamar opened a bottle of wine which he purchased at the restaurant.

Jerry Woodson was a hospice care physician. He made his living trying to help others peacefully accept their impending deaths. He found dealing with Lamar's death was very different. It was as though the roles had been reversed. Lamar seemed at peace and accepted his fate with serenity. He was the one who was comforting Colleen and Jerry. Lamar never said "if only I'd had a chance to...;" or "I wish I didn't...;" or "if I could do it all over again, I would have..." This was the hand which God had dealt him, and that was good enough for Lamar. Several times over the years they spoke of God and religion. Jerry knew from their conversations that his friend felt very close to God. He knew that Lamar had a very personal relationship with his creator. This was the reason that the judge didn't proselytize to others. He believed that it was important for everyone to seek and find God on their own level, and in their own time. Jerry, also, knew that his friend believed that God used life's events and circumstances to bring people to Him. The death of a loved one, the peace of a summer rain, the birth of a child, the love of a pet, or the intricacy of the veins in a leaf, are all somehow part of God's plan. Lamar could never understand those who sought to deny the existence of God when the evidence is all around them- the magnificence of this world...the mountains, the sea and its' creatures, the heavens on a cloudless night. In no way could this be a celestial accident. How about the love which consumes you when your child is born or when you hear them laugh. No, this is NOT the result of thousands of years of the mixing of protoplasm with ocean goo. Only the hand of a loving God could have created this.

Lamar never spoke of it, but Dr. Woodson knew that he had been deeply troubled by the actions of Thomas Hartsell. Everyone struggles to find God, and one man like Hartsell can do irreparable harm in people's search for salvation. Lamar reminded Jerry that, aside from man's punishment, God promised that such charlatans could expect the most severe punishment later on from Him.

The bottle of wine was nearly gone. Lamar said to Jerry, "I feel that you and Colleen would sometimes like to speak with me in an attempt to comfort me or ameliorate the pain that you think I must be feeling because I am dying. Honestly, Jerry, aside from my body rotting from the inside out, I am fine. The new pain medications really take the edge off, but they make me a little goofy. My friend, there is nothing which needs to be said. Over the past forty years, we have said everything already. Well, I'll take that back. There is one thing I will say...and that is goodnight. I am exhausted."

ROOM 113

Saturday morning Joel was showered, dressed, and ready to go by 10:00 AM. Wanting to keep his exposure to a minimum, he ordered both breakfast and lunch from room service. One time, early in the afternoon, Joel did decide to venture out. He wore the same hooded sweatshirt again, but he left the gun in his room. He went to the desk clerk and gave him another fifty dollars and reiterated his need to be notified as soon as the other Council members left the hotel. As before, the desk clerk agreed to phone him. Joel then went outside, and sure enough, Emilio was there waiting for him. Bored from sitting alone for hours in his hotel room, Joel decided to sit with him a while. Joel gave Emilio his room number and instructed him to call him immediately if he saw any of the Council members, who Emilio could now recognize, come out of the hotel. Joel told Emilio that he expected two or more of the people they were following to leave sometime after dinner. He promised to bring Emilio a sandwich and a drink before then.

Yolanda knew that she would have to leave sometime around 6:00 PM, but she had no idea where she would be going. Matt Dwyer always kept the locations of his "sexfests" a secret until the last moment. For security, and to protect the anonymity of his clients, neither his driver nor Jolene were told the hotel name or room number until the last minute. Yolanda amused herself changing her clothes and makeup trying to achieve the upscale call-girl look. Finally, she was satisfied and anxiously awaited the call from Jolene.

Hector was playing the valet of Dr. Neal (Dr. Woodson) in this ruse. He had joined Lamar and Jerry in their room hours earlier for lunch. They had pizza delivered to the room, and they ate as they discussed their respective roles. Yolanda had long since returned to her room to await the call from Jolene which would begin the sting. Shortly after Yolanda left, FBI Agent Mark Mahoney brought them a gym bag filled with miscellaneous equipment used in bondage encounters. "Moe" made it clear that he wanted this stuff back. Hector suggested, "How about I give you my cheerleading outfit as collateral?" Going back to his days as a Navy SEAL, Hector was used to friends' attempts at off-color humor as they readied themselves immediately prior to a mission. An obvious attempt to lessen the tension by changing the subject, Hector never remembered it succeeding. Lamar and Jerry also experienced this "guy thing" as they, like gladiators, got ready to take the field in their high school football days.

There was a loud knock on the door of the hotel room. Hector opened the door and he, Lamar, and Jerry stood there gaping at Yolanda dressed as a hooker. They had never seen the Director of the Santa Molina FBI wearing black tights and a boa. Hector started reaching for his wallet. Yolanda slapped Hector's hand and said, "Stop it. It's show time. I received the call from Jolene. I am to take a taxi to the Remmen Inn on State Street. Room 113 will have a key card under the doormat. I am to wait there for my customer." She turned and hurried off.

Two minutes later, Emilio called Joel who had been watching television, but was poised and ready to go.

"Sir, the black woman is out here hailing a cab and she looks like...like a hooker."

"THIS IS IT, EMILIO. I am on my way." Hector and Dr. Woodson still had fifteen minutes to wait, but Joel did not know that. In fact, Joel knew only one thing for sure. Yolanda had to be dressed like that as part of a charade...a charade which would lead him to Matt Dwyer. He pulled his hat down over his eyes and then pulled the hood over the hat. Joel quickly and quietly closed his room door. There was no one in the corridor except a cleaning woman who was singing to herself as she gathered linen from her cart. In the lobby there were only two children studying the contents of a vending machine and an elderly man on a sofa reading a magazine. Joel hurried to the registration clerk and asked, "Have my friends left for the retirement party yet?"

"No, sir...but a woman, the black woman, just left."

Joel hurried with his head down to Emilio's waiting cab. "Follow her cab," was all he said.

Ten minutes later, Joel and Emilio saw Yolanda exit her taxi and enter the front door of the Remmen Inn. He told Emilio to find a place to park and wait. From outside the building, Joel could see Yolanda walking down one of the hotel corridors. He kept his distance and followed slowly behind her. Outside one of the rooms, Yolanda bent down and reached under the doormat and produced a key card. In seconds she was in the room and all was quiet. Joel crept down the corridor past Room 113 where she had gone. A few more rooms past Yolanda's, there was an open area where there was an ice machine and several vending machines. Ten feet beyond the vending area was an exit to the outside of the hotel. Across from the vending area, there was a stairwell which only led upward. Joel entered the stairwell. He was blind to the hotel exit door, but if he held the stairwell door open just a crack, he could see all the way down the corridor from where he had entered. He decided that this was the best place to wait. As he pondered how Yolanda, dressed as a hooker, could possibly fetch Matt Dwyer, he pulled the gun close to his chest.

It was time to go. Hector grabbed the gym bag and he and Dr. Woodson headed out the door.

"Wait," said Lamar, "I'll walk you outside. I have been in this room way too long." They walked through the lobby, passed the registration desk, and went outside. It was a beautiful summer evening. Hector went to get the rental car and left Lamar and Dr. Woodson talking on the curb.

"Get out quickly," Lamar told his friend. "This Matt Dwyer sounds like a real bad ass."

"Don't worry about me," Jerry responded. "I want no part of him. See you in a few hours."

Hector put the gym bag in the backseat, and Lamar stretched and yawned as they drove away. He wished he could have been a part of this, but he made a promise to Colleen. He decided to return to his room and take a nap.

Finding the Cadillac Hotel proved to be easy. It was one of the tallest buildings in the area and could be seen for miles. As promised, in front of the hotel was parked a late model white Cadillac. Dr. Woodson tapped on the passenger side window and slowly the tinted glass went down.

"I am Dr. Neal."

"Get in." said the driver. "Do you have something for me?"

"Oh, yes." Jerry reached into the breast pocket of his suit jacket and produced an overstuffed envelope. The driver made a cursory attempt at counting the money. Hector opened the back door and put the gym bag on the seat.

"Don't forget your toys, boss. I'll follow you." Hector shut the door thinking what a shame it was that such a beautiful car reeked of stale cigarette smoke.

Dr. Woodson's driver gave Hector a moment to get into the blue Chevrolet, and he then sped off, apparently not caring if Hector chose to obey the speed limits or not. The driver never said a word until they reached their destination, the Remmen Inn. The driver let Dr. Neal retrieve his own bag. He said, "Tell the clerk at the desk that you are looking for Jolene's friend. He will then direct you where to go. Make sure that your friend stays in the lobby until you are done." The Cadillac drove away. Dr. Woodson waited in front of the hotel until Hector parked the car. They entered the hotel together. The lobby was clean, but in serious need of updating. But then, thought Dr. Woodson, the people who frequent such places are probably not interested in the ambiance.

"Good evening, I am looking for Jolene's friend."

Without looking up the registration clerk slid a room key card across the counter. He pointed to one of the corridors and said only, "Room 113, on the left."

"See ya, boss," said Hector, and he looked for a corner to get lost in. "Have fun."

Dr. Woodson picked up the gym bag and walked down the corridor. He used his key card to enter Room 113.

Joel watched in silence as his friend came down the hallway and joined Yolanda in the hotel room. He wondered what was in the large bag he carried.

"What would you like to do for two hours? TV or Sudoku?" Yolanda didn't like the idea of having to wait so long, but the ruse had to appear to be realistic. She said to Jerry, "I called Moe Mahoney, and he is putting men in a car outside the exit door and in front of the hotel. When our boy shows up, this place will be locked down tight. Jerry, please make sure that you and Hector are long gone by then."

5

SHOT DEAD

Lamar felt refreshed from his hour nap. It had been nearly two hours since the others had left the hotel. Bored, he decided to walk down to the lobby. The registration clerk saw Lamar and asked him, "Aren't you going to your friend's retirement party?"

Confused, Lamar asked, "Excuse me? What are you talking about?"

"After you and your three friends checked in yesterday, a young man who said he was a friend of yours, checked in and said he was going to surprise you all by coming to the party."

It took a few seconds for Lamar to process this information. "What did he look like?"

"Tall, thin, and I would guess him to be in his thirties."

Lamar's eyes widened and he said way too loud, "OH MY GOD. NO! JOEL IS HERE!"

"Yes, I believe that was his name."

Lamar ran across the lobby and outside. Mercifully, there was a taxicab which was just finishing dropping off new guests with their luggage.

"Please, this is an emergency. Take me to the Remmen Inn on State Street as quickly as you can."

Yolanda and Dr. Woodson busied themselves trashing Room 113. They wanted it to appear as though some very rough sex had taken place here. Once they were done, Yolanda positioned herself so that she looked strangled. She would pretend to be dead, but her right hand, which was under a pillow, held a gun.

"OK, Yolanda, good luck."

Joel saw Dr. Woodson hurry out of the room and down the corridor toward the lobby. As he peered through the crack in the stairwell door, he decided to wait and see how this played out. He knew that Yolanda was still in the room.

Dr. Woodson tried to appear as frantic as possible. He said to the registration clerk, "Oh my God, I am so sorry. The woman is dead. She didn't tell me that the restraints were too tight. She is dead. I don't know what to do. Oh my God. Please help me. I have to get out of here!" Hector came over and said, "Boss, get to the car. We're leaving, now!" Hector and Dr. Woodson immediately ran out of the hotel and headed for the car.

The hotel clerk was paralyzed with fear. His hands shook violently as he tried to open his wallet. After a few seconds of fumbling through the contents and spilling some onto the floor, he found Matt Dwyer's "special" phone number. He dialed the number and explained that Jolene's girl had been accidently killed during the encounter. Matt was furious. His anger was doing battle with his common sense for possession of his brain. Presently, his anger was winning. He screamed into the phone, "I am going to kill that guy." There was a pause as common sense fought back. "OK, look. Don't let anyone near that room. No chamber maids, no one. I will be right there." He hung up.

Dr. Woodson called Moe Mahoney and alerted him that Matt was likely on his way to the Remmen Inn now. All Moe's men were alerted, but could do nothing until Matt entered the building. Tyler and Marty had given Yolanda and Avery Resque a good description of Matt Dwyer. He was nearly six feet tall and rough looking, but the most distinguishing features they were looking for today were cowboy boots and a pony tail.

The clerk at the registration desk didn't have long to wait. In five minutes, Matt's car screeched to a halt as he slammed on his brakes in front of the hotel. Matt threw the vehicle into PARK and jumped out. The clerk saw Matt and knew he was berserk. To avoid confrontation, the clerk pointed to the corridor and said "113." He handed Matt the key card which Dr. Woodson had left on the counter.

Joel knew instantly that this was Matt Dwyer storming down the corridor toward him. Matt paused and listened at the door as he pulled a gun from the back of his pants.

Joel stepped out of hiding. He opened the stairwell door with his foot, and holding the gun as Hector had taught him, he leveled the sight on Matt. "Stop right there, Matt."

"Are you Dr. Neal? Why do you have a gun on me?" Matt was a creature of the street. He instantly was able to size up Joel and he realized that the man who held him at bay was not likely to shoot. He obviously was not from the world Matt knew. No, this guy was civilized...he had class. Matt could tell that Joel was not a killer. So Matt raised his gun and aimed it at Joel's chest and said, "You should have shot me when you had the chance."

From behind Matt, someone screamed "DWYER!" Matt spun around and shot twice. Both shots hit their mark and Judge Laningham's chest exploded as he collapsed to the floor. Several more shots rang out. Yolanda shot from Room 113, and Moe Mahoney shot from the hotel exit door. Matthew Dwyer was hit four times and was dead before his gun fell from his hand to the floor.

Hector and Dr. Woodson had been waiting in the rental car. When they heard the shots, they ran back into the hotel. Yolanda, Dr. Woodson, and Hector were incredulous that Judge Laningham and Joel had both found their way to Room 113. Moe Mahoney confiscated Joel's gun, but once he came to realize that it was his parents and sister who Matt had brutally murdered, he did not pursue any charges.

The four remaining Council members drove back together in silence in the rental car. Joel had dismissed Emilio since his services were no longer required. He thanked the taxi driver and paid him the second thousand dollars which he had promised him. The four friends met in Joel's room and he explained how Colleen told him where they were staying in Detroit. The one thing the Council members were unable to figure out was how the judge came to know that Joel was in the Remmen Inn.

All of the Council members except Dr. Woodson returned to Santa Molina the following day. It was Dr. Woodson who called Colleen to tell her of Lamar's heroic death. He also told her that Joel blamed himself for the judge being killed. Colleen insisted that Dr. Woodson tell Joel that it was not his fault. Lamar was supposed to have stayed in his hotel room. Dr. Woodson remained in Detroit one extra day. He insisted on staying with his friend's body until it was released and returned to Santa Molina.

6

GOODBYE

Three days after the judge had been shot he was laid to rest. As per his request, only the four Council members and Colleen went to his burial. All five had agreed to bring a personal item to leave with the judge, and one by one, they said their final goodbyes.

Joel thanked Lamar for saving his life. Both the youngest and the newest member of the Council, Joel had joined as a way of pushing back the demons in his own life. Thanks to the Council and to Lamar, those demons were now gone. He never anticipated that the Council would one day seek and deliver justice to the killers of his parents and sister. He stepped forward and placed a pipe, tobacco, a bag of potato chips, and a bar of chocolate on Lamar's casket.

"Goodbye, my friend. Enjoy these simple pleasures which you long ago decided to deny yourself." Joel stepped back and Hector moved forward. He saluted the casket and placed his Navy SEAL trident on the coffin.

"God, country, strength, honor, dignity, and justice. You sir, embody all of these things. I will attempt to live my life as you have shown me through your example." Hector brought his hand down and stepped back.

Yolanda stepped forward. She put the judge's gavel on his casket. "Thank you for bringing justice to places where there was none. Those of us who fight on the side of law and order, thank you for divine retribution." Yolanda touched her heart and then the casket. Tears welled up in her eyes and she stepped back.

Dr. Jerry Woodson moved forward. He held Lamar's well-worn Bible in his hand. He opened it and read 2 Timothy 4:7-8. *"I have fought the good fight, I have finished the race, I have kept the faith. Now there is in store for me the crown of righteousness..."* Dr. Woodson paused. He then removed the *Council Rules* established so long ago by the judge. "You have found comfort and solace in both of these, my friend. Rest in peace."

Finally, Colleen stepped forward. She placed a picture of their son, Ethan Cole Laningham, in his Marine dress blues on the head of Lamar's coffin.

"Goodbye, my love. You have been a good husband and my best friend. For too short a time, you were also given the privilege of being a wonderful father. You can now enjoy your son and never worry about losing him again. I will always love you."

It took the Council some time to get over the death of their leader. They met at Joel's house a few times, both to reminisce, and to discuss the merits of seeking someone to take the judge's place in the Council. They all believed that Lamar would want the Council to continue, but who could possibly take his place?

Yolanda summoned Ruth, her secretary. "Ruth, please have Danno Lockwood come into my office."

www.ingramcontent.com/pod-product-compliance
Lightning Source LLC
Chambersburg PA
CBHW071644260626
47170CB00001B/232